God's Thunderbolt

∽

The Vigilantes of Montana

By Carol Buchanan

ISBN: 1-4196-9709-9
ISBN-13: 9781419697098

Visit www.booksurge.com to order additional copies.

Bud,
I thought you
might enjoy this book
especially since the author
µ from Montana).
Judy

Dedication

∽

To Dick, in loving gratitude for your love and moral support,
and your incredible computing expertise.

Acknowledgements

〜

No piece of writing is ever a solo effort, despite solitary hours at a computer or in a library, and I've had the interest and support of the entire Flathead community.

The Authors of the Flathead honored me by electing me president for 2008, even after they suffered through the early drafts. They are truly a group of "Writers helping writers." Dennis Foley, gentleman and writing teacher, mentors the AOF, and lectures monthly on the craft of fiction. From him I've learned more than I realize.

WEST, the Women's Entrepreneurial Success Tribe, a group of women business owners, heard parts of the book and helped with my decision to self-publish the book. Lynda Collins read an early draft on the airplane and gave me the benefit of her perspective and encouragement. Betsey Hurd, equine artist, and Martin Levy, horseman, read it and reacted with honesty and encouragement. Sylvia Murphy let me read the entire final draft aloud to her. You all have my heartfelt gratitude.

Tom Esch, former two-term Flathead County Attorney, helped with points of Montana law, as well as how lawyers conduct trials and think about the law. If Dan Stark doesn't get it right, it's my fault, not Tom's.

The knowledge of historians and archivists of the Montana Historical Society led me to avenues of research I hadn't considered with the question, "Have you thought of this?"

Joanne Erdall, director of the Thompson-Hickman Library in Virginia City, MT, would say, "We also have ...." The MHS and Joanne both helped to deepen my understanding and research.

Outside the Flathead, Marshall J. Cook, writing coach at the University of Wisconsin (Madison), guided my baby steps onto the path of writing.

To everyone who asked how the book was coming, thank you for your interest. If I've forgotten someone, I apologize.

Part I: Justice for Nick

∽

1: Alder Gulch

A breeze from high country snowfields flowed along the edges of winter into the valley of the Stinking Water, swept aside the horses' tails and ruffled their manes, and carried away the sickening sweet smell of the frozen corpse riding in William Palmer's wagon bed. "Those heartless bloody bastards," Palmer grumbled to the team. Ears flicked back, then forward. "Wouldn't even help load this poor sod, whoever he is, into the wagon, would they? Didn't bloody care, did they? 'Men get killed every day in Virginia City,' they said, 'and nobody minds that, so why should we bother about this one?' Heartless bastards, that's what they are, this poor bugger lying almost in their back yard for days. Had to manhandle him into the wagon myself, didn't I? A nice job that was, I don't think. Poor bastard. I need a drink." At Laurin's, he watered the team, drank a whiskey at the bar, and didn't blame Laurin none when he recoiled, gagging. "Le pauvre batard," which Palmer took to mean, the poor bastard. Seven miles on, where Ramshorn Creek emptied into the Stinking Water, he had another whiskey at Dempsey's to take the smell of the corpse out of his throat. Bob Dempsey, a decent enough chap for an Irisher, reacted the same as Laurin. "The poor fella. They left him lay?" At Pete Daly's, on Alder Creek, the stage driver was changing horses while the passengers stretched their legs, and lost their appetite for lunch. "Poor bastard. Who would do such a thing? They let him lie there?"

The valley floor roughened, lifted, and the sudden hills pinched together in Alder Gulch, where miners and mining camps crowded the creek side. Everyone wanted to see, some excitement to break up the dull back-killing labor of digging gold. "The poor bastard, who could do a thing like that?" With every stop Palmer grew more discouraged. Nobody knew the poor bloke, though how could anyone tell who he was? His own mother wouldn't know him. Men bought Palmer drinks to drown his disgust. "Whoever said a frozen corpse didn't stink was a bloody fool," he told the horses.

At Nevada City he almost quit. Dance music from his own establishment reminded him that just that morning he'd set out happy because the day promised beautiful, more like October than December, and after delivering the beer he could do some hunting. Compromising with himself, he decided he'd drive on to Virginia City, just a mile and a half over the rise. "That bloody grouse had to bloody land right on this poor bugger's breast, didn't it?" The horses nodded their heads and plodded on. "The hand of Providence, it was. Too right. The hand of Providence bloody dropped that prairie chicken on this poor sod." He'd stop after Virginia. Be buggered if he'd drive all the way up the mountain to Summit, someone should know him in Virginia, and if they didn't, he'd bring the poor sod back to Nevada and they'd bury him proper.

જ્જ

Dozens of wagons and mule trains toiled up Wallace Street in Virginia City every day, loaded with the needful — canned milk, hammers, paper, nails, shovels, and silk — because the camp manufactured nothing, produced nothing, had nothing. Except gold. Unloaded, the freighters turned around and drove away empty with new orders, back over pitted roads. Below the confluence of the Stinking Water and the Beaverhead river, they turned toward Salt Lake City, 700 miles south, or toward Fort Benton on the Missouri River 350 miles north across the Continental Divide. Mostly they headed south, because the Missouri was too chancy in its flow.

So why had this wagon caught Martha McDowell's eye, glimpsed as it was between the rump of one ox and the uplifted bellowing mouth of another, over the darky's shoulder as he squatted to heft a hundredweight barrel of flour? Why did it seem to her to turn the corner from the road along Alder Creek and labor up Wallace in its own pool of silence like it carried the world, the two horses and the driver looking like they'd had a terrible hard road? The driver swayed, even sitting, like he was sick. Or drunk. The reins drooped through his hands, and the horses walked with their heads hanging down like they couldn't hardly take another step. Except the wagon seemed empty.

Martha adjusted her grip on the string around her parcel. Her bump of curiosity itched. What was the matter with the driver, the horses? She stuck her head in the door of Ma's Eatery and called for Miz Hudson to come on out and see this.

"Thee don't suppose it's another typhus case?" Miz Hudson wiped her hands on her apron, her other darky, the woman, behind her. Miz Hudson said the two was free, but she'd brought them West, and Martha didn't see why free darkies would want to stay with a white if they didn't have to.

"Could be," Martha said. "Something's sure enough wrong."

Miz Hudson stood a little in front of Martha, not blocking her view, because she was so short, though she weighed considerable more than Martha. If you took a measuring tape to the both of them, Martha thought, you'd get the same total of height and girth, only she'd got some height and Miz Hudson got girth.

The string bit into Martha's right hand so she changed it

to the left. It was a good beef roast, and everyone would relish it, Sam McDowell, the young'uns and the boarders. She'd use the rosemary Miz Hudson had given her. McDowell didn't care about it, but she figured to please Mr. Stark. She wanted to keep his custom. It was good for the young'uns to have a gentleman putting his feet under her table. See how proper folks conducted themselves.

The wagon swung over to stop next door to Ma's Eatery, in front of Kiskadden's Stone Block, the biggest building in the Gulch, or that Martha had ever seen for that matter, with three shops on the first floor, a meeting room on its second floor. Its afternoon shadow blanketed the Eatery's log cabin.

A small crowd of men, always happy for any change in their routine, blocked the women's view, though Tabby, Miz Hudson's other darky, being much taller, might be able to see.

"Albert," Miz Hudson said, "do thee please see about that wagon."

"Yes'm." Albert left the barrel to glance into the wagon and twisted away, muttered through his teeth, "You'm don't want to be seein' this," before he bolted into the shadowed alley between the Eatery and Kiskadden's.

Over the retching sounds, Miz Hudson said, "Takes something mighty dreadful to upset a former slave."

Tabby, the nigger gal, said, "Albert has a tender heart."

"Oh, Lord," said Martha. It was all she could think of, being struck as she was with two new ideas at once, that the wagon had something horrible in it, and a Negro, big and black as Albert, could have a soft heart.

❧

The card, a queen of hearts, fluttered to a landing face up, in front of Daniel Stark. He left it there, stretched out his legs and pushed his chair back. He breathed through his mouth because the man sitting between him and Gallagher wore a buffalo coat that smelled of old rotten meat. He wished the game were over. He should never have agreed to play, but Gallagher would not take no for an answer. Waiting to bet, Dan watched the room in the bar mirror. Behind the thick rope separating the dance floor from the card tables, the hurdy-gurdy dancers polka'd, their skirts flaring like red, yellow, and blue poppies, to a fiddle's scratching, as out of tune as fingernails on a blackboard. A dancer turned a yelp into a laugh as she pretended to have a rousing good time with a clod who paid a dollar a dance to tromp all over her feet. Dan wondered if she let him do more. Maybe not. The Melodeon Hall was not a bawdy house. Con Orem ran a clean place. Then again, what the women did away from here was their own business.

Maybe . . . No, he wouldn't have a whore for fear of the pox. Stories from the War told of a dreadful price paid for taking mercury. Until he could go home and marry Harriet Dean, Dan wasn't likely to come any closer to a naked woman than the two carved bas-reliefs of bare-breasted women, draperies tastefully covering their loins, that flanked the long bar mirror. There Orem kept watch while he poured a fresh drink for a customer. He caught Dan's eye and nodded in a friendly way. Dan smiled and picked up his cards. Back to business.

The cards had a greasy feel, as if too many men had held them in their hot hands, and they were worth damn-all. Nothing higher than the queen. A player folded, Sam McDowell opened for two dollars, and the next player folded. The buffalo coat stayed in, and Dan opened his mouth to fold again, when Gallagher frowned at him.

"Dammit, Stark, you ever going to bet?"

Better to lose two bucks than cross Gallagher. "Call." Dan tossed in two white chips. Coward. Knuckle under to Gallagher. He wrestled the thought down: Where would the family be without the gold he would bring them in the spring?

"That's better, friend." Gallagher glared at his cards.

Friend? Dan snorted, covered it with a cough. They could have been. He'd liked Jack Gallagher on sight the minute he stepped off the express, and found Virginia City's Chief Deputy Sheriff waiting for news. Jack was handsome, "noble-looking" as someone put it, with dark hair, a well-shaped head, and blue eyes set wide above a narrow straight nose. Even his enemies, if enemy was not too strong a word for disliking and fearing a man, grudgingly allowed he could be the hero of novels, the kind bound in lurid paper covers, typographical mistakes six to the page. Dan didn't quite count himself among Gallagher's enemies because his attitude to Gallagher was not enmity, but more like caution, a looking askance, as though he hadn't yet identified the unseen creature moving through tall grass, just that seed heads wavered above a crooked line his path would intersect. Jack Gallagher had more than looks, though, he had an air, he attracted people. He charmed them. At first.

As he had charmed the greenhorn Dan Stark when, still shaking from a shotgun's close-set glare, Dan had found himself at his destination after three thousand hard dry miles. He would have told Jack all about the armed robbery and how he could identify the blanket-covered robbers by their voices and ears, except that the stage driver, stumbling into him, knocked him off balance.

He had been off balance ever since.

Reading the driver's silent warning, he made two decisions: to keep his head down and stay quiet till he got his bearings. That was one thing. The other, to keep the Spencer rifle with him at all times.

Gallagher said, "Call." He tossed in two white chips.

The player sitting between Gallagher and Sam McDowell folded.

Gallagher gathered the cards for the last deal. Not a moment too soon. Dan sat up. He could fold and go outside. Fresh horse manure would smell better than the buffalo coat. Then Gallagher flicked a two of spades to him. A memory flashed through his mind and was gone: (Blood pooled across a polished mahogany desktop, coated the leather chair and spattered the fat law books, gray brain matter invisible on their bindings.) He'd show Father's ghost that it was possible to play poker sensibly. Unless one of the new face up cards doubled someone's hole card, as the two doubled his, he held the winning hand. Someone might have an ace in the hole, but he'd still win, because a lowly pair of two's beat a lordly ace. Unless someone held a higher pair. The blood surged in his veins; a certainty told him to bet, not to fold, this was his chance, he would win.

The bets went around the table, the pot grew larger, and the players called and raised until other men stood around watching, and then a man folded, and another and another and only Dan, Gallagher, and McDowell stayed. Gallagher raised. McDowell said nothing. "Any time," Gallagher said.

McDowell pulled a piece of paper from an inner pocket and laid it on the pile of chips.

In his hazel eyes Dan read a challenge. "What's that?" Dan knew the answer. McDowell was plunging, like Father used to do, so sure something wonderful would turn on the next card, horse, roll of the dice, on a hunch until – (blood spreading across the desk from the ruin of Father's gray head).

"A claim. It's OK, except Fitch owns half, on account of he grubstaked me." He fiddled with a button on his gray Secesh coat.

Dan could not believe it. "You're gambling it away? It could be worth something someday. Your family –"

"They shoulda stayed to home. Hell, maybe I'll win. Twenty dollars against this paper." As Dan hesitated, the button came off, and McDowell threw it over his shoulder without looking. "You got the balls to make a real bet?"

Five months of keeping his head down, five months of

refusing to be goaded, while their contempt grew to this: you got any balls, you yellow or something? Yeah, I'm a coward, I'm not going to fight you, you've got me by three inches and thirty pounds, you're too ready with a pistol. Acting the coward, being a coward because of the family, and their disgrace. Who else would release them from poverty and disgrace? (He ran and ran, the gunshot echoing, toward the closed door at the end of the hallway receding as he ran.) Dan pitched a yellow chip onto the pile. It bounced. "Call." He tossed in another. "And raise." Stupid, he knew, but he couldn't resist, he was looking at McDowell through a kind of mist. The bastard.

Gallagher tossed in two yellow chips. "Call."

McDowell called, Dan and Gallagher both checked, and McDowell checked, and the betting was done. McDowell turned over his hole card, an ace of spades. "Beats anything you got, Stark." Smiling wide enough to show a broken front tooth, he stretched out both hands to scoop in the pot.

Showdown. The mist evaporated, and Dan saw everything as if etched in glass: McDowell's stained beard, a man squinting through tobacco smoke, Gallagher's Union blue coat trimmed with deer hide, a louse crawling among the buffalo coat's hair. "You think so?" He turned over his hole card. A bystander whooped.

"I don't believe it." A vein across McDowell's forehead swelled. "A rotten pair of two's."

Gallagher laughed. Heads turned, and the fiddle screeched, and the dancers stopped. For a minute the only sound was his laughing, that trailed out to a high-pitched giggle, as he wiped his eyes on his shirt sleeve. "I should have known, dammit. I should have known. Stark, you son of a bitch, you can be a sly bastard at times."

Dan smiled. "Thanks. Coming from you, Jack, that's high praise." Hating himself for flattering Gallagher, he stood up to retrieve the chips, the paper. Keep the objective in mind: Get the gold, survive, take it home. Even if he had to be a sycophant to Gallagher.

The fiddle launched the dancers. Talk hummed. A man at a nearby table lit a cigar.

McDowell said, "You cheated. Goddammit, you cheated."

The fiddle player and the dancers leaped to one side of the room, out of a possible line of fire. Men near the door opened it and were gone.

Gallagher said, "No, he didn't, Sam. Face it. You and me, we was outplayed."

McDowell looked around at the other players.

The man with the buffalo coat said, "Gallagher's right. He didn't cheat." He turned over his own hole card, an ace of diamonds. "I figured he had a pair. Nobody stays with as weak a hand as showed unless he doubles one of the cards."

"Yeah," Gallagher said. "I thought it might be interesting to see what he had." The smile vanished, his eyes narrowed, and Dan thought of blue shadows on snow. "Let him go, Sam." He used his official voice, his Chief Deputy voice, that made people call him sir.

McDowell slumped. Dan pressed his heel on the floor to keep it from drumming while he gathered in the chips. Gallagher had changed in a blink from genial to menacing, and Dan recognized the creature sliding through the grass, heard a faint dry rattling.

He put on his greatcoat, shouldered the Spencer, put his hands on the chips. "I'm going back to work." Winning made this an extra payday, but he'd lose a fee if he failed to deliver his survey results.

"Oh, no. You have to give us a chance to get even." Gallagher's voice was still easy.

McDowell said, "You can't quit now."

"I've got work to do," Dan said. "You'll have another opportunity." Miners were always impatient. Every inch of surface ground meant extra feet of dirt below, more gold to be found, and the miners who had hired him wanted to be sure the other men had none of theirs.

Gallagher aimed his Deputy's voice, each word equally weighted, like bullets, at Dan: "You can't quit now."

Dan's gut twisted, and he shifted his weight to his left leg. If he stayed, he knuckled under. Again. He would endure more jokes about his balls. What did it matter about being thought a coward, as long as he succeeded in his mission? Go home with gold enough to restore the family's good name, pay Father's creditors, marry Harriet Dean. He stacked the white chips, counted them, forgot the total. If he stayed, they might clean him out. Legal robbery. He counted again, and McDowell, a corner of his upper lip lifted, tossed him the yellow chip. Coward.

Dan grasped the yellow chip. No. Enough. He brushed the chips into his hat. "I am quitting. Like I said, you'll have your chance another time."

Gallagher put his hand under the table, as if to find a pistol. "'N I said, you can't quit now."

"The hell I can't." Back prickling, Dan walked away, men's stares crawling over him. A smoldering cigar lay on the edge of an abandoned table. The bar, where he'd cash in the chips, was a mile away, and Con Orem brought out a double-barreled shotgun and laid it on the bar.

"The man's allowed to quit when he wants to, Gallagher." Orem's knuckles, gnarled from all his prize fights, stood out as he gripped the weapon. "You'll have another chance to beat him." His lips stretched, mocked a smile.

Gallagher said, "Sure, Con." He met Dan's eyes in the mirror. "Another time, then."

Piling his chips on the bar, Dan said, "You can bank on it," while he thought to himself, Like hell, never again. As Orem weighed out the value of the chips in gold dust, Dan caught his breath. He felt as if he'd run too far too fast. "Thanks."

The piano player hit a few wrong notes in the opening phrases of a new dance. Conversations rose. A man returned to the abandoned table and put the cigar in his mouth.

"Don't mention it. I oughta be thanking you. You didn't use that thing." He pointed his long crooked nose toward the Spencer's barrel rising over Dan's shoulder.

The front door opened on a surge of cold air, and Jacob Himmelfarb made his way among the tables toward Dan. The wide flat brim of his black hat shielded his face, but Dan knew something had happened. "Come now, Daniel. They have a body found. No one knows him." Before Dan could ask, he was already walking away.

"Keep the gold for me," Dan told Orem, "I'll be back for it later." He felt as if his blood stopped, as if the veins had shrunk and would not let it through.

Gallagher stopped Jacob with a hand on his sleeve, asked a question that Jacob answered, and his own question came clearly to Dan. "You come, too, yes?"

"You don't need me." Gallagher resumed shuffling. "The man's dead. What can I do about it now?" He paused to separate two cards that had stuck together. "I ain't paid to be a detective. Just run errands for the miners court."

∾

From where she stood on the corner of Wallace and Jackson Streets, Martha could see when, near the crest of Jackson, Daniel Stark came out of the Melodeon Hall, that rifle like always slung on his shoulder. Martha sidled over to where she could watch him hurry with that long-legged walk of his to catch up with Jacob, the foreign Jew that helped him with the surveying. They made a contrast, those two: Mr. Stark, arrow-straight, and Jacob, some younger maybe and taller, but thin and stooped like he spent too much time squinting at thick books. What folks like them and Miz Hudson got out of books Martha didn't know, but she wished she did.

Palmer, the wagon driver, told over again how he'd found the body, and finished up, "Providence, that's what it was, Providence." Someone handed him a bottle of whiskey, and Miz Hudson protested, "Don't thee think the poor man's had enough?" to which another man said, "Madam, after what he's seen today, there can't be enough."

John X. Beidler, that folks called X, the shortest man Martha ever did see, climbed up onto a wheel hub to peer into the wagon bed. "Oh, my God. Another one." He sketched a cross in the air and kissed his thumb. A Papist, then. "Who do you suppose it is this time?"

Mr. Stark, who barely nodded to her as he come around to her side of the wagon, was tall enough to see into it from the ground, and she heard him gasp, "Good God." He whipped out a handkerchief to cover his mouth and nose. "Look in his pockets. Maybe there's something in them that'll tell us." He put a foot on the step-up, but X stuck out an arm to bar him. "I'll do it. I'm already up here."

So the poor man's face —. Martha couldn't finish the thought.

Jacob peered into the wagon, and clutched his overcoat closer around him, so tight Martha could almost count the little bones in his back. Mr. Goldberg, who owned the Pioneer Clothing Store down toward the Creek, touched his elbow, and Jacob stepped back. Mr. Goldberg murmured something, and Jacob snapped, "Such things the good God allows."

Mr. Stark spun on his heel. "No, damn it, we allow it. We do."

Somewhere a fiddle played a dance tune. An argument rose to a shouting match, and Martha checked her path into Kiskadden's. She'd be safe behind its stone walls if bullets flew.

Beidler said, "He's frozen hard. Been out in the open awhile, I'd say. Ah, here we are. A pocket knife. Anyone recognize it?" He handed the knife to Mr. Stark, who shook his head over it, and passed it on. It went from hand to hand, a small thing to puzzle over, with an ivory handle, three blades. X Beidler crouched in the wagon bed, giving the corpse a close look, his face and Mr. Stark's grimmer by the second. They conferred together in whispers, but Martha caught a word: murder.

"Oh, no!" came a man's cry. "Oh, God, no! Not him!" Mr. Baume, a partner in one of the stores in Kiskadden's, put his hand to his mouth. "It's mine. The knife's mine. I loaned it to Nick Tbalt the day he left."

A woman cried out, Martha didn't think it was her, she couldn't get her breath, and the world was turning wobbly. Not Nick! The big happy German boy that her little Dotty loved, wanted to marry when she got growed. How could it be Nick? A good soul if ever there was one. Murdered and left out so critters could get at him?

A man's strong arm held her upright, and she smelled beer and tobacco smoke in his wool greatcoat, the scent of gun oil, but underneath clean. Mr. Stark. Martha regained herself, stood steady on her two feet.

"Are you all right?" His face was grey as wood ashes, the dark centers of his green eyes big like he'd been in the dark, and his hand trembled as it left her.

"I'll be fine now." She could feel tears on her cheeks. The poor boy. How would she tell Dotty? The child had insisted since Nick went missing that he would never steal the mules and the gold Fitch had give him, never, and she had the right of it.

༄

"Hear my voice, O God, in my prayer: Preserve my life

from fear of the enemy. Hide me from the secret counsel of the wicked . . . . "

Freshening with the sunset, the wind swept up the noises of gold placer mining from the creek below the knoll where Nevada City had laid its burying ground, and whisked away the words of the Psalm. Dan said to himself, That Psalm might be a prayer for all of us, just as Tobias Fitch muttered, "Fat lot of good He did this poor lad." Mrs. Hudson hissed at Fitch to be quiet. The reader's lips moved, but Dan for a moment heard only ten-year-old Dotty sobbing fit to break the heart. Enfolded as she was in her mother's blue cloak, only her face, streaming with misery, showed. Now and then, Mrs. McDowell murmured in Dotty's ear, but the child would not be comforted. Nick's body, wrapped in a Hudson's Bay blanket, lay at their feet in a shallow grave the men had hacked in the frozen ground. Come spring thaw, Dan promised Nick, we'll dig it deeper. Build you a coffin. The blanket's red and yellow and blue stripes on white wool seemed inappropriate to a murdered man, but Major Tobias Wayne Fitch, late of the Cavalry of the Confederate States of America, and Nick's foster father, had said Nick deserved bright colors, he'd been such a cheerful boy.

The wind brought the Psalm to them again. "They search out iniquities; they accomplish a diligent search; both the inward thought of every one of them, and the heart, is deep." The reader, who sold shoes from a street cart, stared about him as if to make Nick's friends repent sins they hadn't committed.

"We been here long –" Fitch began, but Mrs. Hudson glared, and he closed his mouth.

Fitch. Democrat, a Secessionist who had given half of his left arm to the Glorious Cause. Fitch financed McDowell's prospecting in exchange for half shares in any claim he found. What would be Fitch's reaction when he learned that he had a new partner, and a Republican, a Unionist, at that? Dan couldn't find the idea very appealing, himself. Partners with Fitch. There was an unholy alliance for you.

"But God shall shoot at them with an arrow; suddenly shall they be wounded. So they shall make their own tongue to fall upon themselves; all that see them shall flee away." The man's reading voice changed to a shout: "Lord, send down Thine arrows upon the murderers of our dear Nicholas! Send down your thunderbolt."

Across the "Amens," Fitch said, "About time. I want to find my boy's killers."

But it was not over. Mrs. Hudson began to sing "Amazing Grace," and her voice quieted Dotty's weeping, stilled the men's random shuffling, their impatience, and fixed Dan's gaze on the blanket-wrapped corpse whose clenched fists had frozen with sage twigs clutched in the fingers. Dan wanted to believe that Nick was in glory now, that he would live out an eternity as the happy youth they had known, and somehow the hymn made that seem possible.

They crumbled frozen clods onto the corpse while the shoe salesman intoned, "Ashes to ashes, dust to dust, we are as the grasses in harvest that are cut down and thrown into the fire."

"No!" Mrs. McDowell cried out, and he gaped at her, wide-eyed, his lips apart. Dan imagined his shock that he – in his own mind a man of God – should be contradicted, and by a woman, but as for himself, Dan cheered her. "He had the sweetest soul in the world, and the Lord has received him into His bosom and wiped away all his tears." Her slight body tensed forward, a hawk about to drop on hapless prey, and her brown eyes sparked at the men staring at this transformed sparrow. "You-all want the Lord to smite the evildoers, it appears to me like y'all are going to have to be God's thunderbolt."

Dumbfounded, the other mourners were silent, and she looked about at them, the ferocity fading from her eyes, and her cheeks reddening, while tears gathered and her shoulders drooped. She turned Dotty away from them, the child's tears drying on her cheeks.

"Mrs. McDowell," Dan strode after her, where she stood near Palmer's wagon. Palmer had volunteered to carry the women back to Virginia City so they would not have to walk through the semi-darkness of an early winter evening. Mrs. Hudson already stood behind the driver's seat, and Palmer swung Dotty up as Dan approached.

"I shouldn't have spoke so," she said, "it wasn't my place —"

Dan put a hand up to stop her; in his opinion she had nothing to apologize for. "You're quite right, you know. I just wanted to reassure you that we already intend to track down Nick's murderers. They will not go free. Not this time."

He would have said more, but Fitch pushed between them, took both Mrs. McDowell's hands in his own. Dan backed away, but he read her thanks in the straightening of her shoulders, a glow in her eyes that looked past Fitch to him.

He helped Beidler and the others bury Nick, filling in dirt and setting stones down with respect so as not to break the bones of the arms, elbows bent, the fists a clutch of bones and sinews upraised as if to fight. A magic lantern in his mind flashed recollections: Nick's unrecognizable corpse, Father's blasted head resting in a pool of blood, but pushing both away, crowding them out, the image of Mrs. McDowell, fierce and flaming with indignation. With her dark brown hair parted in the middle and pulled firmly back into a bun at the nape of her neck, her drab linsey-woolsey dresses, and her thin figure, he realized that she was beautiful.

❧

The wagon dipped down the hill, its tailgate pointing upward like a diving duck's, toward Alder Creek and Nevada City. Such outlandish impudence, Dan thought, for crude gold camps to call themselves cities, for they were a motley hundreds of people sheltering themselves in tents, the wagons that brought them here, caves, and cabins built of logs with the bark on that shrank from their chinking as the logs dried and the bark, loosened by industrious beetles, fell away. Or perhaps not impudence, but hope. The hopefulness of a new country, as if to think a thing would make it so. Not much to choose between the two "Cities." Even in his thoughts, Dan couldn't resist putting the word in quotation marks. Both were bound by Alder Creek, and slopes and hills rose under them to towering mountains in three directions. Alder Gulch. The Creek escaped southwards, into the Stinking Water Valley, emptied into the Stinking Water river, so named by the Indians. Pas-am-ar-ri. Because they raised their dead along it on scaffolds? That was one explanation.

He picked up a stone and lugged it to the graveside. With twilight, the cold seeped through his boot soles, and soaked up into his lower legs through his pants legs and winter long underwear. A line from Emerson's *Nature* came into his mind: "I please myself with the graces of the winter scenery." Obviously, Emerson had been writing in front of a good fire with a sherry at his elbow. Sweet, no doubt, not dry. For what graces could anyone find in this landscape of forbidding, snow-laden mountains towering over hills of rocks and sagebrush and juniper trees upright in the snow, this scene of sorrow and cold misery? Sunlight and shadow chased across the knoll, across the piles of stones that marked the graves. How many of the occupants had died of natural causes? Dan was willing to bet that gunshot or knife wounds had carried them all off. Like Nick.

He set down another small boulder beside Nick's grave and left Beidler, Fitch, and Jacob to place it while he went back for another. But all the time he sought and carried the largest rocks he could manage, so that animals would not be able to get at Nick's corpse, he was thinking that he did not see how to get justice for Nick. He crouched down and worked his gloved hands under a rock that time and wind had rounded smooth as a cannon ball.

If. If's loomed in an aggregate as heavy as the stone he carried, staggering a bit, over rocks and pits. If they had a police force. If they had a court capable of dealing with matters more important than boundary lines and claim jumpers and petty theft. If the miners court had a judge who knew anything at all about the law, instead of the popularly elected president of the mining district, a medical man by training and a gold seeker by inclination. If they had a jail in which to incarcerate criminals that a police force caught and arrested. If they had police. If they had more than three punishments: whipping, banishment, hanging. If they had any body of law to go by at all, if Congress had allocated the Constitution to the Territory when they formed it. If the miners court had a formal, twelve-man jury instead of the jury of the whole, made up of anyone – drunk or sober – who happened by when the vote was taken for guilt or innocence. If. If. And if.

Then they could find Nick's killers and turn them over to the law. But to what law did they turn them over? Gallagher?

Jacob said, "We have maybe enough rocks now, ja?"

"I think so." Beidler untied his Masonic apron, a small rectangular cloth marked with Masonic symbols, and stuffed it into his coat pocket. He picked up his shotgun as Dan retrieved the Spencer. "What kind of gun is that?"

Dan didn't hear the little man, standing just an inch or two taller in his boots than his own shotgun, until Beidler repeated the question. "Sorry. It's a Spencer repeating rifle."

"Repeating?"

"Yes." Dan showed him how the rifle worked, how it broke at the breech and a seven-shot magazine inserted there, so that he did not have to reload after every shot. And then it would be a simple matter of removing the used magazine and inserting a new one. "It was invented a couple of years ago, and when Spencer got a Navy contract, he made a hundred or so extra so he could sell them to the public. I was lucky to get one. Ammunition's hard to come by, though. I have to make bullets."

"My God," Beidler said. "If the Union Army gets those, we'll win the War."

"An illegal war." Fitch had been listening, his eyebrows closed together over the bridge of his nose. "The Federals had no right to invade the South."

Dan shot back, "Secession is illegal and slavery is immoral."

Fitch gripped a whiskey bottle. "The hell with this. After we get my boy's killers, I'll show you who has the right of it. But first, let's go get them." He raised it to his lips, used his stump to steady it at the bottom.

"Go where? Get whom?" Dan asked.

Fitch pointed at Dan. "Where's your apron?"

Dan knew he meant the Masonic apron. "I don't have one. I'm not a Mason."

"Then you're not coming with us. I won't have a man I don't trust."

What? All this time, Dan had thought men held him at arm's length because of Gallagher and McDowell, and it was not being a Mason? He had surveyed Fitch's claim, and the survey had held up in the Virginia miners court. Damn it, Fitch knew him, but would not trust him even now? Afraid to touch the Spencer's stock, for fear he'd shoot Fitch, he thrust his hands into his pockets, balled them into fists. "God damn it, Nick was a friend of mine, too. I want his killers as much as you do."

The sharp tang of whiskey reminded Dan of deer hunts, fresh killed meat roasting over camp fires in the dark, men laughing as they relived the stalking, played down the mistakes that spoiled their aim, the buck fever they had overcome, the relief that they were known to be men. Bragged about the good shot, the one that brought down the big buck. God, how he missed that.

A stocky man who had stood by Fitch throughout the burial now spoke. "He's right, Tobias. We'll get the murdering bastards and hang them fair and square, but we gotta be sure. That's all this man is saying." He nodded to Dan.

"He ain't coming." Muscles bulged at Fitch's jaws. "He wouldn't move a damn boundary line for me, so how can I trust him?"

"That's exactly why you can trust me," Dan said. "I've never falsified a survey in my life. I won't do it for you or any man. And I won't be party to a lynching."

"He's got a point," the stocky man said. "Listen – "

"This man you do not know." Jacob's voice sliced through their anger. Thin, stooped as if to avoid notice, his sparse beard almost comical, he stood, chin up, confronting Fitch. Nothing comical about Jacob, now.

Looking down at him, Fitch's jaw muscles relaxed. "Well, Jake?"

Jacob spread his hands, palms up, a mute advance apology for his English. Every 'th' was an S. "I come to this country, and nothing do I have. Not a thing. Maybe a few dollars, and some clothes. This man – " he bent his head toward Dan – "this man, he see me, we talk, he offer me job, show me how to be chain man, share his cabin." He paused, and his Adam's apple bobbed. "In the Old Country is pogrom. The Cossacks our rabbi lynch. Our houses they burn. Barns. There, a gentile gives not even a crust of bread to a Jew. Dan Stark says, we are not Cossacks."

Standing quietly, holding his ground while Fitch tried to stare him down, and a gust threatened his hat, Jacob Himmelfarb would not be moved.

The stocky man said, "He's right. We're not Cossacks."

Dan studied the splash of tobacco juice on the toe of his boot. He could think of nothing to say, nothing that would relieve his embarrassment or the tension as they waited for Fitch to react. A hump of snow lay a couple of inches away, and he scuffed the drying yellow-brown mess in it. He felt like a schoolboy waiting to be chosen for a game.

"No." Fitch relaxed his bunched shoulders. "We're not. That wouldn't be Nick's way, either." Taking a long swallow of the whiskey, he passed it to Dan, who drank, grateful for the warmth spreading in his gullet. Along the road, candles and lanterns were being lighted in the cabins and stores and saloons. "We went looking for Nick a couple of days after he was due, starting at Long John Frank's place because that's where Nick pastured the mules. Long John told us that Nick collected them and started back, and he never saw him after that." He paused, and Dan heard a dry swallow or two before he said in a shakier voice, "Then comes Palmer to say he found Nick's – uh, Nick less than a quarter mile from Long John's wickiup. I say we start there and ask some questions."

"For my part," said one of the other men, "I think better when I'm warm."

"Right," said Fitch. "We need a battle plan."

"We're not going into battle," Dan protested. "We're just going to ask some questions."

Fitch's long slow stare, one eyebrow raised, spoke plainer than words: Greenhorn, but he only said, "You never know, Blue. You never know."

As they made their way down the rutted track past miners coming out of the diggings, and lamplight shining from a few windows, the stocky man fell in beside Dan. "Name's Jim Williams. I have a ranch down on the Stinking Water. Fitch gets the mules from me for his freighting business."

"Glad to know you." Dan was not much interested. He watched his footing, busy with the problem of identifying the killer. "Dan Stark." He didn't hear Williams's next comment, but stopped in his tracks so that Williams and Jacob walked a pace or two ahead. He laughed out loud at himself. He was an idiot. This thing was so simple, he should have thought of it at once. "I think I know how to make sure we get the right man. We look for the alibi."

"How is that important?" Fitch asked.

"The only one who knows for certain when Nick was killed is his killer. If he tries to prove he was somewhere else at a certain time, or on a particular day, we have him."

"By God, you're right. But what time? What day?"

"Any time from when Long John Frank says he left until you expected him back."

"Frank said he left midafternoon on the sixth, and I expected him back by nightfall on the seventh."

"All right," Dan paused to flick a match head with his thumbnail; shielding the flame against the wind, he lighted a stub of candle. "It takes what? six hours to ride from Wisconsin Creek to Summit? So he'd stay over somewhere and start back in the morning?" They were all nodding as he groped along the path of his reasoning.

"He didn't." Fitch's stump reached toward his hat. "We asked at Dempsey's, and Laurin's, and Daly's. They never saw him on the return trip."

The moon was veiled in thin clouds. These calculations were not so different from the routine trigonometry he did every day on surveys, except simpler, more arithmetical. "From what I know now, it seems that Nick was murdered not long after he left Frank's ranch. We'll need to know if Frank moved his camp during the last two weeks, but I think Nick died before sundown on the sixth."

∽

Sitting Indian fashion in the wagon bed, Martha wished she'd walked. The rear axle twisted and plunged like a bucking horse, while the front one screamed like hogs at slaughter. The wagon itself complaining. A wheel bounced on a rock, another dropped into a hole, and Martha's hip was one great bruise. Miz Hudson's pursed lips told a world of hurt as she tried to hold her hat and the sideboards, but the colored gal rode standing up like dancing. Martha would have stood, too, but the child needed the comfort of her mother's arm. When they were to home, Martha would give the child another swallow of the tincture of wormwood in a sweet syrup.

They jolted down into Virginia City, noise rising up like to drown them. The distant thunder of blasting powder rumbled, thank the Lord not close, a thousand picks gnawed into the creek, a thousand shovels dropped streaming dirt and rock into contraptions for washing away dirt and catching the gold. Cradles, rockers, sluice boxes. Warped wood against wood shrieked.

Timmy would be working the claim, too scared of his Pap to leave for his friend's burying. Supposedly he helped his Pap, but like as not McDowell went off and left Timmy to gouge out the gold by himself, braced against the current while ice daily grew out a little farther from the banks. Not that the boy minded work. He'd worked hard back home. Nobody liked killing hogs or wringing chickens' necks for dinner or slaughtering a yearling calf, but dying so the rest could live was the way of things. In return, farming meant cows giving milk thick with cream, fat bacon and ham curing in the smoke house, hay filling the barn to the rafters, and sunlight slanting through leaves. No, it wasn't the hard work he minded. It was the lonesomeness. With his Pap there, it might have been joy. Without him, it was misery to drive his shovel into the creek, his feet numb, his blistered hands aching from the cold. Young'uns worked hard like that everywhere, but it didn't make it right.

They said Alder Gulch was a beautiful place before gold. A sweet-running stream with alder trees giving sun-dappled shade along the banks. Then Bill Fairweather found gold, and the stampede followed them, and someone's campfire got out of control. Now men hunted gold amid blackened stumps of burnt alder trees. An ugly place. What folks would do to get gold. Kill a creek, kill each other. Kill a boy. And for what? Gold. Gold the only crop.

Mr. Palmer left them where the main road turned left, uphill, and became Wallace Street. She and Miz Hudson called out thanks, and Mr. Palmer waggled a hand over his shoulder. Miz Hudson rubbed her left elbow. "I declare, from now on it's shanks mare —"

A pistol shot popped. The bullet, where was it? Men yelled. Martha snatched Dotty behind herself, shielded her. Across the street, men in front of Fancy Annie's saloon whooped and hollered at three horses galloping away, past the garbage dump, out into the sagebrush. A race.

Drat these men! Shooting on Wallace Street with folks about, and children maybe getting hurt. Martha shook like her bones would part. The fringes on Miz Hudson's shawl quivered, and she clung to Tabby, who held her round the shoulders. The colored gal looked ready to kill someone with that knife — how'd she come by it? Martha didn't know as she'd blame her none.

"Mam! Let me go!" Dotty squirmed out of Martha's grasp.

"The blamed fools!" Martha said, "Someone could've got hurt." She'd give someone a piece of her mind, she would, tell him just what she thought of him. The very idea —

"Mam, you all right?" It was Timmy, running to her, stumbling a bit, and as she assured him that they were fine, just shook up was all, Martha began to cry, the first time she had wept since they brought Nick in. She didn't cry because she was sad, she was seeing pictures behind her eyelids, pictures that came and went: the farmhouse back home, her own Mam waving goodbye from the porch, Nick laughing, Dotty's sad little face, Tim's chapped hands. The boy had a comforting sturdiness as she leaned against him, her son growing up. The pictures changed about, melded together, not into another picture, but into a feeling, a knowing. Her life was wrong. All wrong, and she had to put it right.

She was drying her eyes, assured the young'uns that she was fine, the storm had blowed over, when Sam McDowell, her own husband, all six feet something, wearing a Confederate artillery man's double-breasted coat, stepped away from the group in front of Fancy Annie's saloon and walked their way. Jack Gallagher raised his hat to her, and Martha gave him part of a nod. With his long grace Sam quick-stepped around a dog that squatted in front of him, dodged a mule that snaked its head out to bite. Time was, seeing him unexpected like this would have made her damp. No more. With him so changed by the War, his face creased and his eyes holding recollections of battle that woke him, shouting, in a sweat. He was not the man she'd married. She'd prayed so hard they could be a family again like before.

He eyed her down a long-necked bottle he lifted for a swig. "You all right?"

"No thanks to you-all. What do you mean, firing off a pistol that way?" She shouted, wanting to embarrass him in front of his friends, to make him look past the bottle and see them, see her, see the young'uns, especially the young'uns. Tim, most of all.

"We was just starting a horse race." He took another drink, swayed a little.

If she'd had a gun, a knife, she might have used it, she wanted to pierce his skin so he'd be reminded of them, if she pricked him he'd have to see her. Or scorch him. She felt like a great balloon filled with flames and she wished she could open her mouth and let out fire, let it pour over him.

"I'll need dust," he said.

"Tell Gallagher to pay his board bill, then. I got just enough to buy supplies." Martha made her hands stay where they were, not touch the poke that lay nestled against her side just above the waistband of her skirt. "Why weren't you at Nick's burying?"

"Yeah, I heard they'd found him. I thought he'd just gone south with the mules and gold."

"He wouldn't do that!" Tim's hands doubled into fists. It wouldn't take much for him to throw a punch at his Pap. Martha prayed he wouldn't. It would be years before he could match Sam McDowell's height and weight.

Miz Hudson said, "Nick Tbalt was as decent a lad as God ever touched."

Late enough, Sam nodded to Miz Hudson, touched his hat brim.

Her lips shut tight against him.

"You should have come to his burying," Martha said.

"If I'd went, it wouldn't do him no good. He'd still be dead, wouldn't he?"

Miz Hudson gasped. "Have you no decency?"

Sam sparked like flint on steel. "Ma'am, I got my fill of the dead on the battlefield. There was too many to bury so we piled them up and burned them. I'll never get that stink out of my nose." He said to Martha, "I got to get back. I'm taking bets." He held out his hand to Tim. "Give it to me."

"Pap, I need boots." Timmy thrust both hands into his jacket pockets.

"What do you need boots for? They won't keep the water out. Give it to me." He waggled his fingers. "Now."

The boy pulled a deerskin pouch out of his pocket, and set it on McDowell's palm. Walking away, McDowell called over his shoulder, "Boy, you better have more for me tomorrow."

Tim opened his mouth to yell something after his Pap, but Martha drove an elbow into his ribs. "You'll do no good." Wrong, all wrong, but there weren't no way to fix it that she could see.

❧

Warming themselves in Lott Brothers' store, the main commercial enterprise of Nevada City, it did not take long for Nick's friends to organize. Some, who had horses readily at hand, would ride with Jim Williams to his ranch on the Stinking Water and get mounts for those who did not keep a horse in town. Williams ran a livery, but he offered horses and tack at no charge. Fitch grumbled that he would pay, dammit, Nick had been his foster son, but Williams refused. Everyone was to meet at his barn at ten o'clock, ready to ride. A night ride would keep their secret. They wanted no one to warn Long John.

In the meantime, they should do what they normally did, to throw off any suspicion that something was up, that might alert the killer's friends, whoever they were. Daniel and Jacob hiked back to Virginia, Jacob to eat his kosher meal with the Morris brothers while Dan took supper with the McDowells. And Gallagher. Maybe he'd have time to retrieve his winnings from Con Orem, add them to his stash at the Eatery.

"How much did you win?" Jacob spoke slowly, feeling his way among unfamiliar auxiliary verbs.

"Last anyone knew, the exchange rate was $18.00 an ounce." Visualizing the chips in the pot, Dan saw his hands stacking and counting white chips, and blue. Two yellow. "Probably about eighty dollars. And McDowell's half of a claim."

Jacob whistled. "That is a great much."

Footsteps charged up the road behind them, and Dan touched the rifle's stock; he would be ready, but Fitch panted from a few steps away, "Wait there, you all, wait a damn minute, will you?"

They waited, from courtesy rather than wanting Fitch's company. Dan forbade himself to laugh at Jacob's quaint phrasing. "Yes. It turned into high stakes at the end. McDowell plunged."

"That's steeper than I thought." Fitch gulped air. "What was it you said about McDowell plunging?" He produced a tin box of matches, patted his pockets till he found a candle, and put it between his teeth, the wick hanging out. "My night vision isn't so good." Dan had to admire his dexterity as he held the candle in his mouth and struck the match on one of the metal buttons of his coat, though the candle flamed so close to the curly bush of his goatee that Dan thought the hairs might catch. Himself, he preferred the old-fashioned tinder box, matches being too hard to come by, another profit item for Fitch's freighting business. But flint and steel took two hands.

"Yes. He bet a claim at the end." As Fitch's head jerked up, the flame described a swirl in the darkness.

Dan added, "I won it." The candle flame made caves of Fitch's eye sockets, his eyes gleamed from within.

"The hell you say." Fitch brought the candle close to Dan's face. "You mean you played poker with McDowell – Gallagher was there, too, I'll be bound – thought so, and you won and walked out with a claim in your pocket?"

Dan put up his hand to shield his eyes, but too late to save his own night vision. "Yes, and your signature is on it, too."

"Christ!" The candle flame wavered on Fitch's bark of a laugh. "You got one of my contracts?" Another yelp, to Dan's ear as devoid of humor as his own feelings. "That makes us partners."

Partners. Neither man offered to shake hands on it, a one-time partnership they did not want.

Twilight thickened around Martha and the others like the dawn of gloom as they trailed up Wallace Street. Martha felt like her life up to now had started in to die the day she waved goodbye to Mam and Pap and Grandmam, standing in the road, until the wagon left them behind the shoulder of Sugar Mountain, and that with Sam walking off to his pals, it was dead and buried with Nick in his grave. Or maybe it died the day Sam come home and told her he'd sold the farm, and she had carried its corpse all this way. Even holding Dotty close on one side, Timmy's arm solid around her shoulders on the other, she felt like a kite come loose and sailing on unknown currents of air to – where? Into gathering shadows that foretold winter, when what was was gone and what would be was not yet.

In this darkness she put down one foot and the next, without seeing where except where light shone from store windows. The stores, Dance & Stuart and Mr. Goldberg's Pioneer Clothing Store, didn't tempt her to look at goods the freighters had brought. Nor Dotty, who loved to peer in the windows of LeBeau's Jewelry and Kramer's Dress Shop, to see the pretties. Glancing in Kramer's, Martha saw two fancy women trying on extravagant hats with ostrich plumes, while a clerk watched with folded lips and a crease between her eyes. Helen Troy, who owned Fancy Annie's, and Isabelle Stevens, one of the girls. Sometimes Jack Gallagher's woman. With Dotty's longing for bright fabrics and shiny jewels, Martha didn't want her envying their kind.

At BAM, Baume Angevine and Mercy's dry goods store, she recollected Tom Baume's anguished cry over the knife he'd loaned Nick, and she wanted to go somewhere and weep alone, but Miz Hudson stopped them at the Eatery. A smile folded her cheeks. "Come in, do. We can stir up some comfort." She laid a black-mittened hand on Martha's arm. "We all need it, especially the child."

"Thank you kindly," Martha said. "We could do with some consolation."

The Eatery, just one room, held two long plank tables. An aisle at either end, wider on the right than on the left, let Miz Hudson and the colored gal serve up the meals. Miz Hudson used the right aisle, and the colored gal, being far less ample, commonly worked on the left. At a small table hard by the door,

Albert collected gold dust from customers, weighed it up on a scale, and gave them a scrap of paper for a ticket. When the colored gal or Miz Hudson brought the meal, they'd collect the ticket. Martha thought she'd like to know how to weigh up dust and give honest measure for it, like the darky did. He could weigh the gold, and convert it to money.

Imagine! A darky knew how to cipher and weigh gold, and she'd just bet he could read, too. Didn't seem right a darky could read and write and cipher, and she couldn't. Didn't seem right at all. She had to depend on the honesty of her boarders. Mr. Stark always gave her the right measure, but Gallagher might pay more one time and less the next, and she couldn't cipher it out, but must tell light and heavy by the weight of the leather pouch, the poke, in her hand.

She hated being so unknowing.

The darky, Albert, bent deep into a barrel, pulled head and shoulders out with a tin in his hand. He looked mighty pleased with life. "It's come," he said, and Martha was struck with the deep richness of his voice, reminding her of her Pap, who sung bass.

Miz Hudson clapped her hands. "Do let's see, then."

He gave her a square red tin with a wreath of bright green leaves and yellow flowers, below large blue letters. Miz Hudson's tiny feet danced. "Ooooh! Chocolate! Dear Mrs. McDowell, isn't it lovely?"

"Chocolate? Oh, my! I haven't eaten chocolate since, since I can't remember when!" But she could, and embarrassment overwhelmed her because she'd tantamount to ask for some instead of waiting for Miz Hudson to offer, and because of that and poor Nick, and Sam, and the life gone that she had wanted – the four of them as a family the way it used to be before the War – and winter coming on, and it was all just too much. She wept while the young'uns patted her back and held her. So she never knew just how the colored gal made the chocolate, only that she did, and they sat as near the stove as might be, tin mugs of hot chocolate in their hands, while the darkies went on working, their chocolate ready to hand. No one said anything special, but Martha, the mug warming her hands, the rich chocolate smell on her palate, somehow felt almost like her soul was on the way to being restored.

"Gold fever's a terrible disease." Miz Hudson sipped, held it in her mouth, eyes closed, before she swallowed. "Some people would sell their souls for an ounce of dust." She sighed. "I'm afraid my price would be an ounce of chocolate."

So unlooked-for a remark from someone she'd thought solemn. Martha spluttered, barely managed not to spit, and everyone was laughing. Even the colored gal, slicing meat for a stew, put down the knife and threw her head back. The laughter died away, leaving the room warmer. Albert prised open another barrel and lifted out a thick wad of crumpled newspaper that he laid on the table.

"Newspaper! Glory be!" Miz Hudson set to smoothing out the sheets, located the date on each one and sorted them into stacks, to begin putting dated issues together again. Tim and Dotty helped, and pretty soon the three of them had a regular rhythm going, the young'uns smoothing and Miz Hudson putting them together.

"Imagine someplace where news is regular and newspaper could be taken cheap enough to pack with," said Miz Hudson. "I'll rent these out, by the issue or by the sheet and folks'll be glad to pay me just to have something to read." She stopped at one page with big black type. "They fought a battle last summer at some place called Gettysburg, in Pennsylvania. The Union won."

"Hallelujah." The colored gal raised her eyes to the ceiling. "Praise the Lord." There was such joy and hope on her face that it fair took Martha's breath away. Then, seeing Martha look at her, she emptied the joy from her eyes and bent her head to the work. It was like Martha had peeked through a window to where people lived their lives, only to have the shutters slammed.

"War's not over yet." Miz Hudson talked like she was breaking bad news. "Seems the Confederates got away, but it was a terrible slaughter. Just terrible."

"Serves them right," Albert muttered, and Martha felt Tim's back stiffen. She patted his forearm and was surprised at how muscular it was, almost like a man's arm, but his hands were chapped almost raw. When they got home, she'd mix a little ground hops in lard and rub it into his hands.

"The slaughter was on both sides." Miz Hudson frowned. "The Lord said, Love thine enemies."

The colored gal glared at her with such fury on her face that fair sucked Martha's breath out of her. "When the overseer's lash tears open your back?"

"Or the crucifier's nails rip into thy hands and feet," countered Miz Hudson.

Thinking of Nick, Martha said, "I couldn't love them as put my son on a cross." She grasped Timmy's hand. "I can't love Nick's killers, neither." Like Albert's scales had to balance. "Them as murdered Nick can't be let to run around loose to kill someone else."

Timmy said, "They have got to be stopped." When everyone looked at him, he gulped, and went on in his unbroken voice, so odd in a boy his size. "You can see that, can't you?"

Miz Hudson said, "The Lord came to show us a better way, but He let Himself be killed because that was the way He wanted us to see." She spoke so soft that Martha felt like they were in church and laid a finger on the newspaper sheet to stop Dotty. "And to follow Him. He rose again, you know."

"I know," Tim said. "That's what the preachers say. But I ain't ready to test that yet. I dare say Nick wasn't, either. Nobody has got the right to make someone else die for his own principle. How do you save my life, considering there could be someone out there that thinks he wants what I have and ain't so particular about how he gets it? Or maybe thinks I looked at him cross-eyed? I want to be an old man someday." The boy's hands gripped the mug. "How do I do that? How do I get old, Miz Hudson? It appears to me right now like my choices are to leave and be murdered on the way or stay and be murdered."

"Mam said the men have to be God's thunderbolt." Dotty squirmed onto her knees on the bench to give her more leverage with the paper.

"You said that, Mam?" Into Timmy's eyes came such pride that she'd never seen before. "Truly?" Love, yes, she'd seen that, but pride? She could only nod, and not just because she had chocolate in her mouth.

"She truly did," Dotty said. "Spoke right up to them all, give them such a talking-to."

Miz Hudson said, "Thee has much courage, the way thee talked up to the men."

"I never thought I'd speak up so," Martha said. "Never would've back home."

"That Psalm is a great favorite of mine," Mrs. Hudson said. "What is thy favorite?"

Martha set her mug down, watched the brown liquid settle itself. Teetering on a confession, she made up her mind. "I can't read."

Miz Hudson went so still that Martha wished she could back time up and unsay it. "Then thee can't know how the light of the Lord shines for thee. Thee must always depend on someone else to tell thee."

A shiver ran down Martha's spine. "You mean, the Lord – " Her throat closed up, and she tried again. "He shines a light for me? Even an ignorant being like me?"

"Thee might be ignorant, but thee are not stupid. Thee must learn to read, for the Lord speaks to each of us out of the scriptures if we listen for Him." She paused. "That is one part. Another part is to pray for correct understanding. A third is to listen. A warped understanding does great harm in the world."

"Yes, but how can you be certain?"

"That is difficult. But first one reads. Would thee like to learn? I will teach thee."

Martha's hand opened and took hold of the mug's handle. Learn to read? To know things. To find out. A world in her grasp, like the mug, and all she would have to do was lift it up and drink. "That would be —" She couldn't find words to say how glorious. She lifted the cup, set it down. "Yes. Oh, glory. Yes. I can pay you some."

"That is not necessary. I will teach thee for friendship."

Martha bent her head, set down the cup, and hid her face in her hands. For friendship. She'd had no woman friend to confide in since Mam and Grandmam, and the women on the long walk across the plains had been going to Oregon or some such place, or died from sickness, or childbirth. She felt Timmy's hand soothing on her back. After a minute she said, "Thank you, but I can't be beholden."

"I understand." Miz Hudson said after a pause, "Very well, I have a proposition for thee. Daniel Stark has said thee are one of the best cooks in the Gulch, and thy pie crusts are tender and flaky."

The praise made Martha squirm. "I don't know...."

"I have two barrels of dried apples in the storeroom. Suppose thee bakes apple pies for me. I'll have the best pies in the Gulch, and we'll split the proceeds."

Timmy said, "Our Mam is a great healer, too. She medicines us till we don't hardly need no doctors."

Miz Hudson sat up straight, like a small animal on watch by its den. "Indeed? I have some small store of information along those lines myself. My late husband was a homeopathic physician."

"I just know what my Mam and Grandmam taught me about plants and such. I'll have to learn fresh here, where it's so different." She knew the deep dark woods of home, where trees lost their leaves every autumn and the ground was rich and soft with leaf mold, but now she lived in this sparse dry country of sagebrush and juniper. A hard, rocky country, except where streams ran, or where gold hunters found color and turned it ugly, hard, and stony.

"As to that," said Miz Hudson, "thee must consult Berry Woman, the Indian married to Toby Fitch. Their wickiup stands at the bottom of Jackson Street, this side of Daylight Creek."

Nodding her thanks, Martha felt a pressure on her arm. Dotty had been clutching it, and now the child shook it; she was impatient at all the talk.

"Please, Mam." Dotty clutched her arm. "I want to go to school. I want to know things, too."

Martha brushed the hair out of the child's eyes, inwardly sighting down the decision as far as she could, to where it forked, one to their lives, her and the young'uns, and the other to McDowell. Their hankerings came from being here, among so many different people, Jews and Christians and unbelievers and blacks and whites and Indians. All sorts. Most of them decent enough, some of them good men like Mr. Dance and Mr. Stark and Mr. Himmelfarb, but some pure evil like that Boone Helm, or the whores. Everyone with different notions, maybe like Miz Hudson's better'n them she'd grown up with, but how to sort through them so as to keep straight, and what did you measure by if not the Bible?

How to divide a pie and get a fair return if you couldn't cipher? Or know how much dust you had?

"Your Pap don't hold with knowing how to read. And the preachers tell us a woman can't go against her husband." What Sam had said was, A woman don't need to know reading to spread her legs for her man.

"What does the Bible say?" Miz Hudson spoke nearly in a whisper, but her question swept through Martha's mind like a strong wind and blew her ideas before it. She would have to disobey McDowell in order to know what the Bible said about disobeying him.

Dotty's round eyes pleaded with her, and Martha knew she wouldn't have the preachers tell her. She would know for herself how the Lord lighted her way. She would make up her own mind.

"You can't tell your Pap," Martha told them.

"We won't, Mam," Timmy said. "I want to learn, too. I don't want to hunker down in some damn creek all my life and know nothing but shoveling."

"Cross my heart." Dotty swiped her hand in an X across her chest.

"Then, yes." Martha lifted her chin. "I accept."

Reaching across the table, Miz Hudson took Martha's hands in her own. "We'll do as the men do, and shake hands on it. As we're business partners and friends now, perhaps thee should call me Lydia."

Martha laughed out loud. "Only if you'll call me Martha."

༄

Trudging up the rise between Nevada and Virginia, Dan kept Jacob between Fitch and himself, and held Jacob's arm as they climbed.

Fitch said nothing until they stopped to get their breath. "Well, well, Blue, if you ain't full of surprises. I didn't even think you played poker, and here you win against that pair, quit while you're ahead, and live to tell about it."

Dan shook his head. "McDowell's a poor poker player, and Gallagher's not much better."

"Yeah? You're too young to have played much."

"Hell, my father taught me to play before I could read." Memories blindsided him: Father's smile over the cards on the table, the rich smell of bonbons awarded for counting the chips correctly; the rotten-egg stink of gunpowder in his nostrils, the sick-sweet smell of blood overpowering all. He had not eaten bonbons since Father —

At the top of the rise, the aspect of the moon enlarged, so that it appeared to rest on the northern shoulder of Baldy Mountain, where Alder Creek began its westward flow. Below them, Daylight Creek burbled into Alder Creek, and they stood where Gallagher's jurisdiction began, the legal dominion changed from the Nevada Mining District to the Fairweather Mining District, from Nevada City to Virginia City. In the camp mellow rectangles of lamplight shone on the snow. Somewhere a chorus attempted a few bars of Handel's *Messiah*. The high notes were missing because the director had rewritten the soprano parts for tenor voices.

Gunshots rang out, and the music stopped.

"Damn it, why did McDowell bring his family here? It's no place for decent women and children, and he doesn't take care of them." Dan kicked a stone, that tumbled downhill. He had won McDowell's claim, and that made him partners with a Confederate, and he loathed the Confederacy. No matter how they couched their damned rebellion in high-sounding principle, there was nothing principled about it. It was base. Immoral. And their preachers, no matter how they twisted their thinking to justify slavery because the Bible — written in times that accepted slavery as a natural state of affairs — appeared to advocate it in the name of the Lord, who must want to vomit every time He heard their self-serving prayers. Yet that was not the worst.

The worst was that McDowell, gambling away this claim, this paper resting now in his pocket, had a family and was not looking after them. A wife and two children, and he gambled away something that might ensure their future. And now it was his. Conjointly with this God-damned Secessionist.

Fitch bit off a chaw from a plug of tobacco, chewed to soften it. "McDowell didn't want her. She brought the children and just tagged along, probably because if he once got away she'd never see him again."

Dan heard the chomp and hiss of mastication, smelled the tobacco. His stomach lurched. "Good Lord! He couldn't stop her?"

Fitch laughed. "You don't know much about women, do you? Once they take a notion, you've got a snowball's chance in hell of stopping them."

The singing started again as the three men walked down the track. "Besides, he'd sold the farm, and told her about it after he'd used the money to buy what he'd need to come out here."

Dan and Jacob spoke almost together. "Gott im himmel," Jacob said. "He would his family leave?"

"But — but she would have nothing. No way to make a living." Dan could not imagine it. A man cared for his family, that care defined him as a man as much as courage in battle, or prowess in bed.

"Yes to you both. That's the sort of first class bastard McDowell is." He stopped, faced Dan, and in the candlelight, his expression was serious and completely without its usual half-sneer whenever he looked at Dan. "It's a good thing you board there, Blue. That family needs someone principled putting his feet under Mrs. McDowell's table."

The compliment was so unlooked for that Dan felt himself gaping like some half-wit, mouth open, lower lip slack.

"Of course, you got completely the wrong principles, you know." Fitch's upper lip lifted at one end. "You say you're a Union man, on the wrong side of this here illegal War and you haven't the balls to fight in it. You just spout poetry."

As a child, he'd played the children's game, all joining hands and running in a crooked line intended to throw the last child off the whip, the snake's tail. This felt like that. He'd been whipsawed. The Atlantic pounded in his ears, the push and drop and long withdrawal of the waves tugging hard at him. He held tight to the Spencer's stock, something solid amidst an undertow of wanting to beat the shit out of Fitch. God damn Tobias Fitch.

"Go to hell!" Dan stalked away, his feet sure in the starlight, Jacob scrambling after him.

Fitch called out, "My boy thought a lot of you, Blue, and for his sake I'll remember that."

Dan stopped. "In memory of Nicholas, then, we'll make a truce."

"All right. Until we've dealt with Nick's killers."

Fitch caught up, and the three men, Jacob in the center, trudged downward.

The claims along the creek lay quiet to the water flowing around mounds and barriers, seeking its way as it always had and always would, the moon glimmering on its surface. Their boots crunched over ruts slimed with ice from mud setting up. They did not speak. Tonight, Dan thought, they would set about the work of finding Nick's killer, and he would lie to Mrs. McDowell about his absence. He had a hunch she would not be fooled. Uneducated, she was not unintelligent, not without spunk and fire as her outburst had proved. He sensed in her a finer spirit trapped in marriage to a drunken oaf. He would see her soon. Would he think her beautiful now? Or would she have turned again into the drab he thought her before she called on them to be God's thunderbolt?

∽

Before turning toward the McDowell cabin from Idaho Street, Dan stopped to catch his breath. It was a bit of a climb from the creek, up Wallace, right on Jackson, left on Idaho. All uphill. Nothing in Virginia City was level; it was all uphill or downhill. The McDowells' dog, a yellow hound named Canary, growled. When Dan whistled to it, it woofed and bounded to meet him, wriggled and squirmed against his legs as he bent to scratch it behind the ears.

He was crazy to come here. He knew it. Take supper with McDowell and Gallagher after winning this afternoon? Just so he could see Mrs. McDowell once more. What had got into him?

He thought he had two plausible lies prepared. One to explain why he wouldn't play cards tonight, and one to explain why he wouldn't be at dinner for the next day or two. Jacob had offered to take a note, but he wouldn't be any more of a coward than he already was. He wouldn't hide behind Jacob.

His hand unsteady, Dan knocked at the door, heard McDowell's shout to come in.

Inside, the aromas of beef stew and fresh bread welcomed him. If McDowell greeted him with a frown and a grunt, his family had a smile for Dan, and Tim, who sat with his back to the door, twisted around and said, "Good evening, Mr. Stark."

McDowell sneered at his son. "Getting fancy are we? 'Good evening, Mr. Stark.'"

"Good evening, Tim. Evening, all." Dan hung up his coat on a peg driven into the wall, between two of the logs. A tall kerosene lamp standing in the center of the table gave enough light to eat by and for the men to see each other's faces. Beyond the circle of lamplight, the beds, a larger one and a smaller one, stood in the two back corners. Between them, along the rear wall, squatted two large trunks whose brass fittings caught gleams. In the corner to the left of the door, a rocking chair and quilt stood beside a round table as if waiting for Mrs. McDowell to pick up the mending heaped in a basket.

Gallagher, one cheek bulging with food, gave him a quarter of a nod. He sat facing the door, had insisted on that chair, claimed he didn't want someone to sneak up on him. Who, Dan wondered, would invade the McDowell house to shoot the Deputy?

She seemed nervous, but the lamp and one candle on a kitchen shelf gave too little light to see her expression clearly. Taking his usual seat at Gallagher's right, facing McDowell, he said, "Good evening, Mrs. McDowell." He felt stiff, knew he sounded stilted, wondered when they would challenge him.

"Good evening, Dotty." For the child he had a special smile. "How are you?" She reminded him, in her countrified way, of his little sister Peggy, who began to think of her womanhood, but yet climbed trees. When he last saw her, nearly seven months ago.

"I'm sad, Mr. Stark," she said. "Poor Nick."

"I'm sad, too," said Dan.

Mrs. McDowell said, "Think of Nick with the Lord. He's happy now, and we'll see him again."

Gallagher snorted, McDowell mumbled, "Damn foolishness," around the bread in his mouth. Dotty's small face brightened, but her brother kept his silence, spooned up his stew.

A pleasant idea, Dan thought, though it wasn't one he could take comfort in. He didn't think Nick had wanted such happiness. Not yet.

"You seen Fitch?" McDowell asked.

"We walked back together from Nick's burial." Dan accepted the thick slice of roast that Mrs. McDowell set in front of him. She had wrapped her hands with a red towel to protect them from the plate's heat. Her hands were long-fingered, but rough from work and cold. His mother creamed her hands and wore white cotton gloves to protect them at night.

He tore a hunk off the loaf of bread and bit into it. Delicious. Everything was delicious. He'd dined in big New York houses where the food wasn't so good. How did she manage on that small stove? She had to kneel to it, or stoop to work.

"He said he'd bring money tonight," said McDowell. "I got a bead on a good thing out aways."

"He'll be along," Gallagher said. "Fitch always wants part of a good thing. McDowell, your woman cooks as fine a meal as I've ever eaten."

McDowell ducked his head once, perhaps agreeing, or maybe just acknowledging the comment.

"Indeed so," Dan said. He glanced past McDowell. Mrs. McDowell stood within the pool of candlelight. Her eyes were huge, deep, and luminous with pleasure, and he thought he'd never seen any woman so beautiful. His tongue dried like lint in his mouth. He cut at the meat without knowing he did so, chewed as if he willed it, while blood pulsed in his ears. His throat balked at swallowing.

He looked at her. She stood as if frozen, the ladle in her hand, her eyes wide and shocked.

God damn it, what was happening? Dan shifted his focus to McDowell, who busied himself tearing bread. Dan swallowed, drank a sip of beer. Breathed.

Gallagher's voice sounded far away.

Dan cut another bite of meat. Married, an inner voice was shouting, married, damn you. Surely the others must hear it. Dear God in heaven. Married. God damn it. He put the meat into his mouth and looked up. No one had heard. No one had seen. But Mrs. McDowell sat on a stool to catch her breath.

It had to have been a trick of candlelight, of scattered and flickering shadows. Nothing had happened. He took a bite of roasted potato. Nothing had happened. Not really.

Thinking so, he dared raise his eyes toward her, ready to shift focus if McDowell noticed, but she was watching Dotty eat, and her face glowed with such a love for her daughter that Dan could not swallow his bite of potato. It was no trick, or if it was, it was a trick of angles and planes in her thin face. Her own beauty. She raised her head and smiled at him, and her eyes were as large and deep as before. He felt his features soften, though he dared not smile for fear McDowell would see, and made himself look away, tried to hear Gallagher over the massive drumbeat in his ears.

He had never seen her before. Not really. Until now. Christ Almighty. He put bread in his mouth.

Gallagher's face turned to Dan, and at the gesture, Dan's hearing cleared.

"You feeling lucky tonight?" Gallagher asked.

He'd been expecting this challenge, had to adjust his mind to it, but he only wanted to talk to Mrs. McDowell. Martha. Talk to her. Hold her. Be with her. Dan chewed on the bread. He needed time to think, to wrench his mind from the woman to the lie he must tell. Convincingly. And all he wanted to do was look at her, test the feeling and know if it were real, had she felt something, too? He swallowed the bread, drank some beer. He wanted her.

McDowell's head was bent over the plate safely between his elbows. Just like his hole card. His head came up, and Tim sat quiet as stone.

"No more than this afternoon." Dan kept his breathing even before diving into the lie, the bluff; he played for higher stakes than gold. "You'll have to wait a day or two to get your revenge." He kept his voice friendly, mild as milk, seemed to concentrate on Gallagher, but at the edge of his sight, he knew she watched him.

Dotty's voice, chatting to her mother, continued on for a few words, something about walking with Molly Sheehan, then stopped. A bucket of water, heating on the stove, bubbled once or twice. The wind probed the chinking between the logs.

"Jacob and I are riding out real early with a prospector who wants a secret survey."

"Where you going?" McDowell glared at Dan.

"Blamed if I know." Dan's uncertainty came from the unaccustomed idiom. He had learned the substitute word for damned since coming West. "He just said to meet him two hours before dawn."

"You ain't taking him to any of my claims." McDowell's fist clenched around his spoon.

"That's not likely to happen," Dan said, "even if I could find your stakes under the snow." McDowell opened his mouth, and Dan decided a little righteous indignation was in order here. "You know very well I've never lied on a survey yet. Or helped anyone to jump a claim. What do you think would happen if the boys thought I was a dishonest surveyor? I'd be a dead man."

He leaned back in his chair, spread his palms, and smiled first at McDowell, then at Gallagher. Sweat dampened his shirt, trickled down his back, but they wouldn't see under his jacket. Some water splashed over onto the stove, and the woman leaped to lift the bucket onto the counter. Dan said, "When I get back you'll have your chance to get even. That's a promise."

"No," said Gallagher. "I think it should be — "

The dog's barking startled them all. McDowell's arm jerked and a few drops of beer spilled into his bowl.

Fitch's voice shouted, "Shut up, you damn yeller coon hound."

McDowell opened the door and yelled at the dog, but Canary growled until McDowell slammed the door behind Fitch.

"I swear, McDowell," said Fitch, "one of these days that dog of yours will come to a bad end." He hung up his coat and hat on the empty peg next to Dan's things.

While Fitch held everyone's attention, Dan dared to look at Mrs. McDowell, who seemed absorbed in Dotty's chatter. He hoped his face didn't betray his longing.

McDowell bared his teeth at Fitch. "Right before him as does my dog down."

"Oh, don't get all lathered," said Fitch. "Howdy, Jack. Blue." He bowed to Mrs. McDowell. "Good evening, Ma'am, I trust you're in good stead after today's sad event."

Everyone was curious in his own way how Mrs. McDowell would respond, and Dan was free to watch her, just one of the men at her table. The Commandment said: Thou shalt not covet thy neighbor's wife. But oh God, he did. He did.

If Fitch had expected a curtsy, he didn't get it. She nodded politely, without warmth. "Thank you, I'm doing fine."

Tim surrendered his chair to Fitch, stood beside his mother. Dotty took her brother's hand, and he put an arm around his mother's shoulders. The three of them made a tableau of closeness that excluded them all. Even McDowell, as if they were a unit, complete in themselves. Dan might long for her as a man in the desert craved water, but he could never come between her and her children. Beyond his reach. By law, by motherhood, and Jesus, by her own wish? God, no. Not that. If she didn't respond, didn't feel with him, then, then what? He knew it was dangerous to wait, but he had to know, had to have a signal, could not ride out on tonight's errand unknowing.

She turned her head toward him, as he thought, with utmost care, her face neutral until in a moment when her husband, Gallagher, and Fitch pored over a small pile of dust that glittered and grew out of Fitch's poke in the lamplight, her lips curved and she allowed her mind to glow in her eyes. It was the answer he wanted, and it unsteadied him.

Dan scraped back his chair. "I'd better be on my way. I've got to look over my equipment, to be sure it's ready." He was confident they would accept that lie, too. No one around here knew anything about a surveyor's transit, or compass, or chain; he could convince anyone that one of them might be out of order. Unless they understood that he would never have any piece in less than tip-top condition, always ready to go.

Retrieving his coat and hat, Dan said, "Mrs. McDowell, don't expect me to dinner tomorrow. I'm likely to be quite late."

Her brilliant glance shook him. "I'll pray for your safety and your success."

Tim said, "We both will."

"Thank you." Dan had little faith in prayers, but he guessed that both of them figured out what was afoot, and would keep silent. For that he was grateful.

McDowell snorted. "Success? He's going to measure a damn claim, is all."

Tim said, "We just hope lightning don't strike him, is all."

"Yes." Mrs. McDowell had withdrawn into shadow. "I thought I heard thunder."

"You're hearing things." McDowell's laugh boomed out. "You can count every star in the sky tonight."

Fitch said, "I've known a thunderbolt to come out of a clear sky."

Gallagher's easy, charming smile was calculated to warm Dan to his wishes. "When you get back, you'll owe us another game, Stark. You promised us, and we'll be sure to collect." But the smile did not go to his eyes, with their chill, warning stare.

"Oh, I'll give you your chance to win, Jack. If you can." Because goddam it, he would not lose on purpose to any man.

2: Wisconsin Creek

Moonlight gave each man a silent escort, a companion rider and horse stretched out across the crusted snow. Would that the actual horsemen moved so quietly, but saddle trees creaked, bit chains jingled, and hooves scraped on rocks. Someone, Dan thought, was bound to wonder why this night ride. Ask unwelcome questions. Under his left knee the Spencer rested in its saddle holster, a comfort and a threat. He had pulled it out quickly enough on hunting trips, but this time the game was human. Could he shoot a man? Point it at him? God forbid. His teeth clashed, and he pulled his collar up against the chill air on his neck.

They rode in quasi-military formation, Fitch in the lead with Jim Williams, called Cap. In an election as a wagon train captain, Williams had faced down his opponent, Joseph Slade, rumored to carry an enemy's ears in his vest pockets. Men paid Williams respect, and the title stuck. Beside Dan, Jacob sat his mount like a sack of potatoes, and Dan worried that he might fall off and be hurt.

Through Junction, past the haphazard and ramshackle tents, wickiups, and cabins along Alder Creek, past the saloons and hurdy-gurdies that poured their raucous laughter out onto the darkness, they rode. If anyone heard, if anyone wondered, no one challenged them.

Leaving Alder Gulch to avoid the roughs' known stomping grounds like Pete Daly's ranch, they traveled cross country where patches of snow formed white islands on a sea of dark ground. They rode into gullies whose crusted drifts hid their secrets like hole cards. When they climbed out on foot to spare the horses, knee-deep snow melted into their boots. Remounted, wet feet chilled them.

Long past midnight, they stopped at a ranch to warm up. When he heard their errand, the rancher brought out two bottles of whiskey. Nick's friends turned their horses into a corral, forked some hay for them to bicker over, and broke the ice on the water troughs. They could not all be in the house, so they stayed in the barn, where they passed the bottles. Warmed by a swallow or two of whiskey they settled into the loose, sweet hay.

Dan dreamed he stood in cold water while Harriet, naked, drifted away on a raft. Pale hair streaming behind her, she held out her arms to him, but he could not move. His feet were blocks of ice and something chipped at them. He awoke to find Williams kicking his boot. "Time to go."

Black silhouettes of the western mountains, twenty miles away, stood out against the stars. Dan wished he could draw or paint, but he had to trust the poor substitute of memory. Daguerreotypes or these new-fangled photographs could not reproduce a scene as well as a good painting.

Frozen over, Wisconsin Creek flowed among gnarled roots of willow trees whose stems were caught by the ice so that Nick's friends had to hack their way through. When broken stems whipped at Dan's horse's face, it shied, stumbled, went to its knees. Half over the horn, Dan pushed himself into the saddle as the horse regained its feet. Behind him, Jacob clung to the saddle horn with both hands, the reins loose in his fingers. Dan followed the others down the bank. They had broken through the ice, and water rose above Dan's stirrups. On the farther bank, Dan looked for Jacob, who was half way across; his horse had followed the others. When they stood on top, Jacob said, "Mein Gott."

Feeling for his footing in the dark water, one of the horses slipped and went down. Jumping clear, the rider landed on his backside, immersed up to his neck. Soaked and shaking, he scrambled after the horse up the bank. Raising his quirt to beat the horse, he bellowed through chattering teeth, "You hog-footed good-for-nothing bastard."

"Shut up!" Williams grabbed his arm. "You hurt one of my horses and it'll cost you a hundred bucks."

Pretty steep for a $20.00 cayuse, someone muttered.

Williams tossed the quirt into the darkness of the willows. "Leave it."

"If you was mine, you'd get the beating of your life," the man said to the horse as Williams walked away.

They waited for light among the willows. Dan's legs, numb from the knees down, nearly toppled him, but he grabbed the saddle horn, clung to it as he shuffled about. Against the slicing pain of returning feeling, he buried his mouth in his sleeve to stifle a groan. Soft cursing around him told the same story from other men, and in a momentary silence, he heard teeth chattering.

No one explained to the horses why they should not move. They stamped their feet, shook themselves, blew out their noses. One animal stretched himself out and staled. Fitch muttered, "That does it, goddammit. I gotta piss." There was the rip of unbuttoning, the sound of the flow, and a long sigh.

Dan laughed, and his sleeve stifled that, too.

The moon sank and black night gathered the willow thicket. Dan tried to find stars, but the leafless branches shielded the sky from view. He scuffled his feet, petted the horse, whispered to

Jacob, listened to the creek burble. Fitch swore, as if hot words could warm him or melt the ice in his clothes, in time with his marching feet and swinging arms.

At last the eastern mountains emerged from night. Williams whispered: "Mount up. Quiet."

Dan boosted Jacob into the saddle. "It's almost over."

They walked their horses toward Long John's camp, where the ragged cone of a wickiup stood against the snow. Dan's imagination conjured an army waiting for them. To him it was impossible that the roughs should not know they were coming, should not have posted sentries.

A dog barked, then another.

"Go!" Cap yelled.

Heels and spurs clapped the horses' sides. Pent up by standing cold after the icy crossing, the horses leaped into a gallop. Jacob's foot came out of his stirrup, and he was falling, but Dan swung his horse close, grabbed his arm, hauled him into the saddle. "Hang on!" Dan grappled with his own fear: that his horse might stumble, break its neck. Break his neck. Then the fear left him for the exhilaration of the ride, as the horse bounded from stride to stride through the snow. With other front runners, he reined in at the wickiup. Mounds in the snow became awakening men, who raised their heads to see what the commotion was about. Hardly thinking what he did, Dan pulled the rifle from its holster and levered a shell into the breech.

"Get down," ordered Williams. They settled back, watchful and tense in the snow.

Jacob, jouncing in the saddle, trotted up and edged in between Dan and Fitch. Dan nodded to him, glad he had made it.

Beidler, on Dan's other side, asked, "You done this before?"

"No." Dan shook his head. "Not with men." On a deer hunt, a blind bend around heavy undergrowth, the horse smelled a bear seconds before it rose up from a rotten log. Dan had discovered a useful quickness with the rifle.

"Ain't a lot of difference, is there? Quarry's quarry." Beidler leaned to the side and blew his nose with his fingers, wiped his face on his sleeve.

"True enough," said Dan, "but the killing is different."

"That depends on who you're hunting," Beidler said.

Fitch laughed, a humorless short bark. "That's the first damn thing you've said I agree with, X."

Dan asked, "Was this where they camped when you found them?"

"No." Fitch pointed his chin westward. "They were over there about a half mile."

The tallest man Dan had ever seen, maybe even taller than the President, ducked through the wickiup entrance. Beidler said, "That's Long John." The tall man scratched his crotch, and ran his fingers through his tangled, shoulder-length hair.

Fitch dismounted. "Let's go have us a little talk. Come on, X. You, too, Palmer."

"Wait a damn minute." Williams called to the rest of Nick's friends. "Don't let none of these fellas think of traveling." He beckoned to Dan. "You come, too."

Fitch frowned, but Cap met him with a hard stare, and any objection died.

So authority is established, Dan thought as he dismounted, surprised to feel his feet. Not by force, except force of personality. Walking with Long John's escort, he stomped his feet to warm them up and wished he could swing his arms, but he held the rifle on Long John.

Palmer led them about a quarter mile toward the main road, where the sagebrush was broken and newer snow lay on old sign. "I found the poor lad right about here. You can see where my team and wagon flattened the brush."

Dan knelt, studied the ground with Beidler. A long crushing in the sagebrush going back toward the road – that was Palmer's team and wagon. Beyond where Nick had lain, in a slightly different direction, he made out a scramble of depressions partially filled with snow. The smaller ones were boot prints, the larger were hoof marks. Blessed snow had kept the marks through melting and more snow and melting again, not clear, not detailed, but Dan, closing his eyes, seemed to see the killer drag Nick here, dismount, walk to the body, remount and ride away. He felt a deep sadness retained in the ground itself, like a battlefield even after grass covered over shell casings, fragments of bodies. Nick had died here, while men counted their takings. In the law, whether they pulled the trigger or not, they were all equally guilty of his death – those who killed him and those who knowingly let him die. His murderer, the depraved, the indifferent.

He pictured Nick's cheerful face and the thing it had become, and rose to his feet in the familiar darkening haze, through which he could just make out the tall form backing away from his intent. A hand on his arm, a voice in his ear, "We didn't come for that." Cap's hand, Cap's voice, and the haze lifted. The other men were staring at him as if they had never seen him before. Dan breathed deep and made his fingers loosen on the stock of the Spencer, allowed the barrel to drift downward. He used both hands to let the hammer down. He wanted to crawl away, he was so ashamed. He had not felt that consuming rage in a very long time, had had it schooled, beaten, out of him, thought he had control of it, but the beast had lain in wait, to claw at him.

It did not help that Fitch nodded to him and smiled.

Cap Williams said to Long John, "You'll give me a crick in the neck looking up at you. Hunker down."

Long John crouched on his heels. Tugging at the sleeves of his Hudson's Bay coat, trying to bring them over his wrists, he pointed at Dan: "Keep him away from me."

Fitch said, "We know you killed my boy. You killed Nicholas Tbalt."

"Who? What? I never!" Long John started up.

Beidler thrust him back with the muzzle of his shotgun, and Long John put a hand in the snow to catch his balance, tucked his hands into his armpits. "I never killed no one. What are you talking about?"

"You know me, you heartless bastard," Palmer said. "I needed help with a body yesterday morning. You said, 'They kill people all the time at Virginia and nobody minds that.' You wouldn't bloody help. I found him, and all the time you knew he was here."

Fitch spoke on top of Palmer's last few words. "When I came looking for him ten days ago, you told me he'd left with the mules. You knew he was here. All the time you knew it." He coughed, wiped his hand across his face. "He was my foster son. He died here, and you did nothing, damn you. Not one God damn thing."

"I never killed him, I tell you. I never. I swear." Long John made as if to stand, but Dan let the rifle barrel drift upward, and its Cyclops eye stared him down.

"We buried Nick Tbalt yesterday," Williams said in a calm, reasonable tone whose menace raised the hairs on the back of Dan's neck. "If you didn't kill him, you did the next best thing. You knew he was here and you let him die. Look around you. There's men here loved that boy like their own son. You know what? They don't care if you didn't pull the trigger. You could die right here, Long John. You'd deserve it. You either killed Nick, or you know who did."

"No, I swear. You got the wrong man." A drop of sweat rolled down Long John's temple and disappeared into his beard.

Carol Buchanan

Dan had been thinking while they talked. He forestalled
Williams and Fitch, pretended to be trying to get something
straight. "Help me out if I'm wrong. Nick came for the mules.
He had a heavy poke of gold dust and when he paid their board
he had some left. You killed ... . "

"I never! I swear it! I'm innocent!"

"Keep your damn voice down!" Fitch said.

Beidler was playing with his lariat, looped the rope around
and around itself, let the loose end crawl and slither while Long
John shivered, watching it.

Dan went on as if no one had spoken, "... You killed Nick,
took the gold and the mules. Then you dragged him here and
left him for the birds and the coyotes. Was he dead yet? You took
your rope off and left him. Only someone utterly depraved
would do that." He inclined his head toward Beidler. "Depraved
killers are not fit to live."

"No, no! I didn't!" Long John screeched. His dark eyes
and beard stood out from his pale face, as on a badly exposed
daguerreotype. An idea changed his expression from panic to
calculation. "If I stole them mules, where are they?"

Williams countered, "If we got the wrong man, who's the
right one?"

"Oh, shit," said Beidler. "Let's get this over with. We know
you done it!" He swung the rope at his side. He had made a
noose.

Long John's cheekbones seemed to thrust against his
parchment skin.

"If anyone hangs him, it's me, by rights. Nick was my boy."
Fitch caught the noose and, by placing part of the loop under
his stump of arm, widened it, took a step toward Long John.
"You have one last chance."

"Yeah," said Beidler. "Make it quick because we're freezing
our asses."

Long John gasped, his head wobbled, and he fell over onto his side. A strong odor came from him. His hands dropped over his crotch to cover the spreading stain.

God damn Fitch. Dan swung the Spencer under his arm and bent to help the tall man up. The son of a bitch had scared Long John so, he'd probably lie, tell them what he thought they wanted to know, rather than the truth. This questioning had to be done right.

Williams spoke in a calm, reasonable voice. "You see how it is, Long John. You know something. I don't know's I can hold these boys back forever."

Long John's tongue came out and circled his lips, reminding Dan of a mouse emerging from its hole and darting in again. "I don't know. I never knew what happened or who did nothing. I didn't even know someone had been killed until he showed up." He nodded at Fitch. "Like I said, where are the mules?"

He had a point, Dan thought. He might be telling the truth. Five determined men pointing guns at him could be powerful incentive. If he stole the mules, where were they? They couldn't ride around the valley looking for them. And they sure as hell couldn't hang Long John on what they knew now.

The sky was lightening. A mist rose from the creek running black a few feet away, willow stems on the opposite bank trailed into the swift water like the train of a woman's gown across a polished floor. They moved in a slight breeze Dan could not feel, and then he realized it was no breeze stirring them, but a dark shadow in the mist, a creature following some path a man would not know, and growing larger as it came toward them amid the crackle of ground ice breaking. Goosebumps rose on his forearms. He stepped away from Long John and raised the rifle to his shoulder, rested his cheek against the stock and cocked the hammer.

"Good God, what's that?" Williams pointed toward it.

"Retribution," Dan said.

"Oh, Jesus, save me." Long John buried his face in his hands.

The shadow emerged, took shape, lifted its mouth, and brayed. Laughing, Dan lowered the hammer, let the muzzle sink towards the ground. He bent over, a hand on his knee. The big black mule brayed again.

"God almighty!" Fitch shouted.

Beidler whooped. "Good God in heaven! That's – that's Black Bess! That's my mule. Bessie! Bessie!"

The mule pointed her nose toward the sky and brayed long and loud.

Williams was the first to recover. He asked Long John, "Do you know that mule?"

"Yeah. It's the mule the boy was riding. The one you're – I mean ...." His voice trickled to a stop.

Dan spoke fast. "So you do know her! You know Nick was riding her! Talk. Now! You said we couldn't prove anything, none of the mules was here, we couldn't prove Nick was here. Well, goddammit, Black Bess is here, so now we can prove you killed Nick!" It was a terrific leap in logic, and he had to hope that Long John's fear would blind him to it.

"I never seen her before. I mean, someone said he was riding a black mule, and I thought this must be the one. She wandered in, I think. Yeah, that's it. She wandered in. Maybe in the night. I don't know."

"First I knew a mule could unsaddle herself," Williams said.

"No, no! I unsaddled her after she come here. I mean – "

"You lying bastard." The words half-strangled in Dan's throat. "You did know he was dead, because you unsaddled the mule he was riding, and you knew he was riding her because you took the gold in payment for the mules he was sent to bring home."

"You son of a bitch." Fitch dropped the noose around Long John's neck. "You killed him."

Long John ducked his head into his collar, and his voice came to them, as if strained through his fingers. "I don't dare tell you. They'll kill me!"

"We'll kill you if you don't tell," Dan said. "Even if you didn't kill Nick, you're guilty of being an accessory after the fact. That's a hanging offense."

Beidler said, "Choose, goddammit. You don't talk, we'll kill you. If you talk —"

"We'll protect you," Williams said. "Your only chance is to tell us who the killer is."

Dan stood the rifle against a log. Crouching beside Long John, he spoke as to a spooked horse. "You see how it is. We're your best hope. You tell us what you know and we'll help you. We'll protect you, but we have to know who killed Nicholas Tbalt."

Long John asked, "You promise?" His chest rose and fell, as if breathless from running. Dan removed the noose. He ignored Fitch's protest, flapped his hand at the others to signal that they should lower their guns.

Hammers clicked into place, and gun barrels looked at the ground.

Williams said, "Dan Stark's right. You'll be fine if you tell us what happened."

"Him, too?" The prisoner jerked a thumb in Fitch's direction, but kept his gaze on Dan and Williams.

"Yeah, me too," said Fitch. "Now spit it out, damn it. It's too cold to chew the fat."

Long John lifted his hand to shield his eyes from the rising sun, and Williams took a step to the side to give him shade. Long John said, "George. George Ives. On account of the mules and the gold. George said it was a crying shame that dumb

Dutchman should have all that and we don't have nothing. And he plumb liked that black mule."

Dumb Dutchman. Dan clenched his hands on the rifle's stock. He wanted Long John to taste the fear Nick must have felt as he looked into Ives's gun. His biceps quivered with the effort of not cocking and firing the rifle.

"The hell with that!" Fitch said. "Do you know who you're a-talkin' to? George Ives is a friend of mine. He's the owner of Cold Spring Ranch. You're just trying to save your own skin."

"No, I'm telling God's truth. I swear. Give me a Bible, I'll swear on it." His tongue circled his lips like a small rodent come out of its den. "Ask Hilderman."

"Him?" Williams asked.

"Yeah," Long John said. "George Hilderman. He was with us that day. He's working for Dempsey building a bridge over Ram's Horn Creek. Ask him."

"We will," Williams said. "Don't your ranch lie next to Ives's?"

"Yeah." Long John pointed with his chin toward the black mule. "The boundary's the creek. Cold Spring Ranch is right across the creek, where that mule —"

Dan felt something move under his collar. Had he picked up a flea from Long John? He scratched around his collar bone while he explained. "Evidence. The mule is found on Ives's property, therefore it's in his possession." They gazed at him as if they had never seen him before. "Had Ives been known to covet the mule?"

"God, yes," said Beidler. "He borrowed her from me once for half an hour, he said, and brought her back after two hours of hard riding. She was all lathered up. I'll never loan Ives any animal, the way he treated her."

"All right," Dan said to Long John. "Now tell us, when did Nick start for home?"

Perhaps sensing that the danger was past, instead of answering the question Long John asked if he could stand up. On his feet, he shuffled his feet and slapped his arms about his body, and only when he was warm enough did he tell them his story, front to back. "Tbalt showed up here to get the mules late the morning of, I guess it was the sixth. It took awhile to round them up, on account of they had drifted on west a ways. He paid for their pasture, and started home, maybe about two o'clock. Little after. Ives saddled up and rode after him right away, like I said." The rodent tongue took its run around his lips. "He come back about an hour later with the mules and the gold." He lifted his hands. "That's all I know. I swear."

Fitch turned away. "I don't believe it. Not George. Not something like this. No, sir." He dug at the snow with a foot, watched the hole he made as if it were the most important thing he would do in his lifetime, and Dan saw a drop of moisture, then another, form at the end of his nose and fall into the snow. "George is my friend. He likes Nick. God damn it. Oh, Christ."

To Dan it sounded like prayer.

༄

The light outlining the eastern mountains promised clear skies and temperatures above freezing, and Dan longed for warm dry feet. At the wickiup, Nick's friends laughed with other men around campfires in the snow.

"Shit!" Williams said. "They could get the drop on us any time." He hurried ahead with Palmer, while Dan tried to prod Long John into walking faster.

"Which one is Ives?" he asked.

"Sitting by Aleck Carter, the big, dark-haired fella," said Beidler. "Decent enough."

"Who? Ives?" Dan squinted against the sun to see the man who had called Nick a dumb Dutchman.

"No," said Beidler. "Carter."

Ives squatted on his heels at one of the fires, his back against a log. He held men's attention, they leaned toward him as he spoke, laughed with him. Ives raised a cup to his lips, and his companions' laughter floated to Dan on the still air. Dumb Dutchman. The bastard.

Fitch said, "I don't believe Ives murdered my boy. I don't believe it. He wouldn't."

Thinking about Ives, Dan only half heard. Ives had a reputation for high spirits, for playing pranks. People shook their heads and said, Boys will be boys. He rode his horse into a saloon and demanded a beer, and the horse shit on the floor, was startled and kicked over two tables. Hijinks were one thing, Dan said to himself, but murder?

"I believe it," Beidler said. "He doesn't give a damn about anyone. He'll do anything for fun and not care who gets hurt." He walked backward, tugged on the lead rope, but the mule stiffened her neck. "Come on, damn it, Bessie. We're hungry and cold. It's been a long night." He faced forward. "What the hell. She's a mule. I guess she's acting mulish." His heavy mustache quivered as he chortled at his own pun. "You watch out, Bessie, or I'll give you to Ives."

Long John slowed. "Don't make me go there, for God's sake."

"I'll keep you safe," Dan promised. "Just speed it up, will you? My feet are cold." He prodded Long John with the rifle, and the tall man lengthened his stride.

"There's plenty don't care about animals," said Fitch, "but they don't murder people."

Some hundred feet ahead of Dan and the rest, Palmer and Cap Williams had almost reached the camp. The big man — Carter, was it? — poked his thumb in their direction. Ives lifted his head on squared shoulders, his body intent, before he relaxed and spoke to Carter, and laughed. Dan had a flash of insight: Ives knew. He understood what it meant that Beidler was leading the mule. Dan recalled Grandfather hectoring Father at dinner after a loss in court: You misread the client's behavior. A guilty man will laugh and joke, an innocent man never, do you hear? Never. Points emphasized with his fist among the cutlery. Innocence is frightened, bewildered, not knowing why the law takes him. A guilty man is jocular, to win over the law.

Ives was joking.

Williams barked: "Men! Look to your guns!"

Once, returning from a deer hunt, Dan had walked past the Deans' house, thinking to let Harriet know he was home, would call tomorrow, but a party in progress, music and laughter and light bubbling into the street, stopped him at their gate. She was waltzing with another man. Old Dean had appeared, spoken, and a servant put up the shutters. The house stood blank and dark.

So now. All laughter stopped. In the act of pouring coffee, one of Nick's friends dropped cup and pot into the snow, grabbed for his shotgun. "You got Long John. What's the fuss?"

"This ain't a social visit, unless you'd like to leave a calling card," snarled Cap.

"What mule is that?" asked a friend of Ives.

"This here's Black Bess." Beidler spoke for everyone to hear. "My mule! I let Nick borrow her the day he disappeared."

Ives spoke to the group around him, raised a laugh.

Frowning, Jacob walked to meet Dan, while Beidler went to picket the mule and Fitch joined Williams and Palmer. Ives called to Fitch, gestured to a place next to him on the log. Fitch, looking to Dan like a man dazed by horse's kick, sat with him.

Williams ordered some men to search the wickiup.

Jacob said, "You get warm. Eat. The food, it is not good, but it fills the stomach."

"Stick by me," Dan told Long John, who mumbled Damn right. Dan sat by another fire with Long John, Jacob on the tall man's other side. Standing the rifle between his knees, Dan rested the barrel against his shoulder while he ate and studied Ives out the sides of his eyes. Jacob gave him a cup of a hot brown liquid that attempted to pass for coffee with whiskey in it, and on a tin plate some tough, gamy venison, an old buck killed during mating season. Jacob was right. Bite by bite, Dan's stomachache eased.

Long John stammered, "He's watching me."

Dan said, "I'm watching him."

Ives raised his voice to be heard beyond his immediate circle. "Did you boys hear the one about the drummer and the farmer's daughter?"

A swarthy man with curly black hair asked, "The one you had, George?"

Long John murmured, "That's Johnny Gibbons. Good friend of Ives. Mulatto."

"Seems this drummer begged a place to stay, and the farmer said, 'Yes, but you'd have to sleep with my daughter.'" Ives wound the story with buttons, a big shaggy dog, and an ugly daughter, but the humor lay in the shock value.

Fitch sat like a stone throughout, his laugh at the end sounded like a pebble in a tin cup.

"You didn't laugh." Ives called to Dan.

Dan said, "Tell a funny one."

"You saying my jokes ain't funny?"

Long John whispered, "Jesus, Mary, and Joseph, laugh."

Ives. Confident. Handsome. A monarch among his friends. Pale beard and mustache, his jacket trimmed—as they said, foxed—with deer hide at the lapels and elbows, his trousers foxed and fringed at the side seams. Supremely confident. Among armed men, eminently sure of himself. Dumb Dutchman. Like Gallagher, accustomed to the respect of others. Their fear.

The hell with this, thought Dan. He was sick of men like Ives, Gallagher, and the rest, the roughs who bullied their way to the wealth that other men sweated and froze to prize out of the earth's grip. He was sick of being afraid, of acting the coward to save his life. He stopped gnawing on the meat, spat out the bite, wiped his mouth on the back of his glove. Dumb Dutchman. "Exactly."

Jacob shifted about, his breath hissed out between his teeth. "Mein Gott."

"Jesus, Mary, and Joseph," muttered Long John, "Jesus, Mary, and Joseph."

"You need a better sense of humor, friend." As if that ended the matter, Ives rose to his feet, yawned, stretched high, then swooped as if to wipe something from the toe of his boot, the connected series of movements flowing together. He was telling Dan, Look at me, I am George Ives, be careful of me.

"Maybe you need a better line of jokes." Leaning forward, elbows on his knees, Dan let the rifle barrel tilt forward, and the breech rested in his hands. Smiling, willing his hands not to shake, his voice to stay steady, he said, "My name's Dan Stark."

"Ah, the surveyor." Ives tipped back his hat. "I'm George Ives, but I expect you know that."

"Yes," Dan said, "I do know who you are." Dumb Dutchman.

The wickiup yielded guns of various types, pokes of gold dust, and several thick packs of greenbacks. A recent robbery of Oliver's stage had netted the robbers $70,000 in greenbacks, no good until a bank was found to honor them. The victim had a list of the numbers and names of the issuing banks; by comparing these numbers with his list, they would know if these bills came from that robbery. Dan was willing to bet they did, but who were the robbers?

As the searchers laid the guns on a blanket, one of the pistols went off. Every man ducked.

"Shit!" yelped Tom Baume, the Virginia merchant who had loaned Nick his pocket knife. "That nearly got me!" He explored his head where the bullet's flight had disturbed his hair. "You want me to part my hair different, there's better ways of telling me!"

"Sorry, Tom," the other man said. "I'll be more direct next time."

To Dan's ears their laughter sounded shaky. It had been a near thing. Too near.

◌∽◌

Steam rose from Dan's trousers, and the sun warmed his face and hands. Riding near the back of the group, Long John between him and Beidler, with Jacob just behind them, he was grateful for the snowmelt that kept the dust down, for the sunshine. Near the head of the group Ives rode with Fitch and Williams, as casual as if he were one of Nick's friends. Amid the jostle of riders Dan glimpsed him, erect, relaxed, the reins in his left hand, the right resting on his thigh, Johnny Gibbons beside him, part of the retinue for the prince. He had made no difficulty about riding with them, but thought he should be tried in Virginia, not Nevada.

The air was so crisp and clear Dan almost expected it to sing, as Mother's wine glass sang when he ran his finger around the rim. On a low rise he could see across the valley to where a jagged outline indicated hills and the mouth of Alder Gulch, nearly hidden among the rock. All around, white mountains guarded the valley, where snow lay in some places a foot or two deep and in others had melted off to a crazy quilt of snow, dead grass and black dirt.

He used to think he knew mountains. After all, he hunted in the Adirondacks, in the Blue Mountains, but he had never truly known mountains until the Rockies. On the trip out, he had stood at the top of a mountain pass while the horses blew and looked out on a sea of mountains, range after range like waves in the ocean, from deep green nearby to blues farther away that paled at last into the sky so that he could not make out the horizon and had the odd sense that this earth was made of sky and not rock.

Just as he had thought he knew the world, knew men, until Father's – death (his mind as ever shying from the word suicide). Did Fitch, riding with Ives, not wanting to believe in Ives's guilt, did he have a similar sense of unreality? Was his confidence shaken, that he did not know men as he thought he did?

And his own inner conviction could hardly be called evidence. Even in a miners court. Ives was a murderer because he told dirty jokes? Nuts. Perhaps Hilderman might say something useful, but they'd question him well away from Long John, and hold all three men separately. No, they had no hard physical evidence.

The search of the wickiup had turned up nothing belonging to Nick. But perhaps the mule was hard evidence. She was stolen property, found on Ives's ranch. On Ives's property, therefore in his possession. He might claim she had strayed there, but from Long John's place, unsaddled? Their horses had been reluctant to cross Wisconsin Creek, and a mule would not do so on her own. Why had Ives not notified Beidler that he had the mule? If he tried to claim that he didn't know she was there, they could counter, how could he not know?

Ives turned in his saddle with a challenge: "I bet an ounce of gold my horse is the fastest in the Gulch."

"Like hell," shouted another man, who kicked his horse into a gallop.

Dan's horse jumped to a gallop, pits and rocks under its hooves blurred, the wind brought tears to his eyes. Trees, a house, swept backward, and other riders fell behind. A mustang, a full hand shorter than Ives's cob, won the race, and the owner petted the animal, held out his hand for payment of the bet. Ives laughed. "When we get to town, friend, where there's a scale."

Having been let out, Dan's mount would not soon settle, but danced along, head up, ears pricked forward. Friend. That word again. What friends did Ives have? Johnny Gibbons rode beside him, the two of them talked as they rode along, and Dan noted how Ives sat his horse with a quiet back, while Gibbons held a stiffer posture. Then Gibbons relaxed, punched Ives lightly on the upper arm and laughed, and the horse began to jog, then loped, and pulled away from the plodding group. Dan tugged at his hat brim to shield his eyes from the sun. He hoped they would come soon to Dempsey's.

⁓

Beside the road, Oliver's stage had pulled into Dempsey's ranch yard to change horses. Nearby, men labored to build a bridge over Ram's Horn Creek.

Well away from the ranch buildings, on the river bank, stood Dempsey's family homestead. Laundry was drying on a line strung between alder trees, smoke rose from the ranch house chimney, and small children chased each other around the house, their squeals echoed in Dan's memories of his small brothers and sister.

George Hilderman. The American Pie Biter. Pathetic fellow, thought Dan. A man with graying hair and a vacant mind. He got along by entertaining people because he had a trick jaw that let him bite into as many as six meat pies at once. He had a good sense of smell, too, and now he smelled danger. When he found he could not joke his way out of it, he made excuses to delay them. He could not ride to Virginia because he had no horse. "You can ride Black Bess," said X. He had no saddle. Dan told him they would borrow a saddle from Dempsey.

As they waited for Dempsey to finish his business, Fitch led his horse over to Dan and Jacob chewed on jerky that Jacob had brought from the wickiup. Dan had purloined a few handfuls of hay from Dempsey's barn for their horses, and he leaned his back against his horse's shoulder while he chewed on jerky and hoped for dry boots.

"That nigger, Gibbons, is up to something, riding off like that. Keep your eyes peeled."

As if he hadn't noticed. "As if I didn't know," Dan snapped.

"Okay, don't get your drawers in a knot." Fitch dismounted and looped the reins around his stump. He hooked one stirrup over the horn, tugged at the cinch.

Fitch loosened the cinch, talking as he did so, not looking at Dan, but as if he talked to himself while Dan eavesdropped. "I've known a few bastards, one way and another." The horse dropped its head to rub its muzzle on a fetlock. "Men do things in war they don't recall except in their nightmares, things they can never talk about. They see things they never imagined men could do to other men." He gazed over the horse's back at some distant country in his mind, a bleak landscape, judging from the way his face sagged under the memory. Dan's horse, grazing, moved a step and Dan caught his balance. Recalled to the present, Fitch said, "You, of course, wouldn't know about that, would you, Blue, because you're rich enough to buy a substitute and pay some poor son of a bitch to do your dying for you." He reached up to the saddle horn and rocked the saddle to settle it on the horse's back. "Betcha Jacob knows more."

Jacob nodded, his jaws working on the dried meat.

Dan said, "To his misfortune, you're probably right."

Fitch retied the cinch as if the task were the only thing on his mind. "This business, though. Nick liked Ives. Hell, I like him. He's a friend." He sounded bewildered, like a man puzzled that life could still show him a new aspect of hell. Then he smiled. "If he did this, shit, then you and me could be friends." He wrapped the reins once around the saddle horn and swung up.

Dan shaded his eyes and smiled up at Fitch, a silhouette against the sun. "When hell freezes over, partner."

Fitch laughed and reined his horse away. "You got that right."

On the road again, Dan found Bob Hereford riding alongside him. The sheriff of the Nevada Mining District dug between his teeth with his little fingernail. "You were pretty smart about the law back there, I'm told. How do you know that stuff?"

Dan sighed. He had thought of this journey to the gold fields as his opportunity to free himself of the practice of law, that if he had to leave his New York life to come West, he would not have to spend his time in an office, but could be out of doors, a surveyor. He had reasoned that surveying would earn more gold more quickly than as a lawyer, waiting for clients. He'd been correct. "I was an attorney in New York. I come from a family of lawyers. My grandfather founded a law firm, and my father was a lawyer, too. So are an uncle and a cousin." Grandfather imposed his will on them all, the law was the only honorable occupation for a male Stark. Had Father wanted to impress him by winning a fortune? Or was gambling the only way he could get some excitement in a mundane life of wills and contracts and sloppy accounting?

"Why aren't you a lawyer here?"

"I was a surveyor before I started reading law." Before Grandfather wore him down. "I don't like practicing law. I like being outside." He remembered summer rain falling through smoke spattering women's frocks with spots of soot. An unfinished brief on his desk, his thirst to be in the woods, to taste clean rain on his tongue. "I like surveying." The peaceful sense of imposing order, lines and measures, on chaotic nature. The math. Certainties of angles, sines, cosines. The law was messy.

"If we're having a trial, we'll need us a prosecutor." Hereford spoke so quietly that Dan barely heard him over the clop of hooves on the stony road.

"Find someone else. Our firm practiced corporate law." He lied. A dispute over vanished profits turned into prosecution for fraud. A rancorous partnership was dissolved by murder, the survivor prosecuted. Though unqualified in criminal law, he had defended both cases. And won.

If he prosecuted Ives, he would be a target. He might as well pin a bull's eye on his chest. Fitch had said some things a man remembers only in his nightmares, but Dan hadn't said what he'd been thinking, that was not only in war. His own nightmares yielded a single gunshot, and blood pooling from Father's blasted head across the polished mahogany desk.

No, he could not risk it, for the family's sake. They needed his gold to survive. Grandfather was too old to start over, his brothers too young. Yet for Nick, how could he not? He could not bring them back, Father or Nick, but he could do one thing for Nick — justice. Yet he said, "Find another lawyer."

Hereford reined away from him, kicked his mount into a trot, and Dan knew he had lost honor. Hereford would never understand that his obligations to the family had to come first. Along with his promise to Harriet.

Good God, Harriet.

Were those obligations, those promises, more important than justice?

Christ, what a mess.

"Race you to Pete's!" came a shout.

In two bounds Dan was leaning into the wind, his horse's mane stinging his face, galloping full tilt over the rutted road. He ducked his face away from the mane, and trusted the horse to save them both. The clump of riders around him thinned, but Dan's mount ran on, passing more tiring horses.

Dan squinted through the whipping mane. Ives led, with others close behind. They topped a rise. In front of Pete Daly's two-story ranch house stood a saddled horse, men on the porch. Ives led by one or two lengths, no one now between him and Dan, who swung a crop against the horse's shoulders and hindquarters, but the animal was running flat out.

Ives was winning. As they neared Daly's, he glanced behind him.

Winning.

Ives must not stop at Daly's.

Dan stood in the stirrups to take his weight off the horse's back, and lifted the reins. The horse shot ahead, a turn of speed Dan hadn't thought he had. His knees pumped like pistons, the saddle horn rocked. Ives could not get away. Another rider pulled even with him. Tom Baume.

They flashed by Daly's and into the Gulch. Wind roared in Dan's ears, hooves thundered. They missed an oncoming wagon, dodged a loaded pack string, and a man leaped out of their way. Ives' horse stumbled and sprawled on the ground. Ives jumped clear and left it lie, sides heaving, bleeding from spur gouges, covered with foam.

Dan yanked on the reins, vaulted off as his horse slid to a stop, stumbled and fell, rolled, stood, grabbed the rifle. Baume ran past him. Where Ives's tracks turned into a mess of boulders, they stopped. "You might as well come out, Ives!" Dan shouted, "There's no back door." He knew this spot.

Ives came out with a shrug and a smile. "I almost won that race, though, didn't I? If I'd been able to change horses at Daly's, I'd be in Dakota by now."

Baume said, "I'm getting too damn old for this. I'll be thirty in a couple of years."

They took no chances now. Nick's friends put Ives on another horse, tied his hands to the saddle horn, his feet to the stirrups, and passed the rope under the horse's barrel. One who rode ahead led the animal, Ives in the center of a phalanx. Williams detailed a man to look after the broken down horse.

Hereford and Fitch guided their mounts beside Dan, who had dropped back with Jacob at the rear. Hereford said, "Thank you for bringing him down."

Fitch said, "I want him tried, but I still can't believe he's guilty."

"You can believe it." Dan hoped there would be no more excitement, no more horse races, or rescue attempts, or even loud challenges. He had never been so weary, sure he had passed his limit of strength some time past. And patience. "Damn it, make up your mind Ives is guilty as sin."

"I do not understand." At Jacob's careful, precise English Dan bit his lip.

"You think he killed my boy," Fitch said.

"I don't think it. I know it. I was sure before. Now I know."

"Why?" Fitch growled, "Goddammit, you been pussying around this all day. Why?"

"Because he jokes, he acts like one of the boys, your best pal. He wants to win us over so we'll let him go. That's what a guilty man does. An innocent man is too scared, and he acts scared. And because Ives ran. An innocent man will stay because he knows he's innocent and has faith in the law to exonerate him. And yes, sometimes that faith is misplaced, but that's how an innocent man thinks. A guilty man runs because he has faith in the law, too, that it will hang him, because he knows he's guilty."

"Oh, Christ, he was my friend. Our friend."

Laughter floated to them, thinner than before, but it proved that some men were yet captivated by Ives, that he had friends among Nick's friends. Dan thought of princes. "Ives has no friends. Only toadies."

Amid a fresh gust of laughter, Ives began a new joke. "Hey, did you hear the one about the whore of Babylon?"

∽

They squeezed through the traffic of riders, mule trains, wagons, and pedestrians. Miners paused, shivering, in the Creek to watch them ride by. In Nevada City they stopped in front of Lott Brothers Store. Some dismounted, but Ives shouted, "No! Take me to Virginia! I can't get a fair trial here!"

"Why not?" John Lott, a thin, dark-haired man, thrusting an arm into his coat, shouted at Ives from his doorway.

"I shot a dog a couple of weeks ago. Damn thing scared my horse."

Someone yelled, "He was a good dog. You didn't have to shoot him up thataway."

Johnny Gibbons, catching up with them, bellowed, "Take 'em to Virginia!"

A slight man sporting a Mandarin goatee and carrying a cowbell, crossed the street to stand with Lott. Fitch told Dan, "Dr. Don Byam, President of the Nevada Mining District." He paused. "Uses the damn cowbell to get order in the court." Men were coming out of saloons and stores, from the diggings. A few women stood to the side, hugged their shawls around their shoulders.

"Try 'em here!" yelled Fitch. "Don't take them to Virginia, for Gallagher!"

Perhaps a hundred men now gathered, with more coming, lured from their work by the promise of excitement. Dan straightened his spine. From the saddle he had a good view of the standing crowd, and he loosened the Spencer in its holster. Some of Nick's other friends were ready as well. Ives must be tried in Nevada, away from Gallagher's control, Plummer's influence. Henry Plummer, Sheriff of Virginia City, and sheriff of Bannack, 80 miles southeast in the Grasshopper Mining District. Gallagher was Plummer's Chief Deputy, his surrogate in Virginia City, and he and all his murderous deputies were friend of Ives. By miners court rules, the sheriff selected the formal jury, or the jury was the crowd, the jury of the whole.

Dillingham. The name was a drum rattle in Dan's mind. A summons to memory, and a warning.

Williams and a second man were untying Ives. Williams coiled the rope, his arms moving with deliberation to make each coil the same size.

"These men belong to Nevada, not Virginia." Lott's high-pitched voice bored into the noise, and men quieted to hear him. "In Virginia they let Dillingham's killers go scot free. Do we want that here? If we don't stop murder here, now, all our sacrifices will be in vain! They'll steal our gold and kill anyone who resists!"

"Yeah!" shouted the men, with a sprinkling of "No!"

"That ain't right!" yelled Gibbons. "You care more about a damn dog than a man!"

"Damn that nigger," said Fitch. "He'll get Ives tried in Virginia, if he's not careful. That goddam Gallagher."

So that was it. Fitch hated and mistrusted Gallagher more than he liked Ives.

Lott was shouting, "They don't care a fig for justice in Virginia, or Buck Stinson wouldn't be a deputy!"

They missed the point. Why didn't Byam say something? Or did he not know the rule of jurisdictions? Dan stood up in his stirrups and bellowed over the hubbub. "Ives can't be tried in Virginia. It's the wrong jurisdiction!" Judge Byam smiled and nodded to him. A momentary silence, before Ives' friends cried out again for him to be taken to Virginia, but most of the men seemed to want him tried in Nevada. Dan pounded his fist on the saddle horn. Damn them! Why didn't they understand?

Sheriff Hereford put two fingers in his mouth, and his whistle startled the crowd into near silence. "Listen to Dan Stark, boys. He's from Virginia, and he's telling it straight!"

Dan raised his voice to be heard at the back of the crowd, already doubled in size. "Nick's body was found closer to Nevada than to Virginia. The rules say a crime outside a mining district is tried in the closest district. That makes it Junction's jurisdiction, and Junction and Nevada have to work it out. Virginia has no say in this."

Byam frowned, and Hereford glared up at Dan amid the commotion. "Why the hell did you have to muddy the issue?"

"Because that's the rule. Get me some quiet, and I'll explain it."

"You damn well better." The Nevada Sheriff whistled, and Byam shook the cowbell. Dan's horse fidgeted under him, and Dan petted it to calm it. He wanted to cover his ears against the din, but didn't dare let go of the reins.

Ives sat his horse as if he paused of his own free will, as if his hands were not tied to the saddle horn, as if another man did not hold the reins. To Dan he seemed unconcerned, as if the debate had nothing to do with him, as if he were indifferent to his own fate.

Dan shouted, "Junction and Nevada should decide who will try Ives for murder. Virginia isn't in it. They're too far away from the crime."

"No!" Johnny Gibbons shook his fist in the air. "Let's vote! Try George in Virginia!"

There was a shout so loud that Dan despaired. Surely they would carry the day, and Ives would be tried in Virginia and acquitted. Like Stinson, who had murdered Dillingham.

Judge Byam rang the cowbell, and the crowd quieted. Before he could speak, Fitch pointed at Gibbons. "You can't vote! You're a quadroon!"

"That's right! Niggers can't vote! You ain't got a say in this!"

A vein pulsed across Gibbons's forehead. He swept off his hat, and Dan thought he would have thrown it into the mud. "It ain't right!" he yelled. "I got as much say as anyone! I say Ives didn't murder that boy, and he ought to be tried in – "

The Nevada president rang the cowbell. "All in favor of Nevada!"

If Gibbons hadn't been trying to obstruct justice for Nick, Dan would have weighed in on his side. Gibbons should have a say in this, no matter how much Negro blood he had, and it couldn't have been much because he looked like a curly-haired, dark-eyed, swarthy white man, perhaps Spanish or Italian. But the law was the law, and it said that coloreds did not have the vote. Any vote.

"Aye!" The crowd's roar rattled Lott Brothers' windows. Miners and merchants alike, standing in the deepening dusk where shadows already consumed the sunlight, voted to keep justice in their own venue.

Johnny Gibbons shouted, "Go to hell, all of you! We'll get you out of this, Georgie! They want a trial, we'll get you some lawyers." With that, he slapped his hat on the horse's rump and galloped off toward Virginia.

∽

"Martha! Wait!" Lydia Hudson, the colored gal walking alongside, hurried up Jackson Street, all the flounces of her black skirt bobbing, the fringes of her shawl fluttering in the wind. Martha crossed over to meet her. "I've been looking for thee." Lydia laid her hand on her bosom as if clutching at every breath.

Behind Martha, Dotty screamed. "Mam! Mam!" and Canary barked his deep-throated threat. Martha pivoted, dodged around a six-horse team pulling a dray loaded with barrels of beer, ignored the teamster's yell. Dotty was holding Canary's rope, the dog jumping and snapping to get at a boy who poked a sharp stick at a cowering puppy.

Martha grabbed the stick and broke it, cuffed the boy away. "I'll let the dog loose!"

The boy, perhaps thirteen or fourteen with greasy hair hanging in clumps, screamed, "I'll tell Gallagher!" His eyes shifted their focus past Martha. "Keep that nigger away from me. Keep her away, you hear?" He edged backwards, turned, ran downhill, and disappeared around the corner onto Wallace Street.

Martha could bring no saliva into her mouth. Dotty threw her arms around her Mam, sobbing, and all a-tremble she folded the child to her. Canary, wagging his tail and whining, nosed at the whimpering puppy. The colored gal crouched down by the little creature.

Martha said, "Thank you kindly."

The colored gal ignored Martha, spoke to Dotty. "He's hurt some, but he'll be fine."

The puppy lifted his long muzzle and licked at Canary's mouth, wagged his tail, gave two or three sharp puppy barks, licked the colored gal's hand, Dotty's face. The colored gal laughed, and Dotty, her tears dried like rain in sunlight, laughed along with her. "Mam," said Dotty through her giggles, "he's thanking us." But there were patches of red on his gray fur. Blood.

Miz Hudson — no, Lydia, it was hard to think of using her given name — joined them. "Nasty horrid boy, that Jacky Stevens. Good thing thee has a big dog." She breathed deep two or three times. "Of course, what can thee expect, with that woman for his mother." When Martha did not understand, she said, "Isabel Stevens."

"Oh." The Stevens woman "entertained" at Fancy Annie's.

The colored gal stood up, held her hands away from her short coat and green skirt so as not to smear them with blood. "Ain't nothing serious, Missus." The pup settled down to lick at a wound. "Whose pup, you s'pose?"

Lydia smiled. "Ours."

"We don't need no dog," the colored gal said. The puppy looked up at her, its brown eyes friendly, and raised a paw.

Martha eyed that paw. "It'll be a big dog someday, maybe bigger'n Canary."

"We can't turn it away. It's hurt and that boy will catch it again." Lydia bent down to let it smell her hand. "I think we have a dog now."

Martha said, "A dog is a useful critter. Keeps varmints away."

"Those with four legs, and those with two," said Lydia.

The colored gal said, "I expect maybe we could use us a watch dog."

"I think so. We'll feed it, and it can sleep by the stove."

The colored gal would not carry the pup. "If I gets blood on, it'll never come out." Even when Martha said, "Cold water takes out blood," she refused and walked ahead with her head up. Dotty followed with Canary to make sure the puppy came along, limping, while Martha and Lydia dropped back to the end of their female train.

Near the corner, Martha's boot came untied, and Lydia stopped with her while Martha knelt to tie it. "She's afraid of it." Lydia spoke softly, though the town's noise would have drowned a shout.

"Scared of that little dog? Why?"

"She's afraid to love it. Afraid if she does, it will come to grief. She had a child sold away." Martha rose quickly enough to be dizzy, cast about to find Dotty, only a mite reassured that the child skipped along, laughter sparkling at the dogs' antics, while Tabby waited, grim about the lips. Dear God in heaven, that a child would be sold away from a mother. Taken from her to Lord knows what? Used however the new owner wanted. Even kind owners were still owners.

Two women came out of Fancy Annie's and strode up Wallace, big as you please, like they owned the street. The shorter, plumper one was Helen Troy, as she called herself, who owned that place, and the taller, redheaded one was Isabelle Stevens. Jacky's mother, Gallagher's woman. Dressed fit to kill in low-cut silk and satin, wearing new hats with tall flat crowns and wide brims curving down on one side and decorated with orange and blue ribbons that flapped down their backs, and wind-battered ostrich feathers. Silly geese had to use both hands to keep the things on their heads.

In her dark blue cloak, thick stockings, and brown linsey-woolsey dress, Martha knew she was no beauty, but she was almost warm, while they'd be chilled to the bone in two steps. Thinking they meant no good, Martha moved close to Dotty, Lydia right behind her. The child's eyes were rounded like full moons. No linsey-woolsey for these women. How to raise up a child like her, that loved pretties so much? Tabby picked up the puppy, and Canary sat at Dotty's feet.

As they crossed Jackson, the Stevens woman said, "That dog of yours ought to be shot, going after my boy thataway."

"That boy is a menace," Martha snapped. "He was hurting that puppy, and if we hadn't been there he'd 've turned his meanness on my girl."

"You hit him! You'd no call to hit him!" the woman screamed.

Passersby stopped, and some smiled, expecting a show, women fighting each other in public, an entertainment good as a music hall. Martha wanted to tell them if they wanted a show, they wouldn't get one from her. Martha wanted to flood this — this whore with words so that she felt what she was, a disgrace to women. She controlled her voice, buried her clenched fists in the folds of her cloak. "You ought to hit him some. Spare the rod and spoil the child. He don't behave like civilized folks." All the time, the Stevens woman hollered, so that Martha knew not a word of hers had got through. Martha stepped away. It wouldn't do to waste more breath on the likes of these.

A gust of wind tore the ostrich feathers from Helen Troy's hat. Laughing, Martha watched them go, served her right, wearing such frippery in the wind. Canary lunged free and raced after them, to the cheers of the watching men, dodged around a horseman whose shying mount nearly unseated him.

"Goddammit," shouted the man, "that dog outgha be shot!"

"You just watch where you're going!" Dotty ran after Canary, and Martha screamed, "Come back!" Oh, Lord, that child would be the death of her. The horseman kicked his horse up Jackson, and Martha found she could breathe again.

The onlookers cheered as Canary leaped in the air and snatched the feather from the wind. Ears and tail up, he trotted with it to Dotty, who petted him, wrapped his rope twice about her hand, brought him back.

Martha took the soggy feather from the dog's mouth, and held it out to Helen Troy.

"I don't want that thing," said the woman.

"You better take it," Martha said. "It nearly got my dog killed."

The Troy woman snorted, but took the feather in two fingers, and said to the Stevens woman, "Let's go." They flounced off down Wallace, or tried to, but the struggle to keep their hats on spoiled the effect, and they could not hold onto both their hats and their skirts, that blew about their limbs and up, to reveal far more than proper. Cheering men watched them go.

Martha turned her back. "You were looking for me?" she asked Lydia.

"Yes. It's the typhus. The doctors can't keep up, there are too many sick."

Dark junipers and silvery sagebrush stood against the snow. "Yes. I'm not surprised. They don't see what's around them." Martha said, "I'll visit Berry Woman."

❧

Like his namesake in the Bible, Dan had stepped into the lions' den. Because of a woman. Pretending that McDowell and Gallagher did not look ready to kill him, that Dotty's jaw had not dropped when he came in, and that Tim's cup did not rattle against teeth when he drank, Dan felt as if the lions gathered themselves to pounce. But he hungered to see Mrs. McDowell, so, though his body screamed for rest, and the blood beat in his neck, he would learn if a spark existed, or he had dreamed the whole thing. He was mad, that's what. Stark raving mad. His own pun on his name almost made him laugh, which he took for hysteria and put him more on his guard, that wound him up even more and knotted his shoulder muscles.

She set down his plate, venison steak and potatoes fried in deer fat. Indian fare. "Sorry your dinner's cooling."

The aromas of her cooking flooded his mouth with saliva, and he had to swallow twice before he could answer. "I'm the one to apologize," he managed to say despite his almost desperate desire to pounce on the food. "It's my fault for being late." She had saved his dinner for him, she had hoped he would come tonight.

She had used rosemary to flavor the steak, it brought out the succulent flavors of the venison, and she had used the herb on the potatoes, too, along with salt and pepper just to his taste. The potatoes were not sliced, but cut into chunks, and he guessed that she had rubbed rosemary on the skins before crushing some into the fat. What a meal for a starving man! There were even a few canned beans that she had cooked with the potatoes, and Dan thought he had never smelled or tasted anything so delicious, he who had eaten nothing but ersatz coffee and boot leather for nearly twenty-four hours.

Mrs. McDowell retreated to the kitchen corner, stood eating her supper and talking softly with her daughter. She did not look at him. He'd been wrong. She would have saved dinner for any boarder. That's all he was to her. A boarder. He'd been wrong. Wrong, dammit, wrong. He was an idiot. Dan cut off a bite of the venison, piled some potato on the meat, and put it in his mouth. His stomach revolted. It tasted as gray as it looked. Focusing on McDowell and Gallagher, he watched her at the edge of his vision.

"We know why you're late." McDowell propped his elbow on the table and pointed his knife at Dan. "You're one of them as brought in George Ives."

He couldn't deny it. The news must be all around the Gulch by now, even if Johnny Gibbons hadn't ridden straight to Gallagher to report. Dan said, "We rode out to Wisconsin Creek to ask Long John Frank some questions, and found evidence that Ives killed Nick." By the set of her head, he knew she listened, even as she whispered with Dotty, as he watched her while he defended himself to the men.

McDowell stammered, "You – you – ."

"You son of a bitch," Gallagher whispered.

Mrs. McDowell gasped, spun about with her mouth open to scold Gallagher.

"Hey!" Tim thumped the handle of his knife on the table. "You watch your language around my little sister."

"Sorry." Gallagher spoke to Mrs. McDowell. "I apologize, Ma'am. He took me by surprise."

Mrs. McDowell squeezed out words through tight lips. "We don't hold with that language in this house. Apologize to the young'un."

Gallagher rose to his feet, made Dotty as elegant a formal bow as any Dan had ever seen. He wished Nick's other friends could see this, the fearsome Gallagher, handsome as a rattler dozing in the sun, who ruled the roughs in Virginia City, bested by a woman.

"I do apologize for my language, Miss McDowell. I hope you can forgive it, and I promise henceforth to behave myself in your company."

Dotty smiled at the charming gentleman Gallagher imitated. "You shouldn't cuss, Mr. Gallagher. It ain't nice."

Gallagher's big laugh boomed out. McDowell laughed a sort of guffaw down his nose, and Tim grinned at the Chief Deputy. McDowell mimicked his daughter: "'You shouldn't cuss, Mr. Gallagher. It ain't nice.'" Only Mrs. McDowell did not smile, while Dotty looked hurt and bewildered. Dan kept his own face straight.

While everyone's attention was on Gallagher, Dan raised the mug to his mouth, so he could look over it past McDowell, who gave himself to his laughter with his head tilted back and his eyes closed. Her modest, high-necked shirtwaist enticed him more than the low-cut fashions of the women in his New York set. Mrs. McDowell's sleeves, rolled up for work, revealed her wrists, thin and delicate and strong. Unknowing, watching Gallagher, she raised one hand to her breast and fingered a button, then turned her head toward him. Her eyes crinkled at the corners, and her lips softened as she peeked at him from under her eyebrows. Her eyes shone in the lamplight.

Dan said, "Delicious." He was talking of more than the food, although that was included. He meant Martha McDowell, and the feeling inside him, for he was convinced that a connection existed between them, a spark, a union of feeling, at least in this, that Gallagher and McDowell should not be laughing so at Dotty. She spoke the truth, and her mother was beautiful to him.

"Do you need more beer?" asked Mrs. McDowell.

"Yes, thank you, I do." He had only drunk half of it, but he held the mug out to her to fill. Her fingertips brushed the back of his hand as across the strings of her dulcimer, and something inside Dan sang. She dipped out more beer for him, and when she brought it back, though Gallagher and McDowell had stopped laughing, he took the chance of raising his eyes to hers, and in them found the answer to his question. The spark existed, was real, and on her side, too.

As if he held a royal flush, he wanted to leap into the air and shout, and never in any game had he worked so hard to prevent his face from telling anything. He cut another bite of meat, rich and succulent. When he could speak, he was any boarder complimenting the cook. "Delicious, Mrs. McDowell. Thank you." As he put the cup to his mouth, he met McDowell's glare over the rim, and turned as cold as if he'd tumbled into Alder Creek.

She was a married woman. There could be nothing between them. Nothing. His stomach clenched. There could be no good end to this. Dan forced himself to chew and swallow.

Gallagher interrupted his thoughts. "Ives did not kill the Dutch kid." The Chief Deputy held his knife ready to cut a piece of potato, forefinger along the top of the blade. With each word he poked the knife into the air at Dan.

A faint echo, as from a distance, an unmistakable warning rattle. Dan felt the unshaven bristles rise on his face, the hairs of his arms prickled against his sleeves. He cut his meat in a steady rhythm and composed a reply as mild as milk. "I imagine the Nevada miners court will consider all the evidence."

"There is no evidence against him." The whirr of rattles insisted.

"As to that," Dan forked a bite into his mouth, chewed until he could swallow, to gain time to think. "It's in the hands of the miners court." Thank God he'd had the sense not to prosecute, or he might be dead now.

"George wouldn't bushwhack a man that way. Shoot him in a fair fight, maybe, but not murder him."

Although George Ives had threatened murder against two men who were reluctant to "loan" him money. Furthermore, he had made those threats in broad daylight in front of witnesses, and they'd been the talk of the town. Dan said nothing, but nodded and took a swallow of his beer. In his opinion, Ives was fully capable of murder and robbery. He knew Ives killed Nick. Knew it from the horse races, the jocularity. Long John's testimony. Tomorrow they'd know what Hilderman said.

McDowell said, "Them other times, George was just joking."

"He's a great joker, is George." Gallagher laughed to show how he appreciated Ives's jokes, but his eyes, watching Dan, did not seem to catch the fun.

Dan had looked on Nick's hideous corpse, understood what it told them about the last moments of a young life, and chased down the killer. His chilled feet rested in damp boots, he craved sleep, and he sat at table with a bully and a man who had threatened to kill him over cards. For a woman he couldn't have. He was sick of this. "Sure. Backing his horse into Morris's windows was extremely funny. I laughed for a week." Words.

He had only words to attack with, as men in battle might form up troops and launch them against the enemy. "It cost Morris a dollar a pane to replace them and several weeks of bad weather. Lord knows how much he lost when rain ruined his goods. Hilarious." Holding Gallagher's eyes, he sipped beer. "I've been told, however, that my sense of humor is deficient. That's probably why I see nothing amusing in a loaded pistol pointed at me by a man demanding money. But then, it probably depends on one's point of view." He smiled at Gallagher. "At which end of the pistol one is standing, the muzzle end or the trigger end. You, apparently, find it highly engaging."

Dan's pulse pounded in his neck as if trying to free itself, but no one could tell because his long hair and high collar covered it. Would Gallagher know he was being accused of being one of the road agents? What the hell. Everyone in Virginia at one time or another had seen Gallagher shoot people when he was angry.

Gallagher sat, breathing hard, the rattling was loud, now.

No one spoke.

Dan listened to McDowell's steady low growl of breath, Dotty's sniffling, Tim's panting. The woman held her fist to her mouth. The cabin walls creaked, wood rubbed against wood. There was food left on Dan's plate, but he had to get clear of these men. He could never eat here again. Then how would he see her? He'd contrive something. He should not contrive anything, but he knew he would not be able to resist.

Gallagher shivered as he laid the knife down. "Whoever said that was right, Stark. You don't have a sense of humor." He managed a smile, all affability and charm as he waved his hand, sweeping away difficulties. "You don't want to mess with that court in Nevada. Bring the trial to Virginia. I'll make sure it's fair."

The effort cost him, Dan knew. Gallagher wanted to kill Dan right there and then, and all that stopped him were the woman and her children and the thought of what McDowell might do if Gallagher endangered his wife and girl child.

This was a poker game between him and Gallagher, and the pot was his escape. Dan let his face assume an expression of deep regret. Easy, considering that he'd miss seeing her every day. "Wish I could," he lied, "but it's out of my hands. The boys voted to keep it in Nevada."

"Why would they do a fool thing like that?"

Because they know you'll rig the jury, because they know all the roughs in the area would congregate here and you'd let it happen, because you take orders from Henry Plummer, because you helped Buck Stinson get away with murdering Dillingham. He said, "Adriel Davis yielded jurisdiction to Bob Hereford."

"Davis might be sheriff of Junction, but I'm Chief Deputy."

"Only in Fairweather District, and it's too far away from where Nick was killed." Dan felt her watchfulness, her stone-like shadowed stillness. What did she think? A woman had to take her husband's part, but she had called on them to be God's weapon.

"Maybe, but Sheriff Plummer's appointment should come through any day. He'll be Deputy US Marshal for the whole region. Then you'll see."

Dan saw. Plummer would rule Alder Gulch through Gallagher. God help them.

Gallagher smiled. "Seems to me you owe us a poker game, Stark. How about it?"

"Not tonight." Dan scraped back his chair and stood up. He looked over McDowell's head, at Mrs. McDowell. God damn it. He pushed the chair in and leaned on it, smiled at her, made his hands relax so they would not reveal his tension. He'd found out what he wanted to know, and now he hated the knowledge, the futile certainty.

"Damn it, you owe us a game, Stark." Gallagher's smile died.

"It'll have to wait." He reached around Tim to pluck his coat off the peg. When the boy would have moved out of his way, Dan laid a hand on his shoulder. "No, Tim, don't get up. Tonight I have too much work to do, and then I'll turn in early."

One last time, he would look at her. He made himself say her name, hating it. "A fine meal, Mrs. McDowell."

Her eyes were incandescent, so luminous that Dan was surprised to see shadows in the corners of the room. How could her husband not see it, her son, even Gallagher? McDowell picked at a scab on his hand, Tim drew rings on the table with the beer glass, and Gallagher cleaned his knife. Dan shrugged his coat onto his shoulders. He had to take his eyes from her to find the first button. When he glanced back, her breath came a bit faster, though her voice revealed nothing, "Glad you enjoyed it."

From behind the safety of his poker face Dan allowed his feelings to shine in his eyes, and was rewarded by a sharp indrawn breath, almost a gasp. He opened the door, ready to step over the threshold. Almost, he was safely out.

"Hold your horses there," said McDowell.

Blood surged in Dan's neck. Stupid fool that he was, he had given himself away to her husband. Worse, he'd given her away.

McDowell said, "What sort of work would a surveyor have at this time of night?"

Dan said, with absolute sincerity, "I haven't had time to do those calculations."

∾

No sooner had Martha begun to recover herself after the fracas between Gallagher and Mr. Stark than Canary started in barking. Sam opened the door without getting out of his chair and yelled at the dog, hollered to someone, "Come on in."

Step stump step stump, and Club-Foot George Lane put his club foot over the threshold and stepped the good one in after it. He stood, not even closing the door or taking off his hat, like he had no manners till Sam said, "Shut the door."

"Sorry." Club-Foot George closed it quick-like.

Martha felt sorry for Club-Foot George, it must be a trial to go through life with that foot. She went on with her women's work, dipped out water from the cold bucket into the wash pan on the stove, while the men went on with their business like she was dead.

"You wanted me?" Lane asked Gallagher.

"Yeah. You know they've got George Ives chained up over in Nevada City?"

Lane nodded. "They're saying he killed the Dutch kid."

Martha turned her back so her face could give nothing away. She wanted to shout Hooray because they'd got Nick's killer. George Ives was the right man. She just knew it. Daniel Stark said so, and he'd put his feet under her table every night for three months, so she knew him for an honest man. Inside she was cheering like at a parade, but she couldn't let them see a hint of it, while she pretended to be about kitchen things they'd pay no mind to. They weren't saying Ives was innocent, that he didn't do it, couldn't have done it. No, they were all of them – Gallagher, Club-Foot George, and even Sam – talking like he might have, could have done it, or it didn't matter if he done it.

Dotty pressed up against Mam. "They got him?" she whispered. "Nick's killer?"

"Seems so." Martha laid her finger against Dotty's lips, quieted the child, stilled her delight, because the men weren't about to give the child any pleasure if she showed it.

"If they aim to have a trial there," said Club-Foot George, "they'll have it tough."

"How so?" Sam asked.

Martha glanced over her shoulder. Club-Foot George had a knowing sort of smirk on his face, like he had a great joke for Gallagher and Sam. "Johnny Gibbons hired all the lawyers in town to defend Ives." His voice became a child's chant: Neener, neener, neener, I know something you don't know. "They can't find a prosecutor."

Gallagher slapped his hand on the table top. "I knew it! No lawyer with any sense will prosecute Ives. Not if he values his skin. The fools! Hah! Look here. Ride over to Bannack and get Sheriff Plummer. Tell him to come and take over jurisdiction."

"But he ain't sheriff in Nevada," said Lane.

"Don't matter," Gallagher said. "We'll have the boys in the crowd to back him up. Tell them at the ranches I said you should have the good relays."

"Will do." Martha heard Club-Foot George's step stump down the path. She made a clattery business of the kitchen work to cover her thoughts: Gallagher could promise the best relays for Club-Foot George? Most folks had to take whatever cayuse was handy. It didn't sit right. Gallagher calling for Plummer, sending orders about remounts at Daly's and Dempsey's ranches. Daly's was a den of wolves, roughs and loafers. Yet Gallagher expected they'd do what he asked.

Not Tim. She heard, "What if Ives killed Nick?" And the muscles in her neck tightened. Oh, Lord, she was that proud of him for sticking to what was right, young as he was, but he was too young not to be foolish sometimes in his bravery, and then she feared for him.

Gallagher said, "It don't matter to Nick what happens to Ives."

"It ain't right," Tim said. "It ain't —"

"You hush up, boy," said Sam, "this is none of your business."

But Tim wouldn't give in. "You can't say it don't matter whether Nick's killer pays or not."

Martha heard a slap and swung around in time to see Sam drawing back his hand, and the boy's head rocking backwards, then forwards, and a print, like an outline of a hand on a slate, stand out red and clear on Tim's cheek

"They won't hang him if I can help it," said Sam, "so you just shut up. You got one thing to do, and that's dig more gold out of that claim."

Dotty frowned. "I hope they hangs 'im," she hissed.

"Hush your mouth, d' you hear?" Martha seized Dotty's arm and shook it a bit. "Now hand me that there towel." She pointed to a shelf where she kept the towels. She could have reached it easy, herself, but Dotty would have to climb onto a stool to reach it, and maybe that would hide what the young'un had said, because she'd scared her Mam silly. She'd bring the men down on them both, like as not.

Gallagher laughed. "They won't get a prosecutor, and won't nobody dare testify against him, either. Not if they know what's good for them."

"You bet," said McDowell.

No matter that Ives might be guilty, they'd make sure by any means that he went free. God's thunderbolt had struck George Ives, and Gallagher and her own husband were planning how to free him, and it wasn't because of knowing Ives was innocent. If they thought that, they'd let him be tried, like most folks did, and wait for the evidence to do its work. They didn't care, not even Sam McDowell.

Wrapping her hands in the towel, she lifted the basin of hot water, all the time a thought rising in her mind like bread dough, filling it, and the daring of it made her gasp.

Involuntarily, Martha's arm jerked, and water just off boil splashed onto her hand, and made her jerk again, spilling more hot water, soaked the towel wrapped around her hand, and she nearly dropped the pan as she set it on the counter, where more water sloshed out but lucky not on her or the child. She knelt, plunged her scalded hand, still wrapped in the towel, into the cold water bucket. She would not cry out. Her hand in the bucket, she unwrapped the towel, saw that the scald to her hand was not as great as the scald to her heart: McDowell in cahoots with Gallagher to free Nick's killer.

She couldn't look at them, especially not McDowell. She wanted to cry, he'd gone so far from the man she'd married. What had happened to him that he'd side with Gallagher against what was right? When did he change so, that he'd free Ives, no matter him maybe being guilty? Where was the justice to Nick? The resolve she'd felt rising in her mind was firm now. She'd help Nick's friends, she'd help Daniel Stark.

෨

Jacob slept when Dan pulled in the latch string and turned up the lamp wick. He set to work without taking off his coat, because Jacob had banked the fire and the cabin already struck cold. Taking up his notes, he began to find where in the calculations he had left off. The bracing air in the room refreshed him, kept him awake, and he took up slate and chalk to work on from his stopping point, and was soon so absorbed in the clear logic of planes and angles that he forgot his chilled feet in their damp boots and clammy socks. He had nearly finished the last calculation when he realized that Jacob was shouting and someone was pounding at the door.

The cabin, called a bachelor cabin because it was built for one man, never seemed so small as now, when Fitch, Sheriff Hereford, and John Lott all crowded in. Sensibly, Jacob stayed in bed; there was no room for him to stand, and no room for them to sit, even if he and Jacob had possessed more than two chairs. So they stood, close enough to smell each other's breath.

"I'll come to the point," Fitch said. "You have to prosecute Ives."

Deep in his secret mind, Dan had been expecting this. Ever since Gallagher said no one would dare to prosecute, he'd known he would have to do it or the world would know him for the coward he was. So now it came, the request — more like a demand — that he must answer.

John Lott said, "Bob here, tells us you're a lawyer, and you think Ives killed the boy."

"Yes," said Dan. How was Fitch taking it now? His friend Ives accused of murdering his foster son. "I'm convinced of it."

Sheriff Hereford said, "All the lawyers in Virginia have signed on to defend Ives. Every damn one of them. Ives and his pals have plenty of money."

"I'll prosecute them," said Dan. "For a fee."

"Ha!" Fitch growled. "Money hungry lawyers."

"Damn it, show me one soul who isn't here for the gold," Dan snapped. "You're asking me to pin a target on my back, so I have to be sure my family has something in case — " He did not have to finish that sentence.

When they left, he made himself finish the calculation and write the report before he pulled off his clothes and crawled into bed beside Jacob, who was already snoring. Tired as he was, he knew he would not be able to sleep for thinking of strategies to make up for the thin evidence, how he would ensure that Grandfather received the gold, who would —

He entered a grand ballroom lighted by a thousand-candle chandelier, with Harriet on his arm, blond curls and diamonds cascading over her shoulders, into the shadows of her bosom, but outside, where a wall should have been, stood a thin woman who wore a plain shirtwaist and skirt, her hair pulled into a bun, whose eyes glowed large and luminous in the dim light.

~9

3: Alder Gulch, Nevada City

The promise of sunrise did not yet separate the eastern mountains from night when Dan and Jacob walked the uncertain road to Nevada City. At Daylight Creek, Dan paused, imagining it to be his own Red Sea: cross it and there was no going back from his commitment to prosecute the three prisoners. Jacob teased him about not wanting to get his feet wet, and with a grunt Dan splashed across, carrying the lantern and leaving Jacob to find his own way through the dark water. On the other side he relented enough to light Jacob's way.

At the crest they paused to catch their breath. Lights – candles, lanterns, torches – streamed from Virginia, from Junction, from camps in the side gullies, flowing through the darkness to converge about a bonfire on the main road between the Music Hall and the Star Bakery, in the middle of Nevada. Like ancient warriors summoned to battle by a beacon fire. Or fireflies swarming.

Some roughs with one or two women companions, caught up with them. "Going to see Ives freed?" one man jeered. "They'll never convict George!" Their laughter floated back as they strode ahead, heedless of the women, who nagged them to slow down.

"God," muttered Dan, unaware that he spoke aloud. "How can we fight that?" The hopelessness of the situation overwhelmed him. No lawyer could win a case against several opponents, with a jury controlled by the defendants' friends, no time to prepare, no library within which to research precedents and find strategies, no time to gather more evidence. His case consisted of an unreliable witness and a mule, certainty based on attempted flight, and bawdy jokes. Christ, did he even have a case?

In Nevada, two freight wagons, one painted green, were drawn up at right angles to each other, tongues crossed, forming a corner. Dan leaned the Spencer against the green wagon and helped to roll a log up to the back of it to form the third side of a makeshift square around the fire. The fourth side opened on a small street that curved behind the Star Bakery.

The courtroom. Good God, Dan said to himself, how could this open space carved out of the road function as a courtroom? Yet it must. There was nothing else.

Sheriff Bob Hereford joined Dan and Jacob near the fire and held out his hands to its warmth. The sheriff's eyes were red-rimmed, and Dan thought they must be as scratchy as his own. Deep lines curved from Hereford's nose around his mouth, and he had not shaved. He said, "We have plenty of men to act as guards. The roughs won't have a look-in." He swept his arm around the court area, and Dan saw that while he had been helping with the log armed men had moved in to guard the entire perimeter. They pointed their shotguns and rifles and muskets at the swarming crowd, faces partly lighted – a beak nose, the gleam of an eye, a long tangled beard, mouths slack-lipped around threats:

"Hang George Ives and you're dead."

"You'll pan fool's gold in hell, you bastards!"

"When Plummer gets here, he'll show you, all right!"

"Yeah, just wait! Plummer will show you!"

Fear ground in Dan's gut, and even standing as close as possible to the fire, he could not get warm. What had possessed him to agree to this?

Hereford cupped his hands around his mouth and yelled at the roughs, "Plummer ain't sheriff of Nevada, damn it. I am. If he tries to take over, I'll arrest him."

Fitch came through the cordon of guards toward them. "If you do, I'll back you up." He held his shotgun against his ribs with the stump and stretched out his hand to the fire's heat.

"You ain't man enough to arrest Plummer!" shouted a voice.

Hereford strode around the fire toward the open side of the square, planted his feet wide apart. "Yeah? Want to try me now?" When no one moved, he spat into the ground, and came back. "Yellow bastards, every damn one. They back down every time. Yellow bastards." Yet Dan saw the fear in his eyes, the thought in the back of Hereford's mind, as it was in his own, that even though their numbers had grown in the night, the roughs outnumbered Nick's friends four or five to one.

And in Jacob's eyes he saw a greater fear, the terror of the Cossacks relived. "It's all right, Jacob. They'll protect us."

Jacob managed a smile, but his hands, outstretched toward the fire, trembled.

Would Hereford have the courage to stand up to Plummer? Given Plummer's undoubted skill with a pistol, could any man arrest him? And what if Plummer's appointment arrived before the trial was over? Could they legally stop a Deputy U.S. Marshal, even one reputed to be in league with the roughs? There was no proof of that, either. Merely suspicion, conjecture, opinion. No proof.

Meanwhile, it was high time he found out what Hilderman had to say. Dan was heading for the perimeter when two men forced their way against the general milling of the crowd, amid threats and a few good-natured jeers. "Hey, Cap, watch it. You can't bull your way through."

"Yeah? You're no china piece, Hank!"

Stepping between the armed guards, riding a crest of laughter, Jim Williams ushered a stranger ahead of him. The newcomer wore a high-ranking Union Army officer's caped greatcoat, open to let the quilted lining of the cape show. Dan envied the man his coat, warm enough for a blizzard.

Fitch whistled. "A goddam Union colonel, looks like."

Williams introduced the stranger. "Boys, this is Wilbur Fisk Sanders, from over in Bannack. Chief Justice Sidney Edgerton is his uncle." When two or three of the other men looked blank, Sanders said, "My uncle is Lincoln's appointee as Chief Justice of the Territory. I'm here on other business, but when some gentlemen in Virginia asked me to prosecute, I agreed."

Tension melted out of Dan's neck. Thank God he wouldn't have to do this alone. With two prosecutors the danger was cut in half. Smiling, he held his hand out to Sanders. "Thank God you're here. Daniel Bradford Stark is my name. I've been asked to prosecute as well." As the two men shook hands, Dan knew he had heard of Sanders in another context, if he could just think of it.

Sanders' grasp was strong without being hard. He smiled into Dan's eyes. "You may wish to await the outcome before you give thanks. This will be my first case as a prosecutor." A lean man perhaps an inch shorter than Dan, he carried himself sword straight. His dark beard was close-trimmed, and his eyes were set deep in their sockets.

"Mine, too," Dan said. "I practiced in New York, but I have very little criminal experience."

"I had a good deal of civil and criminal trial experience in Ohio, but never as a prosecutor." Sanders swept his hand down the front of his Union coat. "Lately, my law practice has been interrupted."

"In a good cause," Dan said.

"Glad you think so." Sanders smiled. "We'll get along." He offered his hand, in an odd position, index finger straight and stiff, the next three fingers bent at the second knuckle, thumb out. When it met Dan's straight hand, the position changed, and Sanders nodded to himself as if he had learned something.

But if they were not both Masons, they were Union men, one a fighting soldier, and Dan regarded Sanders with satisfaction. An ally, he thought. A man to go to war with. For this was war, as were all trials. Civilized warfare, couched in polite language, full of convention and lacking guns, but warfare all the same, needing strategy, battle plans. He had nothing. No ideas as to how to proceed.

Fitch said, "I'm Tobias Wayne Fitch, formerly Captain, CSA." He and Sanders met like two strange horses who inhale each other's breath in wary and tentative exploration to determine what manner of creature this is. Dan waited for the squeal and flattened ears as two men who would try to kill each other on the battlefield extended their hands. Sanders held out his own left as if it were the common thing. Both placed their fingers in that odd position, and their hands made a join.

Dan relaxed. Masons both, their recognition lay in the odd handshake; their mutual commitment to the principles of Masonry overrode their antagonistic allegiances to North and South.

"All right," Sanders said. "Let's get to business. What evidence have we so far?"

"Not much." Dan summarized what they knew. "I was just about to interview Hilderman."

"So you have one man's word against another's. Is that all?"

"No," Hereford said. "We have Black Bess, but she can't testify."

Sanders cocked an eyebrow. "A Negro?"

"Might as well be," Fitch said. "She's a mule."

So Masonry would not stem all belligerence from Fitch. Dan intervened to stave off the anger flaring in Sanders's eyes. "Nick was riding Black Bess when he disappeared. We found her on Ives's land, without saddle or bridle."

"I see." Sanders bared his teeth at Fitch, and Dan was grateful that smile was not aimed at him. "So Ives was in possession of stolen property."

"Correct." On a mischievous impulse, Dan added, "Palmer said the mule was another agent of Providence."

"Providence?" Sanders blinked at them.

Fitch said, "William Palmer, he's a saloon keeper here, found the body. First the sage hen he shot landed directly on Nick's chest, and then the mule appeared. Providence." He spoke in the flat neutral tone of someone holding in laughter. Bob Hereford turned his head away and sneezed.

"I see. Well." Sanders cleared his throat. "So the sum total of evidence is this Long John's story and a mule."

"For the most part." Out beyond the ring of guards, someone sang "Dixie" amid loud cheering. Dan hastened to add, "It's his demeanor. His attitude." He watched their expressions, Sanders raising an eyebrow at him, Fitch glowering, Hereford wondering. Feeling increasingly silly, he told the rest of it, how Ives had joked with Nick's friends, and how he had tried to escape. Sanders listened, his brown eyes seeming to probe Dan's mind. Feeling he would hate to be cross-examined by this man, Dan finished, "That's not evidence, I know. It's too nebulous."

"Not really," Sanders said. "Flight as a presumption of guilt. That's telling, but it might not be enough. We need more." As the song ended in the Rebel yell, he forced words through tight lips: "Your feeling carries more weight than you realize. You're not one to leap to conclusions as a matter of course?"

"Shit," Fitch said under his breath, the word so quiet that Dan almost did not hear it under the fire's growl. Seeing that he had been heard, he said, "Dan Stark is the most finicking man for his damn calculations you'd ever not want to do a survey. He'll retake measurements until I want to shoot him, but he's – " He swallowed, turned his back on them for a second or two, swung back. "Christ. Oh, Christ. It's true. Ives killed my boy. Our friend. Our God damned friend."

If it had ever been possible for Dan to feel sorry for Fitch he would have then, for the pain in Fitch's eyes that they had the right man. Fitch's shoulders sagged, and he looked at the ground, the brim of his hat shielded his face. He drew one long shuddering breath. Dan was afraid to look at Sanders for fear he would say something to ruin this, but Sanders kept quiet. They had Fitch, now. For the first time, they had Fitch.

Fitch said, as if to himself, "They'll pay. They will all pay."

Dan watched what he could see of Fitch's face, shadowed as most of it was under the brim of his hat. The beard quivered, and one end of his mustache moved up and down with the twisting of his lips, as if pain and anger coalesced into something greater than the sum of their parts. Dan thought he would be afraid to come in range of that feeling. He said, "They will pay," and Fitch nodded without looking up, though his mouth relaxed into a steady downward curve.

"Moral certainty is one thing," Sanders was saying. "It's important, vitally important, but it isn't enough to convict a man of murder. Especially not here."

Hereford spoke up. "What if he has an alibi? Does that undo everything?"

"No." Dan and Sanders spoke together. Dan said, "False alibis have been constructed by perjured witnesses."

"That's something I can do," Fitch said. "I can find out if Ives has an alibi. I'll put Beidler on it, too. He can find out anything."

A few men were singing the "Battle Hymn of the Republic" despite the Rebel yells trying to drown them out, and Dan hummed along.

Sanders said, "We need to know if they have an alibi for Ives, who the witness is, and when the alibi is for." The men singing the Union anthem had apparently given up as Fitch walked away.

Sanders said, "I haven't tried a case before the miners court."

"Neither have I," Dan said. "It doesn't matter, though. Our job is the usual lawyer's job. Convince the jury. Get a conviction."

"That puts it in perspective." Sanders rubbed his chin, his close-trimmed dark beard. Everything about him seemed neat, tidy, trim. Nothing wasted. He fell silent, thinking, poked the toe of his shoe at a clod of drying mud.

Hereford tossed a chunk of wood on the fire, and the fire blazed up.

Dan, who wished to hell he'd been thinking like a lawyer yesterday instead of like a damn civilian, saw a strategy in the flames leaping against the lightening sky, a three-pronged battle plan. First, discredit the alibi, impeach the alibi witness. Second, nullify the defense's appeal to the mob, the so-called jury of the whole. Third, bolster their own case. Find witnesses to Ives's other misdeeds, persuade them to the courage to testify. That depended on tricking the defense into allowing prior bad acts. But how? Sanders asked, and as a log broke in a shower of sparks, Dan saw how simple it was. Let the defense open the door.

"Yes, I agree." Sanders looked Dan in the eye. "But how?"

"The devil's in the details," Dan said, and laughed. He no longer felt as if they were on the defensive in this trial, but with a plan of attack, sketchy as it was, they were on the offensive. "Let's go talk to Hilderman."

∾

Crouched over the sock she was knitting for Timmy, Martha listened to Dotty's chatter with part of her mind, while she wished for more light than the candle's unsteady flame. Drat! She had dropped a stitch some ways back, and had to rip out what she'd done. She should have lighted a lamp, but kerosene was so dear, and who knew when the next supply would come in if they ran out? So Martha had wished aloud for an endless and cheap supply of bright light indoors, and that started Dotty wishing, too.

They had cut up a deer carcass McDowell brought in, and while she scrubbed the table with strong lye soap, Dotty was making a list: real cupboards instead of boxes stacked against the wall, furniture you polished. Mirrors. Boughten soap. Martha didn't know where the child had come by such notions, except that's what came of having stores with goods in them from foreign places like San Francisco, or St. Louis. Even New York.

Now Dotty listed the clothes she'd have, and that scared Martha. People like them had to be content with less. She said, "Child, you're getting plumb notional. We got food enough, and a roof over our heads, and enough wood and blankets to keep warm by."

"But Mam, I want more. I want —"Arms outstretched, she twirled, and her skirt billowed around her, and like the blind man whose eyes shed scales, Martha saw the cabin as it was: Bark coming off unpeeled logs, cold lurking in the corners, waiting for them to bank the fire before it crept into the room, dirt sifting everywhere from the ceiling because the roof was made of saplings overlaid with sod. When it rained, mud dripped onto everything. Martha tried not to think about the spring snow melt.

"I want more, too." Martha couldn't bring herself to scold the child.

"What do you want, Mam?"

Martha rested her knitting needles. "A house we can keep clean. Windows that let light in. Mostly, I want to read my very own Bible." She smiled at Dotty. "At least we have a roof. There's plenty around here living in caves." And a good few in the wagons they come in that would be lucky to live through the winter.

"That's 'cause they're greedy." Dotty eyed the table top. "They want gold more than they want to live." She picked up the pan of greasy water and threw it out the door.

Bless the child, Martha said to herself. She had it right. Once they came, men had lit out for the diggings too quick to make proper shelter, and this cabin was a sight better than caves and wagons.

The child stood in the doorway, said over her shoulder, "Pap's coming."

Martha's stomach jabbed at her. What could he want? It wasn't his habit to come home until he needed to eat or sleep.

With hardly even a howdy, McDowell grabbed his musket off its peg.

Martha stuck her needles into the ball of yarn. "Where you off to?"

"None of your damn business, woman, but we're going to free George Ives." He hitched his belt up and turned to go out.

"What for? If he didn't murder Nick, they'll find him innocent."

"Damn right, and we're going to make sure they do."

He was taking his musket to a trial? Her Sam? He couldn't. "You'd use the gun to scare folks into freeing George Ives?" She stood up, intending to placate him, laid her hand on his sleeve.

"Yeah, if needs be. Why? What're you looking at me that way for, like you seen a – Woman, I'm telling you Georgie couldn't have killed Nick. Nossir." He shook her hand off, wiped his mouth on the sleeve.

"That ain't the way to do it," said Martha. "Supposing he did kill Nick?"

"What the hell do you know about it?"

"The men that brought in George Ives ain't crazy." She didn't dare say, if Mr. Stark had a hand in this, it was all right; she couldn't imagine him doing something so wrong as to knowingly hang an innocent man. She started to say it would be best to leave it to the trial, to keep hands off, but she only managed, "It's best you –"

"Best? You telling me what's best?" The skin around her husband's eyes puckered. "What's best is you do what I say!"

Even though what he told her was wrong? Heat prickled Martha's face, swelled outward from her middle until she wondered how she contained it without exploding, that he would order her to do wrong as though she didn't have her own conscience to answer to, like it meant nothing God would hold her accountable. Her. With no excuses like My husband told me to do. She could not speak, so many words crowded at her tongue, it couldn't hold them all.

McDowell must think she was cowed. "You don't talk to that damned Dan Stark, either, you hear? He's in this up to his hair, damn his hide. He's persecuting George. You get me? He's their God damn prosecutor." He yelled, his boots crashed onto the porch, and he slammed the door behind him so hard that the plates jumped in their shelves and dirt sprinkled down from the ceiling.

Martha's feet would not carry her to a chair, and she'd gone cold inside, could hardly feel her innards. Mr. Stark. Prosecutor? Mr. Stark was the prosecutor? Her thoughts spun around, top-like. He was prosecuting, and McDowell was taking his musket to frighten the jury into voting Ives innocent. If they did let Ives go, things would go on. Men would shoot their guns on Wallace Street, pick quarrels in the saloons, waylay folks for money. Nick had not been much older than Timmy. If he could be killed for the gold he carried, so could their boy. His own father took his musket, and Mr. Stark prosecuted. Musket. Prosecutor.

God bless Dan Stark. Martha found she could move, persuade her limbs to bend, and she plumped down onto a chair at the table, rested her head on her arms. God bless Dan Stark. She'd promised herself last night that if she could help him during this trial she would, and she meant that, she'd do it, though she had to be careful with McDowell so dead set —. There came into her mind a memory of Mr. Stark looking at her. She gasped. Her head came up. She stared unseeing into the corner gloom where the bed stood, hers and McDowell's. Mr. Stark had a feeling for her, and she had a feeling for him.

Dotty rubbing her shoulders recollected Martha to herself.

Nothing changed, knowing they had feelings for each other. They couldn't come to anything. They could not. She couldn't help these feelings, but she could help what she did about them. She wouldn't act on how she felt. She would help Dan Stark, if she saw a way. What McDowell aimed at was wrong, but she would do the right thing, for herself, and for the young'uns.

Martha stood up, hugged her daughter. "I think we'd best go for a reading lesson."

༄

The new house smelled of pitch, and George Hilderman stank of fear, a sharp odor as of a skunk some distance away. Dan fetched a meat pie from a sideboard, dipped out a cup of beer. When he gave them to Hilderman, the fool came close to tears. He drained the beer, held the cup out to Dan for a refill. "No more. Maybe later." A nod answered him, but Dan knew he would try to beg more. The American Pie Biter. A foolish man in a country intolerant of fools; a pathetic man in a merciless country. Clowning for pies and drinks, being the center of laughter – all ending in the short days of winter.

Outside the curtainless windows guards kept the crowd back, but Dan heard rumbling like a cougar's growl that now and then rose into a snarl.

The president of the Nevada Mining District, Dr. Don Byam, had loaned them two rooms in his spanking new house to keep the prisoners, and he'd given up his parlor for their interrogations. Dan took his place at a table with Alexander Davis, one of the defense attorneys, and dipped his pen. Davis was new to the Gulch, a Secessionist and an idealist. Though he was only two or three years older, Dan felt ancient beside him. To Alex Davis principle was all; he had not known Nick or seen his body. Dan shuddered. Cold drafts swirled about his neck despite the glowing corner stove. If the house was cold now with its new planed wood, how would it keep out weather when siding and joists dried and shrank? Dan warmed his hands at the table lamp that lighted their papers.

Hilderman gobbled pie, until Sanders ordered him to talk about Nick's murder, and Dan braced himself to hear it again.

"I didn't do nothing." Eating restored some of Hilderman's small courage. He stretched out his jaw. When no one smiled, he put it back in place, looking bewildered that his usual gambit failed, that he could not clown and win them to his side and make all this go away.

"I ain't done nothing," he said again.

"Maybe it's not what you did, but what you know," Dan suggested.

Hilderman squirmed, ducked his head. "I gotta go."

"You can wait till you've talked," Sanders told him. "You have to save yourself, and we're your best hope."

"Now wait a minute," protested other defense attorney. Dan knew HPA, for Harry Percival Adam, Smith, from boundary cases he had testified in before the miners court. He would not trust Smith for an instant, him being an excellent manipulator of juries. "We should let this man relieve himself, and his counsel should consult with him in private."

Sanders and Dan held a silent communication. "One of us will accompany you to guard against coaching him." Sanders rubbed an eyebrow with his little finger.

"That's an outrage!" Davis said. "It's a man's right to consult privately with his attorney!"

"Then do we have your word of honor that you will not tell him what Long John has told us?" If Dan had sized up Davis correctly, the younger man would pledge his personal honor not to divulge Long John's testimony.

"You have my word," said Davis, in spite of Smith's stammered objections.

"Very well." Sanders yawned as if he were too weary to care. "Persuade him to tell the truth."

Guards took Hilderman and the two defense attorneys out. Dan paced the room, ten steps across and twelve steps up, with pauses at the stove where Sanders warmed his posterior.

"Neatly done," Sanders said. "Do you think he'll realize what happened?"

"That he joined with us to deprive his client of information?" Something to smile about. "I'm sure he knows by now, but my intent was to hogtie Smith." Dan loosened his arms in time with his steps. "Don't underestimate Smith. He made a strong emotional appeal to the crowd after they convicted Buck Stinson, Ned Ray, and Charley Forbes of John Dillingham's murder. Smith was the primary defense attorney, and most responsible for freeing them."

"Stinson works with Gallagher," said Sanders, "and Ned Ray is in Bannack, under Sheriff Plummer's wing. Where's Forbes?"

"He met a bad end somewhere in the mountains."

"Smith drinks, doesn't he?"

"Don't be fooled by that, either. He should have gone on stage. He plays sober when he wants to manipulate the crowd with tragic pleadings and crocodile tears. As a drunk, his comedy endears him to the jury. Of course, many of them might be three sheets to the wind themselves."

"Is that how he won over the Dillingham jury?"

"Exactly. With the help of crying women." Beidler had described to Dan the convicted murderers, nooses round their necks, on the way to the gallows, standing in the wagon while the crowd wept and argued with itself and took vote after vote that hours later freed them. One man boasted of voting nineteen times. That must not happen here. He wasn't aware that he had spoken until Sanders said, "Yes, we'll have to prevent that."

Footsteps sounded in the hallway. When everyone was ready, Smith brought out his flask. "Our client will tell what he knows, on condition. That you agree to hold him harmless from all punishment." He took a swallow, smacked his lips.

"I know plenty about this business." Hilderman eyed the table where two pies remained. "Being arrested is a hungry thing."

"You can have more," said Dan, "when you've told us what you know."

"I protest!" Davis said. "It is cruel to starve a man."

"We're not starving him," said Dan. "We're just postponing the next phase of his breakfast." He pointed his index finger at Hilderman. "Talk."

Hilderman talked. In the beginning, his account tallied with Long John's, except for differences in wording. And then: "After Ives and the other two left, me and Long John done our camp chores, and when they come back, Ives told us about it."

The other two. Making notes, Dan's hand jerked, and his pen tore the paper, sank into the pad underneath. A blot spread. Long John had not mentioned anyone but Ives. Sanders's skeptical eyebrow climbed nearly into his hairline. Dan wanted to stop Hilderman, who rattled on.

"Ives told us the Dutchman couldn't believe it, you know, what was happening. He started in to cry, and then he asked for time to pray, so Ives said All right, and he kind of fell off his horse and kneeled down, and took off his hat. Ives was glad of that, on account of it would be easier to kill him because the hat might turn the bullet if he had a bad charge. That happened to him once, and he had to let the man go, but the fella didn't have any money anyhow so it was all right. He thought that was a great joke, you know, pretending to murder the fella. Told him if he didn't have money next time, he would kill him. Anyway, the Dutchman folded his hands and bowed his head and closed his eyes like a little kid. When he started the prayer, Ives shot him. One bullet. That's all it took. He was happy about that." Hilderman wiped his mouth with the back of his hand. "Can I have the pie now?"

"Wait," said Sanders. "Who were the other two?"

Dan could not bear to meet Hilderman's moist, hopeful glance darting from him to Sanders.

"Aleck Carter and – I don't know the other fella's name."

"You're willing to swear under oath that Ives pulled the trigger?"

"Yeah, that is," Hilderman's lips came together, and he squinted at them as he probably thought, with shrewdness. "Only if you promise not to kill me."

"Your lawyers and we will decide what's appropriate." Sanders nodded to Smith. "He can have another pie, and then go back to his room."

It took all Dan's will to watch Hilderman walk away without shouting that he deserved hanging, damn him, he knew beforehand what Ives and the others would do, he did nothing to try to stop it. He and Long John had colluded with Ives in their cowardice.

When the lawyers were alone, Smith asked, "Well? What do you say?"

Dan spoke through his teeth. "We want to re-interview Long John. He didn't mention other men with Ives, and he said nothing about the prayer." His voice stumbled on the word, prayer. That son of a bitch, Ives. That bastard, Ives.

∽

"I don't know." Long John's rodent tongue circled his mouth. "Didn't think of it. Anyways, what's it matter? Ives killed the Dutchman. Ain't that enough?"

Though he corroborated Hilderman's account of the prayer, they could not budge him on why he had not mentioned Carter, no matter how they flogged him with questions. When they had sent him, complaining of its cold, back to his room, Dan realized one benefit to have come out of all this. He believed Long John. The tall man's story was strong, and with Hilderman's corroboration, it went a long way to prove Ives's guilt. What were they to do about Carter? Dan remembered Beidler saying that Carter was decent. Some men wouldn't believe he could be party to such a thing. He must talk to Sanders alone, but before he could winkle Sanders away, Davis fired the opening shot across their bow.

"You can't use their statements to implicate Ives. They're hearsay."

The younger man looked so proud of himself that Dan almost regretted puncturing his certainty. "No, because Ives told them both, he confessed. Furthermore, each statement implicates the other man as an accessory before the fact." Ives shot Nick as he began to pray. Dumb Dutchman. Dan felt a tingling in the tips of his ears. He clamped his jaws shut, shook ink off his pen into the ink bottle and laid it down on the blotter as the anger rose, like an ocean wave. He must not give in to it.

Sanders said, "What my colleague says is absolutely true. We could try all three, and hang them all. However, if these two turn state's evidence that results in a conviction, we might not hang them."

"I don't know," said Smith, "that I can put that over. You're asking us to give up Ives."

"Not entirely." Sanders inspected his fingernails. "The jury might find that even with their testimony and the extrinsic evidence of the mule, we haven't proved our case."

"You'll agree not to hang them?"

Again the silent consultation, a lift of an eyebrow, a nod so slight it could have been a tremor. Sanders said, "Yes, but we'll recommend banishment."

"That's not good enough. Freedom or no testimony."

"For both." Sanders squared his shoulders, upright on the chair, not resting his back. The commanding officer. "There will be no forgiveness."

Dan cleared his clogged throat. His tongue felt stiff. "If either of them comes back, they'll be shot on sight. If Fitch doesn't kill them, I will."

Davis gasped. "You can't mean that!"

"Believe me." Dan met Davis's wide shocked eyes, but he was seeing Nick's faces, the living and the dead. "I mean every word."

"You understand how irregular this is?" Davis's voice trembled. "A prosecuting attorney threatens the life of a defendant? What sort of lawyer are you? You should recuse yourself."

"Oh, yes, you're right. I should step down, leave Sanders to prosecute alone, against you five, with the lives of the entire Gulch hanging – if you will excuse the expression – in the balance. And we should perhaps wait until we have a courtroom, a police force, a jail, a judge who is not a medical man popularly elected, but one who knows the law. We should have a body of law, not just miners court rules. Absent all these things, what would you have us do? Slap murderers on the cheek and tell them not to do it again? Boys will be boys?" He stopped, because he had run out of breath, and because he heard himself shouting.

Smith said, "If anyone should recuse himself, it's you, Sanders. You have history with Ives."

"Oh? Are you referring to the time he tried to kill me at Rattlesnake Ranch?" Seeing Dan's surprise, Sanders explained, "I was spending the night there, when Ives came in drunk and tried to get the drop on me."

Smith laughed. "There was more to it than that, the way I heard it."

"No doubt," Sanders said. "But my colleague's statement goes for me, too. Absent a body of law and a legal system, we must do the best we can."

Dan had to leave this suffocating house, to breathe fresh air. "Let's get out of here. We still have to interview Ives." He gathered up his notes and slung the rifle over his shoulder, heard Davis gasp. Perhaps he would lay a bet with himself how long it would take Davis to carry a gun.

At the front door, Smith said, "Wait." He tried to drink from his flask, shook it, put it into a pocket, and from another pulled a bottle of Valley Tan. "All right. I warn you I can't promise, but this will save the two of them, and besides, we'll prove Ives could not have done it. He will have an unshakable alibi."

As they walked toward the cabin where Ives was being held, Dan and Sanders dropped back, and guards protected them amid the crowd grumbling threats in the growing light. "Why didn't Long John mention Carter yesterday?" Dan fumed. "We could have brought him in. Now we don't know where he is."

One of the guards, who had black shadows under his red-rimmed eyes, said, "We can find out. You want us to go after him?"

"Not yet," said Sanders. "That might only confuse things. If they don't bring in Carter's name, we won't."

"Even if they do," Dan said, "it won't matter now. Ives pulled the trigger."

"But knowing he was there could confuse the issue, can't you see that?" Sanders temper flared. "How do we know Carter didn't pull the trigger?"

Dan's own irritation rose to meet him. "For Chrissake, because both Hilderman and Long John agree that Ives confessed to killing Nick. So stop worrying."

"I can't," Sanders said. "You shouldn't either. We cannot be confident of the outcome."

"I know." Dan's anger ebbed, until it took some strength to support the rifle on his shoulder.

❧

Nick's friends kept Ives in a long, low cabin behind the Star Bakery. Coming in from outside, Dan almost gagged at the stench of unemptied night wastes. The shadowed front room, lighted by one table lamp to the right of the door, seemed full of men – Ives, his lawyers, guards. Ives sat on the dirt floor. Light logging chains around his ankles and waist, anchored around the logs of the wall, kept him from standing or lying full length.

"How do, Sanders," said Ives. "We meet again, in what you might call trying circumstances."

"Ives." Sanders ignored the pun. He was distinctly cool to the defendant, but what, Dan asked himself, was the proper etiquette when meeting a man who tried to kill you and whom you now prosecuted?

Smith introduced Sanders to another of the defense attorneys, who wore a Confederate greatcoat. "My esteemed colleague is the Honorable James Thurmond. Mr. Davis you already know. Our other two colleagues are elsewhere, gathering incontrovertible evidence of Mr. Ives's complete innocence of this dastardly crime."

Dan saw how Davis stepped back into the shadows as if dissociating himself from his colleagues. As well he might, if he wanted to acquire a reputation as a good, responsible lawyer.

Sanders touched Thurmond's hand just enough for a form of politeness. "Naturally, you would have to take that position," Sanders said, "considering that you're being paid to represent them."

Thurmond raised his voice. "I resent that. You're just trying to railroad the boy because he showed you up at Rattlesnake Ranch." He swung round to Dan, "What are you doing in this case, Stark? Didn't know you were a lawyer."

"Life is full of surprises." Dan kept his hands in his pockets. He'd be damned if he'd shake hands with anyone who attacked the honesty of his surveys in court, even if everyone did know it was a ploy to win for his client.

Ives chafed his hands, put them between his thighs. "Sanders is from Ohio," he told Thurmond.

"An Oberlin man," sneered Thurmond. "Niggers and whites sitting together in classes. No decent person would go to school with niggers."

Sanders said, "I never set foot in Oberlin College. I'm from Ohio, and Oberlin College is in Ohio, and there it ends. Dammit, what I think about the Negro people is not germane to this case, but your prejudices will do your clients harm with the jury."

"Like hell," snorted Thurmond. "Folks here are Secesh, and they'll vote Secesh." He laughed. "In fact, you might as well give up now and let the boys get back to work. No jury in the Gulch would vote with an all-Union prosecution. Never!"

Damn, thought Dan. Thurmond could be right.

Sanders fished a candle from a pocket and lighted it from the lamp on the table. He spoke to Ives. "Your attorneys do you no favors trying to play the War card. It would be in your best interests – "

Thurmond broke in: "I'll decide what's in my clients' best interests. Don't believe him, George. They're out to get you."

"We'd like to talk to him," Dan said. "Outside."

Thurmond spoke to Ives. "You don't have to talk to him at all. In fact, I'd advise you to say nothing. Not one damn word, got it?"

"I got nothing to say," said Ives. "I am innocent." He leaned against the log wall, his coat collar raised against the cold air seeping through the broken chinking. Chains rattled as he folded his arms across his chest. "It's all a story, Sanders, and it don't assay pure metal. Fool's gold is what you've got there. I ask you, if I'd done a thing like that, I sure as hell wouldn't lay up there at Long John's nice and cozy waiting for someone to catch me, now, would I? I'd have been long gone."

One of the guards said in a weary voice, "Shut up, Ives. You been panning that claim all night, and it's all played out."

Cozy? Dan wanted to laugh. A brush wickiup or a bedroll in the snow? Cozy? He had his own perfectly good cabin, not half a mile –. Then, as if a kaleidoscope turned and threw its colored pieces into a new pattern, he saw Ives's actions differently. If Ives had wanted to hide from the consequences of a crime, he wouldn't stay home. He'd go where he could expect someone to give him an alibi. But what crime had he been hiding from when Nick rode in?

၅

"I can't help thinking it could be important." Warming himself at the bonfire, Dan hoped no one but Sanders and Hereford could hear him speak over the noise of the fire. "Why was Ives at Long John's place?"

"It doesn't matter, does it?" Hereford's frown seemed to draw his close-set eyes even closer together. "However he came to be there, he was there."

"Agreed." Sanders spread his hands to the heat. "Could he have been visiting? He's often away, including being at Rattlesnake, drunk, in the middle of the night, trying to kill me."

"He did?" Hereford had not heard the story.

Sanders turned his back to the fire. "I thought so. At least I wasn't about to await the outcome. I grabbed a shotgun and forced a stalemate."

Dan hardly heard him. An idea pecked at the back of his mind, but until it had broken through, he saw no way to explain his instinct that it could be important to know why Ives came to be at Long John's ranch.

Two men, one of them a miner with dirt-crusted hair, stood talking to the guards. "Let them in," called Hereford. "That's Judge Wilson, president of the Junction district. I don't know the miner, but if he's with Wilson, he's all right." The miner, as grimy as most from long weeks of digging, boots held together by strips of rag, torn trousers revealing portions of his upper thighs, nevertheless walked with a straight back. A faint butternut showed under the dirt, and remnants of gold braid dangled from one shoulder. A former Confederate officer, turned scarecrow.

When the scarecrow spoke, his voice startled Dan, for it was smooth and mellow like fine old brandy, redolent of culture.

"Good day, gentlemen," he said. "I'm Charles Bagg, Attorney at Law." His brown eyes swept over Sanders's tidy blue coat and close-trimmed beard. "Until recently, I had the honor to serve the Glorious Cause as a Major, CSA." They shook hands all around. "I thought you might need some help prosecuting these criminals. Five to two didn't seem fair."

Sanders introduced himself and offered his hand. Bagg bowed at Sanders's former rank – "Then you certainly outrank me, sir." Bagg turned to Dan, who gave his name, felt excluded from their military understanding because he had not served except to brave Grandfather's copperhead wrath, the exploding legal arguments about why the Federal Government committed an illegal act by invading the South. Yet Bagg's handshake was firm, cool, and dry, and his eyes were friendly, and when they had compared legal pedigrees, Dan knew he was on equal footing with both of them, and the three prosecutors regarded each other with satisfaction. Sanders had greater legal experience, Bagg combined legal experience with knowledge of the miners and mining, and Dan had two successful brushes with criminal defense. None of them had ever prosecuted, but Dan considered that would not – someone plucked at his sleeve.

Fitch stood at his elbow. "Ives has an alibi."

"Shit." Bagg caught the hairs of his mustache in his teeth, and his jaw moved back and forth, while Sanders swore in a steady stream for several seconds without repeating himself.

Dan looked into his thoughts, saw the distinct possibility that he had been wrong, that they had the wrong man. Ives with an alibi. They were done for. It would all be over. They had the wrong man. He hung his head, stared at the ground, felt the solid earth melting away like ice on the puddles.

Fitch said, gloating over them, happy to have been right all along, "It's a solid alibi, too. George Brown and Honest Whisky Joe Basak were playing cards with Ives and Carter on the sixth.

They'll testify that the game went on for hours." He scratched his backside.

"Two witnesses?" Dan's head came up. "Two?"

"You bet," said Fitch. "It was a long poker game. They played all day."

"Good," Dan said. He wanted to dance, scream, shout, but he only rubbed his hands together as if to lather them well. Two alibi witnesses. They had a chance. He turned away to pace along the wagons. Alibis could be broken, or witnesses discredited. Two witnesses. Hallelujah! The most credible witnesses could be brought to doubt themselves, dates, times. Find the weakness. A stick the size of his forearm fell out of the fire. He picked it up, took out his pocket knife. He could play the two against each other.

Rejoining the other prosecutors, he found that Fitch and Bagg had introduced themselves, and all three men waited for him to explain himself. He was the only one with the right criminal experience. He said, "Fitch, could you buy one of the witnesses a couple of beers?"

"Sure. When?"

"Any time, but whichever one testifies first, take the other one for a drink. Don't let him hear what the first witness says."

"What do you mean?" Bagg asked. "Why treat either son of a bitch?"

Dan flipped open his pocket knife. "I once defended a man accused of murdering his partner. He swore to me and everyone that he hadn't done it, he'd been in a meeting with three other men. One had gone out of town, but the other two would testify." Dan made the first cut, his knife peeled away the bark as if it were the skin of an apple. "I was so confident. Both men had their stories straight, but when it was the prosecution's turn, he took the first witness apart, made him look like a lying bastard. I tried to repair the damage with the second witness, but of course we'd had no time to prepare, and the prosecutor annihilated him on the stand." Dan smiled around at them. "What he did, I can do." On purpose, he made himself sound more confident than he felt.

"What if Ives does have an alibi?" Fitch demanded. "What if he's innocent and you get him convicted?"

"If he truly were innocent," Bagg said, "they wouldn't think they needed two witnesses. Stark is right. They're using two witnesses because Ives is guilty. One alibi witness is damn difficult to impeach, but two? That's easy."

"Ives killed Nick," Dan said. "I know he did, and we'll prove it." And while he said that, a small still voice nagged at him: What if Ives were innocent? Dan flicked the voice aside with a stroke of the knife. Ives killed Nick, and he would hang. Suddenly appalled at himself, he made another stroke. Nothing else would be justice for Nick: a life for a life.

Hereford waved at the guards to let Smith and Thurmond in.

Bagg murmured, "Let battle be joined," and Sanders smiled.

Dan's hand worked the knife faster over the wood. He enjoyed Thurmond's surprise when Bagg introduced himself. Now he could not play the Secesh card, try to portray the case as a Union plot against Confederates.

Smith, weaving a bit, fired first. "We have some doubts as to the justice of separating the cases."

Thurmond said, "I have no doubts at all, by God! They'll be tried together!"

"We'd like nothing better." Bagg's voice oozed sweetness as he summarized the choice facing the defense while Dan's knife sliced over the stick and pale curls gathered at the end. Thurmond could not now pretend either to himself or to others that separating the cases was a Unionist plot, Dan thought. His fellow Secessionist was forcing Thurmond to consider that the three defendants had in truth conspired together to murder Tbalt, and the prosecution would like everyone to believe that, and that they should therefore be tried together and hanged together. Diametrically opposite to what in truth the prosecution wanted the defense to think, and even as Dan worried that the defense would take that, agree with it, and leave the prosecution with no witnesses unless they met any of the three on cross, he knew Thurmond hated the idea. Thurmond must consider his primary allegiance to Ives, and as along as he saved Ives the other two could hang.

Then Sanders intervened to suggest that the three could be tried separately, and Dan smiled in himself to hear Sanders imply, without quite saying outright, that they could be sacrificed as scapegoats for Ives. Granted, Bagg again taking up the argument, if the defense agreed, the prosecution might gain two witnesses, but the two could not be compelled in Common Law to incriminate themselves, and they might well choose to take their chances with the jury rather than split against their good friend Ives. Yes, the prosecution had heard their side of it already, but if they did not testify they would be tried for murder. So, as anyone could see, implying that the power lay with the defense, Thurmond's esteemed colleagues would advocate for them.

Of course, Dan chimed in, if Ives produced an alibi to prove he could not have done it, that changed things, and he was rewarded by the change that came over Thurmond's face, from mistrust to satisfaction that the defense had already outfoxed the prosecution by finding an alibi for Ives. Thurmond was too smug.

Fitch opened his mouth, and Dan, as if by accident, stepped on his toe. He apologized, and though Fitch scowled at him, he kept his silence and bit off a chaw. Dan knew his boots would suffer, but the defense must not know that the prosecution already knew about the alibi. Otherwise, they might circumvent the plan to have Fitch take one of the witnesses away.

Thurmond launched into an impassioned speech about Ives's complete innocence, and Dan knew that he would toss Long John and Hilderman away, to save Ives.

Stealing glances at Thurmond from under his hat brim, Dan could almost watch the man think. Thurmond was saying, "Even with them, you won't hang Ives. He'll go free as the air. The jury will see to that."

Two men, one from Junction and one from Virginia, had agreed to take notes, to act as recorders during the trial. Established at a table by the green wagon, they recorded the agreement for separate trials. They blew on their hands, and worried aloud that the ink would freeze in the bottles. The man from Virginia introduced himself as William Y. Pemberton. He was a compromise between the prosecution and the defense, who had wanted him because he was from Virginia and sympathetic to Ives. He looked young enough not to shave more than twice a week. "I'll record this, but George Ives is no cold-blooded murderer."

"Oh?" Pemberton sounded so certain that Dan's confidence was momentarily shaken. "Why not?"

"I share office space with him in Virginia. He is so affable, so strictly honest in his dealings with customers. Men are always coming and going, you know, ordering horses for their journeys, paying for pasture. He always has a jolly word for them. I like him very much."

"Good. That way we'll be sure to have an unbiased record." But Dan was thinking how clever of Ives the highwayman, the road agent. He pastured men's horses when not needed, and retrieved them when wanted. Miners who sold their claims and cleaned up for the journey home would take their gold with them, and they could not hide their joy at seeing their families again. They would confide in Ives. He knew when gold was moved.

Thurmond's colleagues, even Alex Davis, had satisfied looks on their faces. They wanted to try Ives without Long John and Hilderman to muddy the issue. They believed, Dan thought, that separate trials would make everyone's innocence clear, or failing that, the deal they had negotiated behind Thurmond's back at least saved two clients, while the alibi would save Ives. Did they not have witnesses to it? Dan's knife snicked along the wood. He and Bagg and Sanders would break any alibi the defense cared to put up. No, they would not merely break it. They would smash it. Because Ives was guilty as sin.

Meantime, they had separate trials. Round one to the prosecution.

∽

Berry Woman welcomed Martha into her wickiup festooned with clumps of dried herbs on their stalks, bags that held their contents secret, hampers and round containers made of woven strips of reddish bark. By signs and some English, Martha asked and learned. She ventured a word or two of Grandmam's language, Cherokee. Berry Woman listened with her head cocked to one side, her eyes bright and interested, and gave back word for word in her own language, that Lydia Hudson had said was Crow.

After all, it was not so much different from visits between white women, although they sat on the floor, insulated from the cold by the pungent bear rugs that covered every inch, except for the fire in the center. They drank a tea that Martha found delicious, though she had never tasted it before. She asked what was in it, and soon the two women were exchanging recipes for teas to drink for various ailments.

Their talk swung to food recipes, and Berry Woman put her feet under her and stood up. She lifted the lid from a tall, rounded container of woven red bark, and revealed a winter's supply of bricks wrapped in deerskin. "Camas cakes," Martha understood her to say as she unwrapped one. When they were seated again at the fire, Berry Woman unwrapped the cake, and cut off two pieces as if she sliced a pound cake.

Martha found the cake slightly sweet, though too bland for her taste, but when she sipped tea to wash the taste away, the taste burst out on her tongue. Not too sweet, not at all like candy, the camas had more a hint of sweetness in something earthy. The aftertaste laid at the back of her tongue, heavy and tasting of the earth. Delicious. She reckoned not all white folks would like it, but she could make much of it, smiling and nodding and smacking her lips.

When she left, Martha held bags of dried plants, some she could use in treating various ailments, some for eating, and a treatment for typhus that was all around her if she'd had the wit to see it – juniper. Best of all, she had made another friend.

∽

The sun drifted into the sky as if the mythical horses pulling its chariot were tethered to a line just slack enough for them to clear the mountains, drive the night back across Alder Creek. Amid rising ground fog, the crowd milled and shouted, but Dan, no longer worried about bullets from the dark, could see the closer faces, who cursed him, who yelled for his blood. The occasional gleam of an eye, hooked nose, lips distorted in cursing, all resolved themselves into recognizable men. He could be a credible witness at their trials for his – attempted – murder.

Bagg fired the opening question in the next battle. "We are concerned, gentlemen, to be fair to everyone, Unionist" a bow to Dan and Sanders "and Secessionist alike." A bow to the defense. "So, which Constitution do we use?" He beamed at them. "The Federal Constitution, or the Confederate?"

"Oh, shit." Fitch lifted his hat and scratched his head, and his wiry hair stood on end in a way that reminded Dan of Miss Dean's terrier, whose coat bristled in just that fashion. "Why can't we just try Ives and get done with it? This way we'll be here till my boy rises at the last trump."

Dan could not blame him. Having changed his mind about Ives, Fitch wanted the trial over and done with. What would he think if he knew Carter was involved? Would he seize on Carter as an alternative to Ives because he and Ives had been friends? And where was the guard who went to learn Carter's whereabouts?

"Wait a minute." Dan spoke without taking his eyes from the stick. "We have not settled the jurisdictional question."

The lawyers, by unspoken consent, moved farther from the fire to confer by the green wagon. The mining district presidents, Wilson of Junction, Byam of Nevada, who were also the judges of their miners courts, listened. "That's not for you to decide," Byam glanced at Wilson, who bobbed his head once, and said, "That's our decision. We agreed to share it."

"Who presides?" asked Sanders, overriding Thurmond's objections.

"We both will. This thing is too big for just one man to look at."

"I protest!" Thurmond began, but Wilson cut him off.

The Junction president's bass lectured Thurmond. "You been panning that ground all day without striking pay dirt, so you'd best pull up stakes on it. Miners court rules is clear, the boy was murdered closest to Junction. We just got organized, so Nevada's helping us out. Me and Byam will go shares on the judging, and anybody what don't like it can go to hell."

Silence. Thurmond's lips moved soundlessly, Smith smiled down the neck of a bottle, and the corners of Bagg's mouth twitched. The recorders bent their heads to write, and one hid a smile.

"That seems clear enough," Dan said. And it was clear. A few months ago he would not have understood that Wilson was telling Thurmond to stop harping on the same complaint, that he had exhausted it, and should abandon it. Now Dan, too, thought in terms of mines, claims, pans, stakes that marked claim boundaries.

Sanders reminded them, "The Constitutional question."

Thurmond shouted out, "The Constitution of the Confederacy, of course!"

"You bet!" said Fitch.

Dan ground his teeth, and at the same time felt Sanders touch his elbow. Neither of them could bring themselves to call the Secessionists' outlaw paper a Constitution. There was only one – the U.S. Constitution. He drew in a breath, let it out slowly, forced himself to calm, to bank his anger. The time would come.

The judges looked from one group to the other. Did they understand what this meant? Dan wondered. Certainly the crowd did not. Straining to hear, impatient with the lawyers' jabbering, they caught the word Confederacy, and cheered, mixed with some booing. Clearly, the Confederates held the majority.

The defense attorneys, Secessionists all, would argue into the night if they could, to wear down the prosecution, and Thurmond, at least, regarded Bagg as a traitor because he would not side with them. Dear God, let us all hold out, Dan prayed without knowing. Give us strength, or Ives could go free from sheer fatigue on the part of the prosecution.

"Put it to a vote!" Alex Davis surprised them all. He had been quiet up to now, so that Dan had been on the way to forgetting about him, but now one of the other defenders said, "The boy's right! Let the jury vote on it!"

Smith held up a steady hand, palm out. "Not so fast. Why choose a Constitution? Why is this a question?"

"When Congress created this Territory," Sanders said, "it failed to account for the passage of law from the Constitution to the Territory." He rocked on his heels as he waited for them to grasp his point.

Dan said, "That means the Constitution does not apply here."

"It doesn't?" gasped Smith.

"That is correct," said Sanders. "Until the Idaho Territorial Legislature meets in Lewiston to declare the Constitution applicable, no uniform code of law applies to the Territory as a whole. Nothing. My uncle Edgerton feels that until the Legislature meets, any court he presides over might be guilty of applying the wrong body of law, and the proceedings will be null and void."

"Your uncle Edgerton?" Bagg asked. "The Territorial Chief Justice?"

Thurmond laughed, one short, angry syllable. "That radical abolitionist. Rabble rouser. Lincoln's appointee." He spat, and Dan seized Sanders's upper arm, under the cape of his blue greatcoat, and felt hard muscles tensed for action.

Bagg said, "We're in a legal vacuum. We have no governing body of law by which to conduct a case."

"I'll be damned," said Smith.

Feeling Sanders relax, Dan let him go. "As I see it, we're marooned, so to speak, by both the mountains and by Congress's oversight. We can't send a man to Lewiston, five hundred miles across the Divide in winter, to wait for the Legislature to go into session and rule on this."

"We can't hold the prisoners here for weeks while they argue about which set of laws we operate under." Bagg shook his head as if regretting the situation. "Why, the California boys would want to put in an alcalde and go by Spanish law." He inclined toward Thurmond. "Seems hardly fair to your clients." When Thurmond would have blustered, Bagg's voice, under silken sails, cruised by him. "I consider we should try them by Common Law. Of late we in the South have had considerable experience with it."

"What in hell does this mean?" Fitch demanded.

Dan whispered an explanation behind his hand. "When the South repudiated the U.S. Constitution, they set up the Common Law in its place until they could write their own governing paper. It is the foundation of the Confederate Constitution." He had no intention of telling Fitch, or letting on to any Secessionist that while using the Common Law appeared to give the defense the advantage, it underlay the U. S. Constitution as well. Union lawyers were likely to be as well versed in it as the Confederates.

Thurmond began to argue for postponing the trial until the Legislature should have met. Smith and Davis led him aside. Dan watched them gesture at each other, Smith touching his lips to his bottle, Thurmond's arms flailing the air, Davis gesturing with his hands palms down, go quietly.

Fitch ended the argument. "The hell with this," he roared at Thurmond. "My boy lies in his grave, and my friend sits accused. Bagg is one of us. Get this trial going!"

"All right!" shouted Thurmond. "We'll use the Common Law. It's as close to the Confederate Constitution as we can get."

The crowd cheered, as much because the trial was about to get under way at last as because the Confederates appeared to have the advantage. Under the noise, Dan thought fast. Fitch had been able to end the stalemate because he was known as a friend of Ives, and apparently the defense did not know of his change of heart. Dan resolved to talk to him, privately, just to feel him out. Perhaps Fitch knew or could learn something more of Ives's activities. Not that they would be admissible unless the defense opened the door, but it would be useful to know more about the charming gentleman Ives seemed to be. For Dan, out of his own inner certainty, thought of Pemberton and other respectable men who believed in Ives's innocence. He had a hunch there might be two George Ives, and he wanted to know more of the other one.

∽

In measured fashion, as of an academic procession at Harvard College, or a promenade of dignitaries of the State, armed guards cleaved the cheering crowd to make way for Ives, a prince in stately progress greeting his subjects, who shuffled forward, light logging chains on his ankles, carrying the loose ends in his hands, like the ghost of Jacob Marley.

People shouted after him: "We'll get you out of this, George!" "Never fear, Georgie!" "Hey, George, stiff upper lip!"

How could Ives act so nonchalant? Didn't he understand the danger? Or could he simply not believe in it? Did he think these people would free him? Dan swore inwardly: Perhaps they would do just that.

A steady muttering of obscenities sounded in Dan's ear. He must speak with Fitch. Drawing him off toward the crossed wagon tongues, Dan spoke softly. "You found out about the alibi. Could you and X find anyone else who has reason to hate Ives?"

"Why?" Fitch turned his head to spit, but his eyes never left Dan's face.

"Because most people seem to believe he's a good fellow. But I have a hunch that there's a lot about Mr. Ives that people aren't telling."

While Fitch thought about it, a fancy woman called out, "Come see me when you're free, Georgie! I'll show you a real good time!"

Fitch was watching over Dan's shoulder, but Dan did not turn around as Ives's voice came to them. "I'll be there, honey. Hey, Tom, get ready to lose that poke to me when this is over! Bob, you old son of a bitch, you came for the show, did you? You still got that hat you borrowed? I'll need it when we're done here."

"They make me sick," Fitch said. "I'll do it, and I'll set X to it, too." About to step over the small barrier, he paused. "What if I can't find anybody?"

"You will. Ives has extorted money from men at gunpoint. He calls it a loan, only he never pays it back."

Fitch sucked on a tooth. "Sounds like highway robbery to me."

"It is, but no one has had the guts to make him pay it back." Ives never pays for anything. "He's done it in town, on Wallace Street, in front of people."

"And nobody did anything? What, did all the cowards in the country come here?"

He was no better than any of them. Dan gazed into the fire, and saw his own cowardice dancing in the flames. "Maybe some people think there are more important things than proving their courage."

"Yeah? Such as what, perchance?" Fitch's voice held a contempt rich and thick as butter.

"Survival, maybe." Dan was telling himself that to take the gold home to the family was the supreme duty. Survive so that the family would survive after Father had destroyed it along with himself. Beside that, what did his personal courage, or cowardice, matter?

"Hell." Fitch spat yellow-brown tobacco juice through a gap in his lower teeth. "Cowards don't survive. Survival takes courage, and the sooner folks learn that, the better."

∾

Dan watched the group around Ives, who half-turned to smile at Johnny Gibbons, bent over him, with his hand on Ives's shoulder. Gallagher brooded over them both, glanced from friend to guard to friend, as if gauging the chances of a rescue. His face settled into downward lines, and dark pouches sagged under his eyes. His open coat revealed the thumb of his right hand hooked over his pistol grip. McDowell loomed beside him, shoulders hunched in a fighter's pose, his chin thrust out. His hatred leaped out to scorch Dan like an errant flame escaping the fire, and he lifted his middle finger. Gallagher smiled.

Dan's blood seemed to thicken in his veins, and everything moved as through gumbo – men walking, Judge Wilson beckoning to Sheriff Hereford, Bagg scratching through his mop of hair, Pemberton peering at his ink bottle to see if the ink were dry or frozen. Not McDowell, but Gallagher. Dan feared Gallagher's smile more than McDowell's finger. No one had ever hated him so much before. Gallagher would kill him the first chance he got. An open challenge, a bullet through a window.

Gibbons laughed. "I hear old Morris has got his windows fixed. You can try my horse, George, see he's trained as good as yours."

"Wasn't that just a sight?" Ives chortled. "Damn kike run out like his ass was burning. Wanted me to pay for the goddam windows!"

Sanders asked Dan a question. Dan had to ask him to repeat it, made himself concentrate on it and on his answer while Ives and his pals laughed. George Ives never paid for broken windows, never paid back loans extorted at gun point. George Ives never paid for anything.

Until now, Dan promised Nick. Until now.

Yet he watched Ives's pals swagger, thumbs hooked in their belts to hold their coats open and show their pistols and knives, and amid the fluttering in his belly he wondered, if Ives hanged, would any of Nick's friends live? He shook his head. Too late to think of that. It had already been too late when he looked on Nick's dreadful dead face.

∽

Judge Byam climbed into the green wagon, and shook the cowbell to begin the trial. The prosecutors walked to the wagon's front wheel. Dan's right triceps twitched and would not be still. He paused at the recorders' flimsy table to thank them for their service to the cause of justice.

"Listen up, boys!" Byam's tenor voice pierced the milling hubbub. The men quieted. "Settle down and let's get to work." He beckoned to the three prosecutors to stand in the wagon with him and Judge Wilson.

No. Dan did not want to stand in that wagon and make himself an easy target. It was different for Sanders and Bagg. They were soldiers, they were accustomed to being shot at. Not him. There were two prosecutors; they did not need a third. He could resign. He would resign. He picked up a fresh stick, and thinking of resignation, he grabbed hold of the armrest on the driver's box, put his boot on the hub, and leaped up, his legs obeying in spite of him.

The crowd spread across and up the road and down, swelled and shrank at the edges, as people milled about, edged through to hear better, see better, find their friends, avoid their enemies. Perhaps 1,500 men, with a few women. Little boys played tag through newly melted puddles, their whoops echoing around Dan's ears. To hide the quivering of his nerves, he brought out his pocket knife, turned the wood over as if looking for a suitable place to begin, scraped off a piece of bird dung, and drew the blade down.

Byam shouted, "I declare this court in session!"

Thurmond ran forward. "Not so fast! We got to talk this over. We got a lot of Californians here. We should be fair to them and appoint an alcalde!"

The son of a bitch had broken their agreement. Dan said to himself, shit, it would be a very long day.

Bagg stood forward, and his voice carried to the farther edges of the crowd. "Boys, the honorable counsel for the defense says what we got for a miner's court ain't good enough. You elected Judge Byam, and Judge Wilson, over in Junction. You want an alcalde to take over this here trial? I say we go by Common Law, the same as the Constitution of the Glorious Confederacy."

The crowd cheered. The honorable counsel. Echoes of Marc Antony's sarcasm at Caesar's funeral in Shakespeare's play, *Julius Caesar*. Brutus is an honorable man. Bagg's sarcasm painted Thurmond as honorable as Brutus.

Judge Byam swung the cowbell. "That settles it! We won't have an alcalde. Judge Wilson and I preside, and I declare this trial by Common Law." His chin jutted out, the goatee pointed toward Thurmond: Don't trifle with me.

Dan leaned over the sidewall. "Did you get that?" he asked the note-takers. Their hat brims waggled up and down.

"Hey!" Someone from the crowd stood behind the wagon and called up to Judge Byam, who could not hear him over all the noise. He rang the cowbell, but when the shrill clanging quieted the crowd, the speaker was gone. "Probably wasn't important." Raising his voice, he bellowed: "Simmer down, you men! We got to decide on the jury."

Smith and Thurmond jumped up. "Jury of the whole!" Ives's friends took up the cry: "Jury of the whole!" and the crowd made it a chant: "Jury of the whole!"

Wooden curls accumulated like the questions in Dan's mind. Jury of the whole? Hell. Mob jury was more like it. Drunks to decide justice for Nick? They must have a formal jury. The crowd would never agree. How to break the impasse, prevent the defense from appealing to the mob? His mind whirled among the questions.

Thurmond and Smith stalked back and forth, while Davis and the other defense attorneys applauded, and the roughs shouted as if to a drumbeat: "Jury of the whole!"

Dan's knife flashed like a distant signal sending a message, and an idea emerged. He drew Sanders and Bagg toward him. This just might work.

‍⁀

Sitting across from each other at Lydia Hudson's back table, sipping now and then at hot sweet drinks in speckledy tin cups, Martha and Dotty played the alphabet game. Lydia had made it up for them, it pinned letters onto Bible words, starting with A for Almighty all the way to Z for Zachariah. It was Dotty's turn to recite again, but her mind wasn't on it, until Martha reminded her that she had to know her letters or Professor Dimsdale wouldn't take her into his school in January. Didn't she want to go with her friend Molly Sheehan?

Dotty began again with a deep sigh.

Kerosene lamps glowed over their flower-painted bowls, but it was the sounds that comforted Martha: the colored gal and Lydia chopped potatoes and canned beans for tonight's stew, the puppy's teeth chawed on a bone, Albert sawed at the hip joint of a frozen elk carcass. Dotty's voice piped the letters and their words being the tune. Everything blended like the harmony in music, that ran in Martha's mind, in and out, in and out —

"Mam? Mam?" The young'un was tapping her hand. "What comes after Q for Queen Esther?"

Without peeking at the slate, Martha said, "R for Rebecca," and went on to name all the letters, so's she would know she knew them, her memory having failed before on M for Martha. Of all things. She wished she could spur her brain on faster.

Dotty finished saying the letters, and Martha drove her through them one more time before she allowed as to how the young'un could go play with the puppy. Canary growled everyone away when he had a bone, but this little dog welcomed Dotty with happy tail thumps.

A draft of cold air and a squeak of wood behind Martha told her the door was opening, but by the looks on Tabby's and Lydia's faces something wasn't right. McDowell? Here? Martha scrambled to turn and put her feet on the floor.

Lydia said, "We are not open." Her voice, that was mostly warm and welcoming, held no welcome in it, though it was civil enough. "We haven't begun serving dinner yet."

Growling, the puppy abandoned his bone, and stood up, the hairs lifted along his spine.

"Hold the dog," Lydia told Tabby, but Dotty already had both arms around the puppy's neck. Albert rested the cleaver on the rib of the elk. Tabby went on chopping, only faster.

Them two fancy women, Helen Troy and Isabelle Stevens. Martha put her skirt to rights and kept her seat. The women wore the bright sleazy dresses of their trade, that wouldn't keep a louse warm. Their faces were pinched and gray.

"We didn't come for dinner," said Helen Troy. "We come for help."

Wasn't for their gray faces Martha might have laughed, at the thought of them two coming to Lydia for anything but a meal.

The Stevens woman sniffed, and dabbed at her eyes with her bare hand, but tears dropped one by one onto her bosom and stained the shiny fabric. Helen Troy took a clean square of cloth from her net bag and gave it to the Stevens woman, guided her to sit down.

"What kind of help?" Lydia asked.

"It's my boy." Words struggled against Isabelle Stevens's sobs. "He's sick. All of a sudden like. Powerful sick. We can't find a doctor." She gulped and covered her face, said in a muffled wail, "He could die!"

Without them saying it, Martha knew. Typhus. Dear Lord.

Helen Troy said, "They're probably over at Nevada City, where they're fixing to lynch Georgie." She stared at Martha. "At least your husband went with Gallagher to put a stop to it."

So that was why they had come here. On account McDowell drank in her saloon, spent what dust they had to no good, went to Nevada to save a murderer. Martha thought, was she always to be known by her husband's doings? If George Ives killed poor Nick, he deserved what he got, he'd made his own bed, but these women never figured her to be different from McDowell. On account he went to Nevada. Serve them right, was she to say No.

No to these no-count women and that nasty boy. No.

The Stevens woman uncovered her face, tears run through the paint, mixed black and rouge. She hiccupped. "I'd be obliged if you'd look to him."

Her sorrow, her terror for her son touched Martha. This — this easy woman was a mother same as her, and the Bible said, Comfort ye the afflicted. Martha shuddered, almost overcome by shame. She wanted to hide under the bench, hide her sinful face so the world didn't know how she'd had such a thought as to let Jacky Stevens die. Dear Jesus, forgive me. "I'll come."

೧૭

The muttering crowd seethed in the street, shouted an occasional restless opinion. Judge Byam rang the cowbell and yelled for order. "Listen up, all of you!" He coughed. "Drat. If I have to shout all day, I won't be able to talk for a week."

Dan, concentrating on the voices, returned some sort of reply. There was something he should hear, some key to their thinking, that if he could discover it, the prosecutors might unlock their sentiments and turn them toward a result that yielded justice. Because soon they would have a crucial vote on his idea.

Yet, he reminded himself, there was nothing certain in the law.

Byam shouted, "We got to decide on a jury."

Gallagher shook his fist over Ives's shoulder. "We're the jury, all of us!" He swung his arm at the men around him. Cheers rippled to the farther edges of the crowd and lapped at the walls of the buildings lining the road.

Sanders waited until the noise faded enough to let him be heard before he stood up to them Dan's idea: a compromise, a formal jury to act in an advisory capacity to the jury of the whole. In the manner of men seizing on ideas, Sanders and Bagg and the judges had amended it, strengthened it, made it bullet-proof. Or so they hoped.

Thurmond leaped up: "No!"

Dan's knife peeled wooden curls that he let gather on the stick. At this rate, he'd end up with a cluster of curls on a toothpick. He was listening to undercurrents in the crowd.

"We propose a compromise – "

Jeers from the roughs, cries of "Quiet! Shut up! Let the man talk!"

Dan felt a smile begin at the corners of his mouth.

"We suggest an advisory jury to the jury of the whole, and made up of twenty-four men – " Sanders plowed on, against the gumbo of jeers.

Gallagher hollered: "We're the jury and we say, Let Ives go. Let Ives go!" He tried to make it a chant, but it would not catch on.

Thurmond bellowed, "This ain't a trial, it's a goddam charade!"

The cowbell clanged as Sanders, silenced, stood exposed to a mob that would not hear him. God, Dan thought, what he'd give for a real courtroom with its decorum, the certainty of being heard. And then he heard a new note, low and impatient, hinting at a current of another opinion flowing counter to Thurmond and Gallagher. Men booed them, shouted, "Let the man speak!" "Shut up!" "Let him talk!" "Quiet, goddammit!" The crowd settled into an uneasy quiet.

Dan, who had not lifted his eyes from the wooden curls, was suddenly hopeful. "Try again. The crowd is dividing. You were silenced by men who wanted to hear you. They were trying to tell the roughs to shut up."

"They won't listen to me," Sanders said. "Bagg, you talk to them. You speak their language."

"Yes, do." Dan sensed that the opposition to Virginia must have support, but, being mostly Southerners and Copperheads themselves, they would not trust Sanders in his Union army greatcoat, or himself, an educated Northerner from Virginia City. They wanted truth in their own speech. From one of their own.

Bagg raised both arms. "Listen to me, you hard luck cases." Laughter from the crowd. "I'm Charley Bagg, I got a claim in

Junction District, and I ain't a Union man wanting to make you do anything that ain't democratic." He quelled the laughter, the few cheers, with a downward motion of his hands. "Esteemed counsel for the defense is correct. This trial is a sham."

Startled, Dan looked up. Bagg had everyone's attention. "A proper trial means a jury, and trial by jury means 12 men! You voted to use Common Law, and one of the pillars of that system, in use by civilized governments everywhere, is a twelve-man jury. If you want to pan something else, you won't find color."

Thurmond thrust out his long jaw. "Twelve hand-picked men! Bob Hereford will put the damn posse on the jury."

"A hand-picked jury was all right with you when you wanted the trial in Virginia!" shouted Sanders. "You were happy to have Plummer pick the jury."

"Wait for Plummer!" yelled Gallagher, and his cronies took up the cry, "Wait for Plummer!" while others shouted them down, and Judge Byam called, "Order, order!" and shook the cowbell till Dan thought his ears would never stop ringing.

A voice behind the wagon asked, "Where is Plummer, anyhow?"

"Don't know. It's a good day's ride," said a second voice. "He'll be here before long."

The first man said, "He better damn well get here! It's getting late."

And it was. The sun was well into the westward portion of its flat arc and shadows crept outward across Alder Creek. Already the temperature dipped toward freezing even in the sunshine. Dan pulled his coat collar around his neck and his beard rasped against the material. He rubbed his chin. He forgot whether he had shaved this morning, but a blond man did not have to be so careful about a day's growth of beard as a dark man would, and certainly with so many miners neither shaving nor bathing between arrival and leaving months later, a day would not be noticed.

Sanders's voice booming as if in a call to battle roused him from his irrelevant thoughts. "We owe these men a speedy trial. We're not waiting for Plummer!"

Thurmond shook his fist at Sanders. "The gentleman from Oberlin wants to rush to judgment!"

A mixture of laughter, catcalls, booing. "Nigger lover!" someone yelled.

Sanders's temper flared. He put one leg over the side of the wagon, ready to go after Thurmond, but Dan and Bagg grabbed handfuls of his cape and pulled him back. Both feet in the wagon, Sanders boomed, as if he had just thought of it, as if his suggestion had not been in the plan from the beginning, "All right. Let's have an advisory jury of twelve men from Junction and twelve from Nevada."

"And Virginia!" shouted Smith.

Some of the Virginia roughs took up the shout. "Let's pick a jury from Virginia!" Other men echoed it, some calling for Junction and Nevada, others for Virginia, and more for the jury of the whole. The defense lawyers had their heads together, conferring, and Dan could see the whole idea coming apart, leaving them with only the mob jury. He said to Sanders and Bagg. "Most of the men here are from Nevada and Junction, aren't they? They wouldn't be likely to accept a jury from Virginia, so what if they voted it down? Then Ives's bunch couldn't say we wouldn't give Virginia a look-in."

"Too dangerous." Sanders shook his head. "We can't take the chance."

Dan said, "I think it might work." He couldn't explain how he knew, how he felt that the crowd might be ready to listen, because he couldn't explain the undercurrents he'd heard building among the unruly, ragged men who planted their feet and stood with arms crossed on their chests, signifying their opposition to the roughs, to the Virginia contingent.

Bagg said, "Yes, it's dangerous, but it's worth the risk. I'll try it."

"All right," Sanders said.

Bagg held up his hands for quiet, and the crowd silenced itself as pale curls gathered on the stick, and Dan heard a different quality in the silence: an intentness, a concentration. Bagg's Southern drawl thickened, and his voice carried outward, where on the crowd's rim, men ended their conversations, paused in their errands. "You see, boys, here's the way of it. We want to see justice done, don't we?" Not hearing more than a murmur, he shouted: "Don't we want justice?"

"Yes," shouted Gallagher from his stance behind the log. "That's why we don't want no goddam picked jury."

"That's right," McDowell said. "We want all of us on the jury, that's what."

Bagg ignored them. Their shouts were as nothing to him, with his voice honed to shouting orders across battlefields, and he spoke as if in a courtroom merely larger than most. "There's an innocent boy done to death. We've had a lot of that, one way and another. There's many a man has set off for the States with his gold, and his relatives have written months later to ask his whereabouts. There's babies back home whose daddies ain't coming home, women that will never know what happened to their husbands, sons, fathers."

Sanders rocked, heel toe, heel toe, and his fingers twined themselves together behind his back. "Yes," he murmured, "yes, yes."

Something about the crowd drew his attention, and it took him a moment to realize that it was mostly quiet. They listened to Bagg. Dan sent up silent curses that approached prayers: Christ let this be, Jesus make it work, let them go for it, holy Christ Charlie speak to them, hear him you bastards, God damn you, hear what he's telling you. Pale wooden curls gathered on the stick, and the crowd was silent.

Smith lurched up from the log. "George Ives has got to have a fair trial. I say — " He belched and rocked a bit. Several men laughed. "I say, every man jack has the right to be on this here jury. You want justice? George Ives needs justice, because he did not kill Nick Tbalt."

"God damn it, I ain't done yet!" Bagg shouted.

"Order!" Byam reached for the cowbell, but men shouted at Smith: " Sit down! Let him talk! Shut up! We want to hear him!"

In the quiet, Bagg shouted, "You want a fair trial? Let it be fair to all sides. We'll have an advisory jury. Twelve men from Junction, and twelve from Nevada. They'll hear all the evidence and recommend a verdict. Then you boys can vote to agree or disagree with them. You-all will have the final say."

"So moved," yelled Dan. Bagg had not proposed a jury from Virginia City, but this was not the time to bring that in. They had to seize the moment.

Judge Byam shouted, "Second?"

"Second," bellowed a man who stood at the crossed tongues.

"All in favor," hollered Judge Wilson.

Waves of cheers crashed against the building walls, from one side of the street to the other. Judge Byam waited until he could be heard. "Opposed." Loud as the booing sounded to Dan, it was not as loud as the cheering. Byam yelled, "Carried! There will be an advisory jury of twelve men from Nevada and twelve men from Junction, to make recommendations to the jury of the whole, and you boys will have the final say." He rang the cowbell and coughed. "I need a beer. This is dry work," he muttered.

Leaning over the wagon's sidewall, he instructed Sheriff Hereford and the sheriff of Junction to round up an advisory jury and be back before nightfall.

"Bring on your goddam advisory jury." McDowell rested both hands on Ives's shoulders. "If this man hangs, your lives will be fool's gold."

God damn it! Dan was sick of this – this bullying. He would show McDowell. Intent on the big man, full of an anger that freed him from fear, he rested his left hand, holding the stick, on the sidewall and vaulted over. The stick caught on a hook inside the top board, and as he dropped, his weight wrenched his thumb from its socket. Up his arm stabbed a pain so sharp that he wanted to vomit. He went to his knees, held the arm to his stomach, and Sanders and Bagg jumped to help him stand. Cradling his arm, Dan could see despite the glove that the thumb bulged out at a bad angle.

Bagg shouted into his ear: "Is it broken?"

Dan shook his head. Though the first knife thrusts had settled into a hard throbbing, he still could not speak, and he dreaded taking off the glove. "Just the thumb." He had not thought something so small could hurt so much.

X Beidler, whom Dan hadn't seen since in several hours, walked through the cordon of guards with Jacob. Beidler carried his shotgun, a beer, and most of a paper-wrapped meat pie. He offered the pie to Dan, who shook his head. He had not eaten all day, but the thought of food made his stomach turn over. Beidler took a bite of the pie. "How's your hand?"

"It'll do." Anything else he said would be playing the baby. "Where have you been?"

Beidler offered the beer to Dan, who shook his head. "Out there." He took a swig to wash down the pie. "Listening to public opinion." A nod to Sanders and Bagg. "This and that. Looking for Aleck Carter. The Nevada boys're damn sick of the way things have been going in Virginia. They've had too much trouble from roughs like Ives."

Sanders said, "Divide and conquer. Your idea worked, Stark."

"Yes," Dan said. "But what about Carter?"

Beidler mumbled around a bite of meat pie. "Nowhere to be found. Word is he pulled up stakes and went to Deer Lodge when we brung Ives in."

A hundred miles north. "Christ," Dan said. What if Carter got away? He felt as if he traveled on a deer trail that meandered through dense stands of fir and pine, and at each turn, when it seemed the trail must end in a plain clear road, it disappeared through rampant clumps of thorny stems twining through fallen logs.

∾

There he was. Mr. Stark. Sitting on the back bench, close to Lydia's stove. At the sight of him a kind of fog shrouded the room, and the clash of crockery in the wash tub faded. He smiled, and she knew he hurt someplace, on account pain tightened his eyes, but man-like, he wouldn't let himself know how bad it was. She knew that look too well. Hogs had it before dying, and women in labor. Men who hurt. He maybe thought he could hide it, but he couldn't. Not from her.

The fog vanished. Lydia took the pie out of her hands, and carried it high, like a trophy, and the colored gal let plates and cups slide into the wash tub, and people's talk buzzed around her. Tim squeezed onto the bench next to X Beidler, who sat beside Mr. Stark. She suddenly knew that X Beidler faced the door in case of trouble, and Jacob Himmelfarb, on Mr. Stark's other side, hovered over him like a broody hen, even cutting his meat – now why would he do that? She didn't dare take too close a look now, but followed along, Lydia with the pie and Dotty fair bouncing in Lydia's wake, wanting to tell her news, Timmy coming after.

"Gentlemen, we have a special treat," Lydia announced.

Martha put back her hood and untied the cloak as she walked toward him. To the others, she was a woman walking after Lydia, but she felt guilty, like she was meeting him secret-like in plain sight. "Just a dried apple pie," she said.

"Apple pie!" X smacked his lips.

Two or three customers applauded, and Mr. Stark's smile reached into her soul. "Best pie in the Gulch," he said.

Martha shook her head. "It's plain cooking. Not what you're used to." For she had seen the colored gal's narrowing lips, and understood how she'd feel if she thought her pie-making slighted. "Tabby's the dab hand at pies. My crust is always too thick."

She was doing how she'd been reared, not letting herself get puffed up, and hadn't thought about what she was saying until Lydia froze with the knife over the pie, and her mouth opened, and she and the colored gal stared at Martha, their shock turning quick-like into delight. And Martha was shocked at herself. What she had said just popped out. For certain, she'd never have given the colored gal's feelings a bit of attention a few days ago. Wouldn't have thought that a darky had feelings to be hurt, and it wouldn't have mattered none anyway.

Lydia sliced the pie, set out slices on tin plates. "Let's have some of this delicious pie. Tabby, do thee take some to Albert, please."

"I wanted to tell you that I talked to the Professor today." Martha helped Lydia hand out pie to everyone, part of her mind worried that Lydia wouldn't get enough dust for the pie, seeing as how she hadn't quoted them a price.

"Mam said I knew my letters good enough to talk to him, so we did, and he said I could come. Isn't that fine?" Dotty bounced on her toes, she was that excited. "I start in January." She twirled, and stumbled against Mr. Stark, who twisted about and steadied the child. Martha saw that he wore a glove on his left hand but not on his right, that held Dotty's elbow. His nose showed pinched and white about the nostrils. She must have bumped him, but he hadn't let on.

"The best thing you can learn," he said, "is kindness to others."

"Like my Mam?" The child sidled closer into the circle of his arm.

"Exactly so. And Mrs. Hudson." With a smile at Martha, he let go the young'un's elbow, and shrugged her away as he turned back to his dinner.

Martha put up her hands to cool her cheeks. Lydia said, "Sit thee down, dearie. It's not fair for thee to work so hard and not share in the fruits." She laughed like she'd said something clever, and the men laughed with her, but Martha didn't get the joke, for trying to piece her thoughts together. Dotty must have thought she meant to leave, because the child said, "Why can't we stay, Mam? Pap ain't home. He's off somewheres with Deputy Gallagher."

There was a hard silence Martha could have bounced off of. X Beidler's back stiffened, and Mr. Stark's fork stopped halfway to his mouth, and even Jacob Himmelfarb, who was half turned her way, and was about the gentlest thing in trousers she'd ever met, stared at her like he'd found out her dark secret.

Tim spoke up. "We can stay, Mam, can't we?"

Mr. Stark said, "That being the case, please do have some of your own pie. We'll see you safely home afterwards. I have to pick up my winnings at the Melodeon Hall."

"I'll see them home safe," Tim said, and Martha knew he was wanting to be the man of the house and responsible for his womenfolk.

"Of course you will," said Mr. Stark, "but we'll walk along to the Hall."

"Please, Mam." Dotty had a pleading in her eyes, like Martha might be standing in the way of her most important thing.

Pretending that she had been hesitating over stay or go, Martha said, "All right, but you do the washing up when we get home."

X Beidler slid over to make room between him and Mr. Stark. "Sit here, Mrs. McDowell." So Martha felt she had no choice but to step in between them with a prayer that McDowell or one of his friends would not take a notion to eat at Ma's tonight, though once she was settled with her cloak folded across her lap, she thought if he did come in it would be worth enduring his wrath just to be feeling the friendly warmth coming from this man whose pain had carved lines from his nose around the corners of his mouth.

It pleased her how the young'uns, tucking into their pie across the table, looked happy at her staying. They did so like Mr. Stark.

There wasn't much conversation, everyone being content with their own thoughts, mostly, until by ones and twos, the Eatery emptied out, and the men around Mr. Stark began to talk about the trial. A word here and there, a grunt from X Beidler, until Martha could tell who had come from the trial, and with a chill up her backbone she realized without anyone having to say it that these men, except Jacob Himmelfarb, were Mr. Stark's bodyguard. He needed a bodyguard. Or X Beidler thought he did, which amounted to the same thing. And with another of those flashes of understanding like she sometimes got, that had McDowell scoffing that she couldn't possibly know what she did know, she knew Mr. Stark needed a guard because of Gallagher and McDowell. Her own husband.

Dear Jesus, what happened there today? For they were both in mortal danger, not of their lives, but in danger of doing something awful. Lord, keep them both. Keep them in Your care.

A man sitting at the front table called out, "Are you having a second day of it?"

"Yes, we're hearing witnesses tomorrow."

His companion said, "You'll never get anyone to testify against George Ives. People are either too scared of him and his crowd, or they just don't believe he'd do that."

"That's right. Ives couldn't kill anyone," said the first man. "All them hijinks he gets up to, that's all they are. Hijinks. Hell — begging your pardon, Ma'am, he's just full of high spirits. Boys will be boys, you know."

Before she could give him a look that only a mother knew how to give, Tim threw one leg over the bench and snapped, "Maybe some boys would shoot up a dog, mister, or call a holdup a loan, but we ain't all like that. Nossir."

"I think it's time to go. There's still work to do." Mr. Stark got to his feet, and let Jacob Himmelfarb help him with his coat. He held his gloved left hand toward his shoulder.

Beidler, his chin out, said, "Sanders could testify that he's capable of murder. Ives almost killed him over at Rattlesnake."

"There's two versions of that story," said the man who thought Ives's actions were boyish pranks.

"There usually are," Beidler said, "but I'll take Sanders's word for it."

"Yeah," said the man, "you Yanks always stick together."

"And you Rebs never do?" Beidler took a step toward the man, but Lydia stepped in front of him, said to them both, "Take that outside, hear?" and Albert reached for the pistol he kept by the scales.

Martha said to Mr. Stark, "You've hurt your hand."

"Dislocated the thumb, but Dr. Byam put it back."

"Mind if I look at it?" She didn't know why she should, except that with a dislocated thumb back where it belonged, it shouldn't hurt like it did.

He hesitated, she knew because taking off the glove would pain him so.

"Did he put anything on it?" she asked.

"No, just put the glove on. He said to leave it on till it's better." His eyes pleaded with her not to insist, but she braced herself against the necessity to cause him pain, because she had a certainty.

Lydia said, "I have some unguent that'll do it good. Help it heal faster."

"We'd best bind it up, too, hold it in place," Martha said.

He hesitated, and she knew he was trying to decide did he trust her that much, to take off the glove and bind his hand. She felt the heat of him, smelled his clean breath. His eyes were a clear green, like grass in June. Someone coughed. His head snapped up as if he had bent toward her. "Yes, thank you, kind of you."

He was sweating, and so was she, but not from the stove's heat.

Lydia hurried away, all her flounces bobbing.

Martha said, "You best sit down while I take this off."

He removed his coat, laid it on the bench.

She sat close beside him, took his arm into her lap. This close to him, she breathed in his smell, that did not make her want to pull away. She guessed he washed oftener than most men, certainly oftener than McDowell. She clamped his arm to her side with her elbow, and started in to work the glove off of his hand as gentle as she could. Her hands felt trembly because it was Mr. Stark and because his friends were watching. The leather was black and supple, and had a soft fur lining. She hoped she would not have to cut it, because how would he get another one, let alone one as good as this? She paused to let him get ready for what came next, and glanced up to see how bad it was for him. Muscles bulged at his lower jaw, but he took a deep breath, held it, and nodded to her. The trust in his eyes, though he knew it would hurt, made her want to weep, but she dared not, for fear of not seeing clear.

When the glove came away, his chest rose and fell as he let out a slow breath. "That wasn't as bad as I thought it might be." Then Martha was conscious of his arm muscle at her breast. Her face was hot, and she could not look at him, though she managed to say, "Bad enough, no doubt."

"It's all right," he said.

He was bruised black around the thumb and across the back of his hand and into the palm. There was a bump above the thumb joint where there didn't ought to be one. Even touching it like a feather, she felt his whole arm stiffen, heard the short indrawn breath.

She pointed at bump. "That bone's busted."

Lydia was there with a squat brown jar and a roll of bandage. "I can see it. Shall thee put it back or shall I?"

Martha could not bear to hurt him any more. "Don't matter. I'm here already, so I'll hold it and you put it back." She tightened her grip on his arm and hand, held the hand on her knee. The muscles under his sleeve were so tense they felt like a chunk of wood. "Hold still." She felt sorry for him, being a man, because men seemed to feel pain more than women did, probably because they were spared birthing babies. She wondered why Dr. Byam hadn't set this little bone but just put the glove back on, and Lord it was hard to do for a loved one when you had to hurt him, and why did she think of him as a loved one because he never could be never ever but dear God how she hated to give him hurt.

It was done. She pressed the arm tight to her side and kept his thumb in place while Lydia smeared on the unguent and wrapped it snug real careful, oh as gentle as she could. When it was over, Martha could look at him again. He was pale, and he took out a handkerchief and wiped his face, but his eyes were calm. He was no baby about being hurt.

His arm relaxed, and he smiled. "That was worse in the anticipation than in the fact."

She had let go his hand and relaxed her arm so he could pull away, but he let his hand go on resting on her knee, his arm against her breast. She licked her lips. "Are you wanting the glove on again?"

"Not yet. If it gets cold, I'll put it in my pocket. You'll only be taking it off to check the healing."

"Yes," said Martha, happy knowing she had a ready-made reason to see him again.

"Keep that hand up." Lydia reached out a hand, and Jacob Himmelfarb helped her up from where she knelt on the floor. She thanked him and brushed the dirt off her skirts.

"We'd best make a sling." Martha lifted her arm, and he pulled away, but she felt like he had hold of her somewheres in such a grip that she'd couldn't free herself. She'd never known anything like this happiness, it was too big inside her, and it was all mixed up with misery. Worst of it was, she could see in his face, the way his mouth relaxed, that he, too, was asking himself, What in God's name would they do now?

4: Alder Gulch: Nevada City

Martha led Tabby down Idaho Street, cut behind a livery, past a small mountain of horse manure, to the Stevens woman's crib behind Fancy Annie's. Folks called these small cabins cribs because they were not built for living, just for bedding. Given her druthers, she'd bide to home, but when the Lord gave her the gift to tend the sick, He'd included this boy, whose meanness could someday put his head in a noose.

Hoping they'd chewed enough juniper berries to guard them against contagion, Martha knocked. The Troy woman opened the door, and a putrid stink flowed out. Martha shrank away. The Troy woman's eyelids, red as strawberry juice, stood out against her bleached skin. She looked as bad as if the boy was her own, thought Martha, crossing the threshold. With no windows, a lamp standing on an eating table lighted some of the front part, and a candle on a shelf glimmered down onto a brass bed that took up the whole back part.

Martha made out the Stevens woman holding her boy across her lap while he vomited into a basin on the floor. Her voice could have sawed wood. "Took you long enough. Jacky's awful bad."

Folding her cloak over the back of a chair, Martha took a candle from her ditty bag and lighted it at the lamp. Not until she replaced the chimney could she speak calmly, against her own feelings. "It's the typhus. Now, you do what I tell you, or he could die." The woman gasped. Martha put on her biggest apron, that covered most of her dress except the sleeves. As she rolled them up, she frowned at Helen Troy. "You fixin' to be useful?"

"Yes. What do I do?" The Troy woman braced herself with one hand on a chair's back.

Martha hadn't seen much of any cooking utensils at all, nor a trunk for storing extras, only a chest of drawers between the table and the wall. Where did the boy go when his mama was – it didn't bear thinking about. "Boil up a couple buckets of water, and bring us some cook pans and a few jars to put medicines in. Clean blankets and clothes for the boy."

"I'll boil water on the big stove in the saloon, and send someone back with blankets and pots." Helen Troy paused at the door. "Don't know about clothes, less some of the men can chip in."

"Leave the door open," Martha said, and when the Stevens woman protested that the boy would catch his death, Martha rounded on her. "We'll suffocate if we don't!"

The boy's spasm of vomiting ended. Silent tears flowed down his mother's cheeks, like a small child expecting someone to wipe her face.

Coughing took the boy, and dark fluid dribbled down his chin, that Martha prayed was not blood. She sorted through her bag, smelled the herbs. Barberry, what Berry Woman called Oregon grape, to stop the bleeding and the runs. Milkweed for coughing. Prince's pine to make him sweat and get rid of poisons.

When Tabby thrust a piece of cloth at her, the Stevens woman recoiled. "I don't want niggers here."

"You don't want niggers?" Tabby dropped the cloth on the bed. "Fine. I got enough work to do."

"If she goes, I go, too," said Martha. "Make up your mind, and hurry up about it." It was a hard thing to speak so to this scared mama, but Martha needed Tabby's help.

The Stevens woman hunched her shoulders. "All right. I guess."

"Hmph." Tabby set to tie on her apron.

Martha, wrapping her hair in a kerchief, spoke to Tabby, "This will be as ugly as can be, but I'm right happy for you being here."

"I seen ugly afore. All slaves do," Tabby said.

Martha put a few drops of the juice of crushed juniper berries on three kerchiefs, tied one around her own nose and mouth, and gave the others to Tabby and the mother. "Sit you there." She pointed to the two chairs at the table, and to her surprise, the Stevens woman did as she was told.

They weren't done with hearing her, though. When Martha and Tabby rolled the boy into a less soiled blanket and laid him on the floor next the stove, the mother howled that he wasn't no dog to lie on the floor. When they dragged the mattress, crawling and soaked with vomit and diarrhea, she screamed, "It's the only one we got!" When they ripped off the boy's foul clothing, she shrieked, "You can't do that!"

"What do you want?" Martha rounded on her. It was more than a body ought to stand, this place, the disease of filth, and this woman who sold herself to men that used her anyhow. One fist on her hip, she said, "These rags, or your boy? Choose. Now. Or we walk right out that door."

Martha astonished herself at being so hard, but the Stevens woman put up her hands. "Jacky. Save Jacky. Save my baby boy."

"That's better." Begrudging her any comfort, Martha thrust the squirming rags at her. "Burn them." Timmy had a shirt or two and a pair of trousers he'd outgrown. She'd bring them next time.

Without speaking, his mother put the rags into the stove. When Martha and Tabby stripped the boy, he covered his parts with his hands, and cursed them for looking at his secrets. Martha mimicked a laugh. "You got no more secrets than a great baby." She wanted to whale his bare behind, but a sick child —

His mother jumped from her chair and slapped his face, twice, rocking his head back and forth. "Shut up, you little bastard, and show some respect to someone's trying to save your ugly life."

Martha's hands trembled so she could hardly shave soap into them, and Tabby dipped water over them and her own before Martha could say, "See where your friend got to, why don't you?" When the Stevens woman had gone, Martha felt as weary as if she'd been here all day. "No wonder the boy's mean," she whispered to Tabby. "Amen," said the darky.

Martha wiped the boy's face with a clean damp rag. "Your mama's scared. It takes some folks that way. She's scared because you're sick, but you'll be fine if you do what you're told." While she washed him, Tabby cut his filthy hair, and he lay staring upward, eyes huge above the marks of his mother's hand.

The Stevens woman brought two men who carried buckets of hot water and a pile of blankets. They were not clean, but no one had vomited on them. Or worse. They wrapped the boy up, and he submitted without speaking. Afterwards, the men took away the other blankets, and the Stevens woman crouched by her son, stroked his head, and crooned to him, a wordless song, like he was her baby again.

While Tabby went outside to burn the mattress, Martha set to work to make the teas, and Helen Troy brought a basket of bottles and jars. "Sorry it took me so long. I washed them up." When Martha asked if she could read and write, she said, "I know enough to keep track of business."

"I'll tell you the recipes, and you write them down."

"I have a ledger book in my office," said Helen Troy. "I'll get it and be right back."

When the door slammed behind her, the Stevens woman said, "I can do that. You show me how and I can make them. I can't read or write, but if you tell me I'll remember."

It wouldn't hurt to tell them both, one to remember and one to write. "You got to recollect them careful-like, on account of the wrong dose might cause more sickness." Martha peered at her to be sure she understood. "This Oregon grape, now. Use too much of it, and it turns on you and makes everything worse." She explained all of them, the milkweed, the tonic of prince's pine, how to make them, when to give them and in what quantities. She finished, "Don't let him eat food at all until at least two days after he stops throwing up."

The Stevens woman offered no arguments, no spitting curses. She asked questions and repeated everything until she had got it all right. "I'll do it. You just see."

"I expect you will, at that." Martha rummaged in her bag. "These are juniper berries. You chew them, three or four about every three hours, but no more than ten in a day, and they'll keep the sickness off, but you got to clean yourself up, too."

"I will," said the Stevens woman. "Thank you."

Martha watched her feed the boy a bit of the prince's pine tonic. Then, needing air, she left her to watch the teas, and went outside. "You doing all right?" Tabby nodded. Martha lowered the kerchief from her mouth. "This place stinks of sin and sickness, both."

"We about done?" Tabby poked at the mattress to make it burn faster. "I ain't liking it no better."

"When the Troy woman comes back and I give her the recipes to copy down and some of the plants. I want to watch the Stevens woman give the teas, too. Maybe another half hour."

Tabby poked the mattress. "You took care of them, right enough. Miz Hudson say you ain't stupid." Her voice was flat, like telling Martha her petticoat showed, and the remark was so unlooked for that Martha wondered did she hear right. Tabby added, "I guess she's right."

"Oh, my." Martha did not know how to react, she felt a glow spread in her that had nothing to do with the fire's heat. She was that pleased to have their good opinion, though why should it matter what a darky thought? She didn't know, but somehow it did.

"Thank you," she said, and Tabby looked her in the eye for the first time and smiled the merest bit, but Martha knew that sometimes the biggest changes show in the smallest things, a leaf turning yellow on a tree, or a child sniffling. A black woman smiling at a white.

Blinking in the sunlight, the Stevens woman came out. "He's sleeping. I got to thank you." She was talking to Martha, but including Tabby, though she could not admit to owing a Negro anything, much less the life of her son. Her hair was coming down. She wiped her sleeve across her eyes, and the black eye stuff mixed with her paint smeared across her face and soiled her sleeve, but she had no thought for her looks, though the took out the pins and started in to fix her hair. Before Martha could speak, she said, "I got to say this, and fast, so you listen good. And don't you never tell no one I said it. You hear?"

Martha nodded. What on earth could this woman want to say that was so important?

"I know you was a friend of Nick's. He was a good boy. The kind of boy I wisht mine was." She sighed. "That shouldn't ought to have happened to him."

"No, it shouldn't, sure enough." Martha wondered what she was getting at.

"You remember when that fella was murdered on the main road a few weeks ago? Right out in the open?"

"I recollect." Plenty had seen it, but said they weren't close enough to tell who did it. Maybe they were too scared to say, and who could blame them? Who to report it to, anyhow? Gallagher? "About the time Nick disappeared, wasn't it?"

"Round about then. George Ives bragged at Fancy Annie's he done it. Said he was the Bamboo Chief what killed that man and got away with it. After, he went over to Long John's place and laid low in case someone spotted him."

"Dear Lord in heaven." Martha made herself breathe, in and out, in and out, because it was plain there was more to come, and presently, the Stevens woman told Martha how she happened to overhear, her and the man she – and she turned her face away from Martha, while the redness rose up her neck, and Tabby poked the mattress and Martha felt her own face could burn the thing.

In almost a whisper she continued, "Most of the boys are all right, a little woolly around the edges, maybe, but no real harm in them. Some of them others, that Boone Helm, now, they're downright evil. They told me, keep my damn mouth shut about things, but I figure I can trust you. Keep me out of it." She paused, watched toward the saloon, before she added, "I figure sooner or later they'll get Jacky involved in their doings, if they ain't already. I don't know how to stop that. My boy's lacking, poor soul, and he ain't got sense to say no to these fellas, but if Ives is found guilty over at Nevada City it might put the fear of God into him." She sighed.

"You know how it is. You got a boy, too. My Jacky, he wants to be just like George Ives. If he sees it can happen to Ives, maybe he'd turn onto a better road."

"We got to keep our young'uns safe." Martha was thinking how mothers all had something in common, even her and this – woman. They'd do most anything to keep their boys straight. And alive.

"Here she comes." Tabby was looking down the path to where Helen Troy hurried toward them.

"I got to go in. Remember now. I never said nothing."

"I'll remember."

The Troy woman held a poke in one hand and the ledger book and a pencil in the other. She pressed the poke into Martha's hand. "Thank you. You done a brave thing." When Tabby grunted and shifted her feet, the Troy woman said, "You both did. Free darkies don't have to tend white folks."

Martha and Tabby walked up Idaho in the bright sweet air. "Half of what's in this poke is yours."

"Mine?"

"For certain," said Martha, . "You didn't have to stay." Her thoughts ran to how Nick's mother had loved him, and thank God wasn't alive no more to know how her boy had been killed. George Ives had a mother somewhere, too, who loved her boy. What could mothers do to keep their sons safe from being murdered or murdering? How to raise them up right in these violent, troubled times?

Tabby stopped, and Martha walked on. She had to pass on the message. Find a way to tell Mr. Stark without anyone else knowing. McDowell wouldn't like it none at all if he come to know she'd carried information against George Ives. The preachers said a wife wasn't to go against her husband, but the Lord said plain enough: Thou shalt not murder, and she thought that included helping a murderer get away, which was what might happen if Mr. Stark didn't know about the Bamboo Chief.

But how to get word to him?

When she realized the darky wasn't with her, she stopped and waited for the black woman. Tabby began to talk about how to get a message to Mr. Stark, and Martha thought there couldn't be tears in her eyes, but if so, what for? And then Tabby come up with a smart plan for her and Albert to take Martha over to Nevada, and Martha did a little jig, right there on the corner by his and Jacob's cabin. "Tabby Rose, you do have good ideas, don't you, now?" She'd tell Mr. Stark, and the typhus give her an excuse she could use with McDowell if he found out she'd been over there, and she'd see him, but not like this. She'd wash first and put on a clean dress so as not to carry the contagion with her. Or the smell. And she'd see him. She'd see him.

෬

Firelight licked at the stars and wavered over men's faces, along the ground to the recorders' table where young Pemberton tested the ink on his pen's nib. Finding it would not flow, he laid the pen in the gutter of his notebook. Dan thought of reminding him that with sunrise, the ink would blot the book, but Pemberton was not of an age to appreciate such reminders. Out beyond the circle of firelight, the crowd roamed; the roughs in their midst, armed with the courage of darkness, shouted threats: Say your prayers, you'll need them! This'll be the last sunrise you ever see! Let George Ives go or you're dead!

Evil from the dark. The tiger in the night, eyes gleaming, just as he now made out a hooked nose, a button's shine, a bottle uptilted to a mouth. Tyger, tyger, burning bright in the forest of the night. Malevolent glares battered at him. A bullet from the dark would not be so difficult. He willed the sun to rise, but it stayed stubbornly below the jagged rim of the mountains, while somewhere beyond the firelight, the Ives faction skulked.

A voice from the darkness, "Plummer will be here soon!"

"Damn!" Sheriff Hereford beat his gloved hands together. "Plummer could be here any time."

"God help us then," said Judge Wilson, and he looked around, as if Plummer would materialize out of the restless gathering.

Dan touched the rifle's stock, and the hard steel reassured him, but could he shoot fast enough one-handed, to save his own life? Unsling it, lever a shell into the breech, cock, and fire? Could he shoot a man, even in self-defense? In this matter of killing, it was not true what Beidler had said: Quarry was not quarry.

In the darkness lurked the possibility of Plummer's arrival. "'Tyger! Tyger! burning bright/in the forests of the night.'" Dan murmured the lines to himself.

"'What immortal hand or eye/Could frame thy fearful symmetry?'" Sanders's quiet voice spoke the next two lines.

Dan started. "Another Blake reader?"

"Not especially," Sanders said. "He's too fanciful for me, but my young cousin, Mattie Edgerton, loves him. She has recited this poem so often I've learned parts of it." He added, "Rather as one's coat absorbs tobacco smoke."

Bagg took his pipe out of his mouth, assumed an orator's stance, and pointed the pipe stem upward: "'Did he who made the Lamb make thee?'"

Dan laughed until he felt on the verge of hysteria.

Bagg lifted one eyebrow. "I didn't think I was so amusing. Maybe I should go on the stage."

Wiping his eyes, Dan said, "Your imitation of Senator Douglas is magnificent." One-handed, he folded his handkerchief and stowed it away. "I saw him speak in New York." With Grandfather. Douglas had spoken on the subject of "The Rights of Man," specifically property rights, the property, of course, being slaves. Grandfather had hoped Douglas would convince Dan, but Dan had been incensed, and their homeward argument had caused feelings that lasted until Father's fatal bullet.

"We can imagine his subject," Sanders said, with a twist to his lips. "The poem raises an interesting question, though, how a good God could create a world in which evil exists."

"We could propose that at the next meeting of the Philosophical Society," Dan said.

"Oh?" Bagg's pipe was out. He struck a match and puffed to start it again, his cheeks filling and flattening. "There is such a thing here?"

Dan was about to tell him about it when a blast in the diggings not far off startled them.

"Sounds like cannon," Sanders said. "Today is remarkably reminiscent of a battle's second phase."

"Isn't it, though?" Bagg said. Dan felt left out; the two war veterans shared an experience, a perspective, that he never would have. "We won the skirmishes yesterday. Today the battle." The prosecutors met each others' gaze, and read the same understanding: the war could still be lost.

Judge Byam rang the cowbell and called for order. When he could be heard, Sheriff Hereford shouted: "William Palmer!"

Dan admired Palmer's courage. He was the first man who dared to testify to what he had seen and heard. The tall, thin Englishman marched toward the green wagon as if the threats, "You'll pay for this!" and "You're a dead man!" landed in the fire. The cowbell rang out, the judges yelled for silence, miners shouted at the roughs: "Pipe down!" and "Shut up!" The threats died with the cowbell's echo, the crowd settled into stillness so deep that Dan felt he could hear it breathe, as if all the individuals, Union and Confederate, roughs and miners, had melded into a single creature, not so frightening as the tyger.

Bagg looked like most of the men in the crowd. In his ragged grey uniform and his long matted hair, he was the picture of a miner too intent on digging gold even to trim his beard. His Southern drawl and Palmer's London accent caused some comical misunderstandings that had men smiling, until the saloonkeeper came to tell how on Thursday, just four days ago, he had been happy to do some shooting, and how happiness had changed to horror when Providence dropped the sage hen on Nick's body.

His description of the corpse chilled the people as sub-freezing temperature had not. The distant piano music and high-pitched cries of little boys at their games seemed sacrilegious, like spitting in church. A woman sobbed. Dan saw faces rapt with attention, downturned mouths, eyes brimming with tears. Faces. He saw faces. Sunrise.

When Palmer told how Long John Frank and George Hilderman had refused to help him, some men called out, "No!" A woman screamed. A few men booed, at what, Dan didn't know. A deep voice boomed, "Liar! Liar!" Dan swung around. McDowell shook his fist at Palmer.

God! That her husband would be so calloused, so indifferent to Nick's death. McDowell had known him! How had such a decent woman come to link her future with this oaf? Dan's left hand clenched into a fist, and pain stabbed his arm. He opened the fingers, and the pain settled to a hard throbbing.

Several in the crowd shouted at McDowell to shut up, and behind Ives men pushed and shoved, but the guards thrust shotgun barrels between them. Judge Byam rang the cowbell and rang it until quiet returned. Dan dared to admit a small hope; it was the first time miners had confronted the roughs.

Bagg climbed down from the wagon, and Sanders and Dan congratulated him, but Bagg shook his head. "Time will tell."

Thurmond stood within two feet of Palmer and stabbed his middle finger toward Palmer's eyes. "I put it to you, that you are lying!"

"Scoundrel!" Palmer stood his ground. As tall as Long John, he towered over the defense attorney, and shook his fist in

Thurmond's face. "The whole Gulch saw me bring that poor lad's body in."

"Oh, you may have found the body, but you're lying about what Long John said."

"I ain't lying!" bellowed Palmer. "I give full measure in my saloon, and I don't put my thumb on the scales." He appealed to the crowd. "Have I ever cheated you?"

Cheering answered him. Among the advisory jury, several men shook their heads, and one shouted, "Palmer's no liar!" Dan let his small hope grow a little.

The sun traveled southwesterly on its shallow winter arc, as Thurmond struggled to trick Palmer into saying he had misquoted Long John, even by one word, and the prosecutors shouted out the same objection time and again, that he badgered the witness, and the judges ruled in their favor, until at last Thurmond gave up.

Surrounded by guards, Long John walked into the court. Dan thought of gladiators or Christians entering the Coliseum. Would the juries turn thumbs up or thumbs down? He longed for a stick to carve, wished his left hand could hold one. George Ives turned to joke with his friends. Long John climbed into the wagon and took the oath amid jeers and threats, and Ives laughed at a joke, as if all this were a grand party just for him.

"Doesn't Ives understand he's on trial for his life? Has he no fear?"

Sanders said, "Perhaps to him this is some sort of drama being played out, and nothing to do with him except he must sit there for as long as it takes to resolve this."

Bagg put Long John at ease with questions designed to show him in the best light possible. When he led Long John to tell what happened when Nicholas Tbalt was killed, Dan leaned against the green wagon and watched young Pemberton's pen scratch across the page. There was a large blot in the gutter.

Pemberton, Dan recalled, did not believe in Ives's guilt. What would he think when this day was done? The crowd was as silent as a thousand men in one place ever could be. A rough shouted, and other men cut him off. The air stretched tight with listening, and on the benches, men craned forward to hear over the crackle of flames.

Before Bagg finished, Thurmond and Smith began a low-voiced argument, and when Smith attempted to rise, Thurmond jumped to his feet and pushed him back.

"Long John, I put it to you that George Ives did not kill Nicholas Tbalt. You killed the poor lad and are trying to save your skin by blaming Mr. Ives. He's a respectable businessman and rancher here, and you're jealous because he's more successful than you are. That is the truth, is it not?"

"No, by God, it ain't." Long John's voice rang out. "Like I said, George went after him, and I heard a shot, maybe two, and a little later he come riding back with the mules and the dust."

"How many shots were there?"

"I disremember exactly. One, maybe two."

"You remember word for word what Mr. Ives said, but you can't recall how many shots you heard?"

"Like I said, I disremember." His tongue circled his lips. "I was trying not to listen for shots."

"Why was that?"

"I was afeared of what Ives might do to the kid."

"You knew he would kill him, didn't you?"

"I was afeard he might."

"You knew in advance, and you did nothing to stop him?"

"I was afeared, I'm telling you." Long John looked down at his feet. His voice was so low he could not have been heard beyond the fire.

Thurmond shouted at him, "Speak up, man! You knew Ives would shoot him and you did nothing about it. Why not?"

Long John reared up, seemed ten feet tall. "I told you! I was afeared! You ever try to cross George Ives? It's a good way to die."

Thurmond swept one hand to the side. "Never mind that. What happened to the mules?"

"Ives turned them out to pasture. I already said that."

"So you did. Why haven't they been found?"

"He sold them two, three days later to a man heading for Salt Lake."

"I see. Now tell me this. What happened to the dust?"

Long John's tongue circled his lips before scuttling back into its cave. "George kept it. I didn't want nothing to do with it."

Dan snapped to attention. As if a breeze, blowing through a window in his mind, had caught a pile of papers without page numbers and scattered them, so he had now to reassemble his ideas. Long John always licked his lips when he lied. Damn! He lied about the dust. Dan walked aside, away from the defense and Thurmond. Now what? Admit they had made a mistake? Set Ives free? Yet in Dan's heart he was still certain Ives had killed Nick. He thumbed through his memories, rummaged among his recollections. What had Long John said when his tongue came out? For the life of him, Dan could not recall precisely. He had not noticed at the time. Fool!

Sanders joined him, demanded to know what was up. When he explained, Sanders exploded in a whisper, "Christ! Do we have the right man?"

They stared at each other across the yawning gulf of disaster. To admit they were wrong and set Ives free would give the roughs permanent control of the Gulch. Unthinkable. To hang the wrong man? Equally unthinkable. Except, except. Dan knew that in his bones. His brain leaped to comprehend this.

They had the right man. Their main witness lied. But not with every statement.

"Long John has not been lying all the time," Dan said. "If I'm right, they split the gold." He paused to clear his throat. "Damn them, they split the gold." The flames crackled around him, and sweat ran down his back, and Thurmond's voice rose to accuse Long John. Bagg, left on watch, objected, and the judge sustained him. Dan went on, "Four of them at least were in it. Ives and another man went after Nick. Ives pulled the trigger, but Long John and Hilderman shared in the plunder. God damn their souls."

Sanders scuffed a stick away from the fire with the toe of his boot. "It fits. All it means is that Long John is more culpable than we thought. It doesn't change anything." He let out a long breath, relief plain on his face. "We're still trying Ives, we still have Long John as a state's witness. Maybe he was frightened of Ives, but he was greedy as well. Fear and greed. Deadly for Tbalt."

"Yes." Dan stooped to pick up the stick, the thickness of his wrist. "Prosecutors make deals all the time with smaller criminals in order to bring bigger ones to justice. I just wish ... ."

"So do I," Sanders said, "but it's part of war to make distasteful compromises."

Dan curled his fingers around the stick. He made the first cut, winced, cut again. There was some pain, but this would work.

Thurmond roared, "Long John, so far from spurning George Ives' gold, you killed Nicholas Tbalt! You sold the mules! You kept the gold for yourself!"

Long John, goaded out of his fears, bellowed, "Like hell! He'd a killed me!"

Thurmond sneered. "You expect us to believe you were afraid of George Ives?"

"Hell, yes. He'd kill a man soon as look at him. He shot that fella on the road a couple of days before he killed the Dutchman."

"Strike that!" Thurmond leaned over the side of the wagon and waved his index finger at Pemberton. "Strike that from the record! Strike it!" His face swelled and turned bright red as if injected with blood.

Sanders yelled, "The defense asked the question!" And both Bagg and Dan shouted at the same time, "You asked the question! The witness answered!" Thurmond jumped up and down, rocked the witness wagon. Dan knew he grinned like an ape, it was a colossal blunder. For now, the question having come from the defense, it did not matter that Long John gave an unexpected answer. Thurmond had opened the door for the prosecution to introduce Ives's prior bad acts.

The crowd booed and cheered, and Byam's cowbell rang for two or three minutes before the crowd quieted enough that they could hear anyone speak. "Why the commotion?" demanded Wilson. Dan was convinced that the crowd did not understand, either, what had happened. Thurmond shouted as if the crowd still howled, that Long John's answer was inadmissible, and Sanders hollered, that because Thurmond elicited the response in answer to his own question, it opened the door for testimony about Ives's other crimes.

As the two judges whispered in each other's ears, men in the crowd shouted each other into a muttering quiet.

Dan held his breath. Even operating under Common Law, in this miners court the judges could put it to a vote of the crowd. In a proper court, the jury had no say in the matter.

The judges finished their conference. Byam's voice rang out: "The defense asked the question, and the witness answered it, and it stands as is." Thurmond roared, "No! No!" and the roughs booed, but the cheering was louder. Dan, letting out his breath, felt as if he'd run miles. Wilson said to the recorders, "You can leave that be."

"I'm through with this witness." Thurmond jumped down from the witness wagon. "You may get down. Get down, I say!"

"Redirect." Sanders whispered to Bagg, who called out, "Judge, I'd like to ask a question. It's called redirect." From the ground, he asked Long John, "Have you anything to add?"

"You bet," said Long John. "George Ives shot that fella in broad daylight, with travelers about a half mile away. That's why he come to my place. He told me to say he'd been there all the time if someone come looking for him about that."

"Did Ives say why he killed the man?"

"The fella was going to peach on him in the miners court here."

"Peach? I take it you mean the man was going to testify against Mr. Ives over some matter."

"That's right. What it was, I disremember."

"No wonder you were afraid of him. You have a lot of courage to testify today. Your honor, I'm through with this witness."

Before Judge Byam could excuse Long John, Smith waved. "Your honors, I have a question for this witness." He smiled. "It's only fair. You let the prosecution ask one."

"You sure? Oh, very well then. Go ahead." Wilson glanced upward as if to say the sun traveled faster than the trial. "Make it snappy."

"Thank you, your honor." Placing each foot so as to avoid puddles, Smith walked to the wagon, steadied himself with one hand on a wheel. "Who told you Ives killed that man?"

"Why, Ives did. That's how I know."

Dan watched wooden curls gather at the tip of the stick. Damn. Smith was smart.

"Thank you." Smith bowed to Long John. "You'll have to tell the juries to disregard all testimony about the killing on the road."

"Why?" asked Judge Byam.

"Because it's hearsay. A man can't testify that someone did something if the person who did it is the one that told him."

"What?" Byam's face wore a look of profound confusion that would have amused Dan under other circumstances. Sanders explained that indeed Long John's testimony about that incident was hearsay. Inadmissible.

Smith passed the prosecutors on his way back to the log. "Check."

"But not checkmate." Dan's smile was the equivalent of thumbing his nose. They might have lost that testimony, but they had the principle: Ives's other crimes could be used against him. Judges' instructions or not, the jury would remember.

As guards led Long John back to Byam's house, the tall man said, "I done my part. You keep your promise, now."

"Much as it pains us," Sanders said, "we will."

Dan could not look at Long John. The man would go free, because he had testified against Ives, when he was almost certainly more complicit in Nick's death than they had thought. They had made a pact with the Devil, and the Devil was laughing now. How many curls could he carve? It was a question of technique, a nice distinction of angles and depths to gather them without breaking any.

❦

George Hilderman shambled around the fire, watching Ives as he would a snake. Ives sat with his elbows on his knees, a steaming cup in his chained hands, chatting with Alex Davis as if this trial were no concern of his. Hilderman nodded to the oath, and from a faint beginning his voice grew stronger as Bagg took him through his testimony. Dan gripped the stick, almost relishing the pain as a distraction from hearing yet again this account of Nick's last minutes. But he had tears in his eyes when Hilderman described how Ives had shot him as he began the Lord's Prayer.

"Hearsay!" screamed Thurmond and leaped up, fist in the air. "Hearsay!"

"It is not hearsay," yelled Sanders. "It's a confession, and we have corroborating – "

"You got nothing! Nothing, you –"

The two stood toe to toe. Thurmond waved his arms, and saliva sprayed from his mouth. A vein bulged across Sanders's forehead and the cape of Union greatcoat quivered as in a breeze. Dan leaped to separate them, Bagg following, and the defenders came off their log, and all of the attorneys, defense and prosecution, surrounded Sanders and Thurmond, who yelled in each others' faces. Both men's words were lost in their noise, and the crowd encouraged them as if cheering on a pugilistic contest.

Over it all, the cowbell clashed. Both sheriffs shouldered their way into the clutch of lawyers, and as they shifted and parted, Dan glimpsed Pemberton protecting the notebook.

When Judge Byam could be heard, he said, "I can't make heads or tails out of this. Why can't this man tell his story?" Thurmond and Sanders spoke at once. Byam shook the cowbell. "Mr. Sanders will speak first."

Thurmond roared, "I demand – "

Byam waggled the cowbell at him. "Your turn will come. Meantime, shut your face."

Dan's broken thumb jabbed at him. Without knowing, he had clutched the stick. He relaxed his grip and tried to ignore the continuing jolts by picturing Grandfather's face when he told him that a judge had ordered an attorney to shut up. He smiled. The old man would know everyone in the Gulch was a ruffian.

Panting, Sanders said, "In general, Your Honor, the rule of hearsay is that you can't have someone testify as to what someone told him if no other person were present. However, a confession is an exception to this rule —"

"Balderdash!" Thurmond hollered. Alex Davis hissed in his ear, while Smith, on Thurmond's other side, patted his forearm.

Sanders continued, "This testimony satisfies the condition for a confession, in that both Mr. Frank and Mr. Hilderman heard Mr. Ives say he murdered Nicholas Tbalt."

Davis said, "Your hon. —"

Thurmond cut him off. "Bullshit! That's a complete nonsense! Hearsay is never admissible under any circumstances, no matter how many people hear it. I demand you dismiss this spurious case. They have no other evidence."

Dan, studying the growing bundle of blond wooden curls, knew what Davis had wanted to say, that by Hilderman's own testimony, Ives had told him about the prayer after Long John took the mules away. If true, the prayer incident and the outrage of it, was hearsay, and Davis was right, yet both men had now sworn that Ives confessed to killing Nick, and at least one other. Damn it, Ives was guilty, guilty as sin.

"No, your honor." It was his own voice that Dan heard. "We've been through this already. The defense is wasting the court's time. If two people hear a man admit to a crime, it's not hearsay, it's a confession." He added in his most persuasive tones, "Our witnesses differ in some details, but they agree that Ives told them both, at the same time, that he killed Nicholas Tbalt."

Smith tore a corner of his pocket as he yanked a bottle out of it. "You want to railroad an innocent man! What each of them says is hearsay because the other man didn't hear the same thing!"

"Yeah!" Thurmond tugged at his arm, held in Davis's firm grip. "Sanders, you want to murder George because he showed you up." He turned on Davis. "Let go of me, damn you!"

"That's a damn lie! I demand you take it back!" Sanders stuck his jaw out at Thurmond.

"There's lying around here," said Thurmond, "but I ain't doing it."

"You calling me a liar?" Sanders's hands fumbled at something in his coat pockets. "I'll see you anywhere after this trial is over."

Jesus Christ, Dan swore to himself. Sanders and Thurmond would kill each other if they weren't stopped. He moved between them, faced Thurmond. "Simmer down!"

Judge Byam shouted to the juries. "Two witnesses say Ives admitted killing Nick Tbalt, so we're letting you boys consider what they said. Their stories differ a bit in details, but we think that's all right, because the details don't change the issue: Ives told them both he did the killing."

Judge Wilson pointed his finger at Thurmond. "It's done. Quit your fussing."

The lawyers separated, warring armies regrouping for battle.

Judge Wilson said, "Cross-examine, but don't waste time."

Dan glanced toward the sun. While they argued points of law and heard the witnesses, the sun had reached its zenith and begun its downward slide.

"There's no point in a cross," Thurmond said. "He's lying, and this is a kangaroo court! You're all hell bent on hanging an honest businessman... ."

Byam leaned so far over the sidewall that Dan feared he might fall. "Do you have a point to make, or are you just trying to warm us up?"

"You bet I do! We will prove absolutely that Mr. Ives could not have killed that poor boy. Long John Frank and George Hilderman killed him and are trying to pin it on George Ives."

"In that case, the witness is excused." Judge Byam rang the cowbell. "I'm hungry, too."

⁓

Dan felt an urgency in his gut that would not be denied. Excusing himself, he sought a necessary and found a two-holer that faced the creek. It had no door. Sitting there, rifle across his knees, he watched miners work their claims, oblivious to a man's life being decided not thirty yards away. Cold air wafted through the outhouse, floated away the stench but chilled his buttocks. He wished to hell he'd finish faster.

Jacob, who had come along as a bodyguard, stood behind the structure, talked through the wall about the crowd's mood. "Is not that they different think, aber – but, doubts they now have." He spoke slowly, his English syntax even more garbled than usual. "Long John, Hilderman, they speak, and now people Ives maybe so Nicholas killed. Say."

To be sure he understood, Dan said, "Some people who thought Ives could not be guilty now say maybe he could have done it. Is that correct?"

"Ja."

Detecting doubt in the single syllable, Dan tried again. "Most men who thought Ives did not kill Nick now say perhaps he might have done it, because of what Long John and Hilderman said?"

"Ja. You have right." Relief and certainty rang clear in Jacob's voice.

"Thank you, Jacob." The small hope he had nurtured all day grew a little larger. Maybe they could yet swing enough in the crowd for a guilty verdict, but able manipulators like Smith could demand vote after vote until Ives went free. There had to be a way to prevent that. But how?

Voices interrupted Dan's train of thought. A Southern accent, a bass voice rich and thick as heavy cream. Dan tensed, his right hand found the rifle's hammer. Jacob's higher tones, unworried. A friend, then. But who would seek him out now? At this most private time, with his trousers around his ankles and the flap of his long underwear dangling behind his knees.

The deep voice called his name. "Mistah Stark? Mistah Stark? You hearin' me? It's Albert."

Albert? "I hear you." Why was he here? "What's the trouble, Albert?" A sudden sweat made the hammer slippery. Not Martha. Please, God, not her.

"No trouble, sir. It's something Miz McDowell said you have to know. In Mistah William's barn, sir, when you've a mind to come?"

"All right. I'll be there as soon as I can."

Dan stepped over the threshold of Williams's livery barn into sun-streaked darkness. Pausing to let his eyes adjust, he inhaled the good smells of hay and horse manure. Horses in their stalls pricked their ears at him, and satisfied, went back to munching their hay. One nickered softly.

"Mr. Stark? Is that you?"

Dust floated in streaks of sunlight between the vertical wall boards. Back lighted, she was a shadow among shadows in a vacant stall. "Yes, it is I. Dan Stark." He disgusted himself, how stilted he sounded, but he could find no middle ground between seizing her in his arms and treating her with freezing formality. He stepped forward, mindful of where he put his feet. Because she stood against the sunlight, he could not see her face, but he could not mistake the shape of her, or her voice. Seeing her in this barn felt like an assignation, but it could not be. She was not so brazen. A respectable woman, no hussy. Mrs. McDowell. Martha. If he could just once call her by her name.

"This stall's empty," she said, "in case someone comes in."

Her voice was soft, uncertain. He towered over her, leaned toward her, and the rifle slid around so that it hung between them. In his own ears, his laugh sounded like a horse's whinny. He took the weapon off his shoulder, leaned it against the stall partition. She came close, to whisper to him. He hoped she would not think he was – what he was, because he wanted her, oh God, so much.

"How's your hand today?"

She had not come all the way over from Virginia to ask about his hand. "I think it's some better, thank you." He felt his body yearning toward her. "Is there something I can do for you?" Name it, he wanted to say, just name it. Anything. My life.

"You know that murder on the main road a couple of weeks ago?"

Bending a degree or two more, as if to hear her better, he smelled mint on her breath. Never perfume so fine. "Yes. Long John testified a while ago that Ives did it."

"He did?"

Her posture changed, shoulders rounded, and her chin dipped to her breastbone, as if she had braced herself for a difficult task, and found it all for nothing. He wanted to put his finger under her chin and kiss away her disappointment, sought something to say, and found himself explaining hearsay to her when that was furthest from his wish.

She stood straight, tipped her face up to look him in the eye. "I don't know as how this'll help, but there's a woman, Tabby and me, we took care of her boy today, what has the typhus. She, uh, works at Fancy Annie's, name of Isabelle Stevens. She said that George Ives was bragging there that he done that killing. Said he called himself the 'Bamboo Chief.'"

"Good God. He bragged about it? To her?" Dan's mind raced along twisting trails of thought. This corroborated Long John's testimony, but it was hearsay, too. And the trail branched off into another idea: Ives had bragged about that killing. He had bragged about killing Nick. Did he want fame as a corsair of the road? Like a cheap novel? If so, the trial was making him famous. He was getting what he wanted.

"Not to her. She don't think he knows she heard him. She said he bragged to a, a — "

She stammered, as if she were embarrassed, thinking how to describe the situation. "A companion?" Dan suggested, to help her. The blood throbbed in his temples, and he hardly dared breathe. If he was right, this was corroboration and it was not hearsay. He pictured how it might have been, one couple on each side of a flimsy partition on the saloon's second floor, but the Stevens woman had a crib and didn't have to use one of the rooms upstairs. Or perhaps she and the man had wanted to be quick, so they used one while Ives and his whore had the other.

"Yes, thank you, he bragged to her that he was the 'Bamboo Chief' what done it. The Stevens woman won't speak up. She daren't."

"Of course not." Good God! Corroboration, indeed! That's what this was, but not admissible in court unless they found the other man, the man who had been making use of Isabelle Stevens. It didn't matter that the Stevens woman was too frightened to testify. Nick's friends had banned women from the jury because women, with their infernal sensibility, had wept and cried over hanging Stinson and the others for Dillingham's murder, and that gave Smith his chance to manipulate the crowd and free them.

"I guess I didn't need to come, then," she said.

"No, why do you say that?"

"Because even knowing about this, there's nothing you can do with it."

"No, that's not true. Do you know the name of the man the Stevens woman was consorting with?"

"I think his name was something like Marvin or Martin. Like that."

"Maybe we can find him and persuade him to testify about it."

"I best be getting back. I'm sorry I troubled you with something so useless."

"No, it's good you came. It corroborates Long John's testimony. We'll look for this man." And then, somehow, persuade him to testify.

"Won't it be hearsay?"

His face relaxed into a smile. He felt it, and knew why he smiled, because she was intelligent. Uneducated though she was, she understood the concept immediately. "No. His testimony would not be hearsay, because he overheard Ives. Ives did not tell him. It will be admissible. The judge will accept it without question."

"All right. Then I guess it's all right I come – came today."

He allowed himself to touch her upper arm. "Thank you. You have helped a great deal."

"I have? I thought you'd – " She broke off. "Morton. Pete Morton. That's the man."

"Thank you!" He could have hugged her, but did not dare because he would not be able to stop himself, the hug, the kiss, the – "I think you are a very courageous woman, and I'm honored to have your acquaintance." The formal sentence bumped off his tongue, a pale shadow of what he wanted to tell her, as his brief touch had been a mild and unsatisfactory hint of his wishes.

"I should go out first." As she passed by him, she reached for his arm, as if to steady herself, and her fingers trailed down his sleeve, set fire to his arm. She touched the bandage. "You take care of that, now."

"Yes, Ma'am." He waited a time, enough for them to be gone, before he left the barn through the small front door where Jacob waited. His thoughts spun, as if some centrifugal force would throw them from his brain. The flame at her fingertips, why Ives was at Long John's place, corroboration for Long John's statement, her small strong arm in his hand, why the trial did not frighten Ives. Because of Thurmond's error, they could bring in Ives's previous crimes, and now they had the name of a witness to find. Pete Morton.

Thanks to Martha McDowell.

∽

Dan and Jacob pushed through the throng in the City Bakery to the counter where meat pies steamed the rounded glass case, and found Fitch waiting for his beef pie to be wrapped in newspaper. Dan said, "Newspaper's expensive. You could rent that sheet out."

"Hell, everybody's read it or they know what's in it." A drop dangled at the end of the spindly counter man's nose. Just when Dan considered that he'd rather go hungry, the man twisted his head and wiped the drop on his shoulder. Another drop formed. "It's from May 1861. The Rebs fired on Fort Sumter." He finished wrapping the pie, and handed it to Fitch. "I got it memorized, you want to know what happened."

"I think we know that already." Dan said.

"Yeah," the counter man said. "Figured as much."

Fitch said, "You Yanks should have quit right there." He gave his poke to a man sitting at a table that held a keg of beer and the scales. The man said, "Not in here, boys. This here's neutral territory." He drew beer into a large tin mug.

"I'll be outside." Fitch retrieved his poke. A man sitting at a table near the door shouted after him, "Close the goddam door, will ya?" And then got up and slammed it, mumbling, "Born in a barn." He spat tobacco juice on the floor.

Balancing pie and beer, Dan did not wait for Jacob, but managed the door latch and pulled the door shut on the voice inside, "Shut the ... ."

Fitch, standing with some other men around an empty beer barrel, beckoned to Dan. Dan maneuvered pie and beer onto the top of the barrel, folded the paper back from his pie. When he said his name, a corpulent man who wore a well brushed coat at odds with his muddy boots, said, "We know who you are. The prosecutor."

"Only one of three," Dan said.

"What happened to your hand?" asked Fitch.

"Stupid accident. Broke my thumb. It'll be all right in a few days." Dan took a swig of the beer. "That's good beer."

"Yeah," said the plump man. "Charley Beehrer makes it. His brewery's just up the road."

Dan bit into the pie. The air around Fitch and the other men seemed charged, as in the early stages of a thunderstorm, before the turmoil in the clouds has worked itself up, and he wondered if they were Secesh.

Jacob emerged from the Bakery carrying a gray stein of beer. He drank, licked the thick dun-colored foam from his mustache. "Is good beer. Good country, having such good beer." He beamed at the men, at Fitch, who all smiled and drank to good beer.

"I'd like to talk to you," said the corpulent man. "I hope you hang Ives." His chins wobbled as he told a story of robbery at gunpoint in the guise of a "loan," and threats of death if he ever talked. Another man chimed in, "Wait a minute, there, Ives robbed me, too." Talk buzzed as men pushed closer to Dan, jostled each other, excited to find other victims of Ives and his friends, spoke at once so that Dan, by now scrawling notes in his pocketbook, called out, "One at a time," and each man contributed details of stripes on the blankets that cloaked the robbers and swathed their mounts, horses' markings: a white coronet on an off hind, a black tail and two white hooves; a notch in a near fore hoof, sure it could have got another notch as its hooves wore, but it also had a crescent of white hairs on the off fore knee. They described the riders' boots, hats, saddles, and agreed that a man would not give up a hundred-dollar saddle as easy as a twenty-dollar horse. See the saddle and find the man.

Dan recalled the robbery that had been his introduction to the Gulch, and details like pictures came back, above all, a saddle with a metal horn showing through the leather, two broken saddle strings on the skirt and a high Spanish cantle. That saddle was already in his book, more than once.

Scribbling as fast as he could, his pie forgotten, Dan took names, dashed down mnemonics to prod his memory later. He asked each man, "Would you testify?" They shook their heads. The habit of silence was too strong, their fear of the roughs too great, and they were still afraid to talk, to stand up in the witness wagon and be identified.

Walking with Jacob back to court, Dan glanced around him at the crowd. Who was Pete Morton, and would he ever find him, and finding him, would he agree to testify?

∽

Dan met Sanders and Bagg by the crossed tongues and made a summary report in hushed tones, afraid the defense might overhear. He showed them the pocketbook, the scribbled pages.

"That explains it," Sanders said, and when Dan raised an inquiring eyebrow, he said, "Listen."

Voices. Men talking in twos and threes, now and then an exclamation, a curse, bubbling to the surface. The tyger had become merely men who compared notes, kept watch for listeners, spoke in near whispers, but as men had not dared to confide in each other since Discovery brought together thousands of strangers, any of whom might be criminals, who were criminals.

Dan patted the pocket where his notebook rested. Evidence. A prosecutor's dream.

Sanders said, "We have to meet, later."

For Judge Byam rang the cowbell, and court was again in session. Dan tried to breathe. Now they must break the alibi. Fitch walked away with George Brown, whom Dan disliked on sight for his air of self-importance.

Dan said, "I need a stick," and Bagg found him one, opened the knife for him, and relieved him of the Spencer. Curls collected at the end of the stick while Honest Whiskey Joe took the oath. He and George Brown had played cards all day with Ives and Carter and some others when Nick was murdered, on the sixth of December. Ives hadn't even "pissed by himself," and he earned a laugh, a small shriek from a woman, and a reprimand from Judge Byam: "We'll have no gutter language."

At last Smith said, "Your witness," and Dan's mouth dried and a muscle quivered in his thigh as he climbed into the wagon. McDowell swung the shotgun toward him and showed his teeth. Dan swallowed to open his tight throat, and his mind went blank. To gain time, he laid his knife blade against the stick, and made a slice, then another, and men quieted. Listening to the silence spread, Dan sliced a third thin curl, and his mind lurched into motion.

"You testified that you and some other men played cards with George Ives all day."

"That's right."

"Never left him alone for a second." He concentrated on the stick, on carving the thinnest curls possible.

"That's right."

"He didn't even piss by himself?" Dan smiled and winked at Joe, just us boys here, Joe, we don't give a damn what the judge says, and Joe lost some of his wariness, came out of his slight defensive posture.

"That's right."

"What about you?"

"Huh? What do you mean?"

The wink, the smile. "Did you piss by yourself?" Without waiting he asked, "You and Ives always do that together? Look a little odd, wouldn't it?"

"What? Hell, no. Yeah, I mean, uh, maybe. I guess so. Sure"

"Speak up. Maybe? What do you mean, maybe? Did you do that by yourself or not?" Louder, not looking at Joe.

"Yeah, damn right."

"Then you didn't watch Ives all day, every minute, did you? What game were you playing?" The knife stroked the stick, and the curls gathered, and he thought he'd cut them off, one by one.

"Um, stud poker."

"How many cards?" The curls collected midway from the end.

"Seven."

"Seven-card stud?" As if it didn't matter, merely a curiosity on his part.

"Yup. Seven-card stud."

"You've got a good memory." An expansive gesture with the stick let everyone see the curls bunched at the end. While he waved the stick around and let Joe tell him how good his memory was, Dan considered his strategy. Most wouldn't know seven-card lingo, so he'd have to explain, but they'd understand the question, and if he explained it to Joe, they'd understand the term, and they'd know that Joe lied, because he'd have to know the lingo to play the game. If he lied.

Dan lied, help me out here, I'm just a poor dumb lawyer. "I don't know much about seven-card. Five-card stud is my game."

From the direction of Ives's log, "Not for long, it ain't!" Gallagher, or McDowell.

Joe stretched his neck and lifted his chin, preening himself. "Go ahead."

"Thank you. What is the best combination of hole cards and door card, do you think?"

"Oh, I don't know. Um, maybe –" He trailed off.

"You don't know. Do you know what a door card is?"

"Uh, sure. It's, uh, well, it's the card that lets you in the door, into the game."

Dan chopped off a curl. He could feel the silence gather around him. "It's the first card to show face up. How many cards are dealt before that one?"

"One."

"You're wrong. It's two in seven-card stud. Two hole cards." Dan whacked off two more curls. "All right, maybe you don't know the lingo. Doesn't matter. What was your highest bet?"

The witness shifted his feet, his head sank into his coat collar. "Five dollars?"

"Are you asking me? I wasn't there. Tell me, what was your highest bet?"

"Five dollars, I guess."

"You guess? You guess? You can afford to lose five dollars on one bet? You're a richer man than I am. How many hole cards in seven-card stud?"

"Two, like you said. Two."

"Wrong again." Another curl floated downward. "Three. There are three. Three hole cards. When is the third hole card dealt?"

A shrug, and silence.

"On the last deal. The fifth. How much did you win?" Dan cut off two curls. If he didn't slow down, he'd run out of curls.

"I forget."

"You forget? I never forget how much I win. Or lose." Dan waited for laughter to fade. "Did you win?" He hacked off a curl.

"I lost." Honest Whiskey Joe mumbled.

"You lost?" Dan almost shouted. "You lost, but you stayed in that poker game all day? Why not fold?"

"I won some."

"Glad to hear it. How much did you win?" Another curl lopped off.

"I don't know. I didn't count it."

"You don't know how much you won? You didn't count it? Not once, these last two weeks?"

"I lost it again."

"Did you even play?" The knife slashed at the curls, and Dan yelled, "You don't know how many hole cards are in seven-card stud. You don't know what a door card is, though you played seven-card stud all day. You don't know if you won or lost! I say you're lying about all this!"

"I ain't lying! I played cards. Maybe not seven-card stud, but something else."

"Tell us! What did you play? Come on, tell us."

"I – Maybe five-card stud."

"How many hole cards in that game?"

"Uh, two."

"Wrong, there's only one. How many cards are dealt?"

"Five. Yeah, five."

"What's the highest hand you can have?" He cut another curl.

"A flush."

"Wrong. You don't remember what you played, you don't know anything about the games you say you did play." Dan sliced off the last curl. He could feel all the eyes on him, and he shouted, "What were you doing on December seventh?"

"What?"

"December seventh. What were you doing?"

Honest Whiskey Joe craned his neck to make eye contact with the defense, but Dan shifted, and the knife gashed at the stick. His world contracted into thirty-six square feet of wagon bed, and the wood chips dropping fast as rain.

Joe glowered at Dan from under his eyebrows and gnawed on a dirty fingernail.

Dan threw wide his hands, turned away as if he might be finished, swung back, shook the pointed stick at Joe. "What were you doing on the fifth of December?"

Joe glared.

"What about the seventh?" The knife scored the wood.

Honest Whiskey Joe's mouth opened, but no sound came out.

Slicing at the stick, Dan recited all of the dates in early December, from the first to the sixteenth, when Palmer found Nick, each date a cut into the stick, and the knife cut faster, and chips rained down, and Joe took hold of the top sideboard with both hands to steady himself. Dan closed the knife, took the stick, now the size of a sharp pencil, into his right hand, thrust it rapier-like at Honest Whiskey Joe who staggered back. "You don't know what you were doing on the sixth of December at all. You don't know what you doing any day this month!"

The witness's chin sank to his chest.

Dan shouted, "Isn't that true?"

Joe's chin rose from his chest, and his mouth opened, but Dan pressed on, "So how did you come to recall that you were playing cards with George Ives and Alex Carter on the sixth?"

"It must have been the sixth."

"Why?"

Joe licked his lips, glanced toward the defense attorneys, but Dan blocked him.

"'Cause that's the day the Dutch kid was killed."

"How do you know that?"

Joe shrugged.

"How do you know Nicholas Tbalt was murdered on the sixth?" Dan bellowed, "Tell us!"

"Uh, I guess somebody must a tol' me. Yeah, that's it. Somebody tol' me, and then I recollected I was playing cards that day with Ives and Carter and the boys. Yeah, that's it." Looking pleased with himself, Joe shifted, to catch Smith's eye, but Dan threw the next question at him.

"Who told you Nicholas Tbalt was murdered on the sixth of December?"

"I disremember. One of the boys."

"Which one? Who was it?"

"I don't rightly recollect!" Joe yelled back.

Dan hammered on, "Who told you when Nicholas Tbalt was murdered?" No answer. "You don't remember who told you Nick was murdered on the sixth, you don't know what games you played all that day, what you bet, if you won or lost!" He gasped for breath. "You don't know what you were doing on any day this month! Who put you up to this?"

Joe raised his arm to point, and Dan stepped aside just as Thurmond and Smith sprang up. Joe hollered, "It was him! He said Ives told him the Dutch kid was killed on the sixth."

Thurmond gaped. Smith shouted, "Objection! It's all hearsay! He's testifying to what he says someone told him!"

"Who, Joe? Which one?"

"The tall one behind Smith." He meant Thurmond.

The tyger came to life and roared, but mixed with the booing of the roughs sounded a strong note from men who yelled at them to shut their faces, shut the hell up, and the cowbell rang and rang until slowly, slowly the tyger's roar quieted to a growl and Dan could be heard.

"Let the record show that the witness has pointed to Mr. Thurmond."

"He's lying!" screamed Thurmond. "Lying, I tell you!"

Sanders yelled, "Your honors! He's impeaching his own witness." Blank uncomprehending stares came from the judges. "He's accusing his own witness of lying!" Wheeling, Sanders confronted Thurmond, "What else did your witness lie about?"

Caught, Thurmond closed his mouth, at a loss for words and stood mute. The tyger was quiet.

Dan flung the stick away. "I am through with this witness!"

Sanders and Bagg shook his hand, because he had discredited Joe's testimony and established a clear chain of reasoning: Ives had told Thurmond Nick died on the sixth, and Thurmond had told Joe, who then gave Ives an alibi for that date. Thurmond had not talked to Long John or Hilderman alone since they brought Ives in, and if someone else killed Nick, the defense had not mentioned him. The conclusion was inescapable.

Ives killed Nick.

But did the people understand it?

Logic be damned, Dan said to himself, without hard evidence Ives might still be freed. The God damn mob jury.

George Brown carried himself with his torso tilted slightly back, aping a man of affairs, though his appearance was insignificant and he had something dishonest in his air, perhaps a willingness to laugh, to overlook the character of the jokes, so long as he was included. Dan's dislike of the man was sealed.

As he passed the log, he said something, and the Ives faction whooped and slapped his back. Looking pleased to have scored a success with tough men, Brown climbed into the wagon. Gallagher sneered in Dan's direction, said something to McDowell, who looked at Dan and stroked the barrel of his shotgun.

The Spencer once more slung over his shoulder, standing with Bagg and Sanders, Dan was choking on his anger. The stupid bastards, all of them, who believed that they would never have to face consequences for their crimes.

Ives never paid for anything.

No more. This time Ives would pay.

Fitch brought him a pint of beer. "Thank you." Dan gulped down half of it, then sipped it while Sanders and Bagg brought Fitch up to date. His thumb beat hard, and he cursed his stupidity, although it given him license to rest his arm against Martha McDowell's breast. And then he remembered Harriet. Good God, he had made promises to Harriet Dean. Blonde, beautiful, plump Harriet Dean, a treat to escort in her décolletage to a ball, to hold in his arms during a waltz, to imagine in his bed.

She would never have brought him information about these thugs, or acquired it by braving the typhus for a whore's child. Obedient, she would not defy her father even to the extent of promising to wait for him. But he had promised to return to her. Memory conjured her image, waltzing in another man's arms. She was not the kind to wait. Perhaps she did not believe he would deliver the family from disgrace. He must get enough gold to return, and soon.

But Martha McDowell, she of the luminous eyes, had put herself in harm's way to help him. How could he leave her? Yet he had promised Miss Dean, and Mrs. McDowell was – God help him – Mrs. McDowell.

He wished he could get blind drunk. Forget them both.

"Good God." Sanders's heartfelt curse brought Dan out of his black thoughts in time to understand that Brown named Long John Frank as Nick's murderer.

Long John, at once the bearing beam and the frail reed in the prosecution's case. He'd lied about the gold, he had not tried to stop Ives, he was complicit in the crime. But how far? Dan didn't know. Would anyone ever know?

Bagg rubbed his hands together and chortled with glee. "They've thrown Long John to the wolves. Let me at Brown. Just let me at him."

"Go to it." Dan spoke at the same time Sanders said, "Be our guest."

The group around Ives, especially Gibbons, looked worried. Perhaps because, though the sun hovered just above the western horizon, Plummer had not arrived. McDowell drank out of a tall brown bottle as he listened to Gallagher. Ives tried to strike up a conversation with Alex Davis, who laid a finger to his lips.

"Blue, listen." Fitch, standing behind the crossed tongues, twisted the hairs of his mustache as if to make thread from wool. "Brown's lying."

"We know that," said Bagg and Sanders together.

"Oh, yeah? Do you know where he was? I spoke with a fella who says Brown was at Dempsey's that day, on the job just like he's supposed to be."

"Will your pal testify?"

"Hell, no. He's got a family. It'd be his life if them boys knew he'd talked. You ought to be able to shake him loose."

The three prosecutors regarded each other in a silent consultation. "Yes," Bagg said. "I sure as hell can do that."

"Easily," Dan said. "Threaten him with twenty or thirty witnesses who went through on the stage."

Bagg danced a clumsy step or two. "We got him. You bet we do."

"Thank you, Fitch," Sanders said.

Bagg attacked before both feet touched the wagon's floor, a good commander on the offensive. "I put it to you that you are lying through your teeth, that you were not present at any card game on December sixth, you were nowhere near Wisconsin

Creek. You were, in fact, on the job at Dempsey's ranch, serving up beer and lies, just like now."

"I ain't lying," shouted Brown. "I was playing cards all day at Wisconsin Creek."

"With George Ives and Honest Whiskey Joe."

"And Aleck Carter. That's right, by God."

"You leave the Almighty out of this. We know what He thinks of liars."

A voice called from the crowd: "What was the game?" Other voices chimed in, "Yeah! Ask him! What was the game?"

Bagg cocked his head to one side. "You heard them. Answer the question."

"Poker. That's what. Poker."

Another voice came out of the crowd: "What kind of poker?"

"Draw," yelled Brown. "It was draw poker!"

Silence. Silence spread like water over the crowd, and over the group around Ives. Smith put his head in his hands, Thurmond pounded his fist on the log, and Davis half rose with a protest that died stillborn. Someone tried a half-hearted boo that no one else took up.

"Honest Whiskey Joe said it was stud poker," Bagg said. "What do you think of that?"

Brown inspected something on the floor of the wagon.

"Answer the question!" Byam snapped.

"Five-card. Five-card stud."

Bagg said, "Joe said seven-card stud. What about that?" When Brown said nothing, he went on, "We know someone's lying. My money's on you, Brown. This here claim you're panning, why, you won't see any color." Brown did not speak. "We can bring in twenty, thirty witnesses from the stage coaches that stopped at Dempsey's that day."

"No, you can't!" Triumph shone on his face and in his clear, loud voice. "We didn't get that many passengers. It was a light —"

Shadows from mountains on the southern side of Alder Creek eased toward the court, and the sun, sinking below the jagged horizon, set free the chill of winter's long twilight. The tyger breathed in and out, in and out, or perhaps it was his own breath Dan heard rasping in his throat. Beside him Fitch swore under his breath, one obscenity after another, his vocabulary rich and imaginative as he left neither Brown's privates nor his parentage unscathed.

"It was a light day, was it?" Bagg was no longer Brown's adversary, but his agreeable friend. "I guess not too many of the boys want to travel these days, seeing how unsafe the roads are, what with all the road agents around."

Brown's chin jutted out at Bagg. "That's what I was told. I wasn't there. I was playing cards with Ives and Carter at Long John's place."

What was Bagg doing? Dan held his left hand at a level with his heart and longed to attack a stick with his knife. He took the knife out of his pocket and tossed it idly in his right hand. In Bagg's shoes, he'd have stopped when Brown said it was a light day.

"So Bob Dempsey let you off that day?"

"That's right."

"He's a good man to work for, isn't he?"

"He sure is. The best."

"I bet you're a good employee, too. Not the sort to run out on your boss."

"You bet."

"Because you're loyal, aren't you? You're loyal to your boss?"

"Yes, I am." Brown held up his head.

Dan understood. He whispered, "Beautiful. Just beautiful," and Fitch leaned to him, muttered a tobacco-smelling question that Dan ignored. Fitch would see for himself.

Bagg said, "You want to help Ives, don't you? Speak up, now. Answer yes, good and loud, so men can hear how loyal you are."

"Yes!"

"You're loyal to your pals, too, aren't you?" Again yes, Brown's pride clear in his shoulders held back, his head up. And Bagg said, "That's good. You and Ives are pals, aren't you?"

"Yes!"

The next question rode on the heels of Brown's answer – "You'd go out of your way to help a pal, wouldn't you?" – and hard after Brown's reply – "Yes!" – Bagg fired the next question, "Even lie for him, wouldn't you?" and Brown called out, his voice clear and proud, "Yes!" and Bagg shouted, "You lied about Long John, didn't you?" and Brown shouted back, "Yes!" and then, too late, "No!"

Thurmond, Davis, and Smith all jumped up, shouted objections that Bagg ignored as he rushed in with the final question before Brown recovered.

"You were at Dempsey's that day, weren't you?"

"Yes! I mean – No!"

"Which is it, yes or no? Speak up! Yes or no? Yes is right, isn't it? Isn't it? You said it was a light day, and you knew that because you were there, weren't you, it don't do you no good to lie now, we know the truth, we got witnesses, and you might as well tell the truth, you were at Dempsey's on the sixth because you're a good, loyal employee. Ain't that right?"

"Yes!" Brown yelled. "I mean no, I am, I was, no, I was at Dempsey's!"

Bagg stepped back. "I'm through with this witness."

Because it took a hard man to hold onto a lie, Dan told himself, knowing he was grinning like a fool, but he'd seen a master cross-examine and break a witness, and he doubted he could have done it himself, though Brown was no hard man, but an easy-going man eager to please, and Bagg had read him and used that eagerness against him.

Brown walked toward the group with Ives, but no one would look at him, let alone speak to him. After a few seconds, he walked away.

Dan found he could not see his notebook until Fitch lighted a candle and held it for him. Jacob stood close, with the other two prosecutors, and the five men made a tight, closed group. The judges dismissed everyone until the next day, and under the noise of a thousand men going their separate ways, Dan said, "We must talk about this. There's more to these robberies and murders than we have thought of. It looks very much like a criminal conspiracy, and if we're to survive, we must root it out."

5: Alder Gulch: Nevada City

Dan had hardly slept when he forced himself to rise and light a lamp while Jacob went on snoring with his face to the wall. Shivering, Dan pulled on his trousers over the long underwear he had slept in. He broke the ice skimming the water bucket, poured water into a basin, and scraped his razor over the night's stubble of beard. He rinsed his face in the cold water, and emerged, gasping, at last awake. Damn! He wished he had built up the fire and heated the water. He dried his face, and found Jacob sitting up, elbows on his knees, rubbing the sleep from his eyes.

Jacob yawned. "Today, what is happening?"

"The defense will bring in character witnesses and try to show that Ives is a man of good character." Dan slipped his left arm into his jacket and drew the garment up to his shoulder. Jacob did not ask what would happen if the defense succeeded in showing Ives to be a man of good character. He knew. They both knew. Last night, they'd been escorted to Virginia amid threats from the dark: "You bastards are dead men!" "Breathe deep, you son of a bitch, it could be your last!" Today's witnesses could raise a doubt in the juries' minds as to Ives's guilt, and despite the stories he'd heard, those in his pocketbook, he had no rebuttal witnesses. The only hope the prosecutors had was to break today's witnesses as they had broken Joe Basak and George Brown.

Dan's stomach lurched, and he swallowed bile.

When they stepped outside, the Melodeon Hall was quiet and dark. Somewhere, a drunk sang "Home Sweet Home" off key, with now and then a sob. Dan hoped he had someplace to get out of the cold. A dog barked from farther up Idaho Street, and Dan froze, his hand on Jacob's forearm, before he realized it was probably Canary, barking at the singer. A good music critic, that dog.

A soft Southern whisper from the shadows by the Eatery made Dan shy away: "Mista' Stark?"

"What? Who's that?" His right hand had brought the uncocked rifle to bear.

"Don't shoot, sir, it's me. Albert Rose."

"Albert, what are you doing out this early?"

"Looking for you, sir. Miz Hudson, she said I could."

"Why?" Dan slung the rifle. Beside him Jacob's hoarse breath scraped out and in.

"On account you in need of guarding, we figure. Folks mostly think twice about messing with me." He moved forward, in the moonlight looking even larger than he was, a black man six feet tall, who could carry on his shoulder a barrel that Dan would have to roll on edge.

A bullet is so small a thing to bring down a man sizeable as an oak. Thinking that, Dan wondered where he had read it. "Thank you, Albert."

"You welcome, sir," Albert said.

Albert would never know how welcome his help was. Dan, to his shame, was afraid. Not because of threats and evil gestures, though those were frightening enough. But something unseen, unheard? Blake's tyger. An unidentified evil. Unrealized until last night's meeting in John Creighton's store, when Dan and Sanders had pooled their information while Creighton and another merchant, Paris Pfouts, asked hard questions. Creighton had sketched a chart of dates and locations of armed robberies and known murders, and they had noted descriptions of blankets, gloves, horses' markings, types of weapons, features of tack. Listed places where corpses had been found. Organized a list of men whose friends missed them, whose families had written to inquire for them. When the work was done, they saw how blankets, saddles, markings recurred, and they had reached an awful conclusion: A criminal conspiracy operated in the region. Somehow well informed, the robbers knew who would travel with gold and when.

But how? Who was involved? They needed hard evidence. Leroy Southmayde had identified a pistol taken from Long John's wickiup as belonging to him. It had been stolen in November, during the armed robbery of his wagon train, and both he and the merchant who sold it to him identified it from the serial number and markings on the handle. But who were the robbers? Who put it there? The owner of the stolen greenbacks identified them from his list of numbers, but who stashed them? Finding pistol and greenbacks and other items might show that Long John's place was a drop for stolen goods, or a center of criminal activity. Again, who were the criminals?

Knowing about the conspiracy, finding stolen goods, did not give them the criminals. This evidence, their certainty, would not hang anyone. God help them if they hanged a wrong man.

To destroy such a murderous conspiracy, they needed men not afraid to talk, and a force strong enough to protect the witnesses and root out the conspirators.

For the first time, Dan had heard the words, Vigilance Committee.

∽

The Star Bakery did a brisk business in meat pies and beer, and coffee. Real coffee. Dan bought pie and beer for all three of them, and coffee for himself. At these prices, he told himself, he'd soon have to dip into his going-home cache. He sipped the coffee, his first taste in three months. As its warmth settled into his stomach, a surge of hope washed through him, that perhaps he might live to go home. Home. To Grandfather, the Firm, Miss Dean. His mood plummeted.

They carried their food toward the court, where the guards' eyes widened at the sight of Albert, his coat sagging on one side with the weight of a pistol in his pocket. When Dan said, "He's with me," they stood aside. It's a new world, Dan thought. An armed Negro can walk into a court. Let someone now say that Albert is not a person. In this Territory, Albert was free.

The advisory jurymen were taking their places. Lawyers and judges stood together by the fire where Smith regaled them with a story about a mishap in court when he was a young lawyer. When he finished, they all laughed, except for Davis, and Sanders was merely polite. Byam's lips moved as if committing the story to memory. They greeted Dan in friendly fashion, and Sanders offered his hand to Albert, who stared at it as if he could not recognize it. He held up his own hands laden with pies and beer.

Nodding, Sanders withdrew his hand with a smile. "I'm Wilbur Sanders."

"Albert Rose here, sir." Albert ducked his head.

"No need for the 'sir' business, Mr. Rose. I'm not in the Army any more."

Someone in the crowd yelled, "Nigger lover! Union bastard brought a nigger to court!"

Thurmond snarled, "This is an outrage! Get that damn nigger out of here."

Dan ground his teeth. "Albert is with me. To protect me from your client's friends."

"I insist —" Thurmond began, but Smith interrupted. "Speaking of our client, here he is." Ives, carrying his chains, walked through the perimeter, head up, with an air of walking onto a stage. The defense attorneys gathered around him. The minions greeting their prince, thought Dan.

"Curtain going up." Bagg rubbed his hands together and smiled.

"Yes," Sanders said. "It feels the same, doesn't it? Keyed up."

"Yes," Bagg said, "exactly like battle. Win or die."

The phrase resonated in Dan's ears. He and Sanders exchanged a look of understanding. Bagg did not know how true he spoke. Win or die.

Behind Ives stood Gallagher and McDowell just as on the previous two days. Gallagher raised his middle finger at Dan. McDowell stroked the barrel of his shotgun. Dan thought of the schoolhouse good morning song, but with different words: We're all in our places with sneers on our faces. He almost laughed, but a sudden thought stopped him: Were these two part of the conspiracy? God forbid, for her sake.

A delegation of miners collected behind the crossed wagon tongues. One of them, with hair to his waist, was the spokesman. They had come to demand the trial end by three o'clock, because tomorrow their claims could be jumped.

A man whose ragged trousers barely covered his anatomy chimed in, "Three days is plenty time for a trial. You can't make up your minds in three days, let him go."

"Right," said Hairy. "Besides, now he's been caught once, he won't do nothing like that again. You could just let him go."

"We'll do our best," Judge Byam said, but they weren't satisfied until Bagg spoke up. "Don't worry, boys, I have a claim in Junction that I ain't about to lose hold of."

"See to it, then." Muttering among themselves, the group turned away.

Dan suggested passing a rule that no claim could be jumped during the trial, but both judges shook their heads. "By the time our sheriffs posted a notice for a miners meeting," said Wilson, "and we get the boys together to vote on a new rule, claims would have been jumped already, and getting them back would be hell. The claim jumpers would say the claims was theirs to start with, and sometimes that might be true." He scratched under his collar.

Byam added, "Better we get done."

Thurmond, thrusting himself forward, had a sure-fire way to end the trial. "Let the jury vote now." He should have known, Dan told himself.

"Not on your tintype," said Judge Byam, as Judge Wilson added, "We'll play this out." Byam rang the cowbell, and as sunrise glowed behind the mountains, court was in session.

And Dan, who had set his pie on the ground and forgotten it, saw that a dog had dragged it under the witness wagon and now licked the plate. "We'll get you another one, sir." Albert walked away with Jacob before Dan could emulate Sanders and tell him to drop the sir. He had never been in the Army.

∽

The defense brought on witnesses to vouch for Ives's good character. Sanders whispered, "Of course. They failed to prove an alibi, so now they have to prove his character."

Bagg harrumphed. "They can't prove a negative." The prosecutors laughed, but to Dan the laughter sounded forced.

The witnesses' statements had a rehearsed quality, as they told how Ives had helped them with money in their hour of need, how he sent gold home to his widowed mother and sisters. The witnesses wiped their eyes. Behind their hands, their glances were sly. One man blew his nose on a handkerchief that did not quite hide his smile.

Sanders asked, "Have you ever known George Ives to threaten another man's life?"

The witness answered, "No, damn it."

Bagg asked about the time Ives backed his horse into the Morris brothers' windows, the man said, "Oh, that was a boyish prank. You know, just for fun."

"Did he ever pay damages?"

"Not yet, but he will, soon as he gets some money."

"How will he get the money? Borrow it?"

"I don't know nothing about that. It's none of my business."

A tall, strong-looking man in a plaid coat stood at the crossed tongues, arguing with a guard who took Sanders aside, and then left him talking to the man.

How the hell would they refute these witnesses? There was no chink in the testimony they could use for a handhold to breach the stories they told. True, the man whose dog had been shot could testify to that, and one or two of the witnesses to Ives's "loans" would talk. One man, who had tried to get Ives to pay back his "loan" would testify that Ives had pulled out his pistol and said he'd kill the man if he didn't leave him alone. But would it be enough?

Dan sank into a black mood. Damn. So far from proving that Ives had murdered Nick, they had not shown that he could kill anyone even in self-defense, and a killing in self-defense – if they knew of one – would not be held against him. Any man was capable of killing another to defend his own life, the lives of his loved ones. But a cold-blooded killing? To take another man's life as he had killed Nick? To point the pistol and face the terror, the pleading, of a fellow man, and then to pull the trigger and watch as life flowed red from his wounds? People would not believe Ives capable of such evil. Ives's friends would not say it, and his victims would be dead, or too frightened to get up into that wagon.

God, if they could only find Pete Morton. And then, if he would testify.

Dan reckoned they had lost the trial. As he listened to another witness, he watched and listened to the crowd, and saw hardened miners wipe tears from their eyes. Who would not be moved at the thought of three helpless women depending on their absent son and brother for financial support? The story made him slightly sick.

Someone in the crowd wondered aloud where Plummer was. Dan's silent laugh was sour in his mouth. The way the trial was going, Plummer would not be needed.

Jacob, followed by Albert, brought Dan his replacement pie and a beer. "Thank you!" Dan bit into it and realized he was ravenous, so hungry he would have found his boot sole tasty. The sun shone from near its winter zenith, and he'd had nothing to eat since a few bites of jerky amid the press of business last night. Remembering that business, the meeting, his notebook felt heavy in his breast pocket. How to find hard evidence of the conspiracy? It seemed hopeless. When Albert and Jacob stood aside, Dan realized a new witness had taken the stand for Ives.

Like the others, this witness described Ives's generosity, his kindness — which drew shouts of protest from Nevada men who had seen him shoot up the dog. Idly, Dan wondered what the man's name was, not that it mattered, for he was just one more defense liar. Idly curious, he whispered to Bagg, "What's his name?"

Bagg said, "Pete Morton."

Dusty stripes of sunlight. A woman's caped silhouette. She had come to him with her news. She had said, 'Pete Morton.'

A spasm stabbed his clenched left fist. The bite of pie was a lump of coal on his tongue. He looked for a place to set the plate aside, and young Pemberton took it. "I'll guard it from dogs."

Dan stood the rifle against the wagon's sidewall, and picked up a stick. "I'll take the cross."

"You know something." It was a statement, not a question. Bagg reached for the knife in Dan's hand and opened it for him.

"Yes. I have an idea." Seeing that Bagg looked as if he might want to consult with Sanders, still listening to Plaid Coat, Dan said, "You've been mining in Junction District, and Sanders is from Bannack. Neither of you know Virginia as well as I do. This is a Virginia man."

Dan took the first cut at the stick. Bagg said, "When you get to carving, something's up." He waited, perhaps expecting an explanation. "Go to it, then."

"Your witness." Judge Byam sounded impatient. "How many times do I have to tell you?"

Dan climbed into the wagon. He felt as if he'd been dealt an ace for a hole card and would have to play it just right. Use it to get the crowd, the mob jury, on his side. After a swift glance at the witness, Dan watched the knife. A thin strip of wood floated to the ground.

Seldom had Dan seen an uglier man. A large mole disfigured his nose, two vertical creases folded the skin between his eyes, and his mouth was pinched together. A face women would turn from. Good, Dan thought. The knife stroked the wood, long and slow, almost lovingly cut away another thin strip. He waited through yet one more long, slow slice while he listened to the crowd's silence. Silence. Expectation. Expectation of what?

"I don't think I've seen you around Virginia?"

"You would've if you'd been looking." The man spat over the sidewall.

Keeping his face blank, Dan let his gaze begin at the man's left shoulder, slide past his face, to the other shoulder. Suspicion narrowed the man's eyes. Inwardly, Dan rejoiced. He wanted Morton suspicious, wanted him to wonder what Dan might be up to, where the trap was. He did not want this witness to think about the questions. Morton would not willingly testify against Ives, but he would, in the end. Oh, yes. He would.

In this trial that had turned into a poker game, Morton's hole card was the knowledge of the Bamboo Chief. He thought that was a secret, but knowing that secret was Dan's hole card. He kept his voice mild but clear, his questions bland.

"You're a friend of George Ives, aren't you?"

"Damn right. So what?" The witness scowled.

"Just getting the feel of things. George Ives has many friends in the Gulch, doesn't he?" Moving toward the wagon's tailgate, Dan tossed the question over his shoulder like a pinch of salt.

"Yeah. 'Course he does."

Dan faced the witness, and named some whose names he recollected from his notebook, named them one by one as friends of George Ives, and to each name the witness said, "Yeah, sure, guess so," or "What of it?" or "So what?" His suspicion grew with every name. Dan watched the men by the log from his peripheral vision: the defense attorneys ready to pounce, McDowell glaring, Gallagher frowning, puzzled. On impulse, he named Gallagher, then McDowell, and to each name Morton responded, "Yeah."

Was anyone aware that not one name belonged to a respectable member of the community? That each name carried its burden of suspicion and brought knowing looks and wise nods from honest men? By leading the witness down the trail of Ives's friends, Dan knew he would be thought to play into the defense hand, but no one else knew his hole card, and he did not name Boone Helm. Nobody wanted to be known as the pal of a cannibal. At last, Dan sensed that men were about to lose patience, and a defender might jump up and object that this was going nowhere.

Feeling like he was jumping from the quarry's edge into the water, Dan named the last friend.

"How about Helen Troy?"

"Hell, that's no secret. Miss Troy is popular around town."

Thurmond was ready to launch upwards with an objection, perhaps thinking that Dan meant to denounce George Ives by his friendship with a notorious madam, but Dan dodged his expectation. "Miss Troy is a successful businesswoman, is she not?" He could sense everyone's surprise, even bewilderment. Had no one noticed that the madam ran a business? Dan thought of Betty, the madam to whom his father had introduced him on his fourteenth birthday with instructions to find his son a clean girl. But Betty had taken him under her own wing: I like 'em young, sweetie pie, and I'm as clean as they come. If Betty had been a man, she could have run a railroad.

The witness stared at Dan from under his brows. "Yeah, she owns Fancy Annie's, but what does that have to do with the price of tea in China?"

Some of Ives's friends laughed, and the witness peered around with a smirk, proud of himself for scoring one off the prosecutor.

Dan let him enjoy his moment before he asked, "Are you a friend of Miss Troy?"

"Yeah, sure." The witness squared his shoulders, and his chin made a small circle. "Not like Georgie, but yeah."

From a pace away, Dan put admiration into his voice, "You're quite a man for the ladies, I'm sure." The knife's rhythm quickened, the shortened strokes cut deeper, and Dan ignored the pain in his left hand.

"Yeah, I can be."

"The ladies at Fancy Annie's?"

"Sure. I been there lots of times."

Where would he get the money, this man who owned no claim, no ranch, held no job? "You go with the defendant, don't you?" The witness stared at Dan. "I mean with George Ives."

"Sure, I do. Me and Georgie's pals."

Dan sliced off the next question: "Fancy Annie's is a saloon, is it not?"

"Yeah. But —"

"And a house of ill repute?"

"Yeah. Well, what do you mean?"

"Come, come, we all know what a house of ill repute is. We're men of the world here."

When Morton said nothing, Dan asked, "It's also a brothel, isn't it?" Morton didn't speak. Dan, thinking they hadn't coached him for this, shouted, "Isn't it a whorehouse?"

The crowd laughed, and Dan, celebrating inside because he had got the mob jury to laugh, bowed to the judges, "Begging your pardon." He pretended to ignore the laughter.

"Yeah." The man nodded. "I guess so. Upstairs."

"Have you ever been up there?"

"Sure, I have. Lots of times." Reminding everyone that the prosecutor had called him a man for the ladies, forgetting that he was an ugly man who had to pay.

They were circling closer to the hole card, and he plummeted toward the cold, cold water in the quarry, but as he stepped closer to Morton, Dan kept the knife cutting in a steady rhythm, and Morton stared at the blade flashing in the sun. Dan, about to change the angle of the blade, let it be. "Have you been up there with Mr. Ives?"

"Well, not with him, you know, but — "

"Of course. Let me rephrase that." Dan took a step back. Out the corner of his eye, he saw Thurmond gather his feet under him. Dan hurried on. "At the same time, let's say." The knife made another sweet stroke, and Dan risked a glance at Morton, who seemed mesmerized by it. "Well?"

"Yeah, I been up there at the same time."

This was it. Dan felt as if his toes touched water, as if he now called the defense bet, that they would ever show that Ives was capable of cold-blooded murder. The knife cut deep: "Have you ever heard Ives refer to himself as the 'Bamboo Chief?'"

Morton was startled into truth: "Yes!"

Davis and Thurmond bolted up. "You can't introduce that now! There's no foundation for it! None whatever! Your Honor, you can't let that in. It's hearsay!"

"What's wrong with it?" Dan pivoted to look down at them. "A Bamboo Chief is a leader among men, isn't he? Wouldn't you like your client to be known as a leader? Any man would like to be thought of as a Bamboo Chief. Wouldn't he?" He paused for two beats. "Or why not?"

"Yes, why not?" Judge Byam stroked the long hairs of his goatee. "What about it, boys? Can he ask about this 'Bamboo Chief' or not? Seems harmless to me."

Thurmond had no basis for an objection, other than Dan had brought in a new phrase. To insist on having it thrown out would be to give it undue importance. He slapped his hands against his thighs. "Oh, the hell with it. Go ahead." Parting his coat skirt, he sat down.

Dan wanted to wipe away the sweat trickling down behind his ear. If Thurmond had not quit just then, his clean dive would be a belly flop, his hole card useless. "I ask you again, have you ever heard the term, 'Bamboo Chief'?"

As Morton stood without speaking, Byam ordered him, "Answer the question."

"Sure," he said. "That's what Georgie calls hisself sometimes."

"Is it, indeed? What does it mean, exactly?" Dan stepped closer to Morton, stared at the mole.

Morton could not find a place for his hands, let them dangle at his sides, clasped them in front of him, behind his back. "Like you said, a head man, like chief of a —"

Dan interrupted, "Does Mr. Ives call himself that often?"

"Only when he's done something special. Like —"

"Like backing his horse into the Morrises' windows?"

"Yeah, like that, I guess, only he never — I mean, that was just —"

"Just in fun? You were there then, too, were you not?"

"Sure, I was. Me and the boys, it was –"

"And when he rode into the saloon and let his horse do its business on the floor and kick over tables and break up the place, you were there?"

"Yeah, but it was all in –"

"Yes, we know, just in fun. Right? What about the loans?"

"Yeah, well, Georgie sometimes gets a loan when he's out of cash."

"At gunpoint?"

"Once or twice, maybe. But it's just –"

"Just in fun? Boys will be boys?" Dan let the sarcasm drip from his voice like a relentless drop on stone, and then his mind stumbled on a new understanding. We. Morton had said, We. The witness had admitted being present during armed robbery. Robberies. This witness, maybe all of the defense witnesses, were George Ives's accomplices? Participated in robberies? Murders? God damn them, were they part of the conspiracy?

"Yeah, you know, a joke."

"A joke?" Dan let his anger rise, show in his voice. A joke to demand money at gun point, a joke to kill an unarmed boy? "You think destroying property is a joke? Demanding money at gunpoint is a joke? Just good clean fun?"

The witness stammered, could not think of an answer, and Dan's feet slid into the water, and he laid his hand over the hole card. "So it was all in fun." The witness nodded, agreed, and Dan pushed on, "All the other pranks we've heard of. Just fun?" His voice could be heard everywhere.

"Yeah, yeah, like I said. Just fun."

Amid a still calm, Dan turned over his hole card. "George Ives bragged in Fancy Annie's that he was the Bamboo Chief, right?" His left hand hurt like hell now. He stopped whittling and pocketed the knife. Taking the stick in his right hand, he gestured with it as if it were an extension of his index finger, each question stabbing at Morton.

"Yeah, you know —"

"The Bamboo Chief that killed that traveler on the road. Right?"

"Yeah, hey — Wait! I mean —"

"Was that in fun, too?"

"Yeah, no, I mean —"

Thurmond, Davis, Smith jumped up, shouted objections. Dan yelled across them, "You're right! That was not in fun. The man was going to peach on him, wasn't he? George Ives is the Bamboo Chief, isn't he? A Bamboo Chief wouldn't let someone peach, he'd do something about it, wouldn't he? That's what a Bamboo Chief would do. Isn't that right? Isn't it?"

"Yeah, but — "

"That man was killed on the main road, in broad daylight, with people coming from both directions, and the killer got away scot free." Thurmond and Smith and Davis were shouting, and Byam held the cowbell but did not ring it, and while Pemberton and his colleague scratched furiously over their papers, and the advisory jurymen craned forward to hear, Dan bellowed, "Any man that could murder someone like that and get away, he'd be the Bamboo Chief, wouldn't he? You heard him, didn't you? You were on the other side of the canvas, weren't you? You and your whore? You heard him, didn't you? Didn't you? You can't lie in court, you have to answer, you did hear it. Didn't you?" With each question, Dan inched closer to the witness, poked the stick into the air. He fired each question a little faster, and the witness leaned back farther and farther until he trapped himself against the driver's seat, and still Dan shuffled closer, the stick stabbing each question.

Morton broke. "Yeah, goddammit, I heard it!" he screamed.

"Heard what?"

"George Ives said he was the Bamboo Chief that killed that traveler on the road!"

"Thank you." Panting, Dan stepped back. "A man who could shoot a man down in broad daylight, he could kill Nicholas Tbalt, couldn't he, and feel sure he'd get away with that, too, wouldn't he?"

Morton said nothing, but he didn't need to, and Dan did not care. He had done what he set out to do. He gathered up his cards. He understood that the yelling must have gone on for some time, he hadn't heard it, he'd concentrated on breaking Morton. Had anyone heard Morton admit to Ives's confession?

"Objection!" Thurmond screamed, and, and Smith shouted, "Hearsay!" and stamped his foot, and Davis stood in front of the witness table and yelled, "Strike that! Strike that!" All of the defense lawyers clamored at the judges, at the recorders, to strike the entire line of questioning, they objected, they objected, while Gallagher and McDowell, and Ives's other friends raged at Dan, and in the calm center of the vocal storm, Dan looked Morton in the eye and let his anger and contempt show.

"You tricked me!" Morton shook his fist at Dan. "I didn't mean it like that."

"Bullshit!" said Dan. "If you know what's good for you, you'll ride out of here before Ives's friends get after you."

The cowbell clanged. The judges yelled for order, and more voices, now from the crowd, shouted for quiet, yelled at others to shut the hell up.

Dan's thoughts flew, clouds in a brisk wind. If the law was war, cross-examination was a battle. High stakes poker. A deer hunt, without bullets, and for the biggest game of all – criminals. The law had the joy of the kill, the exhilaration of firing the killing shot, turned over the winning card, when he asked the telling question. Father must have felt it, but perhaps only in the gamble, yet for him, his father's son, all the rest – the hunt, the game – paled beside asking the telling question, when the witness must answer and could never take his answer back, for it was in the record.

If they had heard it.

His exhilaration evaporated like a puddle in a drought. They must have heard. Did Pemberton and the other recorder hear? Or was it all for nothing? Christ, no.

The judges had brought the clamoring voices under control, and the last echoes of the cowbell were dying in the cold.

Thurmond, body cocked forward at the hips, arms outspread with fists clenched, demanded that the judges have Dan's entire line of questioning stricken from the record.

Sanders planted his feet wide and thrust his chin at the taller man and asked, "On what grounds?" to which Thurmond yelled "Hearsay!" and Sanders at the top of his voice, "Hearsay, hell!" Bagg chipped in that it was not hearsay but admission contrary to interest, another type of confession. Byam leaned down to the recorders, asked for clarification.

The crowd, and Dan, who felt a muscle fluttering in his triceps, waited while Pemberton searched back through his notebook, and at last read, "The confession rule means that if someone tells you he did something wrong, you can't say so in court, but if he tells someone else and you overhear him, then you can. If he tells you, it's hearsay. If he tells someone else, it's an admission contrary to interest. A confession."

"Okay." Byam stroked his beard flat against his coat. "I think I got this right." He turned to Dan. "You didn't ask what Ives told him, you asked him to tell you what Ives said to the woman?"

"That's right."

"And that's an admission contrary to interest? Is that right?"

"That's correct." Sweat trickled behind Dan's ear, but he forced himself not to wipe it, not to give away how scared he was that all his work might be in vain if Pemberton or the other recorder had not heard. "This man is a character witness, in the defense's misbegotten attempt to prove that George Ives is a man of good character. By bringing him in to prove that, they left the door open for the prosecution to prove the opposite."

"Is that so?" Byam asked Thurmond.

"I protest! It's not fair!"

"Murder ain't fair, either," said Bagg.

"You all step back a ways." Byam and Wilson held a short conference behind their hands, and then Byam beckoned the eight attorneys to come closer to the green wagon. "We say it's all right for the prosecution to ask those questions. That rule is correct, as we understand it–" waving down an interruption from Thurmond "– so we're letting all of this man's testimony stand." He leaned down to the two recorders. "You two getting this?"

"Yes, sir," said Pemberton.

As he retrieved his pie from Pemberton, Dan asked, "Did you hear everything all right?"

Pemberton said, "It was a little noisy, so we might have missed some questions, but we both got the big one." He turned over a page in the notebook and read: "Question: 'Heard what?' Answer: 'George Ives said he was the Bamboo Chief that killed that traveler on the road!'"

"Thank you," Dan said, and added to himself, Thank God. He bit into the pie, congealed now after its long wait on the recorders' table, the crust thickened and hard, fat in grey lumps, but delicious. No conquering Roman emperor ever ate such a feast in celebration of his victory.

Thurmond threw his hands up. "All right, damn it. The defense rests." He yelled, "Let the record show the defense rests under protest. You're railroading an innocent man!" He bent over the table and watched the recorders write as fast as they could dip their pens. When they finished, he flung away from the table, nearly upsetting the ink. "You wait! You just wait till Sheriff Plummer gets here. He'll fix your wagon, but good."

A man near the crossed tongues, who craned his neck to see over the shoulders of the guards, yelled, "Quit your palavering! It's afternoon, already. This trial's about played out."

"Good work." Sanders beamed at him, and Bagg clapped him on the back.

"Thank you. But all I did was pull a thread."

"You pulled it hard enough to hang Ives with." Bagg's face was rosy.

"How did you know it was there in the first place?" Sanders kept an eye on the defense attorneys, now with their heads together.

"A little bird told me." A little sparrow of a woman. Martha McDowell. Silhouetted in shafts of dust-sparkled sunlight. She had braved her husband's wrath to meet him secretly, and without that he would not have defeated Pete Morton, or known this soaring lightness of joy, that he loved the law. Loved the law? The knowledge blindsided him, and he reeled from it. He had practiced law for six years and thought he hated it, so how did he love it now?

Trial work. He loved the hunt, the gamble of a trial. A criminal trial. He had never known such a thrill outside the hunt, away from the poker table, except in –

If it had not been for Martha McDowell's courage, he would not have known this joy, this love of the law. He loved Martha McDowell for her courage. God help him, he loved her.

❦

"Call Anton Holter!"

Dan barely noticed when Plaid Coat walked to the wagon. Love Martha McDowell? No. Never. A married woman, with children? It could not be. He was promised to return to New York. Grandfather. The family. Harriet Dean. Harriet, his reward for suffering through the fear, the grinding loneliness, the over-crowding. The jeers of the roughs. He dreamed of Harriet, their wedding night, her voluptuous body in his bed, his reward for bringing home the gold. She would not marry for love alone. Her father would never let her go to a man cloaked in poverty, with the taint of embezzlement and suicide thick about him. Father's legacy.

The Devil perched on his shoulder, whispered, If McDowell were out of the way – No! God no! He could not be David, coveting Bathsheba, arranging the death of Uriah the Hittite to get his wife. He had to leave. Tomorrow. Early. No, after the trial of Long John and Hilderman.

Fitch shouldered his way between the guards. "Damn cold in these mountains."

"Wasn't it cold on Pike's Peak?" A dog sat in hope by the witness wagon. Dan flung the rest of the pie to it, and the animal snapped it up. Dan's mind was still reeling. He didn't want to love her. He had not been searching for a woman, but discovered her, as Bill Fairweather discovered gold in Alder Gulch, accidentally. A woman he had never imagined, a woman of courage. He loved her. His body ached with it. He must not love her. She was married. Her husband stood behind Ives, shared a bottle with Gallagher. Dan's gorge rose, and he coughed.

"Yeah, cold enough to freeze your piss. Why the hell does God always put gold in mountains? He should put it in Florida. Or on the Platte." His jaws worked on a chaw. "Good work with that bastard Morton, by the way. How'd you know about that Bamboo Chief business?"

"A little bird told me." Martha, the little brown sparrow. Martha. God help him.

Bagg sidled over to them, rubbed his hands together. "This Norsky has got guts, standing up to Ives." He was referring to the man in the plaid coat, who stood in the witness wagon. "We'll see some fireworks now, all right."

"So what? I'd rather see Ives swing," Fitch grumbled.

Anton Holter spoke with a heavy Norwegian accent. He could not pronounce some English sounds, in his mouth a "j" was a "y," and a "th" became a "t."

When Judge Byam swore him in, he laid his hand on the Bible and said, "Yah, I do it."

"Very well. You may tell the jury what you know."

"I know it was George Ives what tried to kill me."

Thurmond bounded to his feet. "Damn it, you had your chance. You can't introduce another witness!" Before anyone could stop him, he clambered into the wagon and confronted Sanders, his fists cocked.

Sanders pivoted, met him with jutting chin, and put his hands in his coat pockets. "You opened the door! You introduced testimony about Ives's character! Your own witness testified Ives never so much as threatened another man's life. We have the right to rebut that testimony."

"I object!" Thurmond pointed a finger at the two recorders. "Damn it, be sure to get it into the record. This is unethical maneuvering."

"Unethical?" Fists bulging his pockets, Sanders stepped toward Thurmond. "You dare – ?"

A gun exploded, and both men leaped backwards, Thurmond nearly toppling over the sidewall, Sanders colliding with the witness. Judge Byam rang the cowbell and yelled for order. Smoke rose from one of Sanders's pockets. Slowly, he pulled his hands out and held them chest high. One hand held a smoking pistol. He stared down at the floor of the wagon.

Judge Wilson said, "Mr. Thurmond! Sit down, sir, and let us finish this trial."

Fitch laughed around the chaw in one cheek. "Sanders almost shot himself in the foot."

All this time, the big Norwegian stood in the wagon as if nothing, certainly not errant shots or lawyers screaming at each other, could faze him. When Judge Byam signaled to him to continue, Sanders repeated the question, and Holter launched into his account as if nothing had interrupted him. "I been here at the diggings, and was on my way to Bannack, not a coin to my name. Downstream, where those badlands are, you know? Yah, men come out of the rocks, and he point his pistol at me, and say have I got any money?"

"Who pointed the pistol, Mr. Holter? Can you show us?"

"Oh, ja, he's over there on the log."

Sanders said, "Let the record show that the witness has pointed out George Ives."

The two recorders bent over their papers, and while Sanders waited for them to finish, Dan heard a crunch of boots shuffling, a cough, a mumbled question and a whispered reply. Someone in the vicinity of the log swore. Dan did not look to see who.

"I say no, just a few greenbacks," said Holter. "He say, Show me. So I show him, they're from a bank in Minnesota. When he see them, he get awful mad. Say go away and don't come back without more money. Minnesota banks ain't no good in Alder Gulch. I lead my horse away, and something – I look back. Ives, he points his pistol at me. I run, and he shoots, but horse and I run fast. Lucky thing, his next ball go around my hat and blow it off. A good hat, too. The third shot, pistol don't go off good. I leave horse and hide in ditch, and they go away. Leave horse."

To himself Dan translated, the pistol misfired, they didn't steal his horse. Lucky Anton Holter.

"Was Ives alone?" Sanders asked.

"No. There was two, maybe three other men with him."

"Would you know them again?"

"Oh, yah, I think so."

"Do you see any of them now?"

Holter looked around the crowd. "I don't think so. I see one, maybe two, when I got up here, but they had business in some other place, I think. They're gone now."

Try as he would, Davis could not shake Holter's story. After the Norwegian bent his head to show everyone the furrow through his hair, Davis flapped his hands. "This witness is excused."

☙

One moment the sun's chandelier lighted the afternoon, and the next, as if someone had snuffed one of the candles, the light sank, and the cold deepened. The moon, in its three-quarter phase, appeared over the jagged northeastern peaks. Now came the moment of decision. Now they would know if it had all gone for nothing. Sanders paced back and forth, mumbling to himself. He would speak for the prosecution, and he scribbled with pencil on pages in a pocket notebook, while Bagg and Dan stood by. The crowd drifted about, muttering low, perhaps debating Ives's guilt or innocence.

"Here we go," said Fitch. "Now you all get to see if you've done any good. I'm going to check on the crowd."

Jacob murmured to Dan across the wagon tongues. "What next happens?"

"Damned if I know, Jacob. It's up to the jury – the juries – now."

Bagg chewed on his lower lip, nodded his agreement, said nothing.

Sanders broke off to join them, drew Dan off to the back of the witness wagon. Lowering his voice so no one could hear him, he murmured, "After we try Long John and Hilderman tomorrow, a few of us will meet in Kiskadden's upper room." He scratched under his jaw.

"I'll be there." Dan patted his breast pocket. Other men had notebooks, too, or memories, and stories like Holter's, like his own, the sum of the information would be piled high. But how high? He had a sense that they stood on top of a mountain, above a fog bank that hid its base, and they must descend through the fog to learn how high was the mountain.

"I'll be there," said Dan.

Someone from the crowd called out, "Make it snappy, boys. We don't want a lot of harangue. It's getting cold."

The crowd grew as word went to the saloons, the dance halls, the stores to say that the trial was coming to its head. Men came out to see the best show in town, the best show anywhere, because it was the chance to vote on a man's life. Dan, listening to the excited mumblings, wondered how many others thought of the Roman Coliseum, where the crowd voted thumbs up or thumbs down on a life.

Albert, towering over most men, had been watching the road. "Mista' Stark? That Morton fellow is headed downstream. He's got his bedroll and a pack mule."

"Morton? Good riddance." Dan smiled. "Thank you, Albert." As an afterthought, "See any sign of Sheriff Plummer?"

"No, sir. Morton, he ain't the first I've seen, sir. There's plenty of the roughs has pulled up stakes and is making tracks."

"That's good, Albert, but you don't have to call me sir. I was never in the Army."

"Yes, sir, Mista' Stark." Albert's slow drawl told Dan that Albert would do as he pleased. A free black didn't have to take suggestions from a white man.

~

The mountains cast long shadows over Nevada City, and matches rasped, flint scraped against steel, and candles and lanterns sprouted a hundred flickering lights. One of the guards brought kindling to the bonfire and took it away, flaming, to light the torches on the wagons. Listening to the crowd, Dan sensed a new seriousness. Men spoke in hushed voices as if in church, and when the judges climbed into the green wagon, they quieted at the cowbell's first ring.

Sanders bowed toward the defense. "Learned counsel for the defense may take precedence."

"Yeah?" said Thurmond. "Mighty generous of you. The defense always goes first." He climbed into the witness wagon, and raised both hands.

"Gentlemen, you've heard the prosecution's case. They say that George Ives murdered Nicholas Tbalt for the mules and $400 in gold dust. On what evidence? I ask you, what proof did they show that George Ives murdered anyone in such a cold-blooded way? I'll tell you what proof. The word of two men who, I say, killed that poor lad themselves. These same two liars – for that is just what they are – liars, these two perjured themselves in this court and before Almighty God. They made a pact with the Devil and his minions, the prosecution, and traded their own freedom for George Ives's life.

"Ah, but the prosecutors say that is not the only evidence. We must not forget the mule. They claim that the mule found on Mr. Ives's property was stolen, and because it was on Mr. Ives's ranch, it was in his possession, and therefore he stole it. There are a myriad ways the mule could have come there. She strayed there. She was put there, and not by George Ives.

"We live in dangerous times, gentlemen. The Federal government is waging war to take away freedom granted to us by the Constitution. They want to take away our property, tell us what we can and can't own, and they want to dictate how this

Territory shall come into the Union. They want to take away our freedom."

Behind Dan Albert stirred, a mere shifting of his feet as anyone might do who sought to be comfortable, but his rasping breath told Dan how he was holding in his anger.

"That's what's at stake here, boys. Our freedom. Not only Mr. Ives's life, but the freedom of every white man in the Territory. How do we know that? Look at the coat worn by the chief prosecutor. It's blue. Union Army blue. He's a servant of the Devil that wants to take away our freedom. He is the Devil that wants to take George Ives's life.

"Why? Because he had a run-in with Mr. Ives. You won't hear the story from him, and the prisoner is too much a gentleman to tell it, but I will tell it in the sacred cause of justice. The chief prosecutor was asleep at Rattlesnake Ranch one night, when my client came in. Mr. Ives was slightly intoxicated, and the learned prosecutor felt threatened, so he got the drop on Mr. Ives. If it hadn't been for the timely intervention of other men, he would have killed George Ives on the spot.

"No one saw the dastardly murder of Nicholas Tbalt. Even the two lying cowards, the only witnesses against my client, don't forget, they don't claim to have seen George Ives pull the trigger. Two wrongs do not make a right, gentlemen! Do not compound the evil of Nicholas Tbalt's murder with the murder of George Ives. I say to you, gentlemen, the prosecution has not proved beyond a reasonable doubt that George Ives killed that poor boy. Don't do the Devil's work for him. Set George Ives free!"

"Free George Ives! Free George Ives!" shouted the roughs, Ives's friends, and some of the other men in the crowd took up the chant until Dan thought the whole mob would seize Ives and strike off his chains there and then. Thurmond climbed out of the wagon and sat down by Ives.

While the judges ordered and cajoled the mob into silence, Sanders stood with bowed head, and when they were quiet enough for him to be heard, still Sanders stood as if looking at some papers in his hand, but whether he was truly looking at them or praying, Dan could not say.

McDowell patted Thurmond's back, and his congratulatory smile turned to a sneer as his gaze crossed Dan's. "Don't worry, George." McDowell spoke loud enough for Dan to hear. "We'll get you out of this yet."

Ives bent over to scratch inside his boot, as far down as he could reach.

Dan could see no worry on his countenance. Why not? Dan wondered. Did he believe that he could yet be freed? Was he so confident? And if so, why? Was Plummer at last on his way? Albert would have warned them. Or Williams would.

In the wagon, Sanders stood at attention. Peering between the wagons, Dan saw X Beidler straddling the ridgepole of a new small cabin. "Friends, gentlemen of the jury, and citizens." Sanders paused, and from the back of the crowd someone – Dan thought perhaps Johnny Gibbons – yelled, "Hey, Sanders, get on with it! We ain't got all night!"

Even so, Sanders let the silence lengthen. With unsteady torchlight flickering across his face, he looked a spectral figure. The recorders paused, and Pemberton blew on his fingers, and on the nib of the pen to keep it warm so the ink would not freeze.

"Oh, God," Bagg whispered to Dan. "He's petrified."

Just as someone might have shouted something, Sanders spoke in a quiet voice that nevertheless could be heard at the back of the crowd. "You have all heard that George Ives is innocent of Nicholas Tbalt's death. That he did not waylay this innocent young man peacefully riding homeward after concluding his business. That George Ives did not shoot young

Nicholas in the head as he knelt to pray. That he did not thereby deprive young Nicholas of the opportunity to cleanse his soul before he met his Maker.

"The defense says that George Ives is innocent, and God knows Mr. Ives is an honorable man."

They could lap up the sarcasm that dripped from his words. Dan recalled Marc Antony's speech in *Julius Caesar* about Caesar's murderer: Brutus is an honorable man.

"The defense says that we have not proved George Ives killed that dear boy, who never harbored a vengeful thought, who forgave the Indians who slaughtered his parents. The defense says that George Ives would not have killed Nicholas Tbalt because he is a man of good character. George Ives is an honorable man.

"They brought witnesses to swear to it. They brought George Brown, and Honest Whiskey Joe, and Pete Morton, among others, to swear that George Ives is an honorable man.

"You have heard other witnesses like Anton Holter, swear that George Ives robbed him, and attempted to murder him. You've heard how George Ives extorted money from men at gunpoint. He called them loans, but not one has he paid back. Not one. One man who asked for repayment was told to get lost or he'd be killed. The defense says that George Ives is innocent, because he did these deeds in fun. Armed robbery, extortion. Murder. All in fun. Good, clean fun. George Ives is an honorable man.

"We say that justice must be served. The souls of George Ives's victims cry out for justice. The soul of Nicholas Tbalt, whose body lies on that knoll, pleads for justice.

"We meet here in the gathering darkness and gloom of night, that justice shall balance her scales. I say to you, gentlemen, let us do our duty to Nicholas Tbalt and to ourselves.

"I call upon you to demonstrate that law and order shall exist, and the assassin, evil-doer and murderer, will be promptly punished.

"I call on you to bring in a verdict of 'Guilty.'"

Now the waiting. The twenty-four men of the advisory jury, surrounded by guards, went off to consider their verdict, accompanied by calls from Ives's friends: "Vote to free George, or you're dead." "Ives is innocent." Talk, low-voiced and intense, buzzed through the crowd, but Dan could get no sense of their feeling: Guilty or innocent?

Fitch returned and came to stand with the prosecutors. When Bagg and Dan praised his speech, Sanders only shook his head. "Thank you, but we won't know if it was good or not until the jury comes back. If they bring in a guilty verdict, it was good. If not…." His voice trailed off.

"How do you think they'll vote?" Fitch's jaws chomped at the tobacco, and Dan thought they worked faster now that the tension was building. So Fitch was nervous, too.

"You never can tell about juries," Bagg said. "They'll produce a guilty verdict because they think someone's eyes were set too close together."

"Or innocent because they like the shape of his head," Dan said.

"Myself," said Bagg, "I think the phrenologists are onto something. The bumps on a man's head are a certain indication of temperament and predisposition to commit crime."

"What do you suppose a phrenologist would make of Ives?" Dan didn't give a damn, phrenology was a lot of bunkum, but this discussion would pass a little time. His left hand throbbed, and the rifle, slung on his right shoulder, weighed him down. Jacob, who appeared to find safety with Albert, thrust his hands in his pockets, took them out again. Albert stood at ease, arms folded across his chest, a good soldier.

"Ah, now, there's a classic case." Bagg's eyes took on a kind of the missionary light, eager to convert his listeners. "We can't know about the phrenologist, but to me it seems obvious – "

Sanders interrupted. "Listen. I have an idea how to make the crowd accept the verdict of the advisory jury."

Dan exchanged a glance with Bagg. "Tell us."

Sanders opened his mouth, but a shout cut him off: "They're coming back!"

"What?" Bagg pulled out his pocket watch. "They were only out half an hour."

"Shit." Fitch spat a stream of yellowish tobacco juice that flew out a good ten feet. "So soon?"

Dan sucked in a deep breath, but the pulse in his throat only beat harder. He thought everyone could see it, and would know how frightened he was. He pulled his scarf higher. Sanders was pale.

The twenty-four jurors took their seats. Some turned up their coat collars against the chill, two or three rubbed their hands together as if to warm them. What had they done? Would there be freedom for the law-abiding? There could be no freedom without law and order. Freedom to go home with one's gold? To travel without fear of being robbed or murdered?

The crowd hushed. From the Music Hall sounded a rackety polka played on a piano and a fiddle that badly needed tuning. The cowbell's strident noise clashed with the music.

"Gentlemen of the jury," called Judge Byam, "do you have a verdict?"

A miner rose from the middle of the front bench.

Byam beckoned him forward. "Would you approach, please? I don't want to have to squint through the fire."

"We ain't unanimous, Judge," the miner called out.

Dan's stomach clenched. Under miners court rules a majority would carry the verdict, even with a formal jury. It didn't have to be unanimous, but was the minority opinion for a guilty verdict? Did the majority vote not guilty? God, no. Not that. Not that.

"What do you mean? You split?" Byam leaned so far over the wagon's sidewall that Judge Wilson grabbed hold of his coat to keep him from falling.

"Just that. We got ourselves a verdict, but we ain't unanimous."

"How? How did you split?"

"One of us says he won't vote. The other 23 say he is guilty."

Fitch let out an exultant Rebel yell that made Dan's ears buzz. "By God, Blue, we got him. We got the bastard!"

"No!" bellowed Thurmond, and the other defense attorneys jumped up, shouted their protests while McDowell and Gallagher shook their fists, and yelled, "You're dead!" and "Murderers!" But it seemed to Dan that other voices, cheering, were stronger. Or was it that he wished it so?

Judge Byam clanged the cowbell, and hollered for order.

Dan stayed quiet, wished he had grown a great mustache to hide the lunatic grin he was trying to suppress. He wanted no one to see what he was feeling. Fitch was right. They had done it! That split still meant, Guilty, by God! But how would the jury, the crowd, the mob jury, the so-called jury of the whole, vote? Guilty or not guilty? Everything came down to this, a great weight balanced on a pinpoint.

"It's not over yet," Bagg shifted from foot to foot. "Damn! If this were a real court ...." His voice trailed off.

Fitch rubbed the back of his neck. "I been listening to the boys. A lot of them ain't happy about hanging anybody. They'd rather banish Ives."

"Christ." Dan knew the others had the same thoughts. Banishment was meaningless. Memories would fade in time, and Ives would be seen here and there, and his charm would once again win men over, they would ask what the fuss had been about. There would be murders, and robberies, and Ives would just be more careful, more frightening to his cronies. A man who could kill in cold blood, who lacked the element in his makeup that enabled him to feel something for another human being, that man would ever consider his own convenience ahead of other people's lives.

Judge Byam asked each man on the advisory juries to state his verdict, and one by one they stood up and answered, "Guilty," like the tolling of a bell, and at each one, Ives's friends let out a sound like a growl, an occasional curse hushed by a guard or someone in the crowd. Dan, as intent as waiting for a deer, felt for the rifle stock, gripped it hard; it was solid, something to hold onto.

One man said, "Abstain." Ives's friends cheered him and Jim Williams and his crew of guards shut them up with leveled shotguns. Why had he voted that way? Dan determined to ask him, later.

The polling done, the crowd let out its pent-up tension, a steam kettle going off in cheers and boos and curses, and a man could not think, dammit, there was so much noise it was like to drown him. Dan tried to hear a sense of the crowd, which way the mob jury would vote, but he could not.

"Order!" shouted Judge Wilson. "Order!"

Sanders climbed into the green wagon, stood with the two judges. He held up his hand, and the crowd quieted, man by man. Dan's breath smoked in the moonlight. He thought he could hear the collective breathing of the crowd, and in that comparative quiet, Sanders's voice rang out: "I move that the jury of the whole accept the report of the advisory jury!"

As he spoke, Dan filled his lungs. He roared out, "I second the motion!" and Bagg immediately yelled, "Question!"

"No!" Thurmond, with Smith, Davis, and the others were all on their feet, all protesting, but Judge Byam shook the cowbell at them. "Sit down! You're out of order! You'll get your chance."

Smith called for adjournment, and Ives's friends took up the cry until Dan thought surely they would prevail. "Finish tomorrow," hollered a voice in the crowd – he thought maybe Gallagher – and the hairs prickled on the back of his neck. That would mean defeat. Certain, sure, defeat. Either Ives's friends would rescue him, or Plummer would at last appear, or men would change their minds, regret their guilty vote, take a new poll and free Ives, because the majority would return to their claims to save them from being jumped, and only those who held no claims, the roughs, would be present in force. They could not adjourn. They must finish tonight, one way or the other. Win or lose, it had to be tonight.

He bellowed at the top of his strength, "No! Finish tonight!"

Someone yelled out, "I ain't coming back tomorrow to listen to lawyers yap."

Amid the laughter, McDowell raised his middle finger to Dan, and shouted, "Adjourn! Adjourn!" and Gallagher and others took up the chant, but more men shouted them down: "Finish now! Finish now!"

Fitch hollered, "My boy is in his grave! Get this trial over with and let's get back to business!"

"No!" McDowell dodged through the small gap between guards, between the jury benches and the log. He charged the green wagon, hands outstretched, a man big enough to seize Sanders and drag him down to the ground. Dan leaped at him, grabbed for his arm, seized a fistful of grey coat. McDowell turned on Dan, kicked at his ankles, and his fist hammered once, twice, on Dan's left thumb. Through raging red pain, somehow Dan held on, and McDowell's fist hit at his face. He felt hands at his back, and thought they were after the rifle, and he couldn't hold on any longer, and then Bagg and Fitch had caught one of McDowell's arms, and Adriel Davis had caught the other, and the fight dissolved into pain stabbing at Dan with every heartbeat, and anger hot as flame pulsed in his eyes and only slowly cleared so that he could see, and hear the cowbell.

The guards seized McDowell, and hauled him back, behind the log.

Judge Byam rang the cowbell until one of the guards fired his shotgun into the air, and for a second or two, men were too busy ducking pellets. And then, silence.

Panting, gritting his teeth against the agony in his hand, Dan heard Albert murmur apologies, and shook his head. He could not speak for the eruptions from his stomach. Jacob held one hand under his elbow, and Dan was grateful for it.

Byam for once not yelling over the crowd's noise, called out, "We have a question, boys. All in favor of adopting the advisory jury's report as the verdict of the whole, say Aye."

Not a man moved, not a voice rose, and in that instant, Dan felt himself collapse inside, as if his bones could no longer support his flesh. They had lost, after all. All the work and the clever strategies, and the courage of witnesses like Anton Holter, had all come to —

"Aye!" The crowd roared, and the sound broke against the log buildings, rolled down the street, and swamped the dance music, the stomping of boots to the polka's beat.

"All opposed," Byam shouted, when he could be heard.

"Nay!" came so small a number of dissenting voices that Dan estimated there could not be more than a hundred votes out of more than a thousand that made up the crowd.

"Carried," bellowed Judge Byam.

Grouped around Ives, who looked disbelieving, his lawyers and friends looked stunned, like the wind had been knocked out of them; they had never expected this. They had believed he'd never be found guilty, he was too popular, or he'd be rescued, or Smith could manipulate the crowd into freeing him, or Sheriff Plummer would take jurisdiction. Behind him, McDowell glowered at Dan, and Gallagher's dark eyes glared out from under drawn brows. Each had Dan lined up in his sight, taking dead aim with their hatred.

Dan straightened, and the Spencer shifted against his back. Come ahead, he told them. Next time, I'll use it. His left hand hurt, but the color of the pain had faded to dull purple, and his stomach had settled. They had got Ives.

"Them boys sure do hate you," Fitch said.

"Sore losers." Dan managed a brief smile. "Can't play poker, either."

"We gotta talk about that." Raising his stump, Fitch rubbed the pinned sleeve across his face.

The advisory jurors rose and threaded their way between the guards, away from the court. Their job was done. "I gotta ask that one why he didn't vote guilty like the others." Fitch hurried to catch the man.

Bagg motioned to Dan to join him and Sanders at the green wagon.

Sanders crouched down to look over the sidewall. "You all right?" And when Dan lied against the aching throb in his hand, Sanders smiled as if he did not believe it. "You probably saved the trial when you jumped – McDowell, is it? You're no shrinking violet, but he's a big one." After a second or two, he added, "Anyway, I certainly thank you." Bagg spoke up with a question, and the prosecutors carried on a discussion about tactics to bring about a hanging, until Dan suggested Sanders invite the jury to vote on it. "Just make sure they're moved to vote our way."

"I'll do my best." Sanders rose to his feet.

The crowd shifted about, laughed at someone elbowing his way through the crowd, a small man who stood between two guards and held up both hands. "I got something to say!"

Wilson called out to him: "Say it, then, but be quick."

"Some of us don't see no need for hanging, Judge. It ain't right to kill a man, we all knows that, but two wrongs don't make a right, neither. Hanging Ives won't bring back the poor lad that got killed." He shuffled his feet, shrugged his shoulders. "I guess that's all I got to say."

Fitch, returned from his talk with the juror, muttered, "Christ! How many more of them feel that way?"

As if to answer him, another miner demanded to be heard. "He's right!" The new man clutched the rags of a brown coat about him. "Now that Ives has been caught and everyone knows him for what he is, he won't get away with nothing like that again. We'll be on our guard, so it don't serve nothing to hang him."

Cheers and boos followed them, the judges rang order into the crowd, and Sanders, head bowed, waited for quiet. His hat brim, with insignia of a high-ranking Union officer, hid his face until he looked up, and his light tenor voice split the night with its call, "Listen!"

The crowd settled back amid the yellow candle lights and lanterns, that glowed in the dark like the black cats' eyes, and prepared to listen.

"Twenty-three men, good and true, after hearing overwhelming evidence, have returned a verdict that George Ives, with malice aforethought, murdered Nicholas Tbalt in cold blood."

As he spoke, Dan listened to the silence, hoping he could gauge the crowd's opinion, and he heard again how Nick's body was found, and how "there were two bullet holes in the brain, and marks on neck and body, of a lariat that the murderer had used to drag the body from the road, and pieces of sage-brush spasmodically clasped in his hands, showing that he was dragged to the place of concealment, in a semi-conscious condition." Beside Dan, Fitch drew out a large handkerchief and blew his nose. He was not the only one. From here and there came the sounds of noses blown, coughing and spitting, but Sanders continued, his voice vibrating with emotion, but as inexorable as a steam engine.

"I doubt, gentlemen, if you search the annals of crime you can find a parallel case, or one that will equal this in bloodthirsty ferocity and wantonness. We must set such an example of stern justice, that there will not, very soon, be a repetition of this act."

In his pocketbook, Dan carried a dozen or two similar wanton acts described by witnesses, and he had the names of men who had not declared their intention of going home before they were missed. He caught the vile phrase that echoed against the walls of his mind: "damned Dutchman." And then Sanders likened George Ives to the wolf that devours the defenseless lamb, and a low growl from the darkness answered him.

Sanders called out, "Wait! Men, wait!"

Fitch muttered, "Wait for what? We oughta just string the son of a bitch up."

Bagg hissed at him to shut his mouth, and Sanders's voice rose: "These are the facts, men, they are all true, as you know. The jury has heard all the evidence, what shall we do?" And some of the crowd called out, "Hang him! Hang him! String him up!" while others cried, "No! Let him go! Let him go!"

Sanders went on, relentless as fire, "The Bible, that Holy Book, says: 'Whosoever sheddeth man's blood, by man shall his blood also be shed.' Let us proceed according to the Scripture." He paused, and Dan heard the crowd breathing in the dark. "In that light, I move that George Ives forthwith be hanged by the neck until he is dead!"

Through a roar from the crowd Dan heard Sanders finish: "And may God have mercy on George Ives's soul."

Byam called for a second to the motion, and Fitch hollered, "Second!"

Dan dared McDowell and Gallagher, and all Ives's other friends, and his attorneys, to make a move, any move now against Sanders, because he was ready, one-handed or not, and he would bring the rifle around, lever a shell into the breech, and cock it. And shoot.

"Question," yelled Bagg, and Judge Byam shouted, "Everyone in favor of hanging George Ives, say so."

"Aye!" The massive cheer roared from hundreds of throats. With a whoop, Fitch pounded Dan on the back. "Yeehoo! Got 'im, Blue, we got that murdering bastard."

"Yes. Yes, we did." Dan shook Bagg's hand, repeated to himself that Ives would hang. The murdering son of a bitch would hang. Ives would die for killing Nick. But instead of feeling satisfied, he felt empty because they were not done, there was so much more to do, and he carried the proof in his breast pocket. The work was just begun.

"Why did that one juror vote not guilty?"

"He said, if the question was whether Ives was a road agent, he'd have voted yes. He just didn't think you-all proved he'd killed Nick." Fitch stared into the night, his face bleak. "I sure as hell hope Ives is the real killer."

⁓

The "no" vote was a pale protest. If Dan could have felt sorry for the defense, he might have done so now. Davis sank down onto the log and stared at nothing, Smith put his face in his hands and wept, and Thurmond howled incoherent threats. Gallagher bellowed, "We'll get you for this!" McDowell shouted, "You goddam sons of bitches, you're dead, you hear? Dead!"

Discordant and off-key, tin dance music mocked them with jaunty rhythms inviting them all to dance on George Ives's grave. But no one would dance tonight, Dan thought, except Ives, in his own Danse Macabre at the end of a rope.

Judge Byam sent the two sheriffs off to find a place for the hanging. And Ives asked to speak to Sanders. "A condemned man has the right to a last request."

Sanders motioned to him to come ahead. Ives climbed into the wagon and seized Sanders's hand. To Dan's total disbelief, the condemned man claimed a sort of kinship with Sanders, as one "perfect gentleman" to another, though he had been "somewhat wild." Pleading his mother and sisters in the States, he asked Sanders, as a favor, to put off his execution until morning so he could write them a letter and make a will. He gave his word of honor not to escape or allow his friends to rescue him. "If the situation were reversed I'd do it for you."

"Jesus Christ." Dan thought that never in the literature of trials had he heard such effrontery.

Sanders hesitated.

No! Dan wanted to shout, but his throat closed up. Sanders couldn't do it. He damn well could not let Ives have until morning on the basis of his word, the word of honor from a man without honor. A convicted murderer. Dan felt the crowd, a thousand people, waiting, the moment teetering on an unmade decision.

"Hey, Sanders," a voice boomed out, "ask him how much time he gave the Dutchman!"

The moment splintered into laughter. The voice came from X Beidler, straddling the ridgepole of a nearby cabin, his shotgun across his thighs.

∽

The two sheriffs returned, and reported to a disgusted Judge Byam that they had not been able to find a tree big enough to hang a man.

"Bull." Judge Wilson pointed toward a cabin under construction by the Music Hall. "What's wrong with that?

Looks to me, we can get a good drop there." The walls were up, and the trusses, but the roof had yet to be put on.

"That'll do," Sheriff Hereford said. "Let's get to it."

With some help, the sheriffs set to work while guards watched over Ives and his friends as they came to shake his hand, and bid him good-bye. Ives said, "It's all right, I had a good run." Tough men, weeping, made obscene gestures and rumbled threats at the prosecutors: "You bastards ain't got long to live," "Make your will, Sanders," "Bagg, you son of a bitch, be careful a shaft don't fall on you," "You're a dead man, Stark." Some could barely speak through their tears.

Jacob said, "You do not fear them?"

"Of course I do." A muscle quivered in Dan's inner thigh, and he could not stop it.

Pemberton stoppered his ink bottle and wrapped the pen in a stained handkerchief. His job was nearly done, and now he could listen to conversations and join in if he wished, without having to listen to the trial. He seemed to have something he wanted to say to Dan.

"A great pity." Jacob polished his spectacles on his sleeve and hooked the wire rims over his ears. "It is all a great pity."

"Fuck that," Fitch growled. "Who wept for Nick? Who pleaded for Nick's life when he died alone in the cold? The pity is that we've let this go on so long. My boy wouldn't have died if we'd had the balls to put a stop to it months ago." He rubbed the stump of his arm against his hand. "I'll get even, though." Dan wondered what else, after seeing Ives hang, would be getting even. "When Byam auctions Ives's ranch, I'll be first in line."

Speechless, Dan gaped at him, and Pemberton muttered. "Good God."

"Well, why not?" Fitch blew his nose on his fingers. "A man's gotta look out for himself in this world. No one else will. They're going to sell the ranch anyway, and pay the costs of the trial, so I'll help everyone – myself included – by buying it." He scowled at Dan. "Hell, Blue, I don't see you waiving your fee so the mother and sisters can inherit more." The stump of his arm made a circle. "Someday I'll be the richest man in the Territory." With that, he walked over to join Jim Williams, who stood with an extra guard around Ives.

Pemberton put the notebook in his pocket. His eyes were red-rimmed, and the skin beneath them was dark and puffy. "I was so sure that Ives could not have committed murder. Any murder."

Dan could think of nothing to say to help the younger man, but Pemberton appeared not to notice. "The worst of it is, I still quite like him." He turned the bottle of ink around and around. "I'm shocked to find that my liking or disliking a man does not prove his character. I shall have to be on guard against my feelings for the rest of my life."

Some ink dribbled out of the bottle. Dan reached for it and tilted Pemberton's hand so the stopper was upright. He admired the young man's courage in admitting he'd been wrong about Ives. Sensing that Pemberton waited for something, perhaps some reassurance, Dan looked into his own life and found words. "We've all been fooled by a plausible liar." Father's eyes brightest, his air of prosperity growing as the firm's assets – clients' assets – shrank and disappeared in the smoke of one bullet.

Dan shivered. The stars twinkled, as though a man were not about to die, and the moon shone down on the Gulch, laid the shadow of the noose across the ground.

The two sheriffs stood in front of Ives. "We're ready for you now."

Ives rose to his feet. "If it has to be, I guess we'd better get it over with." He turned so they could tie his hands behind him, but stopped. "I don't want to die with my boots on."

"OK, fair enough," said Williams. "You can sit down again." He called out, "Bring the man some moccasins."

Two other guards removed his boots and slipped the moccasins onto his feet. "Ready," Ives said. Guards helped him stand, and walked him to the cabin inside a solid square of armed men. The judges followed, with the prosecutors. A large packing crate stood beneath the rope.

Sheriff Hereford placed the noose around Ives's neck, and adjusted the long knot behind his left ear. He and the sheriff of Junction boosted Ives onto the box.

Ives stood on the box, with armed guards around it, facing outwards. Somewhere among the crowd a woman's shriek was cut off as if by a hand over her mouth. Smith and Thurmond sobbed. Tears ran down Alex Davis's face. A squabble broke out: "Don't hang him!" "Hang him!" "Banish him!" "Hang him!"

"You're murdering an innocent man," Gallagher shouted. "Nothing Ives ever did compares to this."

"Do you have any last words?" called Judge Byam.

"Yeah, someone put my boots back on. My feet are cold."

Yet another delay, thought Dan. How many more could he come up with? This or that little errand to gain precious minutes to live, to feel the breath come and go from his body, his heart beating in his chest. It did not matter about his feet. He would be entirely cold soon, yet someone put his boots on while he teetered on the box.

Sam McDowell stood as near as the guards allowed. Every so often he swiped his sleeve across his nose and eyes. Jack Gallagher's curses flowed in a scorching stream of anger at Dan, Sanders, Bagg, and everyone else responsible for Ives's death.

The guards brought their guns level and thumbed back the hammers. The ratcheting clicks warned everyone into silence. Running feet pattered down the boardwalk, and the music stopped. Dan heard nothing but people breathing. Weeping. Ives looked across Alder Creek, as if he had climbed up for a view of the mountains whose snow-capped peaks gleamed in the moonrise.

"Do you have any last words?"

Ives, gazing over their heads at the shining mountains, said, "I am innocent of this crime. Aleck Carter killed the Dutchman."

"Men, do your duty," said Judge Byam.

The two sheriffs, one on either end of the crate, jerked it out from under Ives, and he dropped, with a crack like a dry branch snapping underfoot. The body bounced, and the feet kicked out, and his head, his neck broken, flopped over. The rope cut into his flesh and severed the jugular vein. Blood spurted out and a few drops spattered on Dan's coat and on his face. His stomach jumped, and he saved himself from vomiting by clenching his teeth and swallowing the thin bile as fast as he could. He would not have anyone see him weak. His memory filled with that other violent death – the side of Father's head blown out, shards of his skull embedded in the leather chair, and his brains sliming the gold-embossed law books behind. Ives's swollen, bug-eyed face turned to him, away from him, as the body pivoted. Dan fished out his handkerchief and wiped his face.

"You won't live to the New Year, Stark." The threat came from under the sobs and curses. Gallagher's voice. Albert moved closer; Dan felt the big Negro's chest brush his coat. Jacob stood at his left, with a guard at his right. Dan wanted to tell them to move away, give him room to swing the rifle, but his voice had stuck.

The corpse swung on an ever shortening arc. Just a few minutes ago, there had been a man. Now it was clay, swaying, turning, freezing in the cold. Ives would not worry about his feet now.

There should have been a preacher, Dan thought. But if there were one in the Gulch, he had not come forward to help Ives adjust his soul to its sudden and unexpected journey, to help him approach his Maker. Perhaps someone prayed for him, but no one had offered to pray with him. Nor had he asked for a prayer any more than he had whimpered, or begged, or whined. He had only cared that his feet were cold. Within minutes of death George Ives had thought of his feet, but not his soul.

Fitch conferred with Jim Williams, and after a few minutes, he joined Dan, who wiped Ives's blood off his face, brushed at the drops of Ives's blood on his coat. "A few of us are going after Carter," he said.

"Tonight?" Dan shivered.

"Tonight. Want to come along?"

Dan shook his head. "We have work to do in Virginia." But as Fitch said, "Suit yourself," and walked away, Dan knew he had not refused because of the meeting he'd promised to attend. He needed help to reset the bone in his hand. He needed a woman's smile warm in mellow lamplight. He had to see her.

The need dried his tongue and clove it to the roof of his mouth. Telling himself that she deserved to know how her testimony had helped the outcome, how it had given him the certainty to break down the witness, he knew even as he said it to himself, that was a lie. He must see her.

But how?

McDowell and Gallagher would kill him, if they could.

He had to see her.

჻

In Virginia City, curses and shouts overlaid the usual night noises, laughter and fiddle tunes and the stomp of booted feet dancing. "Get the Goddam stranglers." "The bastard stranglers as murdered poor George Ives." "He never done no harm to nobody." "They'll pay for this, those strangling bastards." "By God, Sanders won't live to see the New Year." "That pansy Stark won't see Christmas." "Bagg's a dead'un."

Bravado. Below the anger sounded a jangling note of fear like one violin out of tune in an orchestra. Why were they not out here if they wanted him dead? Him and Sanders and Bagg? The group that had followed from Nevada melted away into the saloons. Why did they not aim their guns and pistols from the windows, or hide in the dark to kill? Damn it all, he and his small group would have had no chance.

He smelled pastry as they walked past the City Bakery and his stomach growled. Dan said, "God, I'm hungry. We'll stop at the Eatery." She might be there. McDowell was still in Nevada with Gallagher.

She sat at the rear table, facing the door, bent over a book and a slate. The door creaking brought her head up with wide, fearful eyes until she recognized him and a smile shone across her face. She had chalk dust on her nose. As he unslung the rifle he saw other people, Tabby Rose cutting up meat with a cleaver, Mrs. Hudson rising from beside Mrs. McDowell, Dotty and Timothy playing draughts by the left wall.

"How do you do, Mrs. McDowell?" What a damned formal greeting when his need pulsed through his veins. He could not use her given name, could not call her Martha.

"Mr. Stark." At the sight of his face her smile was snuffed like a candle. "Have you finished?"

The room was warm. The muscles in Dan's chest relaxed, and he took what he thought might be his first deep breath since Nick's body was found. "Yes. Ives was found guilty, and he is hanged." Jacob helped him with his coat, and Dan greeted her children, and put a leg over the bench. He would at least sit where he could look at her and talk to her.

"Oh, no," Mrs. Hudson said. "Such a pity." Tears gathered in her eyes.

God damn it, Dan said to himself. Women. Did she think he wanted to be an executioner? Or that the sheriffs had relished their dreadful task? Or that anyone could enjoy Ives's death struggles, or his blood on one's face? Christ almighty! Dan wanted to tell her to save her tears for those who deserved them, but he held his peace.

"What are you-all weeping for?" Fitch asked. "We strung him up fair and square."

A clatter startled them all. Tabby had dropped the cleaver onto the table and stood, panting as if from running; her eyes widened and looked into unseen horrors with such terror Dan had never seen on another human face. Even Ives had looked into death as into a shaving mirror.

Albert set Fitch aside and wrapped Tabby in his arms. She hid her face against his chest, her arms folded like an injured bird's wings. Her shaking subsided as he murmured to her.

"Hey!" Fitch's protest died when Albert raised his head and looked at him, hard, not at all like a slave to the Massa, but a man keeping safe his own woman.

"She fears a lynching," Albert said.

Oh, for Christ's sake, Dan said to himself. How many times would he have to explain it? How many others would not see the difference between a just punishment after trial and murder?

Before Dan could speak, Jacob said, "In Old Country is pogrom." He was talking to Tabby and Albert, and Dan felt excluded somehow, outside the intimate circle of people who suffered from riders in the night carrying destruction on their saddles just because they were a different color, a different religion. Because they were Other. "Pogrom," Jacob repeated. "Cossacks come, burn our barns, burn our houses, lynch our rabbi. Tonight, not lynching. This Ives, he murder boy. He hang."

"Did we lynch Ives, Albert?" Dan asked.

"No, sir, Mista' Stark."

Dan hoped he kept his voice to free of the irritation he felt, because the youngsters were absorbing every word. "Ives had ample opportunity to provide a defense. He had five lawyers, and they could not do it. He was found guilty by three juries, and his punishment was just."

Mrs. Hudson said, "But it's such a waste. Two young men dead, when they could both be living their lives to some good purpose. It's just such a waste."

"Yes. No doubt about that. But Ives made his choice," said Dan. "Rather than let Nick ride home, he killed Nick and stole the mules and the gold."

"I don't hold with killing," said Mrs. Hudson. "Thee may think thee has a righteous cause, but no cause is righteous when there's killing in it."

Dan gripped his thigh with his right hand under the table to remind himself to hold his temper. "Do you really think we could have persuaded Ives out of his ways? If that were so, Nick could have talked Ives out of killing him. We are dealing with murderers who have no conscience, and we have no other recourse." She would not yield, he understood that as clearly as he knew that now it was kill or be killed for him and all of Nick's friends. All the righteous, as she had said.

Tabby tipped her head back so she could look into Albert's eyes. "Yeah," the black man said. "It's like Mr. Stark say. Ives, he could have chose different, only he wanted the gold and them mules. Do you think I'd stay for a lynchin'?"

"No," she whispered, and stepped back from him, stooped and picked up the cleaver.

"Tabby," Dan said, "I did not like doing it." He recalled a newspaper drawing he had seen, of cloaked white men stringing up a Negro by torchlight. An artist's fancy, no doubt, but it had seemed real. He shuddered. God help them.

"No, sir." But she would not meet his eyes.

The others were sitting down, and Mrs. Hudson fetched them their dinners, and the men all gave their pokes to Albert to pay for the meals, and under cover of the hustle and bustle, she smiled at him. "How are you?" she asked. And Dan knew she didn't only mean his broken thumb. He said, "I think perhaps you might look at it again."

Alarm wiped the happiness from her face, but before she could ask a question Dan might have to lie to, Albert startled everyone by speaking in company with whites.

"Mista' Stark is the hero of the hour. He done got the truth out of a witness name of Pete Morton." And though Dan protested that Sanders and Bagg had done far more, Albert went on to tell about the Bamboo Chief.

Martha McDowell covered a squeak with a cough as if chalk dust had lodged in her throat. She asked him a silent question that he answered with a tiny nod and half a smile, and her pride glowed for Dan so that for the first time in weeks he felt warmth under his breastbone. Maybe he'd postpone going home until after the meeting with Sanders and the others.

"How did thee know?" asked Mrs. Hudson.

Dan smiled at Mrs. McDowell. "A little bird told me."

Part II: Vigilantes Rise

❧

6: Alder Gulch: Virginia City

Boone Helm. The hulking figure waited for Dan and Jacob to cross Wallace. When Dan saw him through a break in the traffic, between a man on horseback and a dray, Helm leered and tipped a whiskey bottle to his lips. There was no place to duck into without showing the yellow feather to the whole town. Jacob sucked in his breath. Helm stepped into their path. His beard was long and matted, and as they came nearer, Dan saw things moving among the hairs. Helm's lips, red and moist as a wound, mouthed at him. "I'm the meanest son of a bitch west of the Mississippi, my mammy was a polecat, my daddy was a grizzly bear, and I ain't afraid of no man." Then the raspy voice dropped a couple of notches, the wink. "I eats people, you know. You want to know what human meat tastes like? Sort of sweet. Oh, you watch out for me, strangler. You watch out. I'll have your liver on a spit, I will. Or maybe your balls."

He laughed while Dan wished he could kill him on the spot, and Jacob trembled beside him. He had been angry at men before in his life, but never had murder seemed so reasonable a means of dealing with an enemy. Dan heard himself say, "Out of our way, Helm." And to his great surprise, Helm stood aside with a bow that almost toppled him, and his cackle of a laugh followed Dan and Jacob up Jackson Street. The two men were nearly to their cabin before Dan's fury gave way to a great relief that left him shaky inside: He had not been forced, after all, to see if he could murder Boone Helm.

❧

Imitating a man looking to buy a book, Dan browsed along the open shelves of D. W. Tilton's Stationers. He wished that Tilton had a book to buy. He had never thought how he'd miss bookstores until he came to a place where a book, however dull, however badly written, would be snapped up for an exorbitant price almost before it was unpacked. The lack of books made his small cache valuable. Like Lydia Hudson, he could rent out his books as she rented her wrinkled newspapers, sheet by sheet. He could do that, too, tear the books apart and rent them by the page, or the signature, refusing to give out a later one until the earlier one came back. Some people's books vanished page by page into the maw of starving readers. Still, he could make good money. A fat novel, *Rob Roy* for instance, would earn well. He could charge an ounce of dust a month. People would be happy to pay it just for something to read, though it was highway robbery.

Highway robbery. Dan slipped out the back door of Tilton's, into the hallway to the stairs that led to Kiskadden's second floor. He thought, highway robbery. That's why we meet tonight. Because hanging George Ives had not meant the end of robbery and murder in the Gulch. It had only revealed the discovery of a wild animal's kill, stinking and rotten, that the creature intended to retrieve later.

The big upper room was lighted by a single candle burning on a table near the unlighted stove. Struck by their stillness, save for men's quick breathing, Dan whispered, too, as his feet felt their way to the other men. "Cold in here."

A rich voice answered, "We don't dare start a fire. Someone outside might wonder why."

Dan stood the rifle on the floor and took a chair. Some of the men around the table surprised him. Besides Sanders, an abolitionist like himself, there was Paris Pfouts, the outspoken Secesh. John Creighton was a leader of the Catholics in Virginia, but Pfouts and Sanders were Masons, and Dan recalled that the Order had a reputation for being anti-Catholic. Or maybe the Catholics were anti-Mason. Merchants like Nye, Creighton, and John Lott from Nevada, who had spoken out against trying Ives in Virginia. A clerk from one of the shops, who knew of the Vigilantes in San Francisco and how they worked. War veterans with the rank of Captain, Major, Colonel – from both sides. Noncombatants like himself.

What could this small number hope to do against a conspiracy of fierce men like Stinson and Gallagher, and the crowd of roughs like Helm and McDowell who surrounded them? He caressed the barrel of the rifle standing in the crook of his elbow.

"Do you carry that thing everywhere?" one asked.

"Yes." Dan wiped sweat from his forehead. "It seems a sensible precaution these days." He added, "I don't want it stolen. It's the only Spencer repeating rifle in five hundred miles."

Another man spoke with a flat twang. "You carry the rifle, Sanders carries pistols in his pockets. Creighton keeps a loaded shotgun under the counter."

"Just last night, I nearly had to use it against another man," said Creighton.

Sanders's breath came broken into a soundless wheezing, and Dan realized that he had not heard Sanders laugh before. "Fellow came into Creighton's store with the firm intention of shooting me, but Creighton persuaded him otherwise."

"I and one or two others," Creighton said. "It's no laughing matter. Damn it, this must not be allowed to continue."

"Shhh," someone said. "Softly, softly."

"How can we possibly succeed?" whispered one of the men.

"We can, and we must." Dan surprised himself by speaking. "Consider the alternative. Do we go on as we are and prove ourselves cowards?" The fingers of his left hand played with his coat buttons. "The trial of George Ives has showed us how much there is to do. Men talked, in whispers, and a few in open testimony, and now we know how widespread the rule of crime is."

"And how difficult it will be to root out." Lott's sharp voice cut into the darkness and brought anxious shushing noises from one or two others. "Yet we must. We have no choice."

"Either we root out crime, or we die and this community dies with us."

Dan was not sure who spoke, but the word community made him think of Martha McDowell. Maybe he could not have her, but he could help her by making this place safe to rear her children. Safe for her. "We must make it safe for those who cannot act for themselves. For families."

"Amen," said Sanders, whose wife and small sons awaited him in Bannack.

∽

How to begin?

A Vigilance Committee, Dan had always thought, was fearless, though secret, but he had never stopped to think that its secrecy was bred in fear. We're afraid, he said to himself. Frightened of meeting sudden death. Terrified that Nick's end will be ours. Yesterday Sanders was almost killed, and I faced down Boone Helm. So far from being discouraged by the death of Ives, his faction seemed angrier, more bent on getting even.

Aside from the clerk from California, they had no experience in this. They made it up, and everything was subject to discussion, even argument, because each man had his independent ideas. Through the long cold evening hours they talked about the structure of the group, ground rules. They agreed the clerk would write the bye-laws and bring them to the next meeting.

"We need an oath," said Pfouts. "This is such a dangerous undertaking, we must bind ourselves to the task in the sternest possible way." In the candlelight his dark eyes had a hawk's ferocious glare.

"Agreed." Sanders thought for a moment, while the others waited. "We here tonight pledge our sacred honor to be true to the principles of law and order and justice and to be true to each other, never to violate the sacred trust we give each other or the trust we seek to deserve from the good citizens of this region. So help us God."

"So help us God." Dan raised his right hand as the others raised theirs. He felt disconnected, that the oath was wildly out of keeping with the reality, fewer than ten men who sat in a dark room. Almost, he thought, like small boys in a clubhouse, remembering the hollow in the shrubberies, the little cut on his thumb, bloody prints on a stone. Except that the rifle leaning against his arm comforted him.

Having taken the oath, he was struck by a realization: He was a Vigilante. He, who had always taken for granted the supremacy of the law, the rightness of those in power, because power was granted by the people.

Again that strange disconnected sensation, as the discussion moved to the mundane – how to pay for their efforts because men would have to take time from their businesses, their jobs. They would have to pledge their own funds, dun the honest citizens. Only fair, said one, impatient because some objected to soliciting money. We're taking the greatest risks. Besides, added another man, everyone in the Gulch should pay something for their safety, as they do in civilized places. A kind of minimal taxation.

Agreed.

Who would be members? They would be democratic, would exclude no one who was not a criminal, or suspected of being one.

Agreed.

Deciding guilt or innocence could be as unwieldy as the jury of the whole, so they established an Executive Committee composed of one representative from each mining district, and four from Virginia, in addition to their elected officers.

Dan counted on his fingers. "If the officers are a president, secretary, treasurer and prosecutor, that would make fifteen as I count it."

"We won't need a secretary," Lott said. "We will keep no written records. None at all."

A pause followed, and Dan felt a chill in the pit of his stomach. Paper could be lost, misplaced, stolen. It was safer that way, but it would leave them nothing to defend themselves with, should it ever become necessary. Yet he joined his voice to the others: Agreed.

Lott said, "The exception must be a record of collections and disbursements. We must be accurate in our accounting of funds."

Agreed.

The Major, or perhaps Sanders, who outranked him as a military man, put in that the whole organization, as it grew, should have a structure also. They debated for a time, until Pfouts called for the question and they voted on a quasi-military structure: companies of a hundred men, one from each mining district, each company to elect its own commander.

All evening, Dan thought, they avoided the crux of the matter, their purpose. However they cloaked it in fancy words and rounded phrases, they were talking about men trying other men in secret and hanging them. "How do we find the guilty men? How do we make sure of their guilt? And what punishments do we administer?"

"We'll need a group to ferret out the guilty ones," Sanders said. "Someone to take what evidence we have and investigate."

"A ferreting committee," said one, who leaned against the back of his chair, his face in shadow, outside the circle of candlelight.

"Exactly," Creighton said. "Because we are trying men in secret, we must be absolutely certain of their guilt."

Dan thought he detected a grim humor when Sanders said, "Agreed. They must be guilty beyond a reasonable doubt."

Dan leaned his cheek on the rifle's cold steel barrel. "We are talking about trying men in secret and hanging them. Even though our case against Ives was thin, I am convinced we did the right thing. I always will be." He paused to marshal his thoughts, his eyes fastened on Sanders. "Ives was found guilty and sentenced to hang by the men themselves. He had as much due process as we were capable of. He faced his accusers, he was represented by counsel, the verdict was delivered by no less than three juries of his peers. We protected his Constitutional rights as well as we were able."

"Yes." Sanders held Dan's gaze as if he understood that Dan was saying, be careful, we're treading dangerous ground. "Considering that the Constitution failed us."

"Failed us?" That Dan had not expected. "How?"

"Failed us. Because the Constitution – either one," he said with a nod to Pfouts and the other Secessionists, "does not apply here, it cannot protect us. Despite the Ives trial, we still have no law. We invoked the Common Law for that occasion only. We are left with the miners court rules and the moral influence of the Ten Commandments. And where men flout the miners court and are blind and deaf to the Commandments, there is nothing. We have to put all that in place."

For the first time, Dan had heard someone speak of the tasks that remained for them once they had broken the power of the criminals. "We cannot do it while ruffians rule."

"Precisely. How many more times can we assemble a jury? How many more times will the miners agree to take time off from their claims to attend a trial? Had we not finished in three days, we would have had no jury but the roughs. And who can blame them? No work can be done with six feet of snow on the ground. They must work hard now, while they can."

"That means," said another man, "that if we try men in open court, the juries will be made up of the roughs themselves."

"You are uncomfortable with the idea of a secret tribunal, aren't you?" Sanders asked.

"Yes," Dan said. "I understand what you're saying, and I agree. You know I do. But it's one thing to have a majority in the miners court and quite another to have a majority in a secret tribunal. There is more danger of a miscarriage of justice."

"Yes," said Creighton and Sanders almost together. "We're all uncomfortable with this," Sanders added, "but consider the alternative."

The alternative was the rifle resting against his right arm, and even it was no protection against the odd random shot meant for another target, or the purposeful bullet from a window or a shadowed doorway. Having helped to prosecute Ives, he had made bad enemies who would kill him if they could. Remembering Boone Helm's promise to eat his balls, Dan had no doubt.

"We will carefully consider all the evidence available to us," said Creighton. "If we need more evidence to be certain beyond a reasonable doubt, we will wait until we have it."

Agreed.

"We shall administer only one punishment," Sanders said, paused. "Death."

Dan joined his voice in the combined whisper like a stirring of the air: "Agreed."

∽

Martha lived on tiptoe, afraid almost to think wrong for fear McDowell would know it and explode with that awful battle-rage of his. Since George Ives was hung, McDowell went around like a thundercloud that you never knew for sure where the lightning would come from. He booted Canary in the ribs for nothing more than jumping up like always to say how do. Now when he saw McDowell the dog put his tail between his legs and slunk away. Plumb made her sick, because how the dog acted was how she and the young'uns felt. Like they had so much love for him that he'd just kicked away. None of them, especially the young'uns, had ever done nothing but love him.

Such willing young'uns, they were, too. Potato peelings dropped into the slop bucket set between her and Dotty, and she smiled at the child, who sat facing her by the table. They had a kind of contest, who could peel the most potatoes the fastest, and the child was almost winning. Martha slowed her knife just a tiny bit, and sure enough, Dotty finished first. The young'un sat back with a satisfied smiled on her face.

"That's the first time I won, Mam. I done better'n you."

"You sure did." Martha cut the potatoes into chunks before she dropped them in the pan of cold water. "You had the bigger tater that time, too." It wasn't strict truth, but she figured young'uns needed encouragement to do their best, not just thumping and scolding. Sometimes they needed that, too, but not when you wanted them to learn something from you besides thumping and scolding.

Dotty was looking tired, so Martha said, "I could use some tea. What about you?"

"Yes, Mam."

Martha raised an eyebrow.

"Oh." Sighing like life was just too hard, she got up. "You want me to make it."

Martha smiled to herself as she opened the trunk, pulled out the extra quilts her bones told her they'd be needing soon. Her was head upside down in the trunk when Dotty said, "Mam, I'm missing Mr. Stark something terrible. Do you think he'll ever come back to us?"

Her hands were on the dulcimer, but Martha pretended she was still looking for something so as she could hide the redness creeping into her face and give herself time to allow as how to she missed him, too, without the child reading anything into that. Dotty was plumb too smart for her sometimes. Holding the dulcimer like a baby, she sat with it across her lap. "Child, I'm afraid he won't be back on account of your Pap don't want him here." She plucked the dulcimer's strings and listened, tightened them. When the thrumming stopped, she'd know it was in tune. McDowell liked its music, too. She'd always been able to count on it gentling him, and these days he needed gentling.

Dotty said, "Mr. Stark helped hang that George Ives, didn't he?"

"Yes. They had them a trial over to Nevada, and most folks agreed George Ives done what Mr. Stark and them others said he did. So they hung him."

"Was George Ives a friend of Pap's?"

"Seems like. I don't know who all his friends are."

"I don't like Pap's friends. They're nasty."

The thrumming stopped. Martha took up the pick and let the fingers of her right hand roam over the strings while her left hand moved up and down the neck, stopping some strings at different places. The sweet sounds, like clear water flowing over colored pebbles, carried her into another place, where rolling hills flamed with red and yellow and gold, and the air smelled like flowers. She didn't know when the child set a cup of hot tea next to her, or got up to dance. A warm sun shone on Martha, from someplace inside her because her fingers had not forgotten. When she rested, she sipped some of the warm tea. Her fingertips resting on the sound box brought back the smell of the wood under her own Pap's plane and her breathless fear that she'd made the top too thick or too thin for the music in her heart, but it turned out just right. She played on, and the stream bubbled over blue stones, foamed around snags, down white falls, and she didn't hear footsteps approach the cabin. The stream rushed on into a pool, and quieted because ice at the sides was creeping out into the middle, and all the flow was under the surface of the water.

The door slammed open. Martha's hands clutched the instrument, and it twanged out a loud discord. Only Timmy. Her hands relaxed. She smiled at him, but nonetheless she tucked the dulcimer into the trunk and closed the lid. High time she cooked up dinner, anyway, and why were there tears on Dotty's face? She hugged the child.

"That was so beautiful, Mam," Dotty said.

"I'll teach you any time you want." She smoothed away the child's tears with a thumb.

"Mam, you'll never guess what's happened!" A smile spread all across Timmy's face, but he didn't say any more until he hung up his coat and set a pail of beer on the counter.

"Set that on the floor, if you don't mind." Martha went about fixing dinner. If she didn't press him, he'd tell her sooner.

He did as she asked and filled a dipper of beer for himself, gulped it down and dipped out more. "Boy, was I thirsty!" He swallowed more. "Mr. Dance offered me a job. I start right after New Year's."

The spoon slipped from Martha's hand. Tim swooped to catch it before it clattered on the floor.

"Oh, Lordy, no." Martha shook her head. "No." She pictured McDowell's rage, his big ready hand striking at Tim. "No. No, you mustn't. Your Pap, he'll —"

"He'll tell me I have to go on working the claim, Mam. He'll tell me to keep digging, go on freezing my ass in that icy water, and —" He stopped to catch his breath. "Pap oughta work the claim. I can make decent wages in a store, and stay warm. That hunkering down in cold water makes my bones ache."

Martha wanted to say more, but she stopped herself. The boy had the right of it. McDowell only drank up the dust, or gambled it away, while Timmy hunkered down in that cold dark water. What McDowell was doing to Tim was wrong. Dead wrong.

"There's better ways of getting rich, Mam. I like Mr. Dance's way, and the other storekeepers. They call it speculating, and I aim to do some."

"What that?" Martha gave him a little pat to get out of her way.

He set the dipper of beer in the pail, and pulled out a chair. "It works this way. You buy something, flour or shoes or maybe window panes, have it freighted up from Salt Lake, and sell it here for more'n it cost you, including the freight. Then you got what they call a profit."

"Can you get pretty hats?" asked Dotty.

"You can get whatever will sell," her brother replied. "Yeah, I could maybe get you a pretty hat, when you've growed up some."

"I'll grow up fast," Dotty said. "I have to before the styles change or I won't know what to buy."

"You can't grow up that fast!" hooted Tim.

"Can, too!" Dotty put out her tongue at her brother.

Martha headed off the borning argument. "There'll always be pretty things to buy." She glanced at the square dark opening in the logs where the previous owner had set oiled paper instead of glass. "What if no one wants windowpanes?" There was never enough light.

"Life's always a risk. Farming, ranching, mining. You just got to figure what risks to take."

Martha dipped out a little beer for her and Dotty. What a growed up young man he was getting to be, talking about risks and profits and such like. "How'd you get such a wise head on you?"

He glanced down at his feet and moved his shoulders, the self-same squirm he give for praise since before he could walk. "Dunno. I been listening to the storekeepers. They make sense."

The latch rose and McDowell flung the door open, hung up his coat and hat. "What's for supper?" Dotty quick poured him a beer, and he glared over the rim of the glass at his son. "What are you doing here? Where's the dust?"

"I can't work no more, Pap. It's full dark out. And – "He licked his lips. "I didn't make no dust today."

"You can't have worked very hard, damn it." McDowell frowned at his son, and his voice was a growl deep in his throat. Martha made ready to snatch Dotty out of harm's way, but she went on laying the knives like there was no storm building in the room.

"I did, Pap, only I had to break up country rock, but I didn't get done before dark."

Martha imagined him swinging the pick against the boulders under the surface of the water, and the icy water splashing up on him. His hands were red and chapped, the fingertips cracked and bleeding. They had to hurt, but he'd never said nothing. She'd put tallow on them after supper. He didn't ought to have to live like that. It wasn't right.

Half rising from his seat, McDowell leaned both hands on the table. "You useless, good-for-nothing, you dam that creek when I tell you to."

"No, damn it. You want it dammed, you do it. I'm going to work in a store."

"The hell you are, you — " McDowell stopped himself from using an ugly word against his own son, but it was only a hitch in his get along because he went right on shouting while Martha held Dotty, shielding her against his rising voice. "You ain't going to work in no store. Next thing, you'll wanting to be learning to read and write, and all them pansy things. No real man does that, is that what you're telling me, you're a pansy like Dan Stark, him and them others that hung George Ives?"

When someone pounded on the door, McDowell hollered to walk on in, and Gallagher hung up his coat on the usual peg and sat down without so much as a how-do to her or the young'uns.

"A little family discussion?" Gallagher's eyes were dark with pain, and if Martha hadn't been sure that Ives needed hanging, she'd've felt sorry for him. A terrible hard thing to fight so hard for a friend's life and see him put to death without nothing to do about it.

"Trying to teach this damn stubborn son of mine what a real man is." McDowell drained his beer, held the glass out for Martha to pour more. "Damn it, woman, pour Jack some beer."

It was on her tongue to say she couldn't pour all the beer and tend dinner, too, but she kept quiet and poured. The mood these men were in, it was best to walk real soft.

Gallagher hardly noticed when she set beer down. "What do you think we'd best do about them stranglers?" His voice held a mort of hate, hard as he tried to make it sound like a common question.

"They're gathering, for sure, and they mean business. We'll have to show them who's boss around here."

Martha set bowls of stew in front of them, withdrew beyond the lamplight to pour her own and Dotty's. She was relieved that they appeared to have forgotten Tim, quiet as could be, even as he blew on his own stew.

Gallagher spooned up a healthy bite of stew to chew on, washed it down with a swallow of beer and smiled in a way that gave Martha a tingle of fear. "I guess we will at that. Starting with that goddam Dan Stark."

McDowell laughed, his anger gone like mist in sunshine. "We'll sure do that, yessir. We sure as hell will." He pointed his spoon at Timmy. "And you! You better damn well pan out twice as much dust to make up for today. You ain't too big for me to take a strap to."

Dotty lifted frightened eyes to her Mam, and Martha smiled and shook her head to let the child know she didn't think McDowell meant it, but she knew Dotty wasn't fooled, no more than she would be. McDowell's threat sliced through her heart. Timmy didn't need a strap to work hard, or do the right thing, but the boy couldn't spend his life knee-deep in icy water.

After the men left, Martha tackled the washing up. Timmy went outside, and a draft of cold air brought back the Nevada City barn, the smells of hay dust and warm, fuzzy horses. And Mr. Stark. He'd inclined to her, like he'd wanted to touch her, though he didn't, except for a light brush at her arm. He had feelings for her. Like she did for him. Nothing to do about it, but the knowing gave her a sweet place to go in her feelings. Like the music. It was enough. It had to be.

Dotty, for once without much to say, set to drying the dishes. Martha poured the dirty wash water into the slop pail, and set the dishpan with clean water on the stove to heat. Where could she put the box of contracts where Fitch couldn't find it?

Tim put his face in his hands. "What am I to do, Mam? I can't go on this a way." His voice was muffled.

Martha took down the jar of tallow and a soft rag that had once been part of a skirt of hers before the cloth thinned out too much for patching. Pulling a chair close, she took one of her son's hands in her own. A cold hand. Funny how she'd been fixing men's hands lately. First Mr. Stark, and now Timmy. "Tell me again about this speculating."

She didn't need to listen, because she'd got the idea when he first told her. She dipped her fingers into the tallow, and rubbed it into his skin. His hands were callused and rough and cracked and bigger'n his size. He'd be a big man when he got his growth, but there was a sweetness in him that she needed to protect. Though he'd probably never show it much, it had to be there for the right woman to know about inside herself.

She had dust banked with Lydia. She could let Tim have some. McDowell would be dead against it, and she couldn't have him finding out, but she'd do it because Tim was her son. A wife shouldn't go against her husband, but a mother had to take care of her young'uns.

∾

A Christmas tree, festive with candles and shining red and gold ornaments turning on small movements of the candle-lit air. Fresh logs on the fire, the smell of sweet pitch burning. Father singing Silent Night. One of the tree branches grew, thickened, extended from the tree, and its ornament changed shape from a ball, elongated, became a doll, a man, hanging, and he was hanging, choking, and the rope cut his throat so the blood spurted over Dan. Father sang of moonlit silence and snow, and the Holy Infant, raised the pistol to his temple and pulled the trigger.

Dan thrashed about and sat up wiping blood and brain matter from his face with both hands. He awoke to know that someone was singing, but it was not a song he knew.

The fringes of Jacob's prayer shawl flung out as he swung around with wide eyes, his fingers clutched the shawl about his shoulders. He had lighted one candle on the Menorah, as he called the seven-branched candelabra.

"It's all right, Jacob." Dan gazed at his hands. They were clean. His face was clean. He rubbed his jaw and felt the bristles of his beard, sandpaper on his palms. "Just a nightmare. Sorry I disturbed you."

"Nu, is nothing." He turned his back and resumed singing his morning prayers in their odd minor key.

Lying back, Dan closed his eyes and listened to Jacob singing softly to his God the ancient indecipherable words. He imagined hundreds of Jews singing so in Bethlehem as they waited for their Messiah.

He lay in the welter of blankets. Christmas Eve. The nightmare encompassed everything. Last Christmas, at home, before life went to hell. This Christmas he was in a place that did not exist then. Virginia City. Last Christmas. In New York City he knew no Jews. Would cross the street to avoid meeting one. Today he shared quarters with a Jew. Last Christmas, as Father sang, they had all stood spellbound in a moment of pure beauty. He had never loved Father more than at that moment. Last Christmas he had been, if not happy, at least content. If not content, at least resigned to his future as a lawyer. Because of Harriet Dean.

Last Christmas they had waltzed under her father's glare, her tightly laced body close in his arms as he dreamed of how it would be to hold that body without the stays under his hand. Just the silk sliding against her skin, or perhaps no silk, just the skin.

Dan took his upper lip in his teeth to quell the groan that threatened to break loose. Last Christmas he had danced with Harriet, and soon, when all this was over, he would put most of a continent between himself and this place. If she had waited for him, in spite of her father, he would marry her and be a reasonably good husband to her, because he had promised, and a man's word was his bond. Eventually, he might forget that he loved another man's wife.

He might even forget his newly discovered love of criminal law, the joy of battle in defeating an enemy who would cheat the law. He might find a similar pleasure in torts, in the preservation of capital through contract law, for wasn't the law a constant war against an enemy, and weren't all cases battles in that war?

Jacob's prayers ended.

In the meantime, before he could leave this hell hole, he was a Vigilante.

Dan flung back the blankets and stood up. Tomorrow was Christmas. John Creighton and the other Catholics, like Peter Ronan and the Sheehans, would have prayers at the Sheehans' cabin, and he would join other Protestants at Nick Wall's house where Sanders was staying. After that, he'd signed up for dinner at the Eatery. Even here, hundreds of miles from any church, there would be Christmas.

But in the afternoon, the Vigilantes would meet to approve the bye-laws.

"Good morning, Jacob," he said. "Happy Hanukah to you."

"Ach, ja." Jacob was folding his prayer shawl carefully into its box. "Und you also. Merry Christmas? Is that how you say? Merry Christmas?"

"Yes, Jacob. You have it correctly. Merry Christmas. But it's tomorrow."

The swelling in his left hand was down, though he still wanted to groan when he let it drop down, but the bandage Mrs. McDowell had wrapped to hold the bone in place made it impossible to put on a glove. Jacob helped him with the sling, and the hand burrowed into it like a small animal into a den. When the two men stepped outside and pulled the latch string through, Dan slung the rifle on his shoulder. In civilized places a man did not wear his rifle as he wore his coat, as part of his everyday attire out of doors. He used his teeth to pull on his fur-lined right glove. The temperature was dropping rapidly. How cold did it get here? Large dry snowflakes drifted down from a white sky on light currents of air. "Winter's here." A flake landed on his sleeve, and he marveled at its intricacy. Already the snow was whitening Virginia City, settling on the roofs and covering the rounded shapes of horse manure in the road, that Dan had learned to call road apples.

Jacob, who knew winter from Eastern Europe, said, "Ja. Means businesses." He smiled, proud of his mastery of an idiom, and Dan did not correct him.

They crossed Idaho. From the Melodeon Hall fiddle music and laughter leaked into the street. From somewhere else a fight was in progress. Crooked columns of gray wood smoke rose from chimneys to mingle with the smells of tobacco, and beer and whiskey. It was cold enough to have stifled the smell of old manure. People were friendly, in a good mood, and wished them both a Merry Christmas. More than once a man would stop to congratulate Dan: "You're on a good undertaking," or, "Keep up the good work." Dan didn't know if they meant the trials or the Vigilantes, but he knew the word was going around that a Vigilance Committee had formed.

A tall man in a Union greatcoat cut through Solomon Content's vacant lot at the corner of Wallace and Jackson and walked toward them. He was whistling "Slavery is a Hard Foe to Battle," and the sound pierced the cold air. Seeing them, he stopped whistling and stood still, as if waiting. He opened his coat so that it swung free.

Dan slowed his steps. He felt the air coming and going through his nostrils on short clouds, and deliberately took deeper breaths. People spotted the coming confrontation and waited to see what he would do. What Gallagher would do. If he and Jacob crossed the street to avoid Gallagher, men would see it not as prudently avoiding an unpleasant encounter, but as cowardice. If he had not prosecuted Ives, if he were not a Vigilante, they could do it, perhaps, though they were two men and Gallagher was alone. No, he had to brave the meeting. The roughs could not have bragging rights. Not now. Not ever again. As with Boone Helm, only Gallagher was no empty braggart. Dan walked on, Jacob beside him. "Get behind me, Jacob." He had eyes only for Gallagher, but he knew men gathered themselves to leap out of a bullet's path. They were torn between the excitement of a pending fight and fear for their own safety.

Jacob did not drop back.

Gallagher waited for them. His hat brim was pulled low on his forehead, so that he had to tilt his face up to see them. His eyes were narrow, the brows drawn nearly together over his long, straight nose.

About ten feet away, Dan stopped. Gallagher would have to come to him if he wanted them closer. He needed room to swing the rifle if he needed to. "Jacob, please move to my left."

Jacob crossed behind him and stood at his left shoulder.

All up and down the street, some men ducked into doorways, ran for the Melodeon Hall. Music and laughter died, and a hush fell on Jackson Street, among those men who stayed out to see the action.

Dan's right thumb flicked repeatedly at the rifle stock. It felt like waiting to see if a bear would charge or back away. He called, "Merry Christmas, Jack. May we see a Union victory in sixty-four." Gallagher seemed taken aback, silent for a second, not knowing what to say, off balance. Ha! Dan told him silently. Got you, didn't I? You didn't expect that, you son of a bitch, did you? The Deputy wanted a provocation, wanted a challenge from Dan, but instead he got a friendly greeting, a reminder of the season of peace on earth. Union beliefs in common. A muscle tensed in Gallagher's jaw, and Dan imagined him grinding his teeth in frustration. Asshole.

When Gallagher spoke, his voice had a whine to it that almost made Dan laugh. "Damn it, Stark, you got a hell of a nerve. You owe me money from that game a week ago, and you been too busy strangling good men to pay up."

"I don't owe you a God damn thing, Jack," Dan said. "I won fair and square, and Con Orem will back me up, and so will anybody who was there."

"McDowell won't. He was in the game, too, and he saw you."

Dan saw Gallagher as through a curtain of mist. He forced himself to seize his temper, to ride it because to let it ride him was to lose. Start a fight he could not win, and then Gallagher could claim self-defense. Yet Gallagher had stopped short of outright accusing him of cheating.

The mist cleared. Gallagher stood waiting, and Dan let the moment stretch. You God damn bastard, Dan told him silently. You want me to push this so you can say you never started it. Like hell I'll do that. Dan raised his voice so that everyone on the street could hear.

"Tell you what, Jack. I'll let you get even. How about another game, say on New Year's Eve? At the Melodeon Hall. That'll be a good way to bring in the New Year." So many men heard him, it would guarantee the Hall would be packed. He would have friends there. As many as Gallagher. Maybe more. Men who were not afraid any more. He might even survive the game. In the next breath Dan could not believe he had put himself in harm's way, had set himself up to be killed. Sweat trickled down his back, though he could feel the temperature drop each minute they stood here.

"No, I want this game to be at Cy Skinner's place."

Pretending regret, Dan shook his head. "Can't do it. Con Orem's saloon or nothing."

"Like hell. Maybe I'll take what's mine right here and now."

Dan laughed. He put his head far back, so that his hat nearly fell off, and laughed as if the Deputy had told a very funny story. As he laughed, he moved his shoulder, caught the Spencer as if it had slipped off, brought it around, and levered a shell into the breech in one motion. All those times practicing that maneuver in his law office, imagining he faced a charging bear, and never thinking he would use it this way. Against a man. He had only to raise the muzzle and cock it now.

"Like I said, Jack. Con's place or nothing."

Gallagher spread his hands away from his coat. "Okay, I guess it'll be your way. But the deck better be clean."

"Don't tell me. Tell Con. We always play with Con's cards." He was light and floating, his very being soaring to the skies because he had beat Jack Gallagher at this game. Jack's game. No one would dare accuse Con Orem of running a crooked table, issuing a marked or shaved deck. The man's honesty was beyond dispute, and he was the best bare knuckle fighter in the Territory.

He and Jacob waited on Content's corner for a freight wagon drawn by eight plodding mules to pass before they crossed over. Dan's stomach growled nonstop. Two men, brothers whose claim Dan had surveyed, caught up with them. "Good for you," said one. "You showed him, all right." The other said, "I might sit in on that game. Just to keep it friendly." Crossing the street, both men stayed with Dan and Jacob. "We heard about this Vigilante thing," said the first man. "Yeah," the second said. "How can we join?"

Dan smiled. "Damned if I know." How the hell had they heard? Who had talked about the group they were forming? After all the care during the first meetings, the sheets of tin over the windows in Nye's tin shop, the darkness in which they agreed to the death sentence. He would ask Sanders and Pfouts about them. Did they already have a spy? Was there already an infiltrator? These brothers might be fine men, but he did not know them well, though he knew nothing against them. Or might it be lucky conjecture, a rumor that turned out to be true?

"Count us in," the older brother said, and the younger one echoed him as they parted.

∽

Small, light snowflakes swirled on currents of air under a steel gray sky. Dan tugged down his hat brim and put up his coat collar. Colder today. He took a couple of deep breaths, happy to escape the smoky fug of Creighton's store. Warm though it was, for a man who liked being out of doors it had been hard to bear. Or perhaps it was something in the atmosphere, in the purpose of the men gathered around Creighton's stove. Murder and robbery on Christmas Day. No one reminiscing about Christmas at home, but if they were anything like himself, they could not help thinking about it. Perhaps that was it, an underlying sadness of men who wanted to be at home. Even Sanders, whose wife and family were in Bannack, had a longing in his eyes though he kept strictly to the subject. Murder and robbery, and how to stop it. Speculating on who had done what, concluding they had not enough evidence. Not yet.

If anyone had asked him while he was still in New York, Dan would have said that a Vigilance Committee was a mob of men inflamed by drink, hysterical, morally certain and immorally wrong, spontaneously moving by night to lynch someone – black or white – for their own purposes. Outside the law. He would never in a million years have described a Vigilance Committee as a group of the most sober citizens, lawyers, merchants, and law officers, who organized themselves carefully into an Executive Committee, with companies led in quasi-military fashion by themselves or other citizens of equal rectitude. Yet the meeting today had ground along absorbed in administrative detail. The boring construction of an administration as bound in red tape as any government body. As boring as a legislative meeting, and he was immured in it all. All the discussions, the voting, the agreements never put in writing, but remembered.

The biggest task to separate personal motives from the public good, like curds from whey. Knowing beforehand it would not be perfect.

Old arguments resurfacing that he thought were settled. It is the way of men, Dan thought, to talk a problem to death before proceeding to solve it. The selection of a ferreting committee to ascertain the probable guilt or innocence of those whom people named as having been present at a robbery, or last seen with a man who disappeared, or with one whose body was found later. They did not have enough yet to warrant hanging a man.

But they had Dr. Glick's testimony. Somehow that timorous man had nerved himself to speak up, had traveled all the way from Bannack, and finding himself in time for Hilderman's hearing, had supported the old man's claim that fear had kept him from speaking of Ives's murder to anyone. His testimony finished, he had confided to the prosecutors that he had tended the wounds and injuries of many men who threatened him with death should he say anything. They had come by their hurts in the course of robberies, murders, and bragged to him of their crimes. He had no doubt in the world that they would keep their word to him. He trembled as he spoke, his legs quivered, and he darted looks around as if expecting death at any moment. Yet he talked, and the Vigilantes added his reports to those they already had, those that continued to come in almost hourly, mostly in frightened whispers. All were carefully noted, and the evidence in the stories added up. Dan was delegated, as Virginia City prosecutor, to keep track of these reports, to build on Creighton's chart. In the midst of the administrative work they had stopped to compare notes, to cross-reference what they knew. Again, not enough against many. Not yet. Against a few, more than enough.

The Vigilantes did not want to hang one or two now, and one or two later. They wanted to break the back of the conspiracy forever, and to do that they assumed that they would have to swoop down on several men at once. As yet, though the reports piled up, they did not prove a conspiracy, or tell who the primary conspirators were.

The Vigilantes agreed to wait.

Dan had asked Dr. Glick why Plummer had not come. Glick replied, "He's scared. He thinks there is an army of men against him here, and he told everyone in Bannack that his enemies were massing against him, so men have been standing guard on the hills to warn him when the Vigilantes come." Glick added, "He is a coward. Afraid of the Vigilantes."

Laughing, Dan had lied, "Vigilantes? There are no Vigilantes."

When X Beidler returned from locating the overdue wagon train Fitch had sent him to find, they would ask him to take charge of the ferreting committee. X had a talent for detection and no fear of any man.

Dan huddled into his coat and wished he were at home.

If he couldn't be at home, at least he might look at the gold stashed with Mrs. Hudson. It would tell him when he could leave this place. Flee from what he couldn't have. Martha. She was never far from his thoughts. Every time he recollected what enemies he had in Gallagher and McDowell, she came into his mind. His memories of Harriet seemed trivial to him now, a small matter of braving her father's wrath to look down her neckline as she sat at the pianoforte, pretending he was there to be helpful, turn pages for her. She had no talent for music, but he had hoped she would have a talent for what her plump richness promised.

He no longer cared. His entire being, it seemed, was caught by a woman whose necklines reached high on her throat and whose shirtwaists could not disguise her lack of figure, a woman worn thin with work and motherhood, but whose courage was as great as any man's. She had brought him word of the Bamboo Chief. A woman whose bright honest eyes seemed to see into his soul.

Only he could not stay, and she was married. He wanted to stay with her, and he wanted even more to leave her because she was married. He must keep his promises at home. But God, how he wanted her.

He pushed open the door to the Eatery. This time of day, with everyone out in the mines and about their business, with the gambling halls and saloons roaring with holiday-makers, few people had yet come for a meal. One couple sat at the front table by the far wall. The man held her hands in his, and she wept softly into an empty plate. Three men played cribbage near the stove and barely glanced up as he walked down the right hand aisle.

"Merry Christmas." Mrs. Hudson wiped her hands on a towel.

"Merry Christmas," Dan said, and with a nod included the black couple who sat at the far end of the back bench eating their meal. "Merry Christmas, Albert, Tabby." They smiled and returned the greeting. He sat backwards on the bench between a cribbage player and Albert, rested his back against the table. "Is that coffee I smell?"

"It is, as it happens, and it's the real thing." She took a blue tin mug from a shelf and poured from the pot standing on the stove. "It hasn't been standing very long."

Dan inhaled the rich brown coffee smell. "It's the elixir of life." He sipped it. Thick and strong enough to plow, but he complimented her on it. "I'd also like to make a deposit." He had finished some calculations, written and delivered the reports, and he had the payments in a poke in his pocket. People were asking him for help with legal problems, too, but he did not want to start a legal practice, develop clients only to leave the Gulch.

She reached into the warming oven, and the cribbage players smiled when she brought down a poke and gave it to Dan. "Banking business doing well, is it, Mrs. Hudson?" asked one of the players.

"Well enough," she said with a smile.

"Aren't you afraid you'll be robbed someday?" The second man asked.

Albert cleared his throat, and the cribbage players laughed. "No, we don't suppose robbery is something you'd need to worry about."

Dan had turned his back on them. He poured the gold dust from the payments into the poke he kept with Mrs. Hudson and wrote the amount, date, and total on the tag. Like the evidence they had weighed at Creighton's, it was not enough. Nearly, but not quite enough to pay off the creditors and establish the family in their accustomed style. He leaned against the table and tasted the coffee and made small talk with the cribbage players. Mrs. Hudson was cutting up the haunch of a deer for a Christmas feast. The cleaver made a definably different sound from an axe chopping wood as it chopped through bone and gristle.

Tabby picked up her and Alfred's dishes and went back to her work. Albert leaned toward Dan to ask, "D'you think the Territory will come in free, sir?" The soft Southern voice slurred over the words.

At least this was a change of subject. "It will have to, won't it? Or we'll all be dead." Dan pointed to the empty space beside him. "Do sit down, man. I can't twist my neck this way for long."

"But, sir," Albert began.

The cribbage players looked scandalized, but they knew Dan had prosecuted Ives, and they said nothing. Was he getting a reputation? Dan wondered. If so, he hoped it would keep him alive. He patted the bench. "Sit here. Please." He knew Albert's objection. A Negro sitting with a white man gave an appearance of equality. About damn time, Dan said to himself.

Albert moved over, but perched on the edge, as if he sat on nails.

"That's better. Albert, this is the political situation." Dan shifted the coffee cup to make interlocking rings on the table top. "Over in Bannack we have the Chief Justice of the Territory, Sidney Edgerton. He's a friend, as I understand it, of President Lincoln. He's also a radical abolitionist, and he and the Governor of the Territory do not see eye to eye." One of the cribbage players snorted. Dan ignored him. "The Governor has told Justice Edgerton to remain in East Bannack, and until he is allowed to travel to Lewiston he can't be sworn in and take his rightful place." Dan pretended to sip at his cooling coffee. He wanted to tell Albert about Edgerton's plans to talk to the President, about the Territory of Montana, but what if the cribbage players were Secesh? They had stopped their game to listen to him. "The Emancipation Proclamation took effect on January 1, this year, and all slaves in the Territories were freed. You have nothing to worry about unless —" Dan gulped. Unthinkable! "— the South wins the War."

"But sir, the majority here's Secesh."

"Damn right," said one of the cribbage players. "You Yanks ain't gonna tell anyone what property we can own. And we will win the War."

Mrs. Hudson said, "Don't worry Albert, thee and Tabby have thy manumission papers."

"Who from?" the third cribbage player growled. "You better be sure they's legal, nigger."

"They're from me," said Mrs. Hudson, "and make no mistake about it, they are as legal as thee are, even if this Territory goes Secesh."

The front door opened on a draft of cold air, and Albert stood up as if a string jerked him. His place was at the front table, with the scales, where he could guard the gold and turn away the roughs. He hurried up the left-hand aisle.

Dotty scooted in, clapping her mittened hands. "Merry Christmas." She skipped down the aisle to hug Mrs. Hudson, who laughed and wrapped her arms around the child and sang out, "Merry Christmas!" Even the cribbage players laughed for no reason except it was Christmas.

"Merry – " Dan caught his breath. Behind the child came the mother with a parcel wrapped in cloth that she held in both hands. She was smiling, and when she saw Dan her smile broadened, and her face shone with happiness, and Dan thought a warm sun had risen in his soul and dissolved the glacial burden of arranging for men to die. It was suddenly, truly, Christmas.

Behind Martha came Tim, who closed the door carefully after him and offered his hand to Albert. "Merry Christmas, Albert."

Dan didn't hear Albert's stammered reply. Martha gave her package to Mrs. Hudson, and took a seat next to him, but left a suitable, modest space between them. Dan swung his legs around under the table. His elbow was a few inches from hers. If he could just touch her. He needed all his breath to wish her a Merry Christmas. Tim seated himself across from them, looking like a cat about to eat cream. Behind him, Dan heard a whispered consultation, and Dotty's voice, "Yes, do, now. Please."

Quick footsteps, the door into Mrs. Hudson's private room opened and closed, and more quick footsteps while Dan groped in his mind for something to say, but could not get further than,

"It's getting colder, don't you think?" Stupid. Inane. Damn it, he could talk about the most important things, about ensuring guilt before hanging a man, and freedom from slavery, so why could he not say something memorable to this woman? Or something intelligent?

Dotty squeezed between them. Dan moved over to give her room. The child had a flat package wrapped in a scrap of deer hide tied with a buckskin boot lace, that she laid in front of her mother.

"Merry Christmas, Mam."

"What is it?"

Dan said, "Looks like the youngsters have a Christmas present for you."

"But I don't need nothing." Hands in her lap, she stared at the package until Tim said, "Go on, Mam, open it up."

"Yes, open it, Mam, do," said Dotty. "We been waiting to see d' you like it."

Martha untied the cord and laid aside the folds of deer hide wrapping. She let her fingers feel over the hide. "It's soft, like velvet." The present was a book, bound in black leather. She wiped her hands on her skirt before she turned the book over and touched the two words embossed in gold on the front cover. "Holy Bible."

Dotty said, "We figured you'd like to read that book first."

"See?" said Tim. "You can already read two words."

"But how—?" Her fingers traced the gold letters, over and over.

By Dan's side, Dotty bounced on the bench. "I earned some of it cleaning out sluiceboxes, and I took it over to the paper store, bit by bit, and Timmy, he helped, too, and Mr. Tilton kept it until we had enough to pay for it, and then I brought it over here and Miz Hudson, she kept it till now."

Tim said. "I kept back a few flakes here and there from the claim, and a nugget or two."

She said nothing, only her left index finger traced the letters over and over.

After a bit Dotty said, "Mam?" The child sounded worried. "Mam?"

Martha shook her head.

Dan put his arm around Dotty's shoulders. "It's all right," he murmured. She leaned into the circle of his arm. His left hand, resting on the table, signaled Tim to quiet. Together he and the youngsters waited. This was a family. They, all three of them, were what he had wanted all his life and had not known it. First the woman, but his wanting her was only a prelude to the larger work, as the sound of the big drums heralded the Fifth Symphony. They were home.

Another man's home, if he had the sense to see it. Another man's wife. Another man's children. Martha should have opened the present at home, with McDowell to share her overwhelming joy. It wasn't right. They belonged to McDowell and he cared nothing about them, always off searching as he was for the Mother Lode.

These children, this woman, could never be his. He had discovered the Mother Lode on another man's claim, where he had no business prospecting.

Martha said, "Such young'uns as I do have." And then she wept while the youngsters looked on, horrified that their present had made their mother cry.

Dan said, "Hold her. Both of you. She has too much happiness to be contained." He got up from the bench, stood the rifle against the back wall, turned his back to give the McDowell family some privacy. The cribbage players folded up their board, packed away their pins and cards. They were going to the Melodeon Hall to celebrate Christmas. The couple at the opposite wall had already left. Dan hoped they had settled their business and would be happy now. Mrs. Hudson wordlessly refilled his coffee cup. "I'll hang out the closed sign."

Carol Buchanan

After a while, Mrs. Hudson said, "Tabby, do thee please cut the pie. We'll eat it now."

Martha raised her tear-drenched face. "No, please, we need to sell that pie. For Tim's speculation."

"Speculation?" Dan wanted to give her his handkerchief, but he was not sure how clean it was. Tabby handed Martha a towel, and she buried her face in it.

"Yeah," Tim said. "I ain't going back to that dratted claim, neither. I want dust to invest in a shipment of goods Mr. Dance ordered from Mr. Sheehan. He's leaving soon after the New Year, and Mr. Dance said I could chip in if I got myself a hundred dollars."

"Why a hundred?" Dan asked. Walter Dance might as well have invited the boy to help himself to a piece of the moon.

"He said it would cost that much to spread out the risk among several things. Much less than that might not yield enough of a return to make it worthwhile." He spoke carefully, like someone learning a new language and anxious about saying it right.

Dan thought about that. He knew little about the economics of investing, except the simple mathematics of buying and selling: buy low and sell dear. It would depend on supply and demand, but it sounded right that the boy would be better off to invest in several commodities rather than a single commodity that might or might not sell. Walter Dance's thumb would never rest on the scales.

He was still pondering a decision when Tim said, "Deputy Gallagher's right, what he said last night. There's easier ways of making money than slaving in a mine."

Dan's arm jerked and he spilled a few drops of coffee. As he wiped at it, he heard Martha McDowell say, "Deputy Gallagher's ways ain't our ways. Don't you be listening to him, now."

"I ain't, Mam, but he's right. I don't mean robbing people, or gambling with marked cards, but the kind of work Mr. Stark does. Or Mr. Dance. Educated work. Work you can do when you can read and write and cipher. Dry. Warm. Even in winter."

"Your Pap don't want you speculating, you know."

She was speaking to her son, but it was Dan she was watching as she said it. Warning him.

"Pap don't have the say-so over me."

"He's your Pap and he does as long as you're under his roof."

"Then maybe I'll live somewheres else."

"Where, then?" His mother's voice was tight.

"I don't know where. Somewheres."

Dan cleared his throat. Both of them turned to him. "I'll loan you the hundred dollars, Tim. You can pay me back, plus another ten, from your profits." He added the extra ten percent because he didn't want the boy to know it would be a gift. That ten dollars he would quietly tell Mrs. Hudson to slip into Mrs. McDowell's poke.

The boy's mouth dropped open. Dotty clapped her hands and hugged him around the waist. "Oh, Mr. Stark! Merry Christmas! Merry Christmas!"

"You shouldn't ought to do this." Martha groped for words. "It ain't, it ain't fittin'."

"Mrs. McDowell, this is business. Your son has given me an opportunity to invest, and I stand to make ten dollars simply by lending him a little more than six ounces of dust." He hoped his face did not give him away, because she was very intelligent even if she had no education, and her moral compass pointed true north. He was doing this for her. To win, if not her, to win her children's hearts. Which he had no business doing. Another man's children.

"I was going to give Timmy some dust for this," she said.

Dan smiled. "You can invest next time. Please, I'd like to earn a bit extra."

With one more searching look from those big luminous eyes, that saw so clearly into him, she nodded and turned back to her son. "All right, but you be careful, now. You know what he can be like."

Dan hid his relief behind the coffee mug. He had a feeling she was not fooled one bit. He could not have done anything this Christmas day more calculated to drive a wedge between McDowell and his family. Thinking that, he nearly choked on a swallow of coffee, that burned all the way down. What secret planner was at work in him, that he would do this, that he would act so as to win the children over when he would not be staying in Alder Gulch? By the shining in the boy's eyes, the sister's delighted hug around his chest, he knew he had fooled himself into offering the dust because he had hated how Grandfather bent Father's life, his own life, to his own wishes. He would give anything to be able to take it back, not to raise their expectations, but it was too late. Much too late. And while the children celebrated and their mother thanked him, he was engulfed in shame. They must not be taught to count on him, because he could not stay and come between another man and his family.

"Thank you, Mr. Stark," Tim's mother said.

Her smile made him cringe.

～

7: Alder Gulch: Virginia City

"In the beginning was the Word, and the Word was with God, and the Word was God." Martha paused outside the Eatery door. "W. W for word. W for was. W for water. W for with." She pursed her lips and made the w sound: "Wuh." She'd learned four words for W in this reading lesson, and she couldn't hardly wait to tell the young'uns. Watching her footing so as not to step in fresh manure, she crossed Wallace – another W! – waited to pass behind a dray pulled by six shaggy draft horses with feet the size of plates. She glanced up Jackson, and the hazards at her feet, and the alphabet, vanished from her mind. Darkness loomed ahead. She stopped on the corner to pull up her hood and wrap her cloak snug around herself with the Good Book safe inside. She had almost crossed Jackson when the wind attacked.

Snow bit at her cheeks, the sudden dropping cold made her gasp. She staggered, leaned against the wind. It shifted, and snowflakes swarmed at her from the side, a thousand thousand frozen bees. She fell, got up again, fought the pummeling wind up to the Melodeon Hall, around the corner, onto Idaho Street. Her cabin was gone. The wind wasn't that strong, surely? She huddled against the saloon's long shivering wall, maybe it was her, so cold, but no it was the building, the wind made it shake, and the wind's shriek snuffed out the fiddles, the piano, the stomping boots. The cabin showed itself, and she launched herself toward it, but it disappeared before she had gone two steps.

Don't be letting me lose it, Lord. Her hood snapped back, but she dared not pull it on again, kept her hands inside. The dog was barking. She heard him, but the wind slewed around and she lost the sound, the wind veered and she heard it, changed her course toward it, and stood at her own door as the wind hit her from behind. She kicked the door, kicked again, then a third time.

"Mam!" Timmy held the door from flying all the way open. The shivering dog whined. Martha let him run in ahead of her, then leaned on the door to help her son force it shut. He dropped the bar, and the wind beat at the door.

Martha made out Dotty, wrapped in a quilt, curled on her bed. The child whistled and opened her arms. The dog ran over to her, and she pulled the quilt around them both.

"Thank the Lord, you're to home." Martha pulled up a chair as close to the stove as she could and hunched inside her cloak. She couldn't stop shivering, and her ears hurt something fierce. Timmy pulled a quilt off the bed and bundled it around her. He drew her hands out and rubbed them. She felt tears on her cheeks.

"You'll be all right, Mam. We're both here. We're safe. I brought in enough wood to last till summer, and boarded the window tight, and I strung ropes to the outhouse and the woodpile and the well so we can find them. There's water and I emptied the slop pail."

"How'd you know to do all that? This storm just hit!"

"Canary started in to bark when we were at Dance and Stuart, and I couldn't see no cause until Mr. Dance said it felt like a storm coming, and it could be a bad one. So we come straight home and I did what he said."

Dotty piped up, "One of the miners told me to go home because a blizzard was coming. He could tell by the rim of cloud behind the Tobacco Root mountains."

Tim set water on the stove to boil. "We should have come for you, Mam, but we thought you'd be to home." He looked at the toe of his boot, and his voice was very small. "I should have gone looking as soon as I come home and saw you wasn't here."

"It's all right," Martha said through her chattering teeth. "You fixed things so's we'll be fine." They had food, if the storm didn't go on too long and they didn't have to go for more meat. "We'll just hunker down and wait it out." They'd make it through, she knew they would. "The Lord'll see us through."

But where was McDowell? Lord, keep him safe. For this storm was a killer, and she didn't want to lose none of hers. Daniel Stark. Lord, hold him safe in your hands, do. Please.

"Water's boiling," Dotty said.

Tim threw tea leaves into the pot and let it boil while he watched it. Martha laid the Bible on the table. Her ears throbbed something awful, and her skirt was wet near to her knees, but her hands were warming, and she laid them over her ears. Could they be frostbit in just that short a time? She didn't know. Tim gave her a mug of hot, strong tea, and she cradled the mug in her hands, and warmed her cheeks with it. After a few sips her innards felt warmer, and the shivering stopped. She shrugged off the quilt, hung up her cloak, and wrapped herself up in her thick winter shawl. Timmy poked up the fire and added two more rounds. If they had a big stove they could build a bigger fire.

"You and I have to tend the fire tonight," she told her son. If the fire went out while they slept, they could freeze to death.

"I can do it, Mam." As he spoke, his voice dropped into a new, low pitch. He stared at her, as surprised as she was, and the man he would be looked at her out of eyes that two minutes before were a boy's.

Dotty giggled. "You sound like a man."

Timmy set the bowl on the floor for the dog, that crawled out of Dotty's grasp to drink, then pulled a chair around to set close to the fire. So close to his Mam that their knees would have touched except that his were inches higher than hers. Dotty, maybe a little bit jealous, shrugged her quilt aside and came to sit on her Mam's lap. Martha pulled the shawl around them both.

Martha sensed her ideas rearranging themselves, because her boy was growing, no, had growed into a man or mostly into a man and she hadn't seen it coming, the little signs that gradually come on him and added up to a deep, low voice she'd never heard before, not out of anybody, but something different from any man she'd ever heard, or maybe would hear again. The sound of himself. Resting her cheek on the top of her daughter's head, smelling the child's hair needing a washing and warm sunshine, she looked at her son, her Timmy, Tim, maybe not hers no more, but his own, where he leaned his elbows on his knees, and stared into his mug of tea like he would get his future from it.

"You purely do," she told him. "You got a man's sound."

Without raising his head, he slid his eyes toward her, but said nothing. Maybe he wasn't quite trusting his voice yet. They had a tendency to crack sometimes, early on, she recollected McDowell's done that when they was young'uns. He'd whispered a great deal in them days, being too embarrassed and shy to talk much. Martha sighed. "What say we have a sing?"

"You sing, Mam," Tim said. "I don't know's I can." He opened his arm and let his sister come over and straddle one knee. Just like he'd played horsey with her not so long ago.

Martha, opening up the trunk to bring out the dulcimer, bit her lip to keep tears back. She felt something coming to an end. Little Dotty had got her monthlies, and now her boy was a man, near enough.

With all this, though, the music held the comfort of a familiar forgetting. She began with one of their favorite tunes, and sure enough, Tim couldn't resist joining in. His new voice startled them all, it was a sort of squeaky rumble that after a while leveled out deep and low like his new speaking voice, except when it broke and embarrassed him. After two breaks, he shook his head and was silent.

Martha and Dotty sang two more songs, but it wasn't the same without Tim, and besides they needed to eat. Setting the dulcimer aside, Martha said, "Don't you worry none. That breaking won't last. Your Pap's voice did the same as I recall." It hit her then with the force of the storm that McDowell ought to be here, he ought to be the one to help the boy turn into a man, be easy in himself. She put a hand on the table to steady herself for a second before she went to heating up yesterday's stew for them.

Come bedtime, she piled all the quilts off the bed just as close to the stove as they couldn't turn over and burn themselves, and all three of them laid down together, Dotty next the stove, with Canary curled in the crook of her body, and Martha between the young'uns, dressed as they'd been, even to shoes. She argued with Tim about being on the outside, but he wouldn't hear of her being there. "I'll be warmer'n that creek water, Mam." It didn't matter about his voice breaking, she yielded to his man's insistence.

Sometime in the night, Martha awoke to hear him poking up the fire and putting in more wood. Dotty snored softly. After he'd laid down again, she recalled something he'd said.

"You were at Mr. Dance's store?"

"Yup. Learning what I'll be doing come Monday." His voice, like hers, was hardly even a whisper, though Dotty wouldn't have heard blasting powder go off.

"You'll have trouble with your Pap, you know." Here she lay in the dark beside her son, while the storm shrieked about the house and the cold did its best to freeze them where they lay. Talking of disaster.

"I know, Mam, but I can't go on thisaway. Besides, he don't need me."

His body stretched out so much longer than hers, maybe a foot, and his whisper come from somewheres deep in his chest, and when she reached out to touch his cheek, stiff hairs chafed her fingers. A man, sure enough. Martha's heart stumbled, then took up its steady da-thump, da-thump.

She murmured, "I reckon you'll do what you have to." Like a man would.

The bristles on his cheek rasped up and down against her hand, like he nodded, and before she took her hand away, she felt a drop that escaped the corner of his eye. "Yes'm." She hardly heard him, and then his breathing steadied. But Martha lay awake for a time, trying to see in the dark what might happen.

Round about midday, Canary growled just before someone made a commotion at the door, and McDowell shouted to open the damn door. Tim leaped to open it, and McDowell stamped in, grumbling that it took them long enough to let a man in and he could've froze out there, dammit. He huddled by the stove while Tim forced the door closed and kept it shut with his shoulder while he fumbled with the crossbar. "What's that goddam dog doing in the house?"

Dotty had her arm around the dog. "Same as us, Pap, trying not to freeze to death."

"Good luck to him." McDowell said. "You're all safe." He stripped off his coat, hung it up.

"Yes." Martha's heart opened a little to joy because he'd come home to check on them.

"We got any beer?"

Martha poured him some. He drank it off like he hadn't had none in weeks, never mind she'd smelled it on his breath as he come in the door. "How cold is it, do you know?"

He shook his head. "No one knows. The mercury in the thermometers has done froze up." He took a deep drink of beer. "This can't last very long. Then you can be back on the claim."

"No, Pap." Tim, leaning his back against the door, spoke in his new voice, that McDowell didn't even seem to hear.

"Whaddaya mean, "'No, Pap?'" McDowell sneered. "You ain't got no choice. I'm your Pap, and in my house what I say goes."

Tim cleared his throat. Martha sensed the struggle he had to keep his man's voice. "Come Monday, I'm going to work for Mr. Dance."

"Like hell." McDowell swung around on his chair and half rose. He shook his index finger at Tim. "Goddammit, you'll work the claim. I ain't hiring no help what'll cheat me worse'n my own family does."

"Dammit, Pap, we don't cheat you!" Tim's voice cracked and he went on in his boy's falsetto, "I ain't going to work that damn claim no more."

Martha held her breath and prayed something would turn aside McDowell's wrath. "How about I make some more tea?" The question squeaked out of her tense throat. Feeble.

"Tea?" McDowell shouted. "Goddammit, woman, you talk about tea? It's beer I'm needing, and a good bullwhip to use on this ungrateful bastard that calls me Pap." He was on his feet, taller than Tim, but not by so much no more, and raised his fist.

"No!" Martha backed away from them, took Dotty into the circle of her arm, and crouched with her on the other side of the stove, and grabbed the dog, that growled without letup, and the wind pounded at the door, held only by the latch, demanded to come in.

"I'll be damned if I'll freeze my ass in that water," Tim circled to keep the table between him and his Pap.

Martha held Dotty. Tim's swearing told her this fight between them had something new to it. It was a fight between men, not just a boy against his father, and it was more dangerous, like two stags going at it.

"You said what?" McDowell's right hand swung to his left side, ready to backhand Tim.

"No!" Martha screamed, and Dotty buried her face on her Mam's breast.

The dog barked, and father and son were shouting at once fit to drown out the storm, neither one hearing the other, their voices and their words blended together in rage. McDowell swung, Tim dodged. McDowell paused to draw breath.

Tim yelled, "Work the goddamn claim yourself, for a change!"

"Get the hell out!" McDowell swung at Tim again, but the boy snatched up his coat and thrust his arms into the sleeves. He fumbled at the latch as his Pap charged around the table.

"You can't," Martha screamed. "He could die in that blizzard."

"Get out!" McDowell went for Tim with his fists ready.

The dog broke free and launched himself across the room, snarling, and sank his teeth into McDowell's tall boot. The man kicked at Canary, but the dog leaped aside, ran between McDowell and Tim, who tugged at the latch. As McDowell lunged toward him, the door blew open, and the storm swallowed boy and dog.

McDowell leaned against the door to close and bar it. Swearing, he fell across the bed. After awhile Martha heard him snoring and got up, mouse-quiet, to look at his ankle. The bite had only dented the leather of his boot.

Dotty clung to her Mam. Through her sobs, she asked, "Will Timmy be all right?"

"He's in the Lord's hands now, little darling." Martha smoothed Dotty's hair with a trembling hand. She couldn't shake a dreadful fear that someone would find Tim's frozen body like they'd found Nick's.

∽

"Dear Grandfather," Dan wrote. The candle flame wavered, and he raised one hand to shield it against the draft while the other dipped the pen into the ink and scratched across the paper before he could stop to think. If he did, he'd never write, never try to persuade Grandfather that, nurtured and trained in the law as he was, he could be a Vigilante. Grandfather had never known an absence of law, a void where the law ought to be. Would he understand, an old man not accustomed to warping his mind onto a new tack? Would he believe any place, this place, could be devoid of law? As difficult to believe as that it was afternoon instead of night.

He got up to stoke the stove, as quietly as possible so as not to wake Jacob, who snored in gulps and gasps, napping because there was nothing else to do.

Someone battered at the door, and a dog barked. Jacob sat up, clutched the blankets under his chin, his eyes wide and frightened as from a nightmare of Cossacks.

Who on earth in this weather?

Dan opened the door, and Tim McDowell fell on the floor in a blast of snow-laden wind. His yellow dog bounded to the stove and shook itself. "Quick!" Dan pulled the boy farther into the room. Jacob, fully dressed, leaped out of the bed and pushed the door shut, helped Dan to lift Tim into the bed and cover him. The two men removed Tim's boots and wrapped up his feet. The boy shivered hard enough to rattle his bones. Even clenching his jaws, he could not stop his teeth clashing.

Dan crouched and felt for Tim's hands. "Bring a pan of cool water! Quickly!"

Jacob ladled water from the barrel by the stove, and when he would have set the pan on the stove, Dan stopped him. "It'll be warm enough."

Dan turned the boy onto his side so he could dip both hands in the cool water. What the hell had driven him into this storm with just a jacket and no hat? Martha! A fire? God forbid! Dotty? "How's your mother? Your sister?"

Through his teeth the boy stammered, "F-f-fine."

Jacob dipped a rag in the water and wrung it out, laid it across Tim's nose and mouth, held the ends over his ears. As his skin color changed from white to pink, Tim bit his lip. Jacob said, "The Lord watches over you."

Tim's shivering calmed. He gasped. "Oww."

"Warming up hurts," Dan told him, "but you'll be all right soon."

A single nod. The boy whispered, "Pap threw me out." He shuddered in a spasm of shivering. "I told him I wouldn't work the claim no more."

Dan read the same thought on Jacob's face. What sort of father would drive his son into this blizzard? It could have killed him. No thanks to McDowell that his son lived. And Martha was left in that man's clutches? And Dotty? Jesus.

Dan raised an eyebrow at Jacob, asked a silent question. Jacob said, "Ja."

"You can stay with us," Dan said.

"Ja," Jacob said. "We make room."

How they were to keep a big boy and a dog in a bachelor cabin already cramped for two men, Dan didn't know, but they would manage. Or find a bigger cabin to rent, because this good lad was never going back to his father. Not if he could help it. "Stay as long as you want." It struck him that he had worried about alienating Tim from his father, felt guilty about the secret planner inside himself, and here McDowell had thrown Tim to him. Dan had worried for nothing, he knew, but what would happen to Tim when he left Alder Gulch?

Tears leaked from Tim's closed eyelids, then as if something in him had breached, they flowed down his cheeks, into the rag. "I'm sorry."

Jacob dabbed at the tears with the ends of the rag.

"Nothing better for healing frostbite." Dan hoped it was true. "You have nothing to be sorry about."

If he had defied Grandfather, fled the house to earn his own keep, he might now be well established and prosperous as a surveyor. If Father had had the courage to tell Grandfather to go to hell, as Tim apparently did to McDowell, what might have been the outcome? He might still be alive, and Dan would not be here in the howling center of a dark and frigid storm.

Useless speculation. The past was never to be undone, but a little courage might yet satisfy the future.

∾

If it hadn't been that she could have lost them both, Martha would have taken Dotty and run after Tim. The one time she went to the door to see out, she near froze herself, and saw nothing but the whiteness of thick snow like trying to peer through blowing sheets on a line. She could never have found him. She could only pray.

Sam yelled, "Close the goddam door!"

She closed it without a word to him. Dotty was huddled under the quilts on her bed, and Martha slept there with her when she laid down. From their bed, where he lay to keep warm, Sam said, "It's cold enough in here without you letting the storm in."

"Then go get more wood. It's at the side of the house." She didn't look at him, but at the stew heating on the stove.

"I know where it is." He bundled himself up to meet the ice-laden wind.

"Mam?" Dotty spoke from her nest, a pile of blankets on the floor. "Where do you reckon Timmy is now?"

Martha smiled down at the child, tried to act confident, not an easy thing, as scared as she was. "I reckon he's with friends. Mr. Stark lives closest. He'd take him in."

"You think he's all right?"

Martha paused, one arm reaching under the counter, into the flour barrel. A certainty comforted her as she thought about the child's question. "I do. He's got the Lord to protect him." She poured flour into the sifter. "What do you say to dumplings for supper?"

After a little silence, Dotty said, so soft that Martha almost didn't hear, "I hate Pap. He shouldn't oughta sent Timmy out in this storm."

"You mustn't say that!" A kicking at the door sent Martha rushing to open it for Sam.

He pushed open the door, and leaned against it, wood piled high in his arms, to help Martha shut it behind him. "I got enough damn wood to last till kingdom come."

He dropped the wood into the box. Several pieces spilled over and rattled onto the floor, but he stripped off his wraps and fell into the bed again. Martha stacked the fallen wood, shoved two chunks into the stove. As she went at making the dumplings she was talking to him in the silence of her mind. You fool. You great fool. You don't know what's important.

Flakes of snow blew through the cracks between the window boards, and the wind roared strong as ever all through dinner and into the night. Martha had nothing to say that wouldn't have been prayer. Save my boy, Lord. Save my boy.

Sometime after dinner McDowell spoke in a voice free of its usual growl. "Come on into bed with me, you and the little one. We'll all be warmer."

"The fire needs building up again."

"I'll do it."

She piled the quilts from Dotty's bed onto their own, and they crawled into it. McDowell built up the fire and used the slop pail, then tossed its contents into the storm. When the bed dipped and he slid in next to her, she lay curled around the child, her back to him, and kept her breathing regular and slow pretending to sleep until it was true.

Later on, she dreamed or maybe just remembered when Sam was at the War and Timmy had been her little man, doing his Pap's chores. Now and then someone from over the rise had come to see was they all right, and they always was. They had enough, even to give away. Corn, potatoes, chicken, ham, milk, all the greens of the garden. Given her druthers, she'd never keep hogs again. She hated the killing of them. Dotty wouldn't stay to home when they had a hog to kill, but traipsed into the woods far enough she couldn't hear them scream when their throats was slit, and she and Timmy hauled them up by their back feet to hang and die.

Except for killing hogs, that they only did the once, and praying for Sam to come home safe, she and the young'uns did just fine. The horses threw their heavy bodies against the traces of the plow, and so what if neighbors smiled at her furrows going a little cattywampus? The grain come up just like they'd been straight as string.

McDowell turned over and prodded against her, but she hissed at him to stop. She couldn't lay with him knowing he might have killed their boy. Maybe if she knew Timmy was alive. Dear Lord, keep Timmy safe. She dreamed. Timmy was walking on Jackson with a man who looked like Mr. Stark, and Martha was that relieved she shouted at him to wait for her and the child, and they stopped until she and Dotty caught up, and they were all together. She'd never been so happy, because they were a family.

She awoke, and the cracks between the window boards were black. A family with Mr. Stark? Why had she dreamed that? Why had she dreamed something so wrong? But the dream had told her that Tim was alive, the feeling she'd had earlier was right, she knew in her bones, though the other part was so wrong. Dreams was mixed-up things, she told herself, that's all they was. Tears trickled out of the corners of her eyes. They couldn't be a family with Mr. Stark. Never.

What was she to do? She'd held to a family with McDowell, even after he sold the farm away from them, because it was his right. And what come of it? He'd throwed it into the storm with Tim. Even if she could forgive him, she couldn't never forget. Forgiving would take time. A long time. If she ever could.

Again she slept, and when she woke up, the cracks were still black, but it seemed the wind had died some, though the room was bone-chilling cold. Cussing the cold, McDowell stood out of bed and rebuilt the fire. When he came back, he put an arm around Martha and pulled her close. She let him, because he was cold.

He said, "We should have brought the big stove."

It was a towering thing for him to say, as close to sorry as he'd ever come, McDowell owning up to that, but she'd had to fight him to bring her and the young'uns along – never mind the big stove. He'd thrown Tim into the storm.

He put his hand over her breast and thrust at her.

"It's too late," she whispered over her shoulder. "You done threw our boy away."

He said nothing, only his hand squeezed her breast so hard that tears come to her eyes.

"Don't," she panted, pried at his strong fingers.

He muttered in her ear, "You'll get your comeuppance one of these days," and turned away, so the bed bounced hard on its springs.

Martha wept into the pillow, quiet so as not to wake the child.

∾

Toward mid-morning the storm stopped. The day changed from a blurred pale grey to sharp blue shadows on dazzling snow. The sun might be shining and the wind might be gone, but the cold stayed, and Martha shivered in the doorway and squinted through her lashes at McDowell forging through the drifts. He was gone without a word, and she watched him go, and was grateful he hadn't done no worse than squeeze her breast. It still hurt, but she reckoned it would ease in time. When he turned past the Melodeon Hall, she shut the door on the sunlight and groped for her wraps. The darkness in the cabin confused her eyes.

"Get yourself bundled up, child, we're going to look for your brother."

Even following in Sam's trail, Martha was soon wet from her boots to her knees. His big strides were small help to her as she broke trail for Dotty. By the time they reached Idaho and turned toward Jackson Street, she was weary, and her snow-crusted skirts dragged heavy on her. They'd be sopping the minute she walked inside someplace and the snow melted off them.

A dog barked, and a man hailed her, and she shielded her eyes against the glare to see Canary jumping over drifts to get to her and Dotty. Daniel Stark, carrying a wide-bladed coal shovel, waved. He and Jacob Himmelfarb, shoveling a path through snow above their knees, plowed toward her. Martha tried to hurry to meet him.

The fine, powdery snow flew into the air all around. Martha stopped, confused because if it hadn't been for the snow dragging on her, she'd have run into his arms. She couldn't get her breath, and she pretended it was from struggling through the drifts, and then she saw he was panting a little, too, and from the look in his eyes it wasn't all from shoveling, neither, though it was awkward for him without the full use of both hands.

"You're safe." He took her hand in his before she could speak. "Thank God. Your son's safe, too."

"Praise the Lord," said Martha. "Where is he?"

"Oh, Mam." Dotty began to cry. "I been so scared."

"In our cabin. Would you walk in and see for yourself?" He dropped her hand, and a redness came into his face. Mr. Himmelfarb bobbed his head and smiled, and Mr. Stark reached out to Dotty. "Let me carry you. These drifts are too much for a little girl." It was in Martha's mind to say, Mind your hand, when she realized he wasn't someone she ought to talk to like family, so she watched him lift the child onto his right arm. She hadn't known he was so strong.

They made a procession, suddenly, of joy. Mr. Stark walked ahead of Martha with the child, breaking through the drifts for her, he told the young'un, "Your brother is just fine. He got a little frostbite, so he'll stay inside today, but he should be out and about tomorrow."

The dog capered about, bounding in the drifts, tail wagging, gulping at the snow.

Mr. Himmelfarb, carrying two wide-bladed shovels, kept saying, "Ja, Tim is fine, just fine."

Mr. Stark set Dotty on her feet, and knocked at the door.

"Mam! Dotty! Thank God!" Tim, in the doorway, gathered his sister into a great hug. Martha walked inside, as near to fainting as she'd ever been from too much happiness, and Canary danced around her, jumped up to lick her hands. Her tears come hard now, but Tim's arms were around her and the child. She clung onto him, and let herself be led near to the stove, eased down onto a chair, where she bent over and hid her face in her hands. Safe. Her boy was safe. Truly safe.

"Mam, Mam, why you crying? Mam, it's all right. I'm fine. Mam, please stop." Tim held her and rocked her like he was the parent and she the child. At last she was able to get ahold of herself some.

"You're safe," she said. "Thank you, Lord. Thank you, Mr. Stark." She looked around for him, but she and the young'uns were alone in the cabin.

"Yes. You all right, Mam?" When she nodded, he said, "Truly?"

"Truly. None of us come to harm. Just a little cold, but we tolerated that, and we had wood enough. Your Pap toted it in."

The boy hunkered down in front of her. Dotty was rubbing her back, and Canary sat watching her with his tail beating on the floor. His tongue lolled out the side of his mouth and he smiled a wide doggy grin that made Martha laugh and rumple his ears. She took out a rag from her sleeve and wiped her eyes, blew her nose.

Tim took her hands in his own. "I ain't coming home, Mam." His man's deep voice.

His forelock hung almost into his eyes, like always, even when he was a baby. She brushed it aside in the old gesture, and it felt about as soft as ever. Even knowing how it would be like he said, she couldn't speak, just nodded, trying to hide her despair in the joy of finding him safe. Her family had broke up and they'd never be together like she'd hoped. "I know."

Tim went on like he hadn't heard her. "I can't come home while Pap's there. I won't be a slavey to him and work his claims for no wages. I'll go to work for Mr. Dance stocking shelves, and I'll do like you and learn to read and write and cipher, and do some speculating. And when I get enough money put by, I'll go to school and learn something, and I'll raise horses. There's a need for good horses here. Something besides Mustangs all the time."

"Where'll you live?"

"Mr. Stark says I can live with him and Mr. Himmelfarb as long as I want."

Dotty sat on the other chair and fondled the dog's long soft ears.

Tears stung Martha's eyes. "I was so afraid you was lost in the storm."

"I was, Ma, but Canary brung me here, and they took me in." He paused. "Especially Mr. Stark."

Martha said, "I need to thank them, personal."

"Especially Mr. Stark," Tim said.

"Yes. Especially Mr. Stark."

Tim went to the door and called to him. Mr. Stark stood the shovel in the snow and come in. He stripped off his wraps and hung them all up neat. With the four of them inside, Martha felt how small this cabin was. How could her boy stay here? It was hardly big enough for two men, let alone three, yet they were willing to make room, somehow.

Martha stood up. "I'll never be able to thank you for what you done." When he spread his hands, seeming about to say it was nothing, she stamped her foot. "It ain't nothing. You done sheltered my boy, and you're willing to keep on until he don't need it no more."

"Your Tim is a good boy, Mrs. McDowell. It's no trouble to me, or Jacob, to help him."

She gave him her hand to shake like a man would do. "Mr. Stark, I think you have a good heart. Thank you."

He was standing in a patch of sunshine from the window over the wash stand, and she watched the red come in his face. He held her hand like he'd never let it go. "You're welcome."

She glanced at his left hand, resting in the sling. The swelling was down. "I see your thumb is better."

"Yes, thanks to you."

Conscious that the young'uns were watching, afraid they'd see too plain how she felt about him, Martha groped in her mind for something to say, but found only a calm silence. When she pulled her hand free, his fingertips slid along her palm, and a flame kindled in her belly. "We'd best be getting on," she said just as he spoke: "I'll look for a bigger cabin." They stood there, not touching, just smiling at each other like they shared a happy secret.

༄

Dan's bowels were jelly. Fool. Damn fool. He might be committing suicide tonight. For Christ's sake, whatever had possessed him to challenge Gallagher? All he had done was to postpone Jack's murderous intent. And by taking in Tim, he'd earned McDowell's greater hatred. This night, he'd warned the boy and Jacob that he might not walk home. He'd told the boy to take care of the Spencer; if he didn't come back, the rifle belonged to Tim, and now, without its weight, he felt lopsided. The pistol in his coat pocket wasn't the same.

Jacob walked with him, but he'd forbidden Tim to come. The night was colder than the word cold would bear, and everyone went about with scarves across their noses and mouths, even for short distances, like road agents, nothing showing but their eyes. If he hadn't challenged Gallagher, he thought as they crossed to the Melodeon Hall, there would be no end to the power of the roughs. Like Anton Holter and the other witnesses, he had to stand up before men. He had helped to prosecute Ives, and it did not matter that his gut clenched and sweat trickled down his back. The job was not over. He could not do otherwise than walk through the door of the saloon.

Just inside, Dan paused. "Gallagher's not here yet." He had to shout over the fiddles, the squeeze box, the piano, the boots and the hollow laughter of men trying to pretend they were having fun, and not far from home.

Jacob still looked worried. "How do you know?" he screamed into Dan's ear.

"I can't smell him." Dan ignored Jacob's stare, that said he was crazy. Later he'd explain. The peculiar malevolence of a man who wants you dead carries an odor strong as a wolverine.

Con Orem waved. Dan and Jacob threaded their way among the poker tables to the bar. Maybe a beer would settle his nerves. Con was nearly through the first draw when Dan put a foot on the rail. "Charlie Beehrer makes the best beer in the Territory, but damn, it's slow." The dark German brew had a thick tan-colored head that Orem blew off three times before sliding the pewter stein over to Dan.

"Keep your dust," the saloonkeeper said. "Happy New Year."

Dan licked foam off his upper lip. "Thanks. And Happy New Year to you, too."

Orem cocked an eyebrow at Jacob, who said, "Ja. Please." Jacob reached for his poke, but Orem shook his head.

"Danke," Jacob said. "Ein glückliches Neues Jahr."

"Same to you, Jake," Con said.

Dan laid his poke on the bar. "Have one on me." The poke held his stake for tonight's game. He'd better win because he would not stake more.

"Save your dust." Orem drew himself a beer in his own stein, and set it on the bar while he rolled up his sleeves. Heavy muscle corded his forearms. He leaned on the bar, and in his hands the stein was reduced to a coffee cup. "You know, at first

I never figured you for a gambling man. Thought you were just a tenderfoot."

"The old man started teaching me before I went to school. I thought you counted one through ten, jack, queen, ace." He had managed a joke, though his stomach rumbled.

Orem laughed. "That's a good one." His glance roamed the room, where his men strolled about, on the lookout to stop trouble before it started. "So you're giving Gallagher and McDowell a rematch tonight."

His mouth full of beer, Dan nodded. His stomach lurched, and he almost could not swallow.

"I'll see it stays on the up and up." The brown eyes, hard now as marbles, slid to Dan. "I don't like trouble in my place."

"That's why we're here. You run an honest game."

"A two-edged sword, ain't it?" Orem nodded toward a front table. "That game's breaking up. Two of them are going to find better pickings."

Dan and Jacob carried their beers over to the table. Dan stood behind an empty chair that held a smelly buffalo coat. Another empty chair, between two windows, separated the coat's owner from another player, who had a wild head of dark curly hair. Dan recalled the coat and the smell, rank and sharp, but what was the man's name? Across from him a man sweated in a brightly striped Hudson's Bay coat. Dan kept a blank face, lest a player read on it something about the cards he was watching. Sloan. Jim Sloan. That was it. Only Sloan and Hudson's Bay counted as players.

"Fold." Curly turned his cards face down, and wiped his cuff at the ice on one of the windows. Dan wanted to yell at him to stop. He didn't want anyone to see in.

Where was Gallagher? Maybe they wouldn't come. The cards slapped down, the players said, "Raise." "Call." Round it went until one said, "See you." The hand ended, Sloan gathered in the pot.

One of the losers threw down his cards. "I'm out." He gathered up his things and left.

"I need a beer, gentlemen, if you'll excuse me," said Curly.

"Well, well," Sloan said. "If it ain't the card sharp. You going to give me another chance to clean you out, Counselor?"

So Sloan knew he'd prosecuted Ives. What did he think of that? "Why not?" Dan said. "It's New Year's Eve. You might as well help me celebrate."

Sloan laughed. "I'll do the celebrating." He looked past Dan at Jacob. "What about you, pal?"

Jacob shook his head. "I watch only."

Dan said, "His English isn't so good yet."

"Hoo!" said Sloan. "Don't need much English for raise, call, check. Fold."

Hudson's Bay stood up and smiled at Jacob. "We've plenty of room, old chap." There was a tear in one coat pocket.

"It's worth it just to hear Bob talk," Sloan said. "I ain't never heard nothing like him."

"I'm English, dear boy." Bob folded his coat over the back of his chair. His plaid wool shirt had two small round holes in the left pocket. "Always happy to provide entertainment."

He'd bought a dead man's shirt. "Does that shirt bring you luck?" asked Dan.

"I rather like to think so." Bob smiled winningly, and Dan's suspicions rose. The man was a gambler. A professional, despite the holed shirt and torn coat.

Dan took the chair between Sloan and Curly. Between the two windows, his back to a solid wall. "What's the game?" Sloan's stink made his eyes water, but no one could outflank him. Jacob had taken up a station slightly to Sloan's left and behind him. Thick ice clouding the windows in spite of Curly's efforts prevented anyone from telling who sat there.

"How about five-card stud, aces high, dollar bets?" said Sloan.

"Suits me," Dan said.

Bob held out his hand. "Butler's the name. Benjamin O. Butler. Folks call me Bob. The initials, you see." An unlit pipe lay beside his pile of chips.

Dan shook it and spoke his name. "Glad to know you."

Bob rubbed his hands together. "Well, now, that remains to be seen, does it not?"

Curly came back carrying two beers. Setting both down at his place, he wiped moisture from his hand and held it out for Dan to shake. "Name's Tony Morelli, Anthony Charles Morelli, and before you ask, yes, I'm a wop, but my people have been American as long as yours."

As he shook Morelli's hand, Dan thought of his Mayflower ancestor and said his own name. Then he forgot Morelli.

The door creaked open and two men walked in on a draft of frigid air. Dan's vision narrowed, darkened, and Gallagher and McDowell appeared as at the end of a tunnel, in a spot of light, and the jolly laughter and music faded into a rushing sound like breakers in the ocean. Gallagher's head turned, he saw Dan, said something to McDowell, who laughed. The laughter and music rose, and everything around Dan took on a sharp edge. He had never seen anything to clearly: Con Orem coming to point, his hands sliding off the bar, one of his men giving his beer stein to a customer waiting to dance. Jacob sucked in a breath.

Gallagher and McDowell.

Dan wished himself at home. In New York. Anywhere but here. His right biceps quivered and would not stop when as if casually, with a steady hand, he raised the beer to lips grown suddenly stiff. He curled the fingers of his left hand into his sling to hide their trembling.

"How do, boys," said Gallagher.

McDowell grunted.

"Happy New Year, Jack. Sam." Dan set down the mug without rattling it on the table. He hoped they couldn't see his shaking.

"Care to sit in? There's room," Sloan said.

"The more the better. Have a seat," Bob said.

"You three know you're playing with a strangler?" asked McDowell.

"Hell," Sloan said, "everybody in the Gulch knows about Dan Stark, friend. His dust weighs out the same as anyone's."

Dan felt the smooth wooden grip of the hand gun, Samuel Colt's latest model Navy revolver, in his pocket. God save him from having to pull the thing out. Yet he should be ready. He laid it across his lap. "Mind if they sit in?" Forcing a smile, and looking into Gallagher's eyes, he said, "I cleaned their clocks the day Nick Tbalt's body was brought in."

"That's right, he did." Sloan barked out a short laugh. "Cleaned mine, too."

"You don't say." A frown creased Morelli's face, but his dark eyes were shining with mischief. "Maybe I better drop out now while I still have some dust."

"What about it, Counselor? Think you can do it again?" Sloan scratched his head.

"Depends on the cards." Dan forced himself not to think about what lived in Sloan's hair.

Gallagher shook himself out of his topcoat, laid it on top of Sloan's buffalo coat, then thought better of that and draped it carefully over the back of the chair next to Bob. "What's the game?"

Curly took the mug away from his mouth. "Five-card stud, aces high, dollar bets, five-dollar limit."

"Five-dollar limit? Sounds penny-ante to me," said Gallagher.

"We don't want to start the New Year broke."

"What the hell. It'll just take longer to skin Stark, that's all. We'll get a beer and be with you."

As they walked off, Sloan said, "Those two are after more than your dust. They want your hide."

"I know." Dan flexed his fingers. "If you want to fold now, nobody'd blame you."

Sloan stretched, reached his hands high over his head. "I wouldn't miss this. I ain't been having much excitement lately."

"I'll stay, too," Morelli said. "Just to see what happens."

"If you chaps stay, I suppose I might as well." Bob riffled the deck, first one side, then turned it over and riffled the same side, but it looked like a different side because he had turned it over. "I've never thought I liked Gallagher much."

Dan didn't hear him. Fool. He laid his right hand on the table, willed it not to shake, tried to look calm, as if he merely waited for his cards. Fool. The room was filling with men, and the buzz of talk rose. Men glanced at him, quick looks that ricocheted off and darted back. He thought they were judging his toughness, choosing their bets. Fool.

"He's crazy," Morelli told Sloan, and Dan wanted to agree with him.

"He's better off here than in any other saloon," Sloan said. "He's got friends here. Con Orem's no friend to the roughs. He won't have Boone Helm in the place."

Bob laid the cards aside and put the long, curving pipe stem in his mouth, chewed at it, then began the business of lighting it.

A crowd gathered around the table. Dan recognized the two brothers who had asked to join the Vigilantes the day he challenged Gallagher. They nodded, smiled, gave him a thumbs up signal. Both men carried sawed-off shotguns. Men made way for Gallagher and McDowell, who took a chair and shoved it between Sloan and Sloan's coat. "Christ," he said. "When did you kill that thing? Yesterday?"

Gallagher said, "Get the damn thing away from me."

"Hey," Sloan protested. "That critter never done you no harm. Don't insult it. It has to be somewhere."

"Oh, hell." Gallagher shrugged. The coat stayed where it was, but he shifted his chair closer to Bob, who said, "We've all been treated to its delicious aroma this evening."

Gallagher let out a snort of laughter.

"Delicious aroma? Like apple pie, maybe?" Dan joked, and in the next breath cursed his stupidity.

"Apple pie? Like my wife makes? What do you mean by that? You carrying on behind my back, you and her?" McDowell leaned forward, a knife in his fist. Sloan pushed his chair back, and a leg came down on Jacob's foot, who shouted at the sudden pain.

"Sorry," Sloan lifted the chair leg off Jacob's foot and slid it forward. "Damn it, are we playing cards or tiddly winks tonight?"

McDowell said. "Being in the same room with that thing is bad. My lungs will never be the same."

Bob tamped tobacco into the pipe bowl. "If you fear for your lungs, I recommend you take up pipe smoking. Fumigates a room and your lungs at the same time. Very beneficial."

As if Gallagher and McDowell had not come to kill Dan, they began to negotiate the pot limit, the values of the different colored chips, the value of a dollar in gold dust. Dan kept himself from squirming, held his tongue between his teeth to keep from shouting, Let's play cards, dammit. He broke into one argument on the price of gold by saying, "The price of gold, last I checked, was $18.00 an ounce." At last the wrangling was done, and everyone agreed on the value of the chips: white for a dollar, blue for five, yellow for ten, each man to start with a hundred dollars worth of chips.

One of the onlookers whistled, and muttered to a friend, "That's pretty rich." A month's wages to a miner.

"High card deals?" Bob finished lighting the pipe, his cheeks pulling in as he sucked down the smoke. He shuffled the cards two or three times, straightened them, and ran his fingertips over the edges as if playing with the deck.

"Here," Bob said to Gallagher. "You cut, old chap, and I'll deal for high card."

Gallagher cut. As Bob dealt, Gallagher said, "I think we should make the game more interesting."

"Me, too," Sloan said. "What do the rest of you say?"

Dan stretched his lips into a smile. "Fine with me." He'd had enough of this dancing around. He wanted to get underway, to know the outcome, if he won or lost. Lived or died before 1864.

"Raise the limit," Gallagher's dark eyes were alight. "To the sky."

"My God." Morelli whistled. "That's rich."

No one objected, except that McDowell, for a moment, looked both surprised and panic-stricken, as if he stood to lose everything on the first card. Perhaps he did, Dan thought.

The deal fell to Bob, who shuffled the deck a few times, slid it over to Morelli to cut, rejoined the halves of the deck, and shuffled again. "Ante up, now, gentlemen. One white chip."

They each tossed a white chip into the center of the table. Dan's chip rolled too far and nearly landed in Gallagher's lap. The muscle spasm in his arm moved to his left calf, and his boot heel drummed softly. He pressed his heel down and concentrated on keeping it there.

When the first card dropped in front of Gallagher, the onlookers quieted. The stomping, the music, a woman's squeal of laughter at the back of the room, faded like an old shirt washed too many times, and Dan heard the small hushed sounds of chips falling, Morelli's raspy breathing, Sloan scratching at his crotch. The two brothers stood in the front row, and Dan recognized other men who had been at the larger Vigilante meetings. He was not alone. He smelled Bob's pipe smoke and let his right hand rest in his lap, on the pistol, the wooden butt warm to his touch. His leg muscle stopped twitching. He knew where he was. He had gone into this battle of cards so many times, and tonight, with the first card, a certainty came. This night he would not lose.

He shed his jacket, rolled up his right sleeve, laid bare his forearm. No one would be able to say he held any card up his sleeve. Just to make sure, he pulled his left hand out of the sling and rolled up that sleeve, too. Tonight he would not use the sling. He laid the left on the table where everyone could see the bandage, the hand's uselessness. He peeked at the hole card, an ace of hearts, and looked up to find Gallagher watching him. He made himself smile, and Gallagher's brows drew together over his long thin nose. A silent threat, but Dan looked at his own cards and, from behind his wall of certainty, calculated the value of his first up card, a four of clubs, compared with the other players'.

Gallagher, with a ten of spades showing, checked. So did everyone else. On the second deal, Bob dealt Gallagher a second ten, Dan a five of hearts. Gallagher bet five dollars, and everyone else folded. Gallagher scooped in the chips and stacked them neatly in front of himself.

Dan dropped his right arm to his side and spread his stiff fingers out, flexed them two or three times. Gallagher's deal. One of the men standing behind him whispered something to another man, and Gallagher snarled, "Shut the hell up." The onlookers went very still.

The hole card was a five of clubs, the nine next. Morelli had an ace up, and one by one the players all folded. "You're a lousy dealer," Morelli said.

Dan tossed in his third white chip. The pot was growing, and he was down close to five dollars. He hoped the cards would turn in his favor. He wanted to win, God, how he wanted to win. Nothing mattered but the cards, the winning.

Now Gallagher cut for McDowell. As the cards fell, Morelli scrubbed both hands through his hair, making it wilder than ever.

"Do you ever get a haircut?" asked Gallagher, whose own dark hair lay straight and neatly trimmed. People said that his woman, Isabelle Stevens, cut it for him with a long-bladed scissors she carried in her skirt pocket to tame her clientele.

"I'll have it cut the day before I get on that stage," Morelli said. "Not until."

The hands see-sawed back and forth, no man winning or losing much. The stacks of white chips in front of each man rose and sank and rose again, but their supplies of blue chips and yellow chips stayed constant. It could go on like that all night, Dan knew, until they either wearied of the game and quit or until someone was a clear winner.

The crowd thickened. Dan heard their breathing like that of a large animal, as if the tyger had come back from the Ives trial. Their odor was of rotting leaves. He wanted air, a drink of clear cold water, but he stayed in his chair. Think only of the game. Only the game. Winning. He waited, like everyone else, for something to break. There would be no quitting early tonight, no walking out before the game was up. Tonight he would stay to the finish. And win.

A man tried to sidle around behind Morelli's chair where he could see into Dan's hand. Dan snarled, "Not there."

"Sorry." The man pushed himself away, through the small space between Morelli and the window.

Dan would not help the side bets by letting anyone see his cards, would not help anyone telegraph his cards to another player, or to the men in the crowd who laid side bets. If they wanted to bet, let them get in the game. Let them be players. He glanced up at Jacob, who parked his butt on the window sill. Jacob wiped his hand down the side of his coat. Odd, Dan thought. His own hands were dry.

Dan's backside hurt from sitting so long on the hard chair. He pushed back his chair into the wall and felt it close him into the game. He stretched, and yawned. He stood up.

"Goddammit, you can't quit," said Gallagher.

Dan let Gallagher's voice echo in his mind. A warning. "I'm not. Just resting. Isn't your ass sore?"

"Not yet," Gallagher said. "I have more staying power than you do."

Morelli said, "I gotta piss pretty soon."

"After the next hand," Gallagher said without looking away from Dan.

The deal came around to Gallagher again. Dan checked his hole card – ace of spades. He had the high card. Already. The first up cards fell: seven of diamonds to McDowell, five of diamonds to Sloan, four of clubs to Dan, three of hearts to Morelli, eight of hearts for Bob, ten of spades for Gallagher.

Sloan muttered, "Damn cards ain't running tonight. Fold." One down.

Dan opened. "One dollar."

"Oh, Christ, make it worth staying up for," said Gallagher.

Morelli said, "Call. And raise." He tossed in a blue chip.

"That's pretty rich," Bob said. "What the hell. Easy come, easy go. Call." He put a blue chip in.

Gallagher said, "Call. And raise." He rolled a yellow chip across the table.

Bob whistled.

He must have a pair, Dan said to himself. Why else would he make such an extravagant raise when he's the last man to bet on this round? Except, he was growing restless. Impatient at the conservative play so far, wanting more action, more of a thrill. Very well. If the cards fell right, he'd give Gallagher a thrill, all right.

The second up cards fell now. A jack to McDowell, a four of hearts to Dan, eight of clubs to Morelli, a ten of hearts to Bob for a potential flush or straight. If his hole card were a nine. If. A queen to Gallagher. Everyone checked. Even Gallagher.

The fourth deal gave McDowell a king of hearts, a nine of clubs to Dan, a ten of diamonds to Bob, and a king of diamonds to Gallagher.

Dan now had a pair of fours showing, while Bob had a pair of tens. If he were smart, Dan told himself, he'd fold. He wasn't sure why he stayed, except that he had a feeling. Was this what had suckered Father so often? This feeling that he would win? His pair of fours couldn't beat Bob's tens, or a possible pair of kings or queens that Gallagher might have. Yet if he died tonight, if it were all over, what did it matter if the gold he left the family were poorer by ten dollars or so? Nearly a week's wages for a clerk. "Five bucks to open."

Morelli and Bob called.

"About damn time. Call." Gallagher dropped a blue chip into the pot. "And raise." He flicked another blue chip toward the pot, but it rolled too far. Sloan caught it and placed it properly.

Some of the men drew their breath in a hiss.

McDowell was pale and sweating. "Call." His Adam's apple bounced as he put in a yellow chip and took back some white ones.

"It's a ten dollar bet," said Bob.

"So?" Glaring, McDowell dropped the white chips on a bare spot on the table.

"So a yellow chip is ten dollars, old boy. You have to leave the white chips in the pot."

"How was I supposed to know?"

Dan knew McDowell took the white chips because he was scared. He couldn't count, couldn't read, and in his fear he'd forgotten that the yellow chips were ten dollars. Now he was publicly embarrassed by his own ignorance.

McDowell snarled at Dan. "What the hell are you looking at?"

"Nothing. It's a simple mistake anyone could make."

"Fuck you, you son of a bitch!" McDowell nearly screamed. "You calling me — "

By rights, Dan should be shooting McDowell, or at the least yelling back; men had been killed, were killed, over those words. But Dan just sat. Insults were nothing. The game was all.

"Shut up, McDowell," Gallagher turned the full authority of his office on McDowell. "We ain't going to do nothing except play cards. You hear? You two can have it out later, but right now we finish this game." He added. "Like he said, anyone can make a mistake."

McDowell breathed hard through his nose. "Yeah. Anyone can make a mistake."

"All right. Let's play cards." Gallagher dealt the last round.

Dan watched the cards fall, but his mind was only partly on the play. Why had Gallagher defused the situation? McDowell had a queen of spades. It was the perfect setup, and he had walked right into it, into a beautiful trap. Had McDowell taken the white chips on purpose? Or had he, Dan, just been stupid? Morelli caught a jack of spades: eight, nine, jack. All he needed was the ten and he'd have a straight. A five of clubs to Bob, was his hole card a five? If so, he had two pair. The queen dropped in front of Gallagher. So Gallagher won. A pair of queens beat a pair of tens, and for sure his pair of fours. Or his high card, his ace of spades. Shit. He'd been stupid in cards, stupid with McDowell. Bet so much on an ace of spades, just because he'd hoped something would –

Dan glanced down at his fourth up card. Ace of clubs. Jesus Christ. He had two pair. Aces and fours. Good God almighty. He'd won.

If. If Bob's or Gallagher's hole cards didn't give them three of a kind. Unless McDowell's hole card were an ace or a ten. Or Morelli had a ten. If. If. And if again.

A flea jumped into the back of his neck, but he kept himself from slapping at it. Tomorrow he'd get a bath. Start the New Year right.

McDowell opened. "Five bucks." He laid a blue chip in the pot as if it were fragile.

Dan said, "Call," and flipped a blue chip toward the pile.

Morelli folded. He muttered to Dan, "I'm not throwing good money after bad."

Bob said, "Call." His voice was flat. Then he smiled. "And raise." A yellow chip followed the blue one.

Shit. Bob had something that made him confident. Another eight or a five? Or a ten? There was only one ten outstanding. What if it were Bob's hole card? Dan's neck itched. The flea worked its way up, into his hair; he tried to ignore it.

"Call." Gallagher pitched in a blue and a yellow chip.

A rich pot. Eighty-one dollars.

Now he could scratch his neck, hunt down the flea. He killed it with his nails and dropped it to the floor. Let his right hand rest in his lap. On the pistol. The steel barrel was cold, the wooden butt warm.

McDowell was grumbling under his breath. Sloan murmured to Dan, "Watch out for him. He knows he's lost money he probably doesn't have."

"Thanks," Dan said. "He probably borrowed from Gallagher."

"Shit," Sloan said. "He's in trouble, then."

"Showdown, boys." Gallagher turned over his hole card, a nine of diamonds, and fanned out his hand, the pair of queens above the other cards.

McDowell flung his cards into the middle of the table. "One lousy pair of jacks. God damn it."

Dan held in his laughter. He'd had a feeling, and this was the result, as savory as tenderloin with a good burgundy. "Queens beat jacks and tens, all right, but not aces. And not two pair." He spread out his up cards and turned over the hole card. "Aces and fours, gentlemen."

The other players stared at the cards laid in a neat line in front of Dan.

"An ace in the hole," said Sloan. "You crafty devil."

"You son of a bitch." Bob threw back his head and laughed a great peal that stirred the smoke layering the table. "You beautiful son of a bitch."

"You bastard!" McDowell half rose from his chair. "You son of a bitch."

"God damn you!" Gallagher started up, his hand on the pistol he pulled from his belt.

The onlookers scattered, a collection of frightened men. Dan stayed in his chair, his revolver pointing at Gallagher under the table. He did not want to shoot, to wound or kill another human being, but so help him, he would if it were Gallagher's life, McDowell's life, or his own.

The three men glared at each other, and the dance music from the back sounded incongruous, like an off color joke in a preacher's sermon.

A dog barked. Another snarled, and men dodged aside from a whirling vortex of snapping, yiping fur that careened out of control amid their feet. Gallagher pivoted and fired at the dogs. One dog yelped and cried, and a man bounded out of the crowd, hollered at Gallagher, "You had no call to shoot! We'd have got it broke up."

"The hell with you!" Gallagher turned his pistol on the man, and before anyone could stop it, he fired.

The man shrieked, clapped his hand to his arm. "I'm getting the hell out of here!" People made way for him, and someone pulled open the door for him, and as he stood outlined against the darkness, Gallagher raised his pistol and shot him. The man went down in a spray of blood.

Con Orem vaulted over the bar, shotgun in hand. He leveled it at Gallagher. "Get out of my saloon. Damn it, Gallagher, get out and stay out."

"God damn you, you can't throw me out!" Gallagher's face swelled, and a vein across his forehead bulged. He swung the pistol toward the saloon owner, but two of Orem's men, as big and burly as their boss, shotguns ready, closed in on Gallagher and escorted him to the door, past the wounded man. Two more pinned McDowell's arms behind his back and shuffled him along, grumbling curses until Orem's men pushed them both out into the snow and slammed the door.

People knelt by the fallen man, so that Dan could see nothing but his legs. The wounded dog's owner cradled the animal in his arms and wept. One of the hurdy-gurdy dancers, who wore a yellow dress, shoved through the men, tearing her petticoat into strips as she came. Seeing the dog's distraught owner, she handed him a strip.

Blood soaked the dancer's yellow skirt where she knelt by the wounded man, seeped into the cracks between the flooring planks. The blood, from the dog or the man, was on Dan's hands. He had challenged Gallagher to this rematch. He had won. He knew what Gallagher was like. No matter that he had meant to lose, when the game opened, his lust to win had taken over as always. He had won. And this blood was the cost. Another man and a dog paid in blood, and others paid in grief, but he had won. Jacob touched his shoulder, held his coat when he got up, still watching the blood. One of Orem's men was gathering up the unused chips and the cards.

"Here, these are yours." Sloan gave him the pot.

The pot was just chips. Valueless. It didn't matter. He would not collect from Gallagher or McDowell, and the other three could walk away. Dan pushed Sloan's hand away. "You don't have to pay. Gallagher didn't, or McDowell." Yet Gallagher would pay. This mayhem was the end of it. It was enough. It was a clear case of murder, if the man died.

"No," said Bob. "Those other two may be murderers and welshers, but I'm not. I pay my debts."

"Me, too," said Sloan.

"You won fair and square," Morelli said. "That was brilliant playing. You take it."

When Dan still shook his head, Bob said, "Come on, boys, let's take these over to Con and sort them out."

Dan barely knew they sidled through the crowd around the fallen man. After some time, the packed crowd loosened, shifted, splintered into individuals, moved away. Two men lifted the wounded man onto a table. Someone stopped by Dan. "A genuine miracle. He's going to be all right. A bullet through the neck, and it missed the artery, his spine, and his windpipe. A God-damn miracle is what it is. A miracle."

"Yes," Dan said. "A miracle sure enough." It didn't change anything. He was still to blame. Like Bob had said, debts had to be paid. Gallagher would pay this debt. "Do you know his name?"

"Yeah. George Temple."

The piano struck up the tune, "Auld Lang Syne," but Dan didn't feel like singing.

It was 1864.

❦

The calculations were not coming out right, and Dan could not find the mistake. He'd checked, double-checked, and re-checked the measurements against his notes, but the calculations refused to come out. Every time. Damn. Would he have to measure the claim again? It was under several feet of snow by now. Dan sighed. He laid his pencil in the tray, rose to his feet, and stretched. Then he kicked the empty slop pail across the room.

Outside, the sun turned the world to diamonds in white and snow-blue. He pulled on his coat, hat, and gloves, tucked his pant legs into boots. Lunch time. He'd walk down to the Eatery, and maybe going outside would clear his mind. Even if it didn't, being outside was better than sitting inside a dim and fusty cabin. Maybe he'd be in luck and see Martha McDowell. Maybe something would occur to him. Maybe he'd walk over to Creighton's, and there would be some news from the Deer Lodge scout, gone now ten days. Had they found Aleck Carter? Or had they been lost in the blizzard? Maybe there'd be new evidence he could enter into the ferreting book. Maybe. Maybe. And maybe.

He kicked at the light, dry snow, and it blew about him, powdered his face, momentarily blinding him. The cold seeped down his neck.

A woman laughed. "Look," she said to her companion, "he kicked snow onto himself."

Dan brushed melting snow from his face. Ten feet in front of him Sam McDowell walked arm in arm with one of the whores from Fancy Annie's. McDowell. Pig. With a good wife at home, he took his pleasure – a sudden surge at Dan's groin – had he no decency, to risk infecting his wife and unborn children? How could he put her at risk?

McDowell pulled the woman close to him and casually put his free hand under her coat, over her breast. "You want some of this? Do you? Good meat here. Want to take a turn? I'll make her, and you can make her." His lips twisted in a sneer. "I'll show you how."

"Go to hell," shouted Dan.

Fast steps squeaked on the snow behind Dan. "God damn you, Pap!" Carrying a snow shovel, Timothy charged his father through the snow. Dan snatched at the boy's jacket and missed. "You son of a bitch!" yelled the boy.

"No!" Dan leaped after him, but the boy did not hear him. McDowell was so much bigger, one blow of that fist could do such damage. Damn! How had he forgotten the Spencer? He pictured it standing against the wall near the door, and he had walked off without it.

McDowell flung the woman aside. She fell into a drift and floundered in the powder snow that gave her no purchase to get up. She kicked and cried and screamed about the cold.

"Walk out on me, will you?" McDowell bellowed. "You're no son of mine, you're someone else's bastard."

At the insult to Martha, Dan felt a film over his vision as he roared at McDowell, "Damn you, no!"

Tim swung the shovel in a wide arc. McDowell leaned away from it, seized the long handle as the blade passed him, and wrenched it out of the boy's hands. He threw it at Dan, and the breeze of its flight brushed his cheek. Dan caught it. He was in a nightmare, running and running and never gaining, thrashing through the snow, as Tim's momentum carried him into his father's grasp. McDowell seized the lapels of the boy's coat in one hand and smashed the other fist into Tim's mouth.

"Now, you little bastard, I'll show you who's boss in his own home. You'll work the goddam claim till hell freezes over if I tell you to." McDowell held Tim between Dan and himself, and laughed. Tim kicked at McDowell, punched at his father's midsection, but a second blow, into his right eye and cheekbone, dazed him. Dan dodged around them, behind McDowell, and one-handed, swung the flat of the shovel against McDowell's shoulder.

McDowell yelled and went down, clutching his arm. "You broke my goddam arm!"

"You're lucky that's all I broke!" Dan helped Tim to his feet. The boy's mouth was cut, and blood streamed down his chin, dropped into the sparkling snow as he bent over, hands on his knees, to catch his breath. He spat out a tooth and felt along his jaw, moved it from side to side. "Put snow on it," Dan told him.

One of the town doctors squeezed through the crowd. He looked over Tim's face, felt the boy's jaw, peered at the cut, the reddened flesh around Tim's swelling eye. "You'll live. You won't be a thing of beauty for a while, but eventually you'll look as good to the girls as ever. Put some beefsteak on that eye."

"I got a better use for it," Tim mumbled.

"Good lad." The doctor turned away to McDowell. As Dan helped Tim toward his cabin, he heard the doctor: "Good grief, man. What are you sniveling about? That arm's not broken. You'll be right as rain in a few days."

The sound of the woman's weeping faded behind them. Dan held Tim with one arm about the boy's waist; Tim dragged the shovel. My God, that a father could do this to his son. Unthinkable. And what of the mother and sister? Still in that bastard's house, in his power, for in the law a man's home was his castle, and Dan could not protect them while they lived there. He staggered through the drifts with the boy, who could hardly put one foot before the other. There would be a way, and he would find it. He didn't know how. Not yet. But somehow.

Jacob caught up to them when they were nearly at the cabin. His English failed him, and he could only stammer in German as he took the shovel out of his hand, laid Tim's arm across his shoulders. "Ich hab gesehen – Es ist – Shrechlich. Shrechlich." As they crossed Idaho Street, he found his English. "I saw it. Terrible. Terrible."

The two men removed Tim's coat and boots and undressed him down to his long underwear and laid him in the bed, as if he were a child, and covered him with thick wool blankets. Tim protested, "I'll get blood on – ."

Jacob shook his head. "No matter. First you we fix."

Dan cleaned the cuts while Jacob applied a cold compress to the eye, now swollen shut. There was a quick light tapping at the front door, and Jacob opened it for Mrs. McDowell and Dotty.

"Oh, dear God," said Tim's mother. "I heard over at the butcher shop. Timmy, Timmy, are you all right?" Dan made way for her. She knelt by the bed, lifted the compress to look at the eye, took in the split and swollen mouth, the blood from his nose. She didn't appear to see anything but her son's damaged face.

"I'll be fine, Ma." He smiled at her, and Dan thought few but his mother would know how much that smile cost him. "It's just my face, and I never was no beauty anyway." He coughed, and spat some blood into a basin Jacob held for him.

She looked up at Dan, who said, "He lost a tooth."

The mother's eyes closed on the spasm of anger and fear that twisted her features, and when she opened them again Dan thought he had never seen such ferocity on a woman's face. He knew that nothing in nature was as fierce as a mother defending her young, but he had never seen it, the look of a bear protecting her cubs, in a human being. She said, "First to throw him out into the storm, and now – this." She laid her palm against the boy's uninjured cheek.

A voice beside Dan whispered, "Pap did that?" Dotty pressed her hands to her mouth.

"Yes." Dan crouched down, gathered the child to him. She was trembling, and her little body was so slight, even with the heavy winter coat. She reminded him of his youngest sister, who would climb into his lap with a favorite book and ask him to read her a story. How he missed her! While Jacob rinsed out the basin and poured the bloody water into the slop pail, Dan sat on a stool and took the little girl on his knees.

Mrs. McDowell stroked her son's forehead. "It's the drink, you know." She wasn't looking at Dan, just at her son. "He was all right when we was young. It ain't him — it's not even the War. He did terrible things, feeding great guns that tore men to shreds, so he hates himself on account of killing so many, but it's the officers he hates most because they kept marching their men into the guns, killing and hurting thousands in a day. So when he come back, he wouldn't be told what to do, nohow. He'd took to drink, and it's been growing on him. He's not a bad man, at bottom. It's the drink." She pulled the blanket up under Tim's chin, a gesture so tender that Dan caught his breath. "But he ain't stopping. I think he'll never stop."

He could think of nothing to say, the law so limited him. This family, the woman and her children, belonged to McDowell, not to him. He said, "I'll do what I can," and cursed inwardly because it was inadequate. A mere shadow of what he wanted to do, what he wanted to say.

She rose to her feet. "I don't know how I ever can thank you. You've already done — "

Not enough, Dan told her silently. "There's no need to thank me. I'm happy to help."

"I have some herbs and things at home that I can bring to you for healing Timmy. If — ?"

"Yes. Show us what you want done and we'll do it." He paused, and plunged. "Or come any time you wish."

Mumbling something about tea, Jacob went outside with the water bucket.

"That's right kind of you," said Mrs. McDowell. "You stay here, child. I'll be right back."

When her mother had gone, Dotty looked into Dan's eyes. "Can I sit with Timmy?"

"Certainly." He helped her out of her wraps, and she sat down on the bed, where her brother lay, a stoic, eyes closed, the little girl's hand on his. Every few seconds a shiver of pain ran down his body.

"He's safe here, ain't he?"

"Yes."

"As long as you're here, ain't that right?"

"Yes." He hung up her wraps. They looked as if they belonged on those pegs.

"Only, you won't be here forever, will you?"

"No, I have to take the gold back home to my family. For them to live on."

"Why?"

"They need it and I promised I would."

"You keep your promises, don't you?"

"I try to."

"What'll we do when you're gone?" She sighed. "I wish you was my papa."

8: Alder Gulch, Virginia City

The woman held out her arms to him, to come to her, but a drum beat confused him, and bright sunlight behind her showed him only her outline, and the drumming thundered around her. A dog barked. Dan jerked awake, his heart's pounding joined with the heavy throbbing in his dream. Someone was banging on the door.

Dan stumbled out of the bed, stiff from lying too long in one position, three in a bed, spoon-fashion, and no room to turn. Jacob, awake, lay shivering in the middle, while Tim climbed over him from his place against the wall.

"Shut up!" Tim yelled at Canary. The dog subsided to a low growling.

"I'm coming," Dan bellowed. He pulled on his overcoat and levered a shell into the breech of the Spencer before he unbolted the door. From behind him, Tim raised a lighted lamp to show two men standing outside.

"About damn time you opened up," said Fitch.

"We need you," Jim Williams said. "Come to Kiskadden's."

"My God," Dan said, "you're alive. Come in, come in. I won't be a minute." He pulled on his trousers over his long underwear. He was already wearing his shirt and a sweater. "We were worried you wouldn't make it. That blizzard was a son of a bitch."

Shivering, Jacob poked at the coals and fed more wood into the stove. Tim held the dog's rope, turned the injured side of his face away from the lamplight.

The two men stood close to the stove, their hands held out to the warmth. "You got that right," said Williams. "It hit when we were on the way back, so we hunkered down by Beaverhead Rock and waited it out. No food, no fire, keep moving or die. The horses stampeded, them we couldn't picket, and we had to round them up after. Some of us ain't slept but a few hours in six days." Deep furrows scored his face from nose to mouth, and his lower lids drooped away from his eyes like those of an old man. "You got any water? I'm so damn thirsty all the time."

"I could use something stronger." Fitch peered into the shadows. "Thought you had a dog in here. Ain't that Canary? What's he—Hey, Tim, why ain't you at home?"

Jacob gave Williams a dipper full of water with chunks of ice floating in it.

Dan was pulling on a boot. "He is at home, and all we have is beer."

"Beer is good." Fitch rubbed his hands together.

The heat from the stove brought out a smell from the two men that made Dan's eyes water. "Did you get Carter?" Dan pulled on the other boot.

"No. We was thrown off the track." Williams glanced at Tim and Jacob. "Long story." He gave back the dipper. "Thank you."

Jacob poured beer into it for Fitch, who drank as if he had spent the last two weeks in a desert.

Fitch held the dipper away from his lips. Melting ice dripped from his beard onto the floor. "So, kid, what are you doing here?"

"Me and Pap had a parting of the ways."

"Come at last, did it?" Fitch jerked the dipper aside, toward Tim. Canary snapped at Fitch, and the boy turned his face into the light to grab the dog's muzzle. "Thought so. He do that?"

Tim nodded, turned the injured part into the shadows. "Yeah."

Dan looked for his gloves, rummaged among a rank pile of dirty clothes tossed in a corner to wait for the washerwoman to be in business again. Not there. The hell with gloves. He put on his overcoat, patted the bulging pockets. The gloves. For once he had put them where they should be. Paying attention to each task, he worked one onto his left hand over the bandage, drew on the right glove, took his hat, reached for the Spencer. The sudden night summons had rattled him, and he knew it. What was so important that it couldn't wait until morning? Why the urgent meeting with men whose exhaustion clawed their faces, who swayed on their feet like pine trees in a wind?

"Even if he is your Pa, he's a son of a bitch," said Fitch.

Tim said, "He'd've done worse, except Mr. Stark stopped him."

"Stark did, did he?" Fitch's fingers snagged in his beard. "I'd like to've seen that."

"Let's go," said Williams.

"Obliged for the drinks." Fitch gulped the last of the beer, gave the dipper to Jacob.

With every step, the snow protested in the tight, high-pitched squeak of deep cold. The night sky sparkled, and the waning moon lighted the snow, laundered out all color, like a photograph, but stark in black and white, without shades of gray. Dan held the rifle in the crook of his arm. Wide awake now, he was eager for the answer to this mystery: What was up, that could not wait?

"We saw X," Williams said. "He found that wagon train he was looking for."

"Good. I'm glad you're all right. It's a miracle anyone survived that blizzard."

"We got a little chilly around the edges," said Fitch. "Some of the boys will lose toes, ears, fingers, maybe a nose."

"But we're alive," Williams said.

"Thank God." Dan could not imagine how men could endure such a storm and live.

"X said he bandaged a fella's hands over Bannack way a couple days ago. Damn fool was out in that storm with no gloves, got some bad frostbite. Lucky he met X. He'll lose some skin. Maybe a finger or two."

"Who was it?"

"Don't know. X thought he might be from over around Bannack someplace." Williams kicked snow out of his path, and stumbled into Dan. "Sorry." Regaining his balance, he asked, "What's been happening here? The roughs give you any trouble?"

"A lot of threats. Nobody's been killed yet, though one of them went to Creighton's store to shoot Sanders." Dan avoided a humped mound in the snow, probably a dog burrowed in. "They persuaded him it was a bad idea."

Fitch said, "I heard you played poker with Gallagher and McDowell. Again."

"Word gets around, doesn't it?" Dan did not want to talk about that night. He'd been a fool to bring danger among innocent people. Thoughtless. If he hadn't challenged Gallagher, George Temple wouldn't have nearly lost his life. "Gallagher tried to murder a fellow named George Temple. Shot him in the back. Talk about miracles. The bullet went through his neck, and didn't hit anything major."

"How is he?"

"He's mending. Mrs. McDowell has been looking after him." It was pleasure to say her name.

"That bastard's got to be stopped," Williams said.

Dan did not know if he meant McDowell or Gallagher, but he agreed with Fitch, who said, "Him and McDowell both." Fitch spat a dark stream that stained the snow.

Despite the fire in the stove, Kiskadden's big room had a damp chill about it. Several men gathered close to the stove, a few sitting, some stood. Paris Pfouts sat at a table, leaned on his elbows. A table lamp with a green glass shade gave his face a sickly hue. Most of the Virginia Executive Committee were there, along two others from the Deer Lodge scout besides Williams and Fitch. Dan nodded to them.

Pfouts knocked his fist on the table. "This emergency meeting of the Virginia City Executive Committee will come to order. Thanks be to the Great Architect that you live."

"Thank God indeed," Dan said amidst the others' murmuring. He felt Pfouts eyeing him as if he had made a rude noise.

Pfouts spoke as if there was no time to lose. "The expedition to Deer Lodge has yielded unexpected results, gentlemen. First, I have some good news. Milt Moody and Melancthon Forbes, who left a month ago for home, have apparently reached Salt Lake after being held up south of Bannack." He raised a hand for quiet. "Two men might have succeeded in absconding with a considerable fortune, except that Lank Forbes wounded one in the shoulder, and the other man took a bullet in his chest. So watch for two men whose injuries identify them as the robbers. Now, Cap, the floor is yours."

Dan rested the stock of the Spencer on the floor between his knees.

"We didn't find Carter." Williams waited until the disappointed mumbling had died away. "We got throwed off the track, but we got something else. We got evidence of the conspiracy we all thought was here. There's a gang operating on the roads hereabouts — "

Sitting upright, Dan almost cheered aloud. Independent corroboration of the criminal conspiracy! No wonder this meeting could not wait until morning.

"I knew it!" A man clapped his hands, then rubbed them together. "I knew it!"

"Yeah," Williams said. "A lot of us thought there must be. George Brown, him that lied for Ives, tended bar at Dempsey's — ?" He broke off to be sure they knew who Brown was.

Dan's grip tightened around the rifle barrel. Tended? Had anyone else heard the past tense?

Williams took some small papers out of an inside breast pocket. "Brown wrote a note to Carter to get out of Deer Lodge." He read from one paper: "'Lay low and watch out for black ducks.'" He gave the note to Pfouts, who laid it on the table. "Red Yeager delivered it. The bastard was in such a damn hurry he killed two horses. We met Red on the Divide the second day, as he was coming back. We was pretty strung out, because our horses had a hard time finding forage, and they was weakening. We had to walk some."

Dan pictured a long slow cold hike over the Continental Divide, leading the horses, snow above the men's knees on numb feet, ears and noses freezing under the rags wrapped around their faces. The horses, tough Mustangs though they were, would have had to paw down two feet or more for grass, and then maybe not find much. Not enough to sustain the effort they made.

"Red told us different stories, but the nut of it was that Carter was in Deer Lodge sleeping off a toot. We was pretty far gone, so we laid up Christmas Day and baited the horses. By the time we got to where Red said Carter was, he'd left. The owner of the place give us that note and told us Yeager come with it for Carter."

He paused, swayed a little in his chair. After a moment, his voice flowed on. Hardly breathing, the men closed on him, listening. The lamplight shone on Williams's hands, but his voice came from the darkness. What are we up against? Dan thought of the crimes in his notebook. They were not random, but somehow connected by the conspiracy. Were Yeager and Brown part of it?

"Up on a mountain, just off the trail to Hell Gate, we saw a campfire, but there weren't no point in going on. The horses wouldn't have made it, so we turned around. We got to Beaverhead Rock just before the blizzard hit."

The great rock formation, named by Lewis and Clark, rose beside the Beaverhead river for all the world like a monstrous beaver floating half submerged on the rolling flat land. A few miles north, where the Stinking Water river flowed into the Beaverhead, the road from Bannack turned and followed the Stinking Water toward the Gulch.

Pfouts passed a bottle. Dan handed it on to Williams, who took a drink, passed it to Fitch. Dan heard the glug as he took a swallow, smelled Fitch's belch. He wanted to back up, but everyone stank. Himself included.

Williams continued, "We arrested Yeager at Rattlesnake, and Brown at Dempsey's, and took them as far as Laurin's."

Someone asked, "What did you do with them after that?"

"Hanged the bastards." Fitch gave the bottle back to Williams.

Dan felt a sharp twinge, like the bite of a horsefly, in his triceps. "My God." Hanged them? Without — who — His brain stuttered, and he seemed to see, ahead in time, the accusing finger of history pointed at them. No trial, not even before a miners court? No weighing of evidence? Except by the men who hanged them.

"Damn it! They needed hanging." Fitch nearly shouted, oblivious to Pfouts's repeated damping gestures to keep it down, man, keep it down. "Those sons of bitches nearly killed us. Brown wrote the note that sent Carter away — "

"Out into the cold. Hung over." Williams said. "Who in his right mind would make a winter camp if he didn't have to, unless—" He stopped to let them fill in the blanks for themselves.

Dan obliged. "Unless he felt his life was in danger."

Williams glared at Dan. "You said that Ives was guilty because he tried to get away. Ain't this the same damn thing?

Flight to avoid the consequences of his crime? Ain't that what you called it? Carter ran because he was guilty. Just like Ives."

"You ain't suggesting that we was wrong when we hung Ives?" Fitch pointed his forefinger at Dan as if he leveled a gun. "You ain't telling us – "

"Hell, no," said Dan. "We were right about Ives, and you're right about Carter. Ives stood there with the noose around his neck and said Carter pulled the trigger. That's a deathbed statement. And Carter left the Gulch because things got too unhealthy for Ives's friends around here, and he fled Deer Lodge because he knew you were after him for Nick's murder. No, that's not what I'm objecting to. You hanged Yeager and Brown without a trial."

"Because we had them dead to rights!" exploded Fitch.

"Quiet, damn it!" said Pfouts.

"The hell with that!" Fitch would not be stopped. "Those two almost killed us all. We rode more'n two hundred miles in the dead of winter, and it's a God damn miracle nobody died. Not even a horse. When we hung Yeager and Brown we had Yeager's confession."

"But did you have it when you decided to hang them?"

Silence. A piece of wood broke apart in the stove, and pitch popped like gunshots. Dan flinched.

"No," Williams said. "What we had was the attempted murder of twenty-four men. All of us. We could have died in that storm, we could have died any time from the cold and – and Yeager knew that and he didn't give a God damn."

"We told Yeager and Brown we were going to hang them, and then Yeager confessed." Fitch leaned forward, propped himself by his elbow and the stump of his arm on his knees.

"It's all right," Dan said. "I don't know if I'd have done anything else if I'd been in your boots." He could picture how it went, how exhausted men, having narrowly escaped freezing to death in the high country, would feel when they met up with the men who had made their harrowing journey a wild goose chase and nearly killed them. Dan wished they hadn't done it, but they did not know the Vigilantes had formed in Virginia, didn't know there was an Executive Committee whose job was to weigh evidence, to prevent summary hangings. And pass sentence of death. Brown's attempt to gives Ives a false alibi and his note to Carter put him squarely in a conspiracy to help Nick's killers go free. And Yeager's ride put him there, too.

But who told Brown to write the letter? Who told Red to deliver it? Did they on their own initiative love Carter so much that Red would ride two hundred miles through the snow in such a hurry? Dan doubted it. There had to be more.

Williams handed the other pieces of paper across to Pfouts. "When Red knew the game was up, he gave us a list. It's members of a gang that's been responsible for most of the robberies and murders around here. He said – " His lips compressed for a moment. "He died like a man."

Fitch shook himself, like a horse shakes off excess dirt after rolling. "Yeah, it was a damn shame. If Red had just went straight. He said he deserved what we were going to do."

"What about Brown?" came a voice behind Dan.

Fitch spat on the floor. "Sniveling bastard. Screamed and cried and begged till he swung." He spat again. "And then some."

"Red said –" A jaw-cracking yawn stopped Williams, and Fitch finished, "Red said Brown was the secretary of the gang. That's why he wrote the note."

Pfouts scanned down the paper, read one name. "Henry Plummer, leader."

"Sheriff Plummer?"

"Good God!" said one man, while a second said, "Can it be true?"

A third snapped his fingers. "I knew that bastard had to be involved."

"I don't believe it!"

"Yes," said Williams. "Believe me. It's true all right. The gang is led by Henry Plummer." He added around another yawn, "Someone should ride over to Bannack and take care of that situation."

Dan held the papers under the lamplight to read: twenty names, their positions in the gang, crimes, dates. He visualized the notebook in his pocket, in his mind turning pages to locate names, the information against each name. Club Foot George Lane, Boone Helm, Frank Parish, Hayes Lyons, Ned Ray, Buck Stinson. Others.

"Sanders is organizing a Bannack company of the Vigilantes," Pfouts said. "We'd better report to him, but I can't leave."

Dan wasn't paying attention. Already there was one glaring omission.

"Why isn't Jack Gallagher on the list?"

"Damned if I know." Williams's voice was thick with the need for sleep. "Red didn't say."

"Must have been an oversight," said Pfouts. "If Plummer's the leader, Gallagher's his second-in-command. He has to be."

Pfouts's reasoning was good, but not good enough. Why would Yeager overlook Plummer's surrogate in Virginia?

"Looks like you're our man, Stark," Pfouts said.

Dan pulled himself away from his train of thought. "Your man?"

"To carry the news to Bannack. You have that notebook and the list. Tell Sanders what we know now." Pfouts drew in a deep breath. "And bring those criminals in Bannack to justice."

"Even if it means hanging the Sheriff?" Dan waited for their verdict. He would not do this solely on his own authority. Hanging Plummer would put them over the line. Up to now they'd had the law to go by, and Ives's hanging had come after a trial, and the elected officials of both Junction and Nevada had sanctioned it. Now, true, they had Dr. Glick's statements, and other men's, and Yeager's list. But to arrest, accuse, hang Henry Plummer? Sheriff of Bannack and Virginia City?

Pfouts, having consulted silently with the other men, spoke. "Even so."

∾

Martha ran plumb out of thread in the middle of darning McDowell's sock, and what with paying Dotty's school fee, she had no dust to spare. Thinking to maybe trade, she wove two darning needles into the collar of her shirtwaist and wrapped herself up snug in her cloak.

The Lord had been extravagant with diamonds in the snow and pieces of blue sky for shadows. She kicked up a sparkling burst and skipped along like a girl instead of the mother of a grown son. Timmy. In clean trousers and jacket and collarless shirt, he rearranged lanterns on a high shelf in Dance and Stuart. His face made her heart lurch to see how stiff his mouth was when he smiled.

Club Foot George, who'd gone for Sheriff Plummer, mistook her smile as being for him. Martha gave him just a little of it.

Way at the back, where Mr. Oliver's stage office was, he and Mr. Dance discussed something in a ledger book. Both men broke off to say hello.

"Mam!" Tim climbed down from the ladder. "What brings you here?"

"I'm out of thread, and if I don't find some there'll be buttons missing where they oughtn't."

Timmy glanced at Mr. Dance. "The thread's on the dry goods side, Tim. Under the counter in a box for men's boots, size eleven."

As Timmy retrieved the box, Martha asked Mr. Dance, "Would you be willing to trade needles for thread?"

"Yes, indeed." Mr. Dance came to her with his hand out. "May I see them?"

Tim straightened with the boot box. "But – " Mr. Dance looked at him, silently telling him not to interfere.

Martha took the needles out of her collar. "They're darning needles."

Mr. Dance held one up. He was such a big man, even bigger than McDowell, but with a far different spirit in him, like Mr. Stark, a gentleness, a kindness. "Excellent! Good and straight. How about one needle for three spools of thread? Would that be fair?"

"That's too much!" Martha.

"I can always sell them for a good price, dear lady. Needles are scarce."

So the trade was done. Timothy followed her out the door, clutched his jacket around him. "I got something to tell you, Mam. Pap's been gambling with the claims."

"No." Her blood seemed to chill in her veins. "He can't."

"He did. He lost two to Mr. Stark, who said he's keeping them till he can sign them over to me. Said they're rightfully mine."

Her mind slid on what Tim was telling her, like she walked on ice. "No. Not the claims."

"He does. Mam, please, I'm telling you. It's true. Mr. Stark showed 'em to me."

"He took them out of the box?" Her teeth chattered, and it was cold, but heat built under her skin. "He wouldn't." Yet a hard kernel of belief was forming in her mind. He could. He did. Legally. Just like he'd sold the farm without telling her.

"What'll we live on?" She didn't know she'd spoken out loud.

"I have a good job, Mam. We'll get by," Tim said. "We don't need him, nohow."

Martha did not hear him as she walked up Jackson in a thick gray cloud, and took up the dulcimer and played, hardly knowing what her fingers did, but let them move on their own, the music finding its way into her heart so that when Sam crossed the threshold she was almost herself again.

"Where's our baby girl?" He looked around for Dotty, a half smile on his face.

"What do you care? You've been off in some saloon throwing away her living."

He dropped into a fighting pose, fists doubled at his sides, his chin tucked into his chest. "What in hell are you talking about?"

"You been losing claims, gambling. Gambling." She laid the dulcimer on the eating table and stood up. "Like, like some wastrel."

"So what if I did? I'll find more when it thaws."

"Maybe. Maybe not. The way the country's filling up with people looking to strike it rich, you might never find color again."

"I know where to look, dammit."

"You looked there already, and whatever you found you threw away."

"I didn't throw it away."

"Might's well. You gambled them away. Why didn't you just take them and burn them?"

"Woman, you don't know what you're saying! I'll win them back and more."

"When? You promised that before. Make a strike. Find the Mother Lode. Now you're gonna win back the contracts. How?"

"My luck will turn. It always does."

"When? What're we supposed to do while we're waiting? I can't earn enough baking pies to keep us from starving. You got to do your share."

"We'd be all right if that lazy son of ours would come home and do some proper work, stead of poncing about clerking in a goddam store. 'Yessir,' 'Nossir,' 'We can get it for you sir.' That ain't no way for a man. It's a sissy way."

"You say that to Mr. Dance, and see what happens. Nobody calls him a sissy."

"What do you know? You're just a female. Good for nothing, for making babies and washing the shit out of my drawers."

"I may be just a female, but I ain't the one gambling away our tomorrows." Martha clamped her lips shut. Almost, she'd told him about the poke of dust in Miz Hudson's warming oven. The thought of it brought her head up and straightened her spine. Just a female. Who made money instead of losing it in silly games? "You ain't getting us ahead. Your way is leading to the poorhouse."

"Ahead! Ahead! What do you know about getting ahead? Putting on airs, like you do. You. Baking pies, slaving over a stove. Slavey." He paused, looked around. "Where's Dotty?"

"What do you care? You've done throwed away her future."

"Where is she?" His big voice boomed out, and Martha took a step backward, was nearly tripped up in the rocker.

"At school, so she won't be ignorant like you and me."

"What? School? Girls don't need to read and write. Just spread your legs and make babies. Boy babies." His lips stretched out in a nasty grin, his yellow teeth gleamed through his beard. "'Bout time Dotty was married."

"No! She can't. She ain't proper growed yet."

"She can finish growing when she has a baby to suck. Maybe then give her some tits." He put a hand on Martha's breast, squeezed hard. "Ain't done you no good, though."

She pulled away from him, swatted his hands. "Don't touch me!"

His lips twisted, the grin made a snarl. The dulcimer lay where she had forgotten it, and he snatched it up. She sprang to grab it, but he pushed her aside, and she fell against the table and slid to the floor. He held the instrument over her. "What you doing with this thing?"

She tried to rise, but her foot caught in her skirt. "Give it here. It's mine." Her mouth was dry, and her blood thundered in her ears. He couldn't! Not that! It was soft summer nights back home, music and moonlight. He'd said it soothed his soul.

"Your'n? Your'n? You ain't got nothing. It's mine. Everything's mine on account I'm the man of the house, and don't you forget it. Women don't need frippery music." He flung the dulcimer onto the floor and stomped on it. "There. That'll learn you." He was panting like he'd run for miles.

Martha stared at the wreckage. One of the strings, still attached to its pegs, vibrated like a lost kitten mewing. He tromped past her and out the door, slammed it behind him. She had no power to move. She felt as if she had no blood in her veins, that it had all drained away, leaving her alone in this snow-covered wilderness of silence.

9: Bannack

They rode 80 miles southwest on roads cut and pounded by wagon wheels and countless hooves. Slow was an inadequate word for the pace of horses picking their way through the darkness, because the men, Dan and Fitch and Beidler, did not want to stop at the places where roughs were known to congregate. They stopped for a short while at other ranches, to rest and take care of the horses, but they were in a hurry, and any progress was better than none. When he reached Bannack, half frozen, wearier than he had thought possible and still remain upright, Dan forced his back to straighten and his legs to carry him. He would not play the weakling in front of Fitch and Beidler, who had survived the Deer Lodge trip.

Having stabled the horses, they sought out Sanders, who greeted them like messengers from Heaven and took them straightaway to his uncle Edgerton. The Chief Justice reminded Dan of an eagle in the carriage of his head, the prominent nose, the fierce eye. He doubted the word compromise was in Sidney Edgerton's vocabulary. Having heard their report, uncle and nephew agreed at once: Convene a meeting. Sanders had talked to men in the town, but they were not convinced that enough evidence existed against any of the suspects to warrant forming a Vigilante group.

In truth, Dan thought, they were afraid.

"It adds up." Sanders pinned each man with an implacable stare.

Seeing their reflections in the window panes of Francis Thompson's store, Dan thought, we look for all the world like men chewing the fat around a warm stove, entertaining each other on a winter evening with tall tales. Instead we weigh men's lives in a scale. In one pan is a life. In the other flakes of gold: witness reports, coincidences, conjectures, small facts, and Dr. Glick's corroboration. Yeager's list. Each of us held a flake or a nugget that meant almost nothing until we put it all in the same pan, and it sinks under the total. Armed robbery. Assault. Murder.

Guilty or not guilty?

Dan touched the notebook in his breast pocket, mentally ticked off names in it. Buck Stinson, Ned Ray, Henry Plummer. Dutch John Wagner. He crossed his legs, shifted on the hard wooden chair. A long meeting, but no longer than it deserved to be when they were preparing to hang men. Across from him, Beidler, frowning, swung his feet. Dan wished they would finish. He pinched a fold of skin on his left hand, so the pain would keep him awake.

God, that he would be party to hanging a man without trial. Yet Lincoln suspended habeas corpus in this crisis of War. And we have done the same in our crisis. His reflection stared back at him. With the knowledge of Chief Justice Sidney Edgerton. He shifted his gaze to the Justice's hawk-nosed reflection. This is no less war than that conflict back home. This war with lawlessness unites us. Edgerton and Sanders, radical abolitionists. Myself. Beidler, who sympathized with John Brown. Fitch, who gave half an arm to his Glorious Cause. George Chrisman, who brought his slave into the Territory. Frank Thompson, moderate Republican. Chrisman and Thompson were both friends of Henry Plummer.

"It's highly circumstantial." Chrisman raised his chin, as if daring them to hang anyone on such evidence. Chrisman's store housed Plummer's office. One of Bannack's city fathers, Chrisman. No wonder he had been terrified when he heard the Vigilantes were coming for Plummer. Enough to beg Edgerton's protection. Though doubting the rumors, Edgerton had reassured him.

"Yes, it is," said Sanders, "but so is most evidence that convicts criminals."

And what is evidence, after all, Dan asked himself, except a deadly aggregate of small nuggets dropped onto a pan until it sinks into certainty?

Stinson's guilt was not at issue. He had twice committed daylight murder in front of terrified onlookers. In Bannack he had shot Old Snag, the Indian, uncle to Bob Dempsey's wife. In Virginia he had helped murder John Dillingham. An impartial murderer who spread it around like a whore.

Ned Ray aided the others, connived with them. A facilitator. Co-conspirator. An occasional robber. He was on Yeager's list. No one here doubted the justice of his death, even if no one had seen him commit murder.

Joe Pizanthia, Mexican, known as the Greaser. The total on him was inconclusive, and they would talk to him later. Perhaps the man merely had the wrong friends, though a man is known by the company he keeps.

But Henry Plummer? Sheriff of Bannack? Sheriff of Virginia City? He had friends and allies around this stove. Thompson, Chrisman. If they were not convinced, Plummer would not hang, despite Yeager's list, despite everything else.

Dan's throat was desert-dry. The notebook named no sources, in case. In case he lost the book. In case his murderers found it on his body. "There's Dr. Glick's evidence," he said. "The injuries he treated, the men who warned him that talking meant dying. Plummer did, when Glick treated his gun arm. And when the doctor treated Jack Cleveland in '62, after Plummer shot him. Plummer threatened to kill Glick then if he repeated any of it. He enjoys reminding Glick from time to time." Keeping the doctor frightened for his life. We can all understand why Glick said nothing.

Thompson leaned forward, elbows propped on his knees, his hands dangling. He stared at the floor. "I've known Plummer nearly two years." He labored to bring the words out of his mouth. "He told me something about his earlier life, and from others I learned more. The murders he committed in Nevada Territory. California. He broke out of prison. Killed a guard. Ended up here." He folded his hands, the joints of his fingers whitened, his nails dug into the backs of his hands. "I tried to convince Electa Bryan not to marry him, murderer that he has been, but she would have him." His lips twisted. "I stood bridesmaid at their wedding. Her sister, Mrs. Vail, would not do it. She has never said why. There were no other white women."

Another little mystery added to that of Mrs. Plummer's visit home three months after her wedding. No word to Mrs. Vail about returning. Both women kept their own counsel.

"I board with the Vails," Thompson said. "Along with Plummer. He said he would mend his ways, and for a while I think he honestly tried. But something went wrong, even before Mrs. Plummer left. He started gambling again. More of his old cronies appeared. I began some time ago to notice a disturbing consistency about his absences from Bannack. He's always gone when someone is robbed."

Chrisman said, "That won't wash. He lived in the other Virginia City, in Nevada. He's an expert on silver. He's often asked to inspect sites for silver ore."

"Shit," Beidler said. "I lived in Kansas, but I know damn all about corn."

"Even more disturbing," said Thompson, "is that he never pursues the robbers, and he never enforces laws for public safety."

Like Gallagher, Dan thought. "We have no laws of public safety. We have no laws at all, not even since the Ives trial." That, too, remained to be done.

"The Legislature may already have taken care of that," said Chrisman.

Beidler snorted. "That bunch? What do they know of conditions here, five hundred miles over the Divide? Before they act, we could all be dead."

Dan said, "Or Plummer could be a U.S. Deputy Marshal."

"God forbid." Edgerton and Chrisman spoke at once, stared at each other in surprise.

Thompson unfolded his hands, his nails had scored the back of one, and a thin line of blood welled up. He wiped his thumb at it. "I've felt certain for some time that a gang of robbers is operating around here, and Henry might be involved, but until you brought Yeager's list, and Dr. Glick's evidence, I had no thought that he might be their leader."

"I don't believe it," said Chrisman. "You'll never convince me."

Beidler said, "He don't seem likely, for sure. Too much like a molly for roughs like Buck Stinson, or Gallagher to respect." The little man stood up and sidled closer to the stove.

Judge Edgerton rose and waved Beidler to his chair. "I'm far too warm. Sit here."

"Thank you," Beidler said, as he changed places with the Chief Justice. "I don't think I'll ever get warm again."

"Plummer may be effeminate," said Dan, "but he has that pistol."

Fitch, who had been silent, uncharacteristically for him, said, "Yes. And he's got a mean streak a mile wide. He killed Jack Cleveland, who was supposed to be his pal."

"That was self-defense," said Chrisman.

Dan wanted to laugh. Self-defense made a murderer's ploy. Lure a man into a fight, make sure he tries to shoot first, then claim self-defense.

Thompson said, "Hell, George, Cleveland's death was a put-up job from the start."

"But why?"

"Because Cleveland was a rival for Miss Bryant's affections." Thompson spat on a handkerchief and dabbed at the scratch. "He knew Henry from California, and he could have told Miss Bryant a thing or two about her love. While Cleveland was dying, Henry expressed no remorse. He just worried about what Jack might say about him."

Chrisman's mouth opened, but Thompson overrode him. "He persecuted Hank Crawford. He wanted to be sheriff."

"That's not fair!" said Chrisman. "Hank tried to murder him, shot him in the back."

"Yeah?" Fitch's chin jutted out at the Southerner. "If Plummer was out to murder you, you know any other way to even the odds? Hank wasn't a good enough shot, was his problem. His tough luck he only got Plummer in his gun arm."

"It's what Plummer did next," Sanders said, "that troubles me. I wasn't here, so correct me if I'm wrong, but I believe he taught himself to use the pistol left-handed in order to maintain his superiority, then drove Crawford out."

"He's the best man with a pistol in the Territory," Fitch said.

Dan asked himself, what would Plummer's skill be if he could use his right hand? "Just like in Virginia City. Persuaded the sheriff at that time to resign in his favor."

Sanders cleared his throat. "Yes. He showed me his handiwork. He took me to the recovery and bragged that most of the wounded were there by his hand." He thought for a moment. "He was trying to deliver a suave warning. Or a threat."

Thompson sighed. "Nobody ever said Henry lacks courage. Or charisma, or charm, or generosity, or a host of other good qualities. That's what's so God damn hard."

"It is a hard thing to learn that he is such a villain," Sanders said. "He gave us an excellent Thanksgiving dinner, with butter and a turkey he ordered especially."

Thompson said, "I believe Red Yeager and all the rest of it. I hate believing it, you don't know how much."

"It won't get any easier." Dan wanted to end this. Listening to Plummer's friends had not changed his mind. Balanced against Plummer's readiness to commit murder for his own purposes, charm and charisma, even generosity, flowed off the scale like water in a sluice carried away dirt, leaving only nuggets of guilt. He began to turn over each nugget, and his mind wandered onto its own trail of thought amid the undergrowth of speculation and hearsay, and evidence, until it broke out as if on an outcrop, the conspiracy spread at his feet in a great web. "No wonder Club Foot George rode all night to fetch him to Nevada City."

"Oh, God," Chrisman buried his face in his hands. "It is a conspiracy. He fooled me. Utterly." He raised his face, stricken and gaunt. "Unsavory characters visit the Sheriff. They discuss people's travel plans. How much gold they carry. Routes, when they're leaving. All under the cover of providing protection."

Another nugget, Dan said to himself. Perhaps the biggest of all.

∞

Henry Plummer had a headache.

"He hasn't felt good all day," Mrs. Vail stood aside, gracious, polite, her smile bewildered at so many men intruding into her parlor, their boots tracking her carpet. The Spencer's stock bumped a gleaming lamp table. Dan caught the lamp before its oil spilled and the flower-painted shade smashed. He rubbed the bruise in the wood, ashamed; couldn't they have caught Plummer in his own cabin? Their odors of sweat and unwashed clothes did not belong amid the gleam and scent of polish. "Why did Mrs. Edgerton cancel choir practice?" she asked Sanders. "We always practice on Sunday nights."

"I believe something came up." Sanders scooped up Plummer's pistols, that he had laid on a chair. "They'll resume next week."

"We need you, Henry." Thompson held Plummer's coat.

Dan hated knowing the sorrow to come to this nice woman. Damn Plummer for his charm, his good manners, his violent ways. They should have had to walk over gunmen to seize him, not a little lady whose puzzled frown furrowed her sweet countenance. Good God, what had they come to, to invade her home? Dan wanted to put down the rifle, back away, tell her it was all a mistake, sorry to have bothered her.

"He's not well," Mrs. Vail said. "Why do you want him? Frank, what is the matter?"

"Don't worry, Mary," Thompson said. Plummer stood up, turned his back to Thompson, put his arms down into the sleeves.

As if seeing the sheriff for the first time, Dan thought we could almost be twins, we are the same age, twenty-seven, have the same rangy build and coloring, though his eyes are blue, his hair is redder, and I'm bigger and he's better looking.

Chrisman, a Southern gentleman at his courtliest, spoke. "We have to borrow the Sheriff, Mrs. Vail. We have urgent business with him."

"Can this urgent business not wait until he's feeling better?"

Thompson took her by the arm, drew her aside. "I'm afraid not, Mary."

Plummer buttoned the coat. "It's all right, Mary. I'll be back soon." Not until the second group had joined them at the ford with Buck Stinson, did he begin to understand danger. "What's going on, boys?"

As they splashed across the dark water, Sanders said, "I'm afraid this is the end, Henry."

"No! It can't be! I'm innocent! Innocent, I tell you!"

He yelled at the top of his voice as they walked down Main Street, where lamplight streamed from windows, printed mellow rectangles on dark blue snow. Dan, ahead of Plummer, rifle under his arm, scanned the buildings, on guard against a rescue. They turned uphill on Second Street.

Thompson said, "Good God!"

"What?" Sanders asked.

"We forgot the rope."

Stinson laughed.

"I have plenty." George Chrisman beckoned to his slave, a Negro perhaps 30 years old also named George, as if Chrisman did not think enough of him to give him a name of his own. "Boy, run to the store and bring back enough rope to hang three men."

Dan stood close enough to Sanders to hear him grinding his teeth. "First things first," he whispered. After they had destroyed the conspiracy of crime, they would enforce the Emancipation Proclamation, keep the Territory free.

Plummer shouted, "No! It can't be! I'm innocent! Innocent, I tell you!"

"Shut up, goddammit," said Stinson.

Across the Bannack Ditch, intended as a giant sluice to bring water for dry claims, they turned left, onto the Virginia City road. The sluice ran uphill, an engineering miscalculation. Dan concentrated on the error, come from an incorrect calculation, or misreading of the elevations? A flaw in the instruments? He did not want to think of what they were about.

The third group joined them at the next corner. Fitch had one of Ned Ray's arms over his shoulders; another Vigilante prodded Ray along with a cudgel.

"Son of a bitch is drunk," Fitch said. "We found him passed out on a pool table."

Seeing Ray, Plummer yanked against their hands. "No! I am innocent, I tell you! I am innocent!" The gang's watchword, Yeager had said, to bring immediate help. People, curious, came out, or stood at their windows. The Negro George among them carried three coils of rope. People trailed after them as they turned uphill again. Dan's breath came shorter, from the incline or the anticipation? He did not know. Past a barn, the gallows, erected by Plummer to hang a horse thief on, loomed up against the snowy hillside. Dan caught his breath.

Plummer begged, "Cut off my arms, cut off my legs. I can't do anything then! Just let me live!" His tears glistened in the torchlight. "Sanders, can't you do something for me? I've always been friendly to you. Help me now!"

"I can't do it," Sanders said. "No one can feel worse about this than I do, but there's nothing I can do. The weight of evidence is against you."

"Then at least give me a jury trial, like you did Ives. Surely I deserve that much. Chain me down in my own jail until you can get it done. Please! I'm begging you here. Please!" The last word was a scream.

"No," said Sanders, at his most formal. "Your pals would pack the jury. You've been tried and found guilty of being the leader of the road agents. Red Yeager gave us a list, and we've gathered a great deal of evidence against you. You've been identified in numerous armed robberies, and you've killed a

number of men in gunfights both here and in Virginia. It won't
do, Henry. It just won't do."

"No, please!" shrieked Plummer.

Thompson's young clerk, who had come out to see what
was the fuss, burst from the thickening crowd to wrap his arms
around Plummer. "You can't do this! He's done nothing wrong!
Frank, dammit, you're his friend, you can't do this. You can't!"

Dan poked the rifle barrel between the young man and
Plummer. Fitch pulled one arm away, and Beidler pried the
other arm loose. Thompson said, "Someone take him over to
my store and keep him there until our business is done."

Plummer wept and shook so that two of the Vigilantes had
to hold him upright.

"Shut the hell up, Plummer!" Buck Stinson yelled. "Live or
die, it don't matter."

Ned Ray said, "We'll all burn in hell anyway."

"No, we won't burn in any damn hell." Stinson squirted
tobacco juice through a space in his bottom teeth. "There's no
God to reward anyone or punish us. That's a damn fairy tale.
There's nothing out there."

"Oh, shut up. You don't know for sure. Nobody does," Ned
Ray said. "This ain't no time for talk." He said to Sanders, "Let's
get this over with. Take me first."

Plummer said, "I need time to pray. I can't meet my Maker
this way."

"Certainly," said Sanders. "That we can do. We'll take these
two first."

A woman shrieked, pleaded to let Ray go. She struggled
through the crowd, demanding to embrace him one last time.
"That's his doxie," Beidler whispered. "She whores out of –" he
named a saloon, that Dan did not hear.

Plummer knelt, prayed partly to God and partly to the
Vigilantes. "Oh, God, forgive me, forgive me. Oh, God, forgive

me. I am too wicked to die. Let me live. I'll pay it all back, I'll pay everyone back. God, forgive me."

"Better just pray for your soul." Dan didn't think Plummer heard.

The Negro had piled all the ropes at Beidler's feet and stood aside. Beidler's short thick fingers wrapped the end of a rope around and around itself in a hangman's knot. He slipped the loop over Ray's head, worked the long knot behind Ray's left ear.

Sanders motioned to Dan. "You're tall enough. We need help with this. You and him." He gestured at a Bannack man about Dan's height.

Dan gave the rifle to Sanders and ground his boots into the snow to gain purchase. When he was ready, three men lifted Ray up, but he struggled and squirmed and they could not make him stand. After several sweaty moments, they lowered him to the ground and one of the men said, "You can go easy, or you can go hard. You can die quick by jumping off these men's shoulders, or we can hoist you up by the neck and let you strangle. Up to you. Now which is it to be?"

"I'll jump." Ray said, and soon he was standing on their shoulders, while men held his legs. Ray wobbled, his boot heel gouged into the point of Dan's shoulder. How had he earned this, Dan asked himself as he sought to balance Ray's weight. The sins of the fathers are visited upon the sons, to the third and fourth generations. Was he paying for Father's dereliction, by standing as a drop for a hanging? Beidler took up the slack in the rope, tied the end around an upright. Dan wished he would hurry, then repented; he had no wish to shorten Ray's life.

"Do your duty, boys," said Sanders.

Dan leaped aside, slipped in the snow and fell to his knees. Ray plunged down, feet flailing, and a beat of air puffed at Dan's cheek. He rolled away and stood up. Ray had forced his fingers between the rope and his neck, and he thrashed about, gargling and choking. His face swelled, turned blue, his eyes bulged from their sockets and his tongue, swollen and purple, escaped from between his teeth. The woman, held firmly back, sobbed. As Ray died with one final wild kick, her shrieks clawed at the night.

The stench of voided bowels stained the air. Dan tightened his jaw against the convulsions of his stomach. He stooped to retrieve his hat, and tasted bile.

Beidler said, "I won't let that happen again."

Stinson's mouth ran streams of curses like dirty melting snow. "You sons of bitches, you goddam fucking bastards...." He kicked at them when they tried to raise him up, and someone punched him in the jaw, but he fought too much to stand on their shoulders, so the Vigilantes seated him there and held his ankles, but still his heel hammered on Dan's chest, and he twisted his head so that the noose caught under his chin and when they dropped him, he dangled, kicking and strangling.

He was killing three men. Dan thought he should have felt something, some horror at the sight of men dying hard by his hand, but his feelings were as numb as his toes. They had earned their deaths.

Plummer rose from his prayers seeming a different man. "All I ask, boys, is give me a good drop. I want it to be quick." He bent his head to receive the noose, like a well trained horse puts its nose in the halter.

Tears ran down Thompson's cheeks. Chrisman stood someplace back in the crowd. Fitch at Dan's back helped Plummer balance, while Beidler tied the rope around an upright, tugged it tight. Dan imagined Plummer taking his last look at the rounded hills, juniper trees jutting up through the snow, their conical shadows black and sharp-pointed, the town below with snow piled on the roofs. A little town lying still.

"Stop! No! You can't do this!" A man stumbled up the slope.

"Good God, it's Vail." Thompson swung away from Plummer. "He must have just come in on the stage."

"Please, you can't," Vail shouted, "let him go, he's innocent, he's innocent, he committed no crime, goddam you let him go, let him go." Thompson caught him, held him back, other men seized his arms, his coat, and he struggled and shouted, but no one could stop him screaming Plummer was innocent, damn you all, innocent.

Biedler signaled and Dan leaped aside, ready to dodge Plummer's feet, but he dropped straight down, hit the end of the rope with a jerk. A loud crack and he was gone.

"Oh, God, no! Murderers!" Vail turned away, sobbing, Thompson's arm around his shoulders. "Murderers!"

Thompson said, "I'll take care of him and break the news to Mrs. Vail."

It was done. Dan retrieved the Spencer from Sanders, Vail's cry ringing in his ears: Murderer.

❦

Together with Biedler and Fitch, Dan ate breakfast in a restaurant where other men smiled and pointed their chins at them, whispered, "Vigilanters," stopped to shake their hands before they left the establishment. Fitch and Beidler preened themselves, but for Dan, pushing the fried bread and venison around on his plate, Vail's accusation drowned out their thanks: Murderer.

He had heard it all night.

Fitch aimed his knife at Dan. "You're death at a party, Blue. We done good work."

"That doesn't mean I have to like it." Dan chewed on a piece of tough venison.

Beidler lifted his coffee cup to his mouth. "It's a dirty job, cleaning up criminals. You oughta be proud you're one of them as has the balls to do it."

Around a chunk of fried bread, Fitch said, "He died game in the end."

They all knew he meant Plummer. "Not a bad epitaph," Dan said, but the venison tasted like boot soles, and the bread had been fried in axle grease. He pushed away his plate. "I'll be at Chrisman's."

Maybe he should be proud, Dan thought as he crossed Main Street toward Chrisman's store, but he could find no cause for pride in helping to hang men. Besides, how many thank-you's were sincere, and how many were sucking up to power? For the balance of power in the region had shifted, too small a word for the revolution they had wrought. They had taken power from the criminals, the ruffians, the roughs.

In the middle of the street he gave way as three riders, leading a pack mule, trotted out of town. One of them spat in his direction, and another raised his middle finger.

His face hot, Dan watched them ride into a white world, the snow-covered hills blending into a white sky without a horizon. He walked on. In the flat light, it was hard to see the ruts.

Chrisman's store occupied a large, false-fronted building that seemed to break in the middle, as if two small log cabins had been pushed together end to end and not matched well. Near the tall front windows Chrisman and Sanders listened to a miner, who stopped talking when Dan pushed open the door.

The miner thrust out his right hand toward Dan and said his name, which Dan instantly forgot. "I been telling these gentlemen, you fellas done good work last night. For months we been scared even to walk around in broad daylight, or have a drink in a saloon, or eat in a restaurant. One of them gets drunk, he's picking a fight, maybe he don't like how I part my hair. I had to tell Stinson I was too much of a coward to fight." He stared into the back of the store, his jaw muscles working. "Goddammit, I ain't no coward, but I was outgunned. I'd have murdered myself if I'd have fought him." He turned toward the door, but not before Dan had seen the sheen of tears in his eyes.

Sanders said, "I've made a tactical retreat from time to time myself."

The miner nodded, pulled the door open and was gone. For a moment, none of the three Vigilantes could think of anything to say.

Two more men rode by, on their way out of town. "They're leaving," said Dan.

"In droves," Sanders said.

"Good riddance." Chrisman sat on a stool behind the counter. "I was always scared when some of them came in here to talk to Plummer."

Dan, thinking to change the subject, waved at the loaded shelves lining the long windowless walls. "You have a veritable R. H. Macy's here."

He didn't think the Southerner heard him. "I can't get used to him being gone." Chrisman stared toward the back of the store, where Plummer's desk and chair stood between two windows set at eye level in the back wall. Dan walked back, nodded to the Negro, who was unpacking a box of canned beans. What did he think of last night's events, of having to fetch the rope for a hanging, when his people were lynched in the South? Dan wanted to say, It's not the same.

He looked out one of the windows. Some twenty-five feet behind the store stood the little jail Plummer had built. It had two doors, so two rooms, each one not much larger than a three-hole outhouse. What had his idea been? To keep suspects a few hours until trial in front of the miners court? It was no prison. Boot heels thumped across the floor.

"How are the Vails?" Dan asked Sanders.

Sanders shook his head. "It was a horrible shock to them. I doubt they'll ever get over it. Thompson is with them now, and my wife. Mrs. Vail fainted when Thompson told her. They'll bury him tomorrow."

"A dreadful business." Dan's shoulder ached where Stinson's boot heel had dug in. He would have to find a seamstress to mend a tear in his coat.

Sanders's brows drew together. "You never served as a soldier, did you?"

"No. My grandfather paid a substitute." Grandfather, at dinner, jabbing the air with his fork: This War is illegal! Some wars, Dan would tell him, we have to fight. Legal or not. Communal self-defense.

"You'd have seen far worse, on the battlefield," said Sanders. "A soldier is frightened all the time, and the fear makes him ferocious to the enemy. At least in this War our cause is just, as our cause is just in this little war against lawlessness. Keep in mind that we did what we had to do, that if we had done nothing the robberies and murders would continue."

"We are soldiers in a righteous cause," Dan said, "but I regret the necessity."

"So do I, but they could have mended their ways a dozen times."

"Yes, I understand that. They made their own wrong decisions." If only they had not chosen the easy way of getting the gold.

"Exactly." Sanders squeezed his sore shoulder, and Dan managed not to flinch. "We have to talk to Pizanthia." His footsteps receded toward the front of the store, where men were gathering. Dan stood a few seconds longer at the window.

He was not seeing the empty jail, but the round white hills beyond, and heard a sparrow of a woman say: You got to be God's thunderbolt.

Martha, my dear, would you say we are doing God's work now?

∽

Joe Pizanthia's cabin lay down a small slope near the creek bed, behind the Bannack Bakery and a saloon. Smoke rose from the mud chimney.

Sanders cupped his hands around his mouth. "Pizanthia, come out. We want to talk to you."

No response from the cabin.

"Maybe he ain't there," a man said.

Another said, "He's there. He ain't stupid enough to go off and leave a fire burning."

Sanders bellowed, "Pizanthia, come out! We want to talk."

Snow fell into the rising smoke, but no sign came that Pizanthia had heard Sanders. Yet how could he not have heard him, or the crowd's jeers and shouts?

Two men volunteered to go down and knock on the door. One man, George Copley, said, "I've had fairly friendly dealings with him. He's rough, but you can't condemn a man merely because he has the wrong friends. I think I can talk to him. Convince him we just want to question him."

"I'll come with you," Dan said.

A voice hollered, "Be careful, George. You don't know what you'll find."

"Yeah, we don't want to lose any good men," came another shout.

Copley held his hands out to his sides, and the other man, Smith Ball, held his shotgun in both hands, low and in front of him, uncocked, pointed leftward toward the ground. Dan carried the Spencer slung on his shoulder.

When they stood in front of the door, Copley shouted, "Pizanthia, we want to ask you some questions." Big snowflakes drifted down, as if aimlessly, but more thickly, and Dan blinked them away. Amid the silence of the snow, the crowd, grown to more than a hundred men, watched. Copley raised his fist and pounded on the door. "Come out, Pizanthia, we want to ask you – "

No reply.

Again, Copley shouted, "Come out, Pizanthia."

"Maybe he really isn't here," said Smith Ball.

"Maybe not." Copley pushed open the door, and a shotgun blast knocked him back in a spray of blood. Dan leaped aside, tasted Copley's blood in his mouth and unslung the Spencer, levered a shell into the breech even as another shot boomed and Smith Ball sank into the snow, yelling with pain, and Dan felt a hard blow in his right thigh. He fired through the doorway, pumped the lever, and fired again. He had no target, only the rose-colored vision of Copley being blown back, his blood in Dan's eyes, and even as he sank to his knees in the snow, he levered another shell into the breech, the rifle so heavy, but he put it to his shoulder and squeezed the trigger, and the recoil knocked him back, which had never happened before, and he toppled over onto his left side. Pain sliced his left hand, and a door slammed.

Hands reached for him, grabbed the rifle, and he was being carried up the slope, laid on the ground, and someone wrapped his leg. "He's lost blood, but it didn't hit an artery."

"Get him to the doctor."

Someone washed his face in snow, and they would have carried him away, but the snow cleared his vision. "I'm all right," Dan said. "It doesn't even hurt that much." He sat up, dizzy, reached for the Spencer. "Where's my rifle?" Someone gave it to him, and he laid it across his lap.

Copley lay beside him, his eyes wide open, disbelieving, while men worked to fashion a stretcher for him. His chest was awash with blood, and sharp white ends of his ribs stuck up amid shreds of flesh and cloth. He coughed, and blood bubbled up between his lips and ran down the side of his face.

Smith Ball limped over to them, another man supporting him and carrying his shotgun, still not cocked. It had all happened so fast.

"That murderin' bastard!" someone yelled. "Let's get him!"

"Wait!" Sanders shouted. "If you charge the cabin, more men will be shot." When they waited for him, he said, "Go to the Chief Justice's house and bring up the howitzer. If Pizanthia wants war, we'll give it to him."

With a cheer, men ran to get the small mountain howitzer standing in front of Judge Edgerton's cabin, ready for an attack from the roughs or the Confederates who nightly rode through Yankee Flats whooping and firing their guns at the American flag on the ridgepole.

Dan waited in the snow. Some men carried Copley away. "Glick is good with wounds," Dan heard, but he thought no human healer could help Copley now.

Fitch crouched beside him, offered him a flask. "Thanks." Dan took a sip; it was a decent brandy. Surprised, he took another, then gave the flask back. "I'll drink it all if you don't take it." Fitch put the flask in his pocket.

The snowfall thinned to only a few flakes. The crowd paced about, muttered. Men came by Dan, knelt, shook his hand, mumbled at him.

Sanders hunkered down next to Fitch. "I'll never forget how you stood there in the doorway, shooting into that cabin. It gave us time to grab Copley and get everyone away." He gave Dan his hand. "Thank you." He looked up the hill. "They're back."

"That goes double for me," Smith Ball said. "You'll forgive me if I keep standing." He leaned on a stick.

With Fitch's help, Dan stood up. Where he had sat, the packed snow was red. "Shouldn't you see the doctor?" Dan asked.

Ball smiled. "When you do. You're hit worse than me." His dark eyes were full of pain.

"Never thought I'd see anyone could handle a rifle like that," Fitch said.

A few former artillerymen, wearing blue and grey parts of old uniforms, set the gun, blocked its wheels, and cranked its barrel into position. A man in grey sighted it, and flapped his hand to the right. Men dragged it rightward a few degrees. The man in grey sighted down the barrel and gestured palm up, squinted through the sight, as two men in blue turned the crank until he flattened his hand, palm down. They stepped back and the man in grey took another look, nodded, and stepped back. Now the blue men loaded it, and a man in blue stepped up with a burning rag on the end of a stick. "Clear away," he yelled at those standing behind the piece. He touched the torch to the fuse, and a second later the gun boomed and leaped backward, then settled.

The fuse tore out, and the ball bored through the wall, but did not explode.

"Shit!" one of the gunners said.

A second ball ripped through both walls of the cabin and exploded on the other side.

Sanders sent some men with rifles to fire on the cabin through the shot holes. "He won't be able to use them to shoot any more of our men." He ordered the artillerymen, "Aim for the chimney. He might be hiding in it."

They hauled the little cannon about, sighted it, and lit the fuse. The gun boomed and recoiled over one of the gunner's feet. The man screamed, and others leaped to roll the howitzer forward for another shot, but the chimney blew apart, and logs splintered. The door fell inward, and the one window shattered.

"Follow me!" Sanders ran down the slope. Yelling and whooping, dozens of men charged with him, including Smith Ball, who limped in their van, his pistol ready.

"Guess he ain't hurt so bad." Fitch turned his head and spat a yellow-brown stream.

Two men lifted the door, and two others dragged the Mexican out. Dan saw one of his arms move. He had apparently been behind the door when it blew in on him.

Smith Ball emptied his pistol into Pizanthia. "You son of a bitch, you killed a good man."

Someone produced a rope, tied it around Pizanthia's neck, and hauled the corpse up a pole. Men began firing at it, and soon more blazed away at the corpse dangling like an obscene flag.

Dan turned his head away. Men were dismantling Pizanthia's cabin, laying the logs on a great pile, bringing out everything Pizanthia had owned and tossing it among them. Someone lighted them, and a bonfire blazed up.

"Burn the Greaser!" came a shout.

The crowd responded, "Burn him! Burn him!"

"No!" yelled Dan. "No!"

"Shut up!" Fitch shouted in his ear. "You can't stop it. Can't you see they've gone mad? Look at Sanders. He knows better. You want them to burn you, too?"

Men cut the rope, and took the corpse's arms and legs, swung it back and forth, and tossed the body into the flames.

Dan was watching the fire. "God in heaven, what have we come to?"

Sanders, walking up the slope, heard him. His face was pale. He had lost control. Pizanthia's murder was a blight on his leadership, and he knew it. "Nothing like this must ever happen again," he told Dan. "We must set up a court system, or this entire enterprise could degenerate into mob action, worse than the roughs and road agents."

"What about Dutch John?" asked Fitch.

Sanders's eyes glowed, live coals in the caves of their sockets. "Now it's his turn."

෴

X said, "If I'd've knowed you was a road agent, I wouldn't have fixed your hands, John, I'd have shot you instead." X Beidler stood in front of Dutch John Wagner and pointed his finger at the German.

Even sitting, Dutch John could look X Beidler in the eye, but big as Dutch John was, Dan didn't doubt but that the little man would have done exactly as he said. The German held up his hands, mittened in dirty bloodstained cloths. He had surrendered two days before. He squirmed from one buttock to the other, and his feet kept up a constant dance, tapped softly from side to side, toes in, toes out. He lowered his hands to rest on his heavy thighs, winced as the blood flowed into them, and raised them again.

He said, "Aber, vielen dank, anyway."

"No need to thank me. I just postponed your hanging awhile, is all," said X.

"Let's get on with this." Dan sat in Chrisman's own easy chair with his right leg resting on another chair. His wound burned, and periodic nausea swept through him, but he clamped his jaws shut and tried to focus. He wanted to go home, to Virginia City, where Martha could tend to him. Not Dr. Glick. He wanted Martha's healing touch. He wanted Martha.

You're lucky, Dr. Glick had said. He had not had to dig for the bullet, thank God, but he had used pincers to pull out tiny threads and bits of cloth, and poured whiskey into the wound to cleanse it while Dan clenched his jaws to keep from yelling. Now and then a moan escaped. You'll live, said Glick, because you're young and healthy, but keep this clean or it'll fester and you don't want to lose the leg. You're lucky I'm here. I may be the most practiced doctor with gunshot wounds in the Territory.

I had to be, the doctor had said. They'd've killed me if I'd lost a patient. They loved it, you know. They bragged about the crimes they committed, and they laughed because they had everyone scared witless and nobody could prove a goddamn thing. They flaunted their crimes, because I was too scared to talk. Besides, who would I have told? I knew the Sheriff was in it.

So Dan, bandaged and with his ordeal over, wanted to be done here. If they'd had a legal system, they could not have used Dr. Glick's knowledge because it would have been judged hearsay, but it was enough for the Vigilantes. Enough for justice.

"Right," Sanders said. "We don't have all night."

Wagner licked his lips and hitched his right shoulder. "I ain't done nothing. I never killed nobody, so you can't hang me. I ain't a murderer."

"But you're friends with them as is," said Fitch.

"You see, John, we have to check up." Sanders, a reasonable man, made a good point, Wagner nodding agreement. "Make sure you're in the clear, if nothing else."

Good God, Dan said to himself. Was Wagner really as stupid as that? "Have him show us his right shoulder."

Wagner crossed his arms over his chest. "No, I ain't taking my shirt off."

X pressed closer to the big man's right side. "John, open your shirt. One of them as robbed Lank Forbes's train a few weeks ago got shot in the right breast. It's real simple. If you ain't wounded, you ain't the man."

"I can't." The prisoner waggled his hands. "Can't work the buttons."

X said, "I'll help you."

Wagner shook his head vigorously. "No, you can't."

"Like hell I can't. There's another way, though." X balled one fist and punched toward Wagner's right shoulder. Wagner gasped and shrank back.

Dan flinched, but the fist stopped an inch short of the wound.

A man asked, "Wouldn't there be a hole and bloodstains on the shirt?"

Dan said, "You never heard of changing your shirt?"

Wagner lifted his tied hands away from the plaid flannel shirt. X unbuttoned it, eased it down from Wagner's shoulder, and stepped aside. Underneath, dried bloodstains surrounded a ragged hole in his dirty undershirt, unbuttoned to the waist because of the thick pad of bandage. Dan caught the stink of spoiled meat and nearly choked.

Dan said, "I think we've seen enough."

X pulled up the shirt and buttoned it as Wagner said, "I was not there, I tell you! I was not there." The th's sounded like soft z's.

"Give it up, John," Sanders said. "We know you're a road agent. You're on Yeager's list, you were caught stealing a horse, enough to hang you right there, and you have a wound that identifies you as one of the robbers. You'd best make your peace with God."

X hitched one buttock onto Plummer's old desk, and swung a foot like a pendulum. Wagner's eyes followed the foot, back and forth, back and forth. The Vigilantes waited. They had no other evidence, and the lack of a confession would not save Dutch John, but if the man confessed some would be easier about it.

For himself, Dan did not care. The rancher who owned the horse had been kind in letting Dutch John walk away when he caught him, even if he had kept John's saddle. We can't afford kindness to thieves and murderers, Dan told himself. They earn their fate.

Wagner took a deep breath and slumped. "Okay. Ja. Is so."

"What is so?" asked Dan.

"What you say. Is true, ja? But don't kill me, please. Do anything, but don't kill me."

"We have to vote, John," Sanders said. "We'll be quick about this, and you can rest in the cabin you've been held in."

Two men led Dutch John out of Chrisman's store.

When the door closed, one of the men who had caught him said, "He's got his good points, you know. He could have killed one of us a couple of times, but he didn't."

"We could banish him," said one of the new Vigilantes from Bannack.

"Oh, Christ," Dan said. "Banished crim – " He clamped his jaws together as a spasm of agony swept through him, tightened the muscles of his leg in a pain like burning. When it was over, leaving him sweating, he took a breath down to his toes, ignored a couple of odd looks. "Banished criminals come back," he said. "Like Stinson did. Or they prey on people elsewhere. We have the evidence. Let's get the job done."

"Are you sure?" Sanders asked.

"Well, well," Fitch arched one bushy eyebrow at Dan. "Getting shot usually makes a man more cautious. Not less."

"Maybe, but this is more evidence than we have against some others on the list." Dan had wanted certainty, he'd tried to keep his conscience clear, to give history nothing to condemn them for, but after the last two days in Bannack, he wanted it over with, the killing, he was sick of it all. Sick of the excuses they gave as long as they were on top and had men afraid of them, sick of their terror when they had had no pity for their victims, and sick of the reek of shit and the piss on the front of their trousers. The jerking bodies and purple swollen tongues would live in his mind and foul his dreams until he died.

And it was not done yet. After Dutch John, eighteen men were left on Yeager's list. Gallagher. His gut clenched. He had liked Gallagher. Gallagher, the charming, handsome, deadly man whom he'd wanted for a friend.

As if they sat in a courtroom and he was polling a jury, Sanders said, "We've had a call for the vote. Is there a second?"

"Second." Fitch brought out a much traveled handkerchief. He blew into it, all the time watching Dan, who felt the stare at the edge of his vision. What was Fitch thinking?

One by one, the guilty votes came down, tolling Dutch John's death knell. Even the new volunteers understood that the Vigilantes passed only one sentence: Death.

∽

They brought Dutch John to an unfinished house, where beams across log walls lay ready to support the roof. The bodies of Plummer and Stinson lay waiting for burial, Stinson's corpse on the floor, and Plummer's on a work bench. Ray's woman had taken his body for burial.

Dutch John stared at them. X uncoiled a new, stiff rope and threw one end over a beam.

Fitch, standing close to Dan, muttered, "That rope will be all stretched out after this."

In spite of himself, Dan saw the humor. "A new way to break in a rope?"

"Why not? Good as any."

X made the noose, and the big man bent to let him slip it over his head.

"Maybe I can pray now?"

"Of course." Sanders steadied him as he knelt.

Dutch John crossed himself and prayed in a low-voiced mumble, his eyes closed. Two or three others knelt and prayed with him, the rest removed their hats. "Hail Mary, mother of God, blessed art thou ...." Snow swirled around them, and the wind thrust down the back of Dan's neck. "Hail Mary mother of God be with us now and at the hour of our death."

When Dutch John said, "Amen," Sanders took Dutch John's good arm and helped him to his feet. X felt for his left ear, and slid the noose into position, worked the hangman's knot along the rope until he had taken slack out. "That comfortable?" X asked.

Dutch John nodded. "I think maybe I don't worry about that soon." His eyes were full of humor, and the corners of his lips turned up.

Fitch and Sanders boosted him onto a flour barrel. X took up the slack in the rope, and anchored it with several turns around the beam.

"How long does it take to die?" Wagner asked. "I have not seen a man hanged before."

"It won't be long, just a matter of seconds and it'll be over," Sanders reassured him.

Dutch John nodded. "All right. I guess I'm as ready as I'll ever be."

They jerked the barrel out from under him. His neck broke with a crack, but he refused to die. His feet flailed in the air, and he turned and twisted, struggled to free his hands, fought even as his head bent to one side, his eyes bulged from their sockets, and his face swelled to a purplish tinge.

"My God," said Fitch. "Why don't he give it up?"

Another man muttered, "Die, damn you, die, you son of a bitch."

Dan wanted to turn away, back out of the building, run back to Virginia City and bury his mind in calculations, in sine and cosine, and his body in Martha's arms. But there was no escape from this futile battle against death.

At last, the feet slowed, the shoulders relaxed, and the air was stained with the outhouse stench of death. The corpse turned, swung, and sank toward the floor as the rope stretched.

10: Alder Gulch: Virginia City

If there were degrees of hell, Dan thought, then he was down around level three, though after a couple of days the wound was not festering, and he could limp with a stick. The journey back by way of the express stage was not much better than if he'd ridden a horse. The coach's leather shades protected him and his companions somewhat from wind, but the springless coach jolted them over ruts of frozen snow. More than once Dan landed on his wounded leg. To keep from yelling, he said, "Damn, it's not cold enough. My leg isn't numb yet." Beidler laughed, and Fitch eyed him with something like respect. Each time they stopped to change horses, Fitch and Beidler helped him into the ranch house where he warmed himself by a fire and took hot food, or whiskey. Underway again, the warmth soon leaked out of him, leaving him colder than before. A level of hell only slightly above Dr. Glick's treatment.

Fitch's attitude toward him had changed some, maybe from the night of Plummer's hanging, the night that left his shoulder so sore he could yet hardly sling the rifle. There were no more jibes. Though the Southerner still called him "Blue," he had a different tone in his voice. Shortly after they passed through Junction, Dan pinned down the difference. The sneer was gone.

When they arrived back in Virginia, he found himself in a much lower stratum of hell. Tim insisted on going for his mother, and Dan tried to stop him with as much success as if he'd tried to stop the snow.

"Ain't nobody better'n Mam with hurts," the boy said.

Which was why he came to be lying naked except for his wool shirt, the quilt covering him up to the armpits, his right leg exposed to her while she tended to the wound. He hadn't shaved, he stank, he couldn't have her, he wanted her to go away, he wanted her to never go away, the touch of her fingers on his thigh was cool, unbelievably intimate, he wanted her to stay, wanted the others to go away. Oh, God, he wanted her. He put his arm over his eyes.

෨

Martha's breath fluttered in her throat, but her hands held the scissors nice and steady, snipping away the blood-crusted bandage from Mr. Stark's thigh. She shouldn't ought to be here, see him like this, yet she should be tending to him like she'd tended to others in the recovery with bullet holes in them, only not in this man's leg and seeing what this man was made of, strong muscles and the light hair on him, and lying back with his arm across his eyes and nary a twitch as she peeled away the bandage and sniffed at the wound. It bled some more, but it was clean. Like the man himself. Even unshaved, needing a bath, his smell was clean to her.

"You're lucky." She couldn't keep the quiver out of her voice, but it didn't seem like he noticed, on account of he took his arm away and smiled. And so am I, she told him silently, because whatever would I do if they'd buried you out there? It was that shook her so, knowing how close she'd come to seeing him no more, like seeing him now and again was the most important thing in her life. Dear God, was that how it was?

"So I'm told," he said.

She felt him watching her as she put on a poultice and wrapped the leg again. She kept her eyes on her hands so's she wouldn't see what she shouldn't, but she knew anyways what was happening, his body speaking its own language, telling her what he felt for her. He shifted under the blanket, turning away some.

"Tim shouldn't have bothered you with this." His face was bright red.

She pretended like she thought maybe it was windburn. Only a decent man would blush now. She felt her own skin heating up.

Her son sat in a chair behind her, and Martha glanced over her shoulder. "No, he done the right thing." To fill the silence, she said, "This poultice is lily-of-the-valley. Berry Woman give it to me."

"Thank you," he said.

༄

"We must not trifle with men's lives." Paris Pfouts's small mouth set in a line like mortar between bricks. The Vigilante president's fingers toyed with a piece of paper, a list of names. Yeager's list, and others. Members of the Executive Committee discussed the names, voted, and Pfouts tore off a scrap, put it in his coat pocket or in the stove. Crumbled to black ash, the names disappeared. Only a few were left, but Beidler and Fitch, allies since Bannack, wanted to cut discussion short, get out of Kiskadden's upper room, that was too big for the stove to warm. Two lamps crowded the darkness back, but not far enough.

"Damn it," Beidler said, "when did they ever care where their bullets went?"

"Yean, hang the bastards," Fitch said.

On the street, horses whinnied, men called out to each other. Whips cracked, sounding too much like gunshots. A mule brayed. Somewhere, out-of-tune fiddles challenged a jolly piano. Outside, the sun shone, though the mercury stayed frozen in the thermometers.

Nobody wanted this over with more than Dan did. In the night he had dreamed of Pizanthia's corpse flung onto the bonfire, and Dutch John's boots thrashed about, and he had awakened, sweating. He'd be damn sure that if he stepped in blood, it would be unavoidable. Necessary. Not because he wanted a death, even if he did.

Something like a fist clenched in his stomach. God. Gallagher. It could have been different.

Pathways of time. He must have read it someplace. "What we do here will track us forever," Dan said. "You want history to charge you with murder?"

"Not me," Williams said. "I want my grandchildren to hold their heads up when they say, My grandfather was a Vigilante, and not be afraid to look anyone in the eye."

"I don't give a damn about posterity," Fitch said. "Or history. Hell, I won't be here."

Beidler said, "We ain't got all day. Let's get on with it."

"Thank you." Pfouts was sarcastic. "With your permission, we'll proceed."

Dan's leg, propped on a chair, throbbed. Martha McDowell's face shone in his mind, her touch soothing him, but when he recalled his own response, his face felt hot.

Pfouts read from the paper: "Jack Gallagher."

"Aw, hell," said Beidler. "Gallagher shot George Temple, and he helped Dillingham's killers!" His feet in lumpy, cracked boots swung like a child's, and with each swing, his chair creaked, a small, irritating noise. Snow buried his signs: Graves For Rent.

Dan's mind was full of memories: Gallagher's hand on his shoulder – the Chief Deputy advising the tenderfoot, Be careful, choose your friends right. Gallagher smiling, charming, handsome, a magnetic personality. A Union sympathizer. Noble-looking, as someone said, as if the phrenologists were right, that a man's looks revealed his character. But villains could charm your socks off, and likable people could murder you.

It could have been different. God, Jack, we could have been friends. Dan held up his fist, raised his index finger. "One. Gallagher has to be part of the gang. He was too close to Plummer not be part of whatever Plummer was doing." He raised his middle finger. "Two. He has shot and killed several men." The fourth finger. "Three," a nod toward Beidler, "Temple was damn lucky the bullet in his neck didn't cut the artery or his spine. Attempted murder." The little finger. "Dillingham." He swallowed, held out his thumb. "He tried to set me up for murder. If I hadn't challenged him to that card game, he'd have shot me down."

Pfouts smiled. "From what I hear, with that rifle of yours, a man would be a fool to try that. Anything in Gallagher's defense?"

Several men shook their heads. Fitch called for the question.

Voting was quick. "Guilty." Pfouts tore off Gallagher's name, put it in his pocket, squinted at the list. The paper was nearly a scrap itself. "George Lane." He looked each man in the eye. "I know, this is a tough one, gentlemen. We've all pitied Club Foot George, and admired his willingness to earn his own living shining shoes."

Dan rubbed the back of his neck. He didn't see the difficulty. A club-footed man could be as wicked as a man with two good feet. Had he been coerced? He could have talked to Walter Dance, as good a man as God ever made, and tough. The roughs let Dance be. No, Lane was on Yeager's list as a road agent, and he was an accessory before the fact. He had assisted the robbers by marking the stages that carried valuables, knowing that his marks could lead to murder.

Pfouts was saying, "With travelers buying tickets at Dance and Stuart, Club-Foot George's shoeshine stand is an excellent place for a robbers' lookout."

Williams said, "Don't forget he's the one Gallagher sent to get Plummer when we arrested Ives. His foot don't stop him riding a horse."

Another man said, "You know, when I took the stage over to Bannack, when we got held up, you know when I'm talking about, right? Well, when I got my bag off the stage, I noticed it had a funny mark on it. Kind of a circle with a X inside. I asked Ives when I got back, and he said it was just a counter, that they had to be careful not to overload the coach. Only there weren't no danger of that, that time. We only had three passengers." He sighed. "Shit, the bastards got all the gold I dug out of my claim for six months. Now I got to start over."

The guilty verdict came quickly. Pfouts put Club-Foot George's name in his pocket.

Dan squirmed. His backside felt squashed, his leg ached, and he was desperate for sleep. Fortunately, the next names went quickly: Boone Helm, though not on Yeager's list, openly bragged of eating human flesh and made dire, frightening threats. His name went into Pfouts's pocket, as did those of Hayes Lyons, the second of John Dillingham's murderers, and Frank Parish, who was on Yeager's list as a road agent and horse thief besides having been identified by victims in robberies with violence. Ed French had collected suspicion about himself as a wheel gathers thick clay mud after rain. No wonder they call it gumbo, Dan thought.

"Sam McDowell."

"What?" Dan's skin prickled, and the hairs on his forearms stood up. Martha, widowed. Martha, available. Martha, his. He saw himself comforting her in her grief, and recoiled from the thought. David and Bathsheba again? He would not.

If he helped to hang her husband she would never be with him, never forgive him.

"I put McDowell on the list," Fitch said. "He helped Gallagher set you up."

"Wait a God damn minute." Dan's mind roiled around. "McDowell's chimney needs sweeping, but he wasn't there when I challenged Gallagher to the poker game."

"For Christ's sake!" Fitch nearly shouted. "Sometimes you ain't got the sense of a louse. You can only carry Christianity so far, you know."

"I never claimed to be a Christian!" Dan started to say more, but Fitch cut him off.

"McDowell hates you. He was pals with Ives, and you go and prosecute Ives. He thinks you're sweet on his wife. His boy runs to you when the old man throws him out. He's pals with Gallagher and Boone Helm and them boys. And he's always out on the trail. Prospecting. Or so he says. We all know how close he sails to the truth."

"God damn it!" Dan pounded his fist on the counter. "You know damn well he's prospecting, because you grubstake him. There are contracts between you and him for claims he's staked out."

"Good story, ain't it?" Fitch spat tobacco juice in the general direction of a bucket. "I ain't never seen one of them claims. Did he ever ask you to survey one?"

"No," Dan said, "but that may be because he's afraid someone will jump them."

Another man spoke up. "That don't wash. You find a promising claim, you register it first thing, with a survey, on account of we have a surveyor now. Then you work it so's you can keep it. If you have more than one claim, you make damn sure someone don't jump the others while you're working one. Maybe hire somebody on shares."

Another man said, "Or get your boy. What I hear, is Tim don't like hard work."

"I don't believe you'd pay out good money without seeing a return," Dan said. "Not you." Fitch was too close with his dust not to know exactly what he paid for.

The Southerner said, "I've got written contracts giving me half shares and general locations, and when the snow melts, you can be damn sure I'll have surveys done on ever' damn one." He turned his head and spat again, and another man yanked back his feet just in time to avoid the gob. Only the fire's crackle disturbed the silence.

"Well, well." Pfouts blew out air. "I'd like a motion that we bring McDowell in with the rest tomorrow morning. We'll get at the truth then."

"I so move," Fitch said. "When you talk to him, you'll see I'm right."

"Second." The only way out of this, Dan thought, was to bring in McDowell and clear him.

"Good." Pfouts said when his motion had carried. He put McDowell's name in his pocket. "Now, about tomorrow."

Dan's throat clogged. He wanted Martha, God knew how much, but never over her husband's dead body. Never by murder. He had joined the Vigilantes to stop murder for gain. Oh, God. A new fear shivered through him. Christ, if we knowingly hang an innocent man, what separates us from Plummer, or Stinson, or Gallagher?

☙

In the night a sudden warm wind had come up, melted much of the snow, and layered gumbo over ice. Feeling the warmer moist air, Martha cheered up some. She took the deep cold hard, even in winter back home she'd never knowed such cold.

Outside, the dog set to barking, and Martha, ladling flapjack batter into the frying pan, started, jerked the ladle and splattered batter sizzling onto the stove. Running steps sounded up the path, more steps than one man. McDowell jumped up from his place at the table and grabbed his shotgun off its pegs. Dotty slid from her chair and crouched in her safe corner behind the stove. The running stopped.

"McDowell," shouted a deep voice, "I want to talk to you. Come out and shut the damn dog up."

"It's the stranglers." McDowell laid down the gun across the table and leaned both hands on it. His eyes, black in his blanched face, stared at something unseen. He wiped his mouth on the back of his trembling hand. "Why are they here? Why do they want me? I ain't done nothing."

"Come out, McDowell," another voice shouted. "Now!"

Stranglers. A word like a wool blanket thrown over her, dark and stifling, and she was frantic to get clear of it, it lay on her, and she couldn't beat it off, but it thinned out so she could see McDowell as through gauze, a long ways off. His mouth changed shape, he was making words, but she couldn't hear him proper, and she couldn't breathe right.

Dotty's scream shredded the gauze. "Pap! Please, Pap! They'll hurt Canary!"

The bowl slipped out of Martha's hands and smashed on the floor, and she gasped for air, and she heard everything – the dog barking, Dotty crying, McDowell trying to make himself heard, his hands reaching out to her.

"You got to believe me." His eyes begged her. "I never done nothing. No matter what, you got to believe I never done nothing!"

He was her husband again, the father to her young'uns. No matter that he ranged far from her, or didn't want the burden of them. He was their Pap. She might not love him no more, but she couldn't desert their father.

"I believe you," she said, and found it was true. Wild though he'd turned, and some violent, he was no murderer, no thief. "I do believe you. I truly do."

"McDowell!" came the shout again. "Come out with your hands up, or we'll shoot the goddam dog."

"Pap!" Dotty screamed. "Pap!"

"You care more for the dog than you do your Pap!" he said, with a look in his eyes like he'd seen a truth, then he squared his shoulders, and grabbed his coat. "I'm coming." He blew a kiss to Dotty and walked out the door.

From the doorway, Martha held Dotty to her and watched the armed men receive him. They patted McDowell's pockets, his trousers, his arms and legs, tied his hands behind his back, and marched him away in the middle of their group, head and shoulders over most of the men. He did not look back.

The dog broke loose and charged after them, making no sound, head lowered, the fur along his back standing straight up. The child squirmed out of her mother's arms and ran after him, shouting for the dog to come back, and Martha raced after her with no time to breathe, let alone think, and as one of them raised his pistol and cocked it to shoot Canary, Dotty flung herself onto the dog and drove him down into a pile of melting snow. Martha felt her heart squeezed like someone had grabbed hold of it. The man yanked the pistol up, so it pointed into the air, and his finger came off the trigger as Martha crouched over the squirming pile of child and dog, shielding them both. She and the man looked into each other's eyes.

"My God, that was too close." Hands shaking, he let down the hammer, oh so slow, with a slight rasp, and the click as it slid into place resounded in the silent, clear air. He helped Martha to her feet, "I'm sorry, missus, you'd best get into the house."

Canary was still snarling at the man, would not let him near Dotty. Martha took a hold of the rope around Canary's neck, dragged him off aways, and the man who had come so near to shooting her lifted Dotty to her feet.

Brushing at her clothes, he said, "You shouldn't oughta get in the line of fire, missy."

McDowell yelled, "You bastards, you nearly killed my daughter." He was still cussing at them as they led him away.

Martha shepherded the child and the dog toward the cabin. McDowell's yelling stopped. She had no time to think about that, just to get Dotty into dry clothes, warm them both. "Hurry, child, do! We'll catch our death out here." She knew she must think, but her mind reeled like she was dancing too fast, and why was —

"Mam, look!" Dotty pointed uphill, where, at the end of Idaho, armed men stood across the road, each carrying a long gun, and Martha wheeled to look downhill toward the Creek, and men stood shoulder to shoulder there, too. Not even a cat would escape.

Martha's thoughts splashed around, the common stream running in her mind broke on rocks like her fingers playing on a smashed dulcimer, misshapen chords jumping up and falling back, their scales flashing until one clear thought leaped the rapids as she buttoned a clean skirt round herself, Dotty already in dry clothes (washday coming up too quick): Find Dan Stark.

She had one arm in her coat, Dotty all wrapped up to go, when running steps froze them until Tim flung open the door. And she relaxed into tears because her son was here. "Mam, they got Pap."

"We got to find Dan Stark," she said. "Your Pap is no murderer, and he's no thief." She squirmed out of his grasp, because a new idea had jumped the tumbling rapids of her thoughts, and she knelt in front of the lowest shelf in her makeshift cupboard, reached far back, and pulled out the cigar box of contracts.

Tim held Dotty, stroked her hair, made soothing noises like someone might make to a fractious filly, gentling it.

The contracts would all have different dates on them; she'd seen them signed and dated at her table at different times during the last months. They'd prove that McDowell had been out prospecting. Not killing, not stealing.

"Here." She thrust the box at Tim. "Run quick. Give it to Mr. Stark. Nobody else. Just him. He'll know what to do. They're the contracts between your Pap and Fitch."

"But – " Tim frowned, like he didn't know what a bunch of papers could do.

"For the love of God, run! They'll prove he was out looking for gold."

Tim's face cleared. Tucking the box under his arm, he shook off Dotty's clinging hands and ran.

Martha watched him run. "Your Pap will be all right now." Now she could hope. Now, she'd done everything she could to help McDowell live. It was up to the Lord now, what the Vigilantes did, but she'd done her best and the wish she'd had wouldn't count no more. "Let's go."

∽

"No!" shouted McDowell. "I tell you I never! I ain't a thief, I ain't a murderer."

Paris Pfouts banged down his gavel, banged it again, but McDowell, straining against the ropes and against the charges holding him, hollered: "All you got on me, it don't amount to a pile of shit, and you sons of bitches know it!"

From behind the partitions strategically placed to separate the prisoners from each other, came shouts: "You tell the bastards, Sam! Go, Sam!"

They might have been cheering a horse race, Dan said to himself, except the prize was McDowell's life. The feed store fronting on Main Street was new enough that the smell of green wood stayed in the walls, as if the logs remembered their lives as trees, their damp pungent aroma mingled with the dry smell of oats and corn. A window gave him a sight all the way up Wallace Street, and the weak morning sunshine cut the guards' silhouettes against the panes.

He did not see her on the street.

"Gag him!" said one of the Vigilantes who stood behind Dan.

Pfouts said, "McDowell, if you can't be quiet, I will do just that."

In the comparative quiet, Dan said, "I haven't changed my mind, either. I can't believe Sam McDowell is a murderer. Or a thief. If he had money, his wife would not be taking in boarders and baking pies to sell." He felt strange, curiously separated from himself, as if he watched through his own eyes and at the same time from someplace outside himself, as from a box and he were a player on a stage acting a life.

"He's gambled it away," said Fitch. "You won his share of two of those contracts."

"Yes." Dan still watched up Main Street, but he could not see her yet. "I've played some poker with this man, and believe me, he's not very good. He's a sore loser, besides. But, gentlemen," and now he turned to look at the other Vigilantes, "he's not a card cheat. He loses, or he wins, fair and square. Now I ask you, would a man who loses a claim at poker be a man who robs people at gunpoint or kills them to steal their gold?" Almost holding his breath, he waited, but no one could think of an example. Being a thief, a killer, and an honest poker player did not go together. "Nor has he once tried to take back the claims by force. Sam McDowell is a prospector. He's not a killer, and he's not a thief." He's the husband of the woman I love.

"He tried to kill you," Fitch said. "You know he did."

"I'd have killed him, too, if I could have." Dan was lying, but once mounted on it, he could not get off; the lie had its own momentum. He would have killed McDowell if he'd had to, he still wished the man were out of the way, but he knew that to kill McDowell would be to lose Martha before he had – what? Won her? Impossible even to try. "It was a fight that got out of hand, that's all."

"What is wrong with you?" Fitch jerked his head toward McDowell. "Why do you defend him? There's not one shred of proof that he was really prospecting."

Why did Fitch keep on with this? Why did he keep prodding at it, as if demanding that he help Fitch murder McDowell for his own reasons? Damn it! He would not be complicit with Fitch. He held hard the reins on his temper, felt it fight against the curb. "I don't have to. You prove him guilty." Proof. Something clicked into place, and he cursed himself for a God damned idiot. He'd been too preoccupied with Martha to pay attention, was letting the secret planner work out McDowell's doom while hiding from himself the simple fact that he would have Martha McDowell, hiding his own King David.

The contracts. He had them in his pocket. They were proof, maybe not in court, but here they would be enough, perhaps, to throw doubt on Fitch. He took the two pieces of paper from his pocket and flapped them at Fitch. "Here is proof. I have signed and dated contracts between you and McDowell. They prove he was prospecting." Duly witnessed by Con Orem, assigned to Dan by his signature and McDowell's mark.

"The hell! They don't show a damn thing." Fitch's voice was rising. "He gulled me!"

The two men might have been alone in the big room, the Vigilantes and the prisoners alike quiet and waiting to see how this would pan out. McDowell, looking from one to the other like a spectator at a tennis game, yelled, "I found them claims! You know I did!"

Dan's mind leaped and skidded into an understanding. The claims were valuable. Did Fitch want them all to himself, so badly he was willing to portray himself as gullible, discredit his own cleverness, to have them? He knew what Fitch would say next, and sure enough, Fitch said to McDowell, "I believed you then, but I've never seen a flake of dust."

"You're too smart to be taken in," Dan said.

"Anyone can be bamboozled sometimes," said Fitch. "There's no proof he did anything but take my money. Those contracts are just paper."

There was movement in the street, where people were gathering, and figures separated themselves from the crowd, a man carrying something. Tim. Armed guards stopped him. The man pointed down the hill toward the feed store. Dan didn't have much time to finish this. It had to be himself that freed McDowell. Not Tim. Otherwise, she would forever brand him as one who had tried to murder her husband. "'Those contracts are just paper,'" Dan repeated.

"That's right. Just paper. Worthless paper."

"How many are there, altogether?" Dan made his question as neutral as he could, against the rising excitement that beat in his ears. Fitch couldn't bear to be thought stupid; he was confessing to having been fooled in perfect grammar, unlike his usual ungrammatical speech.

"Oh, I believe he brought in about eight so-called claims."

"Eight times he humbugged you? You? Major Fitch? 'Fool me once, shame on you.' Or have you never heard that saying?"

Dan swung around, turned his back square to the window, to address the other Vigilantes. "Gentlemen, I propose we release Sam McDowell. By the testimony of his partner, Major Fitch, formerly of the Confederate States of America, eight contracts exist that the Major grubstaked and signed." He held his breath. Would they understand? Would they realize the contradiction that a Major in either Army could not have achieved that rank on such stupidity and gullibility as Fitch now pretended to? This was not England, after all, where a well-born idiot could buy his way to high command. Would they have heard Fitch's educated grammar? Education, rank: Had Fitch been graduated from West Point?

He glanced over his shoulder, up the street. A woman and a young girl had joined the man, and argued with the guards, who restrained them. Clouds had covered the sun. Vote, dammit!

Fitch did not quite shout, "You're making a big mistake, if you let a road agent walk free!" He glared at Dan. "You'll regret this, Stark. By God, you will."

Dan stared into Fitch's eyes that were cold as pebbles under a winter stream: You don't know how I already do.

Pfouts said, "Gentlemen, Dan Stark has asked for a vote of acquittal. What say you?"

The Vigilantes, judge and jury alike, muttered among themselves, until X Beidler spoke up: "All in favor of acquittal say, 'Aye'."

"Aye!"

"Opposed?"

"No!" The no's were not as strong as the Ayes, but the Vigilantes required unanimous votes to convict. McDowell was free.

Dan let out his breath as Cap Williams led McDowell aside to wait until the others had been dealt with. He kept his back to the window, he did not want to know how McDowell's family waited, did not want to see her frantic waiting for her husband.

Christ, if they had voted to convict he would at least know he had done his best, but she would have been just as far out of reach. He had little to say about the others, their crimes; his job was to evaluate the evidence, to make them corroborate Yeager's list. Guards came and went outside, changing places as their stomachs, or nature, called. The angle of the sun shifted, sunlight came and went, with intermittent gleams from the side, then casting long shadows of the afternoon down Main Street as the Vigilantes pressed the remaining men, played them off against each other, to trip them up. At last Dan could ignore his need no longer, but went out to stand against the back of the building, where Cap Williams joined him.

"Gallagher's next," said Williams.

Dan, buttoning his trousers, nodded. The cold air, smelling of wood burning and fresh dug earth, felt good. Behind him, Alder Creek flowed around miners at work.

Williams said, "We ain't going to get corroboration, are we?"

"Doesn't look like it," Dan said. "But we have enough to hang them anyway. Eyewitness accounts of their participation in robberies, shootings, Boone Helm's confession to those murders in Oregon, back East."

"Except Ed French. I think he had some of the wrong friends. Like McDowell."

"Same here. He's careless, but he's no criminal."

"Acquittal, then?"

"Yeah."

Williams pushed open the back door. "I still would have liked to get them to admit the conspiracy exists."

Dan said, "Oh, it exists all right. Or how did Club-Foot George know that marking a stage would tell someone to rob it? I'd like corroboration, too, but we have enough." His wounded leg bumped a box, and he gasped at the scorching pain. "Like with Plummer. We had enough to hang him."

They were questioning Gallagher. Across the street, George Temple paced back and forth by the Leviathan Hall, his arm in a sling, bandages around his neck. Even from here, with the guards blocking much of his view, the man's anger vibrated in the air, in the angle of his back, his abrupt turns, the stiffness in his shoulders. Dan told of the shooting, how Gallagher shot Temple in the arm and then, as Temple, clutching his arm, his back to Gallagher, paused at the saloon door, the Chief Deputy had carefully lined up his sights and fired. Dan's glimpses of Temple between the heads of the guards were like watching a moving card show that was missing a few cards here and there. It didn't matter about connecting Gallagher to the gang. Shooting Temple, on top of other killings, was enough to hang him. Gallagher had meant murder, Temple's luck that he lived.

When Dan had given his testimony, Gallagher sobbed, "I thought you were my friend." Dan stared at him. Why did Gallagher think that? Did he think friendship could be built on intimidation?

Ready to go, the Vigilantes released Sam McDowell and Ed French first. Martha and her children stepped out into the street, but there was no reunion as McDowell backhanded his son, knocked him aside, and strode up Wallace, his family trotting after him.

༄

Martha stumbled after McDowell, who stormed past her and the young'uns like he didn't see them, like the clotted mud didn't catch at his boots and fair trip him up like it did her, so that she had to slow down, her and the child both, blowing like a horse, to watch him turn up Jackson. He was making for home. Tim, holding the box under one arm, gave her the other and helped her along. She couldn't seem to mind where she placed her feet.

All she could think of, he'd been spared. Thank you, Lord, you delivered him. Thank you, Lord. She repeated that all the way home, it kept away the knowledge she didn't want to face: she had wanted him dead so's she'd be free. But if they'd hung him, she would never have been free. Never. On account of she'd wished it.

He'd left the cabin door open, and was stuffing his spare shirts and other things into a gunnysack, all helter-skelter, and the skin of his face all dark like there was too much blood under it.

"What are you doing?" Her voice wasn't hardly more than a whisper. Off to the side of her knowing, Tim followed her into the cabin, shut the door, and stood in the back corner with his arms around his little sister.

McDowell ransacked the kitchen corner for the smaller frying pan, a pot, a knife and fork and spoon. One of the blue tin cups. "What the hell does it look like? Getting out of here. They almost hung me. Don't you understand? Them stranglers almost hung me. The bastards! Your pal Stark among 'em."

"Mr. Stark?" She hugged her arms around her, wrapped in her shawl.

"Yes, Mr. Stark." The name was a sneer. "Oh, he argued some and got them to let me go, but he's a strangler right enough. Didn't lift a finger for Gallagher, or the others."

"Gallagher? They're hanging Gallagher?"

"Yeah, Gallagher, and Club Foot George, and Boone Helm, and Frank Parish, and Hayes Lyons. They let me and Ed French go, but them others – if they ain't dead now, they soon will be. They'd have hung Bill Hunter, too, only he got away somehow."

"Oh, dear God." Martha collapsed onto a chair.

McDowell picked up his bag. "I'll send word where to find me, then you and the young'uns come." He glared at Tim. "'Cept you. I can't abide a man don't dirty his hands."

Martha took in air. She had a sudden vision of how it would be, her life traipsing after him, setting up and him drinking and getting into trouble, and them moving on, and him getting ever meaner, and what of the child then, because they'd have nothing, and where would Timmy be? "No."

"Whaddaya mean, no? You're my woman, you go where I go."

"No, not this time. You go now, and you go alone, because I'm not following you hither and yon. I want to put down roots, and make a home, and so what that I didn't want to come here, you were coming and I wanted to keep the family together, but you never wanted us, and you don't want us now. Here's where I am and I'm staying put."

"You can't do that. You got to come. You can bake pies anywhere, but you'll give me the money."

"You just want me slaving for you, that's all!" Her temper was rising to meet his. That was all he thought of her, was it? A slavey, to make him money to drink up?

He bent over her and she wanted to bolt, but she stayed put on the chair, held fast to the seat. She'd been so happy he wasn't hung, hoped during the long waiting that coming so close to death might have changed him, but no, it just made him worse. He didn't want a family, a home, he wanted to be free except she could earn money for him.

She tipped her head back so she could look him in the eye, and all her frustration and the pent up anger that she'd stored these last months erupted. "No! You stay here, and stop drinking and gambling in the saloons, because I won't leave."

The blow struck her fast as a snake, knocked her to the floor, someone was screaming, and McDowell was shouting, "You whore, you're staying with that bastard Stark, he's hanging my friends and he nearly hung me, and he's been having you behind my back." Half-stunned she could not fight him, even if she could have fought against the strength of him. She heard her dress rip as he straddled her, and her head rocked back and forth as he slapped her.

Boots thundered across the floor, and she heard a clang, McDowell lifted off her, and then a man's shriek. Timmy was shouting, "Yellow bastard, hit Mam will you, get out of here, I'll kill you next time I see you, I swear I will even you are my own Pap, I'll kill you so help me God, I will."

Dotty kneeling over her, crying, Martha barely aware when Timmy said, "I'll fetch Miz Hudson. And Tabby." She wanted to tell him not to leave her, but the darkness was fast coming over her, and she had to yield to it, let it come. She couldn't fight it off.

∾

There should have been drums. Men walking to their execution should march to drums beating a slow cadence marking the solemn occasion of death amid an awestruck silence. Five men about to die. Dan, limping behind the Vigilantes holding on to Gallagher, the Spencer ready to cock and fire, heard again their sentences, in Paris Pfouts's precise, dry words, echoing where drums should roll:

Boone Helm, public nuisance, self-confessed murderer, and cannibal.

Frank Parish, road agent, stage robber; specifically, robbing the stage on the thirteenth of November; co-conspirator with Henry Plummer.

Club-Foot George Lane, road agent, co-conspirator, telegraph agent for the Plummer gang, warning gang members when valuables were being carried on a stage.

Hayes Lyons, road agent, guilty of robbery and murders, specifically the murder of John Dillingham.

Jack Gallagher, co-conspirator, accessory before and after the fact of robbery and murder, specifically covering up the murder of John Dillingham by cleaning one pistol and shuffling them all so that no one could tell which had been the actual murder weapon; and finally, attempted murder on the person of George Temple on December 31st.

But there were no drums. No awestruck silence from the people on the street, who called to their friends while armed Vigilantes scattered throughout the crowd kept order.

The procession halted while men ran ahead to prepare the place of execution, a new building on the corner of Wallace and Van Buren streets, the next street beyond Jackson, the future home of Rank's Drugs. The log walls were up, and the main support beam was in place. A good place for a hanging. The beam would hold the weight.

Walter Dance came out of his store and stood among the crowd, his head in the clear above the other men. Club-Foot George called to him. "Mr. Dance, can't you help me? I'm innocent. I swear I am."

Dance shook his head. "I'm sorry, George. You've been all right to me, but the evidence is overwhelming."

He'd heard it from his partner, Jim Stuart, a Vigilante. Which did Dance regret more, Dan wondered, the execution of a man he had befriended or knowing that Club-Foot George had taken so great advantage of his kindness?

"Then will you pray with me, sir?"

"Gladly."

Dan said, "Let him kneel," and Fitch, holding one of Club Foot George's arms, helped him to his knees. Fitch's face showed his disgust, but he dared not refuse.

Gallagher said, "Me, too. Take off my hat."

Dan swept off Gallagher's hat, and his guards helped him to kneel in the cold mud.

"Would you take off my hat?" Hayes Lyons asked the men holding him.

"Sure thing." One of them removed Lyons's hat and held it for him.

"Obliged." Lyons did not ask to kneel.

Frank Parish wept steadily, tears ran down his cheeks and dropped onto his coat. Dan guessed that he might not even know the prayers were being said.

"Almighty God," said Dance, "we beseech you in the name of your only Son, our Lord Jesus Christ, that you forgive these men – "

"Hey," Boone Helm said, "did you hear the one about the traveling drummer who arrives at the farmer's house – "

"Shut up," said Fitch and Dan together as Dan brought up the muzzle of the Spencer. Helm spat at them, muttered under his breath as Dance prayed.

"– and receive their souls into your everlasting peace and love. Lord, you know we have all sinned and come short of the glory of God, but that in your unbounded love of mankind you sent your only Son to die for us."

Helm called out to a friend in the crowd of onlookers. "Hey, Bob, they got me this time. Say goodbye to Jim for me, will you?"

"Shut the hell up," said Fitch.

Dance had continued the prayer as if he had not heard them. "Forgive our sins, Lord, and receive these men today into your loving Presence. In Jesus' name, Amen."

The prayer finished, Dan helped Gallagher to his feet and put his hat on again. Dance lifted up Club Foot George and set him on his feet. Lane said, "Thank you, sir. I guess I'll see you in heaven someday."

"I'll look for you there, George. We'll meet again."

Dan envied them their belief in life after death, of living beyond this life even though the body was left in the dirt, that what was to come would be a world of quiet waters and green pastures.

"Hey, Jack," Helm said to Gallagher, "that's a fine coat you have there. Why don't you give it to me? You never gave me nothin' and now's your last chance."

"Damn sight of use you'll have for it. You won't need a coat where you're going." Gallagher's eyes were red-rimmed from crying, but his voice was steady though the corners of his lips quivered.

"Forward!" The procession picked up its march.

Someday, the building would make a two-room store, but today the condemned men and their executioners crowded through the door to the back room and squeezed themselves into it. Five crates stood in a straight row beneath five ropes that dangled over the main bearing beam. The hangman's knots were already tied. Sunlight slanted onto a wall through a crack in the clouds, and a breeze, heavy with the threat of snow, touched Dan's cheek.

Outside, the crowd shouted, cried out, called for the release of the five, for their deaths, and a woman's high-pitched wailing sliced through the noise. Vigilantes surrounded the building, guns, like Dan's own, ready to cock and fire.

Frank Parish sobbed, and his legs shook so that he seemed to stand in a breeze rippling his trouser legs. X put the noose around Frank Parish's neck, snugged it against the back of his left ear. Vigilantes boosted him onto the box nearest the west wall and braced him, so he could not slump down and choke himself. When he could muster a few coherent words, he asked for a mask. His own black neckerchief was draped over his head, and it puffed in and out with every breath.

Next to him stood Boone Helm rigid as a pole while Cap Williams placed the noose and tightened it. "Hey, leave a little slack there," said Helm. "You want to strangle me?"

Scrabbling noises from the wall, grunts and gasps, and onlookers' heads appeared over the topmost log. They did not want to miss a bit of the excitement, and their ghoulish glee

turned Dan's stomach. Even murderers deserved to die with —
he could not think of what, and turned his back on them to tend
to Gallagher, in the middle.

Another Vigilante held Dan's rifle while he removed
Gallagher's hat, laid it on the box, took the noose in both hands.
The rope felt stiff and bristly as a hostile hound's back, and
Gallagher dodged and twisted to avoid the noose until Dan's
patience snapped. "Hold still, damn it, Jack. You're not gaining
anything with these maneuvers." His hands were so cold he
could hardly grasp the rope to widen the loop.

Gallagher quieted while Dan fitted the loop over his head.
The condemned man's hair, slicked neat as ever, shone black. A
drop of sweat trickled down through one sideburn. He said in
a low voice that Dan almost did not hear, "It didn't have to be
this way."

Dan could not use his left thumb, and both hands shook
when he tried to tighten the noose. Did Gallagher mean that he
could have been one of them? That Jack would have accepted
him then? It would have been so simple, just tell them things —
where new claims lay, which ones held promise, which did
not. Not much. Just a minor dishonesty here and there, like
Club-Foot George had marked the stagecoaches, or Brown had
passed on information communicated over a friendly drink,
and all of these choices led, on a path as twisted as a deer trail,
to this moment on a winter afternoon. In the deep night hours
Dan had thought he could never bring himself to hang Jack
Gallagher, a man he could like despite everything, but now his
anger beat a drum in his ears. Damn Gallagher for bringing
them both here. He tugged at the noose, and the knot tightened
with a jerk and pain flared in his left hand and with it his anger.

"God damn it, Jack. You could have done things differently,
and you know it. You could have lived an honest life."

"You think so? You can let me know someday if it was worth
it, walking the straight and narrow."

Dan's laugh held no humor. "I know that now. Look where you're standing."

"You got a point." Gallagher rubbed his ear against the knot. "That's a little tight, ain't it?"

"You'll be glad of it soon." Dan stepped away.

Two other Vigilantes helped Gallagher onto the box, and another took up the slack in the rope, looped the free end around a log in the back of the building. The sun came out, and cast long afternoon shadows sideways across the floor. "Do you want your hat?" Dan asked, but Gallagher shook his head. "I'm not likely to need it now, am I?"

Hayes Lyons was begging to have his woman brought so he could say goodbye.

"You tried that before," Cap Williams said. "We'll give her a message, though."

Dan remembered that women's tears had stirred the crowd to free Lyons from hanging for Dillingham's murder.

"Tell her – " Almost, Lyons broke down. His face worked, his eyes squeezed shut, and his lips trembled. Taking hold again, he said in a rush, "Tell her I loved her."

Club-Foot George, whose hands were tied in front, dashed his hat to the ground. A Vigilante placed the noose and tightened it, helped Lane onto the box by the east wall.

When all was ready, Cap Williams said, "Any last requests?"

Gallagher glared at the Vigilantes. "Yeah, damn it, I'd like a drink. And make it decent whiskey." Dan had a flask that he uncorked and someone climbed on the box to help him drink from it. "That's better." Gallagher said, "I hope forked lightning strikes every God damn strangling one of you sons of bitches before this day is out, because then you'll join me in hell and I'll get you there, you bastards." He looked directly at Dan. "You especially, you son of a bitch."

Williams said, "Men, do your duty."

As if he had been waiting for that signal, George Lane leaped up and came down at the end of the rope with the sharp crack of a broken neck, and enough force nearly to decapitate him. Blood spurted against the wall, and Dan was reminded of Ives, whose blood had sprayed him. Lane's body swung free, his boots kicking and twitching a few seconds until at last they stilled.

Vigilantes snatched the box from under Gallagher's feet. He dropped, and again there was the bull-whip crack of a broken neck. Dan coughed and stepped aside from the stench, dodged the swinging feet. He had done the job right; Jack died quickly.

Boone Helm watched Gallagher's feet. "Kick away, old boy. I'll be in hell with you in a minute." He raised his voice: "Hooray for Jeff Davis! Let her rip!" He jumped out high and hard, and the rope twanged as he hit the end of it, and his body swung in a wide arc, his feet knocked against the box.

"Any last words?" X asked Parish, who shook his head. A corner of the neckerchief fluttered. When X and another man yanked the box away, he dangled, jerking and shuddering for several minutes before he died.

Hayes Lyons talked nonstop to the Vigilantes and the onlookers peering over the top to see five men hang. "One bad step leads to another, and I never thought I'd end up this way. Tell my woman she's to see me buried decent, and not leave me hanging here too long, and to take her gold watch, she let me wear, do you promise?" X promised. Hayes said, "I knew you would. You're a square shooter, X."

X said, "Time to go." He and four Vigilantes jerked the box from under Lyons, who plunged toward the ground, and his neck snapped, his feet dangled quietly.

"He went easy, at any rate," said Fitch. Dan started; he had forgotten the Southerner.

Trying not to inhale the stench of death that fouled the air, Dan watched the bodies sway in ever smaller arcs until they stilled. A bystander called down to X, "Didn't you feel for the poor boy as you put the rope around his neck?"

X gave the man a long, considering look. "Yeah, I felt for his left ear."

What was there to feel, anyway? Dan asked himself. They had hanged ten road agents. Who among the hanged had given a thought to their victims? As well ask Club-Foot George if he had ever thought that a chalk mark might give someone terror in the night. Or George Ives if he'd felt sorry for Nick when he shot him down. Or Gallagher if he'd felt for George Temple when he nearly killed him, or Hayes Lyons if he'd pitied John Dillingham when he put a slug in his chest. What ye sow, ye shall reap.

Women's wailing at a distance told Dan that Gallagher's woman, and Lyons's, would shortly claim their bodies for burial. Had those slatterns ever wept for the men whose gold they had been happy to spend?

He had now helped to kill as many men as some of these men had killed. More, perhaps, and maybe now he was a murderer himself, but someone had to risk his life, risk his soul, for other people's safety, other people's lives. Dan wished he could manage not to regret what he had done, but he couldn't. He regretted it to the bottom of his heart, because it had to be done, and more besides. And he would do it.

But it was all such a God damn waste.

∾

The five corpses hung, as if their clothes were empty, motionless at the ends of their ropes. The onlookers climbed down from the log walls. Watching men being killed might have some entertainment value, Dan thought, but watching their bodies freeze did not. From time to time someone else boosted himself up to look, but as the sun slid down, the Vigilantes were left alone in the building with their newly made dead.

Daniel pulled the flask from his coat pocket, mindful that Gallagher's lips had touched it, but he needed it now, and he took a swig, a good single-malt Scotch he'd bought at Trottman's liquor store, but it didn't help to dull the pain of his leg, of Gallagher's death at his hands. It just made him belch. Someone should say something, there should be some sort of epitaph, but he couldn't think what it should be. He gave the flask to X, who took a swallow, rolled the single malt around on his tongue, his eyes widening, and passed it to Fitch.

"They died well," Pfouts said.

"Better'n they lived," X said.

"Hell." Fitch gave the flask to Williams. "Dying well doesn't mean a thing in the balance of their lives. Besides, we're short a couple." He thrust his chin out at Dan, who returned Fitch's glare with a face blank as a wall.

"Oh, it's not over," said Pfouts.

"Yes." Dan thought of Aleck Carter and Bill Hunter, and the others on Yeager's list. "There's work to do yet." The cold congealed the stink of death, and he wanted to go where he would not see five corpses in the thickening gloom. Especially Gallagher, whose handsome face was distorted and bluish pale, all mobility drained away, all the jokes, all the meanness, all the possibilities that had inhabited the man, leaving only inert matter freezing fast. It could have been otherwise. Dan knew that he would grieve for Gallagher even as he regretted the necessity to put the rope around Gallagher's neck. And he would do it again. Grief, regret, and resolve – together, all his life.

Outside, men muttered and grumbled together, and women wailed.

He did not want to listen to that. "They're on the other side now, if there is one."

Fitch said, "If there's a hell, they're in it, sure enough."

"Oh, there's a hell," said X. "A heaven, too. But only one man's come back to tell about it."

"I wasn't there," said Fitch, his voice disgusted as always when religion came up.

Someone else said, "That's why we read the Bible. Them fellas was there."

"It's getting cold," X said. "It'll freeze deep tonight, sure. Give it a few days and we'll be having winter again. This has just been a little thaw."

"Cold enough for hell," Dan said.

"I thought hell was hot," Fitch said.

"According to an Italian poet, the bottom circle of hell is ice. Guess he thought being cold was worse than being burned."

"Oh," sneered Fitch, "poetry."

"I can't say nothing about that," X said, "but the bottom circle is about where these boys belong." He jerked a thumb at the five corpses.

Williams said, "Some of us will be riding up to Hell Gate after Carter and them."

"Can you leave in the morning?" asked Pfouts.

"Sure," Williams said. "Might's well get it done."

"That'll be a long, cold ride," said Beidler, "a hundred and fifty miles north."

Dan began to ask a question, but Williams said, "Not you, Counselor. Not with that leg. You stay here and keep order. We can't have the roughs making trouble."

"They won't." Dan felt as if he'd taken a solemn oath, that never again would honest men and women fear to travel, or walk on a street. The work of God's thunderbolt, as Martha had said. Martha, now reunited with her husband. Martha, lost. We are God's thunderbolt, he said to himself, looking at the five corpses now yielding to darkness, and this is our work. The lines from a poem by Emerson came into his mind:

My will fulfilled shall be,
For, in daylight or in dark,
My thunderbolt has eyes to see
His way home in the dark.

Someone lit a stub of candle, and another man lighted a lantern. Their shadows sprang across the floor, across the corpses' feet. Dan shivered. A small breeze stirred among them, and a rope creaked on wood, Gallagher's body turning slightly away, swinging back. A small motion, but the hairs rose on the back of Dan's neck. "Jesus."

Perhaps a half hour later, Cap Williams said, "That's enough, boys. Let's let their friends have them. We've done our duty here."

In the street, a few people waited: friends of the five and other Vigilantes among them, watching. Jacob stepped out to walk beside Dan. From among a small knot of tearful women, one broke away, screamed at the Vigilantes, "You goddam stranglers! They didn't deserve to die! Stranglers!" It was Isabelle Stevens, her hair coming down around her face, her eyes puffed and red from weeping. Her son, Jacky, stood with her and shook his fist at them. "Stranglers," he yelled, and other friends of the hanged men shouted, "Stranglers!" Hatred contorted their faces.

Dan swung the muzzle of the Spencer across the crowd, and a man shushed the Stevens woman. "Don't give them trouble," he said. "Pipe down."

Jacob said, "There is more trouble."

"Trouble?" Dan could not quite grasp what Jacob was telling him. His leg ached, every step on it a blow.

"Sam McDowell. He has hurt his wife."

Dan forgot the leg, the pain, quickened his step, slipped on some icy mud and nearly fell, grabbed Jacob's shoulder to steady himself. The wound burned, and tears came to his eyes.

"Hurt his wife?" Despite the pain, he hurried, Jacob's shoulder under his arm, helping him. Oh, God, let her be all right. "That God damn son of a bitch." He had not freed McDowell so the bastard could hurt Martha. Dear God, Martha. He'd kill McDowell. He'd kill him. The anger swelled inside Dan, so that he felt it about to explode.

Perhaps Jacob guessed. He said, "McDowell, he is gone."

"Gone?" As if from a sucker punch, Dan's breath burst out, leaving him spent, collapsed inside. "Gone?"

"Ja. Where, no one knows. But he is gone."

∽

The cabin was crowded with women, and lamps and lanterns had been lighted as though lamp oil were cheap and would last forever. When Dan threw open the door, Lydia Hudson bent over the bed and stretched out her arm to shield Martha who lay – oh, God! – too still, though he could see only the quilt pointed where her toes raised it. An Indian woman squatted at the stove, stirring a pan of some fragrant liquid. Dotty, sitting on another woman's lap, scrambled down to run and throw her arms around him, and he lifted the child up on his right arm, where she clung to him, a terrified baby bird fluttering against his chest. He pushed Lydia Hudson and Tabby Rose aside, or they made way for him, and he looked down at Martha, who lay on her back, her face bruised nearly out of recognition. She was breathing, her chest rose and fell. He wanted to bury his face in her hair and weep.

Lydia Hudson touched his arm. "She will be all right. No bones are broken, and her face will heal. He had no time to do more damage."

"Why? Who?" Dan heard himself stutter. He couldn't look away from Martha. McDowell, that son of a bitch had beaten

Martha, left her for dead. Left her, his children in this state. Left his wife — Ah.

Left his wife.

Dan set Dotty on her feet. He laid the back of his hand against Martha's hair. The women had let it down, and the thick braid lay down her shoulder, over her breast. Almost to her waist. McDowell had left his wife. Her hair was a dark rich brown, and Dan had never touched anything so soft. Thank God he was not riding to Hell Gate in the morning with Williams and Fitch. He would protect her in case McDowell, damn his soul, came back.

Mrs. Hudson said, "Timothy got shut of him."

"He did?" Dan looked up, saw Tim for the first time, sitting at the kitchen table.

"Yup." The boy held a steaming cup in his hands. "I hit him over the head with Ma's frying pan, and when he got up, I kicked him."

Dan did not need to ask where. "Good for you."

"He had it coming a long time."

Mrs. Hudson bumped at Dan with her hip. "Go sit down there, thee wants to talk."

Dan obeyed her. Dotty came to sit on his lap, but he fended her off. "I took a bullet, little one, so it'll be a while before you can sit on my knee."

The Indian woman set a mug of tea in front of Dan. It was strange stuff, but after the first sip, tasty and soothing. "Thank you," Dan said, and she ducked her head and smiled. A pretty woman in her deer hide dress, who somewhat resembled Martha in the dark eyes and high cheekbones. Dotty poured herself a cup and sat on the fourth chair. "Her name's Berry Woman," Dotty said. "She's Fitch's wife." The Indian woman nodded and smiled. Dan held out his hand and said his name. Dotty added, "She's Mam's friend."

Dan smiled to see how grown up Dotty acted, sitting there with two men, one her brother. But her eyes were big, the pupils dark and fearful. "What if Pap comes back?"

Tim said, "I'll kill him, he comes back here."

"No, you won't." When the boy started to protest, Dan merely looked at him, and Tim nodded as if he understood that he wouldn't have to. Because I will, Dan said silently. This woman, this child, and the boy would never face that bully alone again. "You don't need to worry. I doubt very much your father will ever come back here. We've taken care of his friends."

"Oooh!" Dotty's heels beat against the rung of the chair. "You hung them?"

The room hushed as Dan said, "Yes, we did. This afternoon."

After a moment, the little girl said, "Good. I didn't like them one bit. That Lyons, he looked at me funny."

Dan's jaw tightened. "From now on, if a man looks at you funny, you tell me."

Beside the bed, the women stirred. Dan straightened, craned his neck to see past the curtain of their skirts. A thin trickle of a voice called: "Dan? Daniel?"

Mrs. Hudson said, "She's asking for thee."

All the uncertainties of the last month sloughed away in the few steps to the bed, where he went down on one knee and took her hand and laid it against his cheek. In calling his name, this plain sparrow of a woman had wrung out his heart and pinned it on her life.

❧

Yet there remained unfinished business in New York. Each evening, as he sat at supper with Martha and the youngsters, the knowledge of it pecked at him, but Dan did not know how to broach the subject. Truth to tell, he feared going back to confront Grandfather's expectations, Mother's tears, the children's disappointment. Miss Dean. He did not think of her as Harriet now, she had become something else, a woman of his acquaintance with whom he had once fancied himself in love. All of that paled before the larger fear, that Martha might in her turn become someone he had known during his sojourn in a faraway place. He must tie himself to her somehow. Somehow.

As her bruises faded, she became more beautiful to him than ever. Some strain wearing away from her face relaxed her features into sweetness, and she put on a little weight. Not that she would ever be plump, but her body softened. Not that she changed her mode of dress, for she was a modest woman, but that occasionally she would move, all unconsciously, about her activities in such a way as to weaken his knees so that he regretted having put away the cane. As she leaned forward to lay a plate on the table, her shape under the blue shirtwaist would alter. Or, as she peeled one last potato into the slop pail with quicksilver strokes of the knife, her skirt might flow in a certain way against her rounded posterior.

At those times, he would make haste to shift his eyes to the youngsters, and do his best to appear fascinated by something one of them said. Or ask Dotty how she was doing in school, or suggest to Tim a card game after dinner. He was teaching the boy to play poker, both so that he himself would have someone to play with away from the saloons, and so that a card sharp would not humbug Tim.

They spent comfortable snowy evenings that way, sharing the pool of lamplight on the table after dinner, Dan and Tim at their cards, Dotty and Martha taking turns reading aloud from Martha's Bible and sewing. He helped them with the hard words, and when the sewing basket emptied, Martha asked if she could mend some of his garments. He brought her two shirts and the trousers he'd worn when the Mexican shot him.

It felt like a family, because he was the only boarder. Not long after she was able to get about, he had found her rolling out pie crusts when he came to pay his board bill in advance. Pressing the poke into her hands, he'd said, "You don't have to work so hard any more." Then he held her while she sobbed against his coat. Lest he do something to make her despise him, he had pleaded the press of business and gone back to work.

Without his active encouragement, people were bringing him legal work. Because he had helped to successfully prosecute Ives, the problems came in thick enough that he had to rent an office on Jackson, below Wallace. He found that he liked practicing law here, enjoyed solving the problems they brought, was interested in them. These cases were not the dry leaves of contract law; they were flesh and blood and mattered to people, affected people's lives.

Away from Grandfather's overpowering control, the law was his vocation.

Sanders sent word that he would soon move to Virginia from Bannack, and Dan looked forward to having another Union lawyer to talk things over with. The roughs melted away from Virginia as they had melted from Bannack, and the town settled into quiet. Alex Davis stopped by Dan's office from time to time, and they discussed establishing a "people's court." Dan proposed Davis as its judge, and the other Virginia Vigilantes agreed. They would not hold his defense of Ives against him, for he was an honest man.

Somewhere, in the snow-piled mountains, companies of other Vigilantes rode, and Dan, hurrying between business and Martha's cabin, tried to imagine the storms, the darkness, the cold at seven or eight thousand feet. If he'd been a praying man, he would have spent hours on his knees, but he knew Martha prayed for them.

All the month after he'd hanged Gallagher, he postponed the distasteful task of telling the family he must make the trip to New York. Then a man who owned a dry goods store and wanted to leave the Gulch, offered to sell his cabin. Without thinking twice, Dan bought it, along with some furniture, and moved in. Jacob, now working for the Morris brothers, could keep the bachelor cabin for a nominal rent, and share it with Tim.

The first night in the double bed he rejoiced at the pure luxury of so much space to himself. The next day he began his campaign.

It was his deal, and the rhythmic slap of cards onto the table did not falter. "I have to make a trip." He spread his up-facing cards as he spoke. By the way their heads lifted, alert as deer scenting danger, he knew this would not be easy. Dotty, who had trusted everyone before McDowell left, now had the wary look of the puppy she and Tabby Rose had rescued. Tim held the beginnings of anger in his clenched hands. And Martha's head, bent over her Bible, stayed down as if to ward off a blow. Damn McDowell anyway, wherever he was. Best place, in hell.

"I will be gone at most four months. A month to travel to New York, a month to travel back, two months there to situate my family and take my punishment."

"Take your punishment?" That caught Martha's attention.

"Yes, because they are expecting me to stay, and I shall return to Virginia City. To you." He inhaled to the limit of his lungs. This was the hardest to explain, considering what came next. "I have also to break my word. To a woman."

"What woman?" Tim's man's voice rasped, and he cleared his throat.

"Her name is Harriet Dean, and we were engaged to be married." How much easier it was to say it than he had anticipated, as if the regret and the pain had all drained away.

Dan faced Tim's next challenge, aware that this boy was growing fast, and filling out, and could soon grow to a man bigger than his father. He had assumed a man's role, protector of his mother and sister, and Dan knew that if he were to gain the mother he would have to convince her son. He could not hope to conquer the mother without Tim's approval, or offer himself as head of the family unless Tim willingly allowed him.

"You come here and forgot you was promised?"

"Not quite. Before I left New York, Miss Dean returned my ring and would not promise to wait for me." Confronted by Tim's skeptical silence, Martha's wary expression, and Dotty's bewilderment, Dan began to disrobe, to relate the entire sordid story, and with every piece of it revealed, he felt more naked. He related how Father's suicide revealed that he had gambled away not only his personal fortune, and the Firm's funds, but their clients' money as well. How Grandfather had bankrupted himself and sold the family home to pay back the clients, and it had not been enough. How he had charged Dan with bringing home gold to repay the rest of the clients' funds and restore the family to honor, if not to their former social status. How Grandfather expected he would take over the Firm. How he had promised Miss Dean to return even though she returned his ring.

"Have you enough gold?" asked Martha.

"Yes." Dan removed another garment. "From survey fees, a little speculation in claims, winnings at poker, and legal fees."

Tim said, "And you expect punishment from what? Not taking over the Firm, as you call it, and not staying to marry a woman who maybe didn't wait for you?"

"That's right. Grandfather is very strong-willed, and I gave my word to Miss Dean. I shall break it while I'm back East, and come home to you three."

"Home?" Martha asked. Her eyes had that luminous glow about them. "Here?"

"Yes." Dan stripped himself entirely naked to them, let them judge for themselves the build of him, the set of his shoulders, the width of his chest, the tapering of his belly toward his loins.

He spoke to Martha: "Because I have come to love you, you and your children."

In the following silence he had time for the beginning of despair before Martha rose from her chair and gathered him to her, rested his head against her breast, kissed his hair. Dan, closer to tears than he had been since he was four, wrapped his arms around her thighs. He nestled there, and watched Tim, who appeared to be adjusting his ideas to the sight of his mother holding Dan to herself.

The younger man nodded. "Very well. I'm believing you, Mr. Stark." He pointed his index finger at Dan. "But if'n you don't come back in five months, allowing for accidents, or if'n you hurt my Mam, I'll travel back to New York City and I'll find you, so help me God I will."

❧

He'd said he wanted her to look the new cabin over before she and the youngsters moved into it, to keep it for him until he came back, but that was a ruse, to hide the question burning his throat since McDowell left. Now, some days after he'd told the family he had to go back to New York in the spring, Dan considered the time was as right as it ever would be. McDowell was still absent, everyone on Yeager's list had been accounted for. The Vigilantes controlled an outwardly peaceful region, and the new "people's court" with Alex Davis as judge, had begun regular sessions.

In the early evening, Dan walked Martha toward the cabin on Jackson Street, opposite the Melodeon Hall. Plump snowflakes sailed in the lights from windows, and Dan guessed the temperature hovered somewhere around fifteen above zero. Give or take. He only half-heard her chatter about Dotty's progress at school. The question choked him, so he could not speak. Would she share this cabin with him? Unmarried, scandalous, beyond the pale in all decent society, would she live with him as man and wife though married to McDowell? If she did, he would keep her safe. Or if she did not. If McDowell came back, he would kill the bastard. He could do it. He had hanged fifteen men. Gallagher. Such he had become, that he could know himself able to take another man's life.

Inside the house, he lighted a lamp, gave it to Martha. His leg quivered where Pizanthia had shot him, and fear fluttered its wings in his stomach, seeking escape.

Martha looked around. This main room had chairs and a table, and a cook stove any woman in the Gulch would envy. Even Lydia. Proper cupboards, too, though not much in them. A pot, a pan, a few mismatched plates. What she'd expect from a single man who put his feet under her table every night.

"Do you like it?"

She could hear the hope in his voice, and knew like a revelation that he'd be wanting her to share it with him. How she would love that! Like she loved him, though she hadn't said it to him yet, being cautious, and because he was aiming to go back to New York. Tears stung her eyes, so all she could manage was, "It's real nice." It was, too. A big cabin, well chinked, with a lamp hanging from the ceiling beams, and two doors that led to other rooms. A real window, with glass, on either side of the front door. But it had a waiting feel to it. Like something was missing. From his silence she felt his disappointment, so she turned around and smiled at him. "It's beautiful. There'll be lots of light." His own smile told her how relieved he was, how important it was that she like it, and she knew that her revelation was true.

He did not touch her. "There's more," he said. "Would you like to see?" The next room might be a child's room. It had two windows, one on each wall facing south and west, night-black now but in the daytime bright as outdoors. Light. She craved it as a starving person craved food, her little cabin being so like a cave. She pulled herself back from thinking that – this cabin, this small house, was not hers. She did not live here, could not live here, not with him, they were not married, could not be married as long as McDowell lived because she could not divorce him. The preachers said so. Once married always married, till death do them part, and the world had words for women who went to men they were not married to. Adulteress. Whore. She was afraid, like standing on a cliff, or running toward a buffalo jump, only maybe she wouldn't jump. She didn't have to, did she? She could stay like she was. In her cave. Waiting for McDowell to come home. Dreading that.

Dan saw the fear in her corded neck and stiffened shoulders before she turned to him with the eyes of someone facing a precipice. He knew that fear, had felt it when he accepted the other boys' dare to jump into the quarry pool. He wanted to seize her, crush her to him, but he knew he had to move softly, for she was intelligent and she knew where they were going, what choice he would ask her to make. Seeing her fear, an answering fear pecked at his stomach. He had not been so afraid when Pizanthia shot him, or when the water closed over his head.

"There's another room." He nearly whispered the words, so intent he was that she not run. "Will you see?"

She nodded, and he led her to the third room.

It was larger than the other bedroom. In one corner stood a round stove, banked for safety, and some warmer than the other. The iron bed, with four tall legs, stood fully made up. What a tidy man he was. He poked at the ashes in the stove, and put in two or three more sticks. Martha trembled at the edge of the buffalo jump.

He set the lamp on a chest of drawers and stood by it, like he was waiting for her to say something. She could feel him holding back, while she stared at the bed.

She turned her head to see on his face such a longing that she felt she might see the blood move through his veins, she saw him that plain, or like he was naked, and she wanted to see him that way, oh Lord, she wanted to be with him, just the two of them a new Adam and Eve, and it could not be while McDowell lived.

She fled. From him and from her own wanting, away from the edge of the buffalo jump. His steps, halting because his leg was still healing, came after her, but stopped before she put up the hood of her cloak and reached for the door latch. Martha half turned toward him. "I will not be your —" She could not bring herself to say the word.

He heard what she meant as if she'd said it, and it knocked the wind out of him, though when he had caught his breath he cursed himself for a fool. She thought that could be what he was asking of her. How could she think he would do that, that he only wanted to make her his whore? How could she? She was fastening her cloak.

"Wait!" he said. "Please!" This pain was worse than any bullet, and in his pain he opened his mouth to accuse her, when he realized she mistrusted him because he was a man, because of McDowell, what a man might be capable of. And herself because she had been wrong about McDowell and feared the same mistake again.

As gently as might be, though his voice shook, he said, "I am not asking you to be my — anything else. I am asking you to be my wife."

"How?" Martha pivoted, the table between them, and flung the word at him. She was so cold, with a chill from inside her, because if he only wanted her that way, she might as well have packed up and gone with McDowell. She looked over the edge of the buffalo jump to the animals below, where wolves and coyotes fed on them, tearing living flesh from their bones. What would Isabel Stevens's life be now?

"When Chief Justice Edgerton returns from Washington, this will be Montana Territory," he said. He would talk politics, now? She and the young'uns heard it every night at supper, and she swung away from him, heard him plead, "No, please, wait, I've thought it through. How we can marry. Please, listen. Please." She turned back, but her hand rested on the latch. "The law here says a husband or wife can sue for divorce on grounds of desertion after two years. After two years, you can divorce McDowell and we can be formally married."

"Two years! How can we wait two years? What if he comes back?"

"When this becomes Montana Territory, we'll have our own Legislature, and I'll run for representative. If I'm elected, I'll get you a legislative divorce."

"What if you're not elected?" He would not hold her hostage to some bye and bye, to all them if's, she wouldn't have it.

"I can get you a legislative divorce even if I'm not elected. I'll lobby them until they agree. They won't dare say no to me. Then, if you'll have me, we will marry. But in the meantime, what shall we do?"

If, he'd said. If you'll have me. The lamplight showed clear the planes and angles and shadows in his clean-shaven face, too thin and drawn with everything that had happened since they'd found Nick, and the fear darkening his eyes. He was plumb scared. She'd never had a man afraid before of what she might say, not even McDowell. But she wasn't the only one in this. "I have to think of the young'uns." Something in her voice must have made him bolder, because he moved toward her, lifted back her hood, and took her face in his hands.

"I want us to be a family." He looked into her eyes. "You know that. I've said so, and they understand it, but if we have to keep separate until we can make it legal, then we will."

It was a supreme offer, and his hands trembling on her face told her what it cost him. As she thought it over, he waited a moment before saying, "We can marry sooner."

"What on earth do you mean? There's no preacher in five hundred miles, and no real preacher would marry us, currently."

"I know. How about an irregular one? A lay preacher, maybe?"

An irregular marriage. She watched his face, how his eyes looked over her right shoulder as he thought, and she waited for what he would say. "Someone can do a form of words in front of our friends. People will know that I take you for my wife. We'll do it right when we can." He bent his head toward her. "It will change nothing, because right now, for better worse, richer or poorer, till death do us part, I give you my life." His voice broke, and he blinked fast.

He held her face up so she had no choice but to look at him while she poised on the edge of choice. She thought of the dark little cabin, of waiting in fear for McDowell to come back, of how tongues would wag, of the words they would call her. Of life without Daniel. What the preacher said. How she loved his narrow face, the blond hair falling across his forehead almost to his green eyes. What the preacher said. How she loved him. "The preacher back home said this was wrong. But he also said slavery was right, God's will. It appears like some folks can find in the Bible anything that's convenient for them."

She put her arms around him, under his overcoat, his jacket, and laid her palms against the strong muscles of his back. Resting her head against his chest, she said, "Yes." Her voice croaked, and she cleared her throat. "Yes."

Dan threw back his head and let out a great booming jubilant laugh that caught her and carried her with him. They clung to each other, all the weeks of uncertainty, of wanting, dissolved in their laughter. Dan kissed her. Her lips opened to him and he felt her tongue exploring behind his teeth. She would have him. They would be together.

"Shall we be together, now?" he asked, and shouted with laughter when she whispered, "Yes." They went into the room the stove had warmed.

Martha soared over the edge of the buffalo jump, and music caught and held her like an eagle's wings and flowed like water to quench her long thirst, while his shadow made from firelight moved on the pale, muslin-covered wall, his shoulders over her protected her, and she welcomed him, and floated on the music until she settled to earth and folded her wings.

He leaped from the quarry rim into the water, and gathered all the cards into his hands, the full deck, dealt them, picked them up, laid them down, one hand dissolving into the next, and he bet, called, raised, and did not check, and the stakes were richer than he'd ever dreamed, and he risked it all, terrified and thrilled at once, while the firelight in the round stove romped against the walls, across her face and her wide, dark, unseeing eyes whose depths promised undiscovered seams of gold deep, so deep underground; and he augured down, probed and thrust down and down, drilled hard toward the gold. Her thighs vined about his body, twined about him as he dove deeper, delved down to the earth's core, drowned in her and lay on the floor of the quarry with long water vines above him, and resting beside him, all the gold. He had found the Mother Lode.